Birthdays for the Dead

Stuart MacBride is the bestselling author of the DS Logan McRae series, the most recent of which, *Shatter the Bones*, was a *Sunday Times* No. 1 bestseller.

His novels have won him the CWA Dagger in the Library, the Barry Award for Best Debut Novel, and Best Breakthrough Author at the ITV3 crime thriller awards.

Stuart's other works include *Halfhead*, a near-future thriller, *Sawbones*, a novella aimed at adult emergent readers, and several short stories.

He lives in the north-east of Scotland with his wife, Fiona, and cat, Grendel.

For more information visit StuartMacBride.com

By Stuart MacBride

The Logan McRae Novels

Cold Granite

Dying Light

Broken Skin

Flesh House

Blind Eye

Dark Blood

Shatter the Bones

Other Works

Sawbones

12 Days of Winter

Writing as Stuart B. MacBride

Halfhead

STUART MACBRIDE

Birthdays for the Dead

HarperCollins*Publishers*

This is a work of fiction. Any references to real people, living or dead, real events, businesses, organizations and localities are intended only to give the fiction a sense of reality and authenticity. All names, characters, places and incidents are either the product of the author's imagination or are used fictitiously, and their resemblance, if any, to real-life counterparts is entirely coincidental. The only exception to this are the characters Royce Clark, Andy Inglis, Janice Russell, Julie Wilson, and Sheila Caldwell, who have given their express permission to be fictionalized in this volume. All behaviour, history, and character traits assigned to these individuals have been designed to serve the needs of the narrative and do not necessarily bear any resemblance to the real people.

HarperCollins*Publishers*
77–85 Fulham Palace Road,
Hammersmith, London W6 8JB

www.harpercollins.co.uk

Published by HarperCollins*Publishers* 2012
1

A catalogue record for this book
is available from the British Library

ISBN: 978 0 00 734418 5

Set in Meridien by Palimpsest Book Production Limited,
Falkirk, Stirlingshire

Printed and bound in Great Britain by
Clays Ltd, St Ives plc

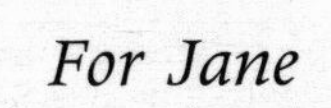

For Jane

Without Whom

As usual I'm indebted to many people for their assistance, information, and patience while I've been writing this book. People like Ishbel Gall, whose knowledge of the dead knows no bounds; Dr Lorna Dawson and Margaret McKeen – soil science gurus; Professor Dave Barclay – physical evidence superstar; and pathology legend, Dr James Grieve.

A big cheer goes out to Matt Wright for all his fishy help; Sergeant Gordon Fowler; Donald Anderson for the hospitality, and the song; and everyone at Shetland Arts. And another for Jennifer, Sue, and Caroline at Talking Issues, for their help and the tour of Bath.

The excellent team at HarperCollins all deserve a medal for their patience and encouragement: Sarah Hodgson, Jane Johnson, Julia Wisdom, Alice Moss, Amy Neilson, Laura Mell, Damon Greeney, Oliver Malcolm, Laura Fletcher, Roger Cazalet, Kate Elton, Lucy Upton, Sam Hancock, Emad Akhtar, Anne O'Brien, Marie Goldie and the DC Bishopbriggs posse. More medals to Phil Patterson, Isabella Floris, Luke Speed, and everyone at Marjacq Scripts.

Many hats off to Dave & Maureen Goulding, Molly Massie, Michelle Bruce, Alex Clark, my little brother Christopher, and

Roseanna Massie; Jim Duncan and Carl Wright for all their help; Allan, Donna and Edward Buchan; Andy and Sheena Inglis; and Mark McHardy.

A number of people have helped raise a lot of money for charity by bidding to have a character named after them in this book, so many thanks to the winners: Royce Clark, Janice Russell, Julie Wilson, and Sheila Caldwell for donating so much.

And saving the best for last – as always – Fiona and Grendel.

please…

1

Flash. It's like an explosion going off in her head, knives in her eyes, broken glass in her brain. Then darkness. She rocks back in the seat; the wood creaks under her.

Blink. Blink. A hot blue-and-orange glow painted across the inside of her eyelids. Tears rolling down her dirty cheeks.

Please…

She drags a shuddering breath through her nose, wet with snot. The smell of dirt and bitter-onion sweat, dust, and something pissy – like when that mouse got trapped behind the cooker. A little furry body hidden in darkness, going rancid with mould, stinking of rotting sausages, roasting every time they turned the oven on.

Please… Her mouth makes the word behind the gag of sticky tape, but all that comes out is a muffled moan. Her shoulders ache, both arms twisted behind her back, wrists and ankles stinging from the cable-ties that hold her to the hard wooden chair.

She throws her head back and blinks at the ceiling. The room fades back in: bare wooden joists stained almost black; spider webs; a neon strip-light, buzzing like a wasp trapped in a glass. Walls smeared with filth. A huge camera mounted on a tripod.

Then the noise. He's singing 'Happy Birthday to You', the words coming out all broken and hesitant, like he's scared to get them wrong.

This is fucked up. Completely fucking fucked up. It's not even her birthday yet: not for four more days...

Another shuddering breath.

It can't be happening. It's a mistake.

She blinks the tears from her eyes and stares into the corner. He's getting to the big finale, head down as he mumbles out the words. Only it's not her name he sings, it's someone else: Andrea.

Oh thank God.

He'll get it, right? That it's a mistake? She's not supposed to be here: *Andrea's* supposed to be here. Andrea's supposed to be the one tied to a chair in a manky little room full of dirt and spiders and the smell of dying mice. He'll understand.

She tries to tell him, but the gag turns everything into grunts and nonsense.

She's not Andrea.

She shouldn't be here.

He stands behind the camera again, clears his throat a couple of times, takes a deep breath, licks his lips. His voice sounds like one of them kids' TV presenters: 'Say "cheese"!' Another flash, filling her eyes with burning white dots.

It's a mistake. He has to *see* that – he's got the wrong girl, he has to let her go.

She blinks. Please. This isn't *fair*.

He comes out from behind the camera and rubs a hand across his eyes. Stares at his shoes for a bit. Another deep breath. 'Presents for the Birthday Girl!' He thumps a battered old toolkit down onto the creaky wooden table next to her chair. The table's spattered with brown stains. Like someone spilled their Ribena years ago.

It's not Ribena.

Her mouth tightens behind the gag, tears make the room

blur. Air catches in her throat turning everything into short, jagged, trembling sobs.

She's not Andrea. It's all a mistake.

'I got...' A pause while he shuffles his feet. 'I've got something *special* ... just for you, Andrea.' He opens the toolkit and takes out a pair of pliers. Their rusty metal teeth shine in the gloom.

He doesn't look at her, hunches his shoulders, puffs out his cheeks like he's going to puke, scrubs a hand across his mouth. Tries for that barely there smile again. 'You ready?'

sometimes it's better not to know

Monday 14th November

2

Oldcastle FM droned out of the radio on the kitchen work surface.

'*...wasn't that groooooooooovy? It's eight twenty-five and you're listening to* Sensational Steve's Breakfast Drive-Time Bonanza!' A grating honk, like an old-fashioned car horn.

I counted out thirty-five quid in tens and fives onto the reminder notice from the Post Office, then dug in my pocket and made up the balance in change. Forty pounds eighty-five pence. Enough to keep Rebecca's mail being redirected into my PO Box for another year.

This week's haul was a Next catalogue, three charity begging letters, and the Royal Bank trying to flog her a credit card. I dumped the lot in the bin. Everything except for the birthday card.

A plain white envelope with a second-class stamp and a stick-on address label:

Rebecca Henderson
19 Rowan Drive,
Blackwall Hill,
Oldcastle.
OC15 3BZ

It'd been done on a typewriter, not a laser printer, the words hammered into the paper, the letter 'e' a little out of line with everything else. Just like all the others.

The kettle rattled to a boil, filling the air with steam.

I took a tea towel to the window, making a gap in the condensation, sending droplets running down the glass to pool on the mould-blackened wooden frame.

Outside, the back garden was a tangle of jagged silhouettes – the sun a smear of fire on the horizon, painting Kingsmeath with gold and shadows. Grey-harled council houses, pantiles jaundiced with lichen; the glistening slate roofs of the tenements; a primary school surrounded by chain-link fencing – squat and dour, its windows glowing.

'Haha! Right, it's Straitjacket Sweepstakes time and Christine Murphy thinks the answer is "Acute Polymorphic Psychotic Disorder".' An electronic quack. *'Looks like the voices in your head got it wrong, Christine: better luck next time.'*

The cigar box was rough beneath my fingertips. A little bit bigger than an old-fashioned VHS case, decorated by someone only just old enough to be trusted with round-nosed scissors and glue. Most of the sequins had fallen off years ago, and the glitter looked more like grit than anything else, but it was the thought that counted. The perfect size for storing home-made birthday cards.

I opened the lid. The woody smell of old cigars fought against the kitchen's mildew fug and whatever the hell was wrong with the drains.

Last year's card sat on top of the little pile: 'HAPPY BIRTHDAY!!!' scrawled above a Polaroid photograph – a square picture set into a white plastic rectangle. Thing was virtually an antique, Polaroid didn't even make the film-stock any more. The number '4' was scratched into the top-left corner.

I picked up the latest envelope, eased a kitchen knife under the flap, and tore straight along the fold, then pulled out the contents. A flurry of dark flakes fell onto the work surface

– that was new. They smelled of rust. Some hit the edge of the tea towel, making tiny red blooms as they soaked into the damp fabric.

Oh God…

This year's photo was mounted on plain white card. My little girl. Rebecca. Tied to a chair in a basement somewhere. She was… He'd taken her clothes.

I closed my eyes for a moment, knuckles aching, teeth clamped hard enough to make my ears ring. Bastard. Fucking, bloody *bastard*.

'Stick with us folks 'cos we've got another heeee-larious *wind-up call after the news, but first it's a golden oldie: Tammy Wynette and her crash-helmet hairdo, with "Stand by Your Man". Good advice there, ladies.'* Another comedy horn noise.

Rebecca's pale skin was smeared with blood, slashed and burned and bruised, eyes wide, screaming behind a duct-tape gag. '5' scratched into the corner of the picture.

Five years since she disappeared. Five years since the bastard tortured her to death and took photos to prove it. Five birthday cards, each one worse than the last.

The toast popped up, filling the kitchen with the smell of burnt bread.

Deep breaths. Deep breaths.

I lowered card number five into the box, on top of all the others. Closed the lid.

Bastard…

She would've been eighteen today.

I scraped the blackened toast over the sink as Tammy got into her stride. The butter turned yellow-grey as I spread it with the same knife. Two slices of plastic cheese from the fridge, washed down with milky tea and a couple of anti-inflammatories. Chewing. Trying to avoid the two loose teeth on the top left, the skin tight across my cheek – swollen and bruised. Scowling out through the window's new clean patch.

Light flashed off the King's River as the sun finally made

it up over the hills, turning Oldcastle into a patchwork of blues and orange. In the middle distance, Castle Hill loomed over the city – a thick blade of granite with a sheer cliff on one side, steep winding cobbled streets on the other. Victorian sandstone buildings stained the colour of dried blood. The castle's crumbling fortifications looked like broken teeth, perched right at the top.

That was the thing about living here – you could get up every morning and look out across the crumbling concrete boxes of your crappy council estate, at all the pretty parts of Oldcastle. Have it ground in your face every day: that no matter how long you spent staring out at the nice bits, you were still stuck in bloody Kingsmeath.

She would've been eighteen.

I spread the tea towel out on the work surface, then pulled the plastic ice-cube tray out from the fridge's freezer compartment. Gritted my teeth, and twisted. The ice cracked and groaned, a better soundtrack to my aching fingers than Tammy Bloody Wynette.

Ice cubes tumbled into the middle of the tea towel. I folded it up into a cosh, then battered it off the worktop a few times. Fished a used teabag out of the sink and made a fresh cup in a clean mug – laced it with four sugars and a splash of milk – tucked the cigar box under my arm, then took everything through to the living room.

The figure on the couch was huddled beneath an unzipped sleeping bag. I hauled the curtains open.

'Come on you lazy wee shite: up.'

Parker groaned. His face was a mess: eyes swollen and purple; a nose that would never be straight again; split lips; a huge bruise on his cheek. He'd bled during the night, staining the sleeping bag. 'Mmmmnnnffff...'

One eye opened. What should have been white was vivid red, the pupil dilated. 'Mmmnnnfff?' His mouth barely moved.

I held out the tea towel. 'How's the head?'

'Fmmmmmnnndfff...'

'Serves you right.' I stuck the icepack against Parker's cheek until he took hold of it himself. 'What did I tell you about Big Johnny Simpson's sister? You never bloody—' My mobile rang – a hard-edged rendition of an old-fashioned telephone. 'God's sake...'

I put the mug on the floor by Parker's head, pulled a blister pack of pills from my pocket and handed them over. 'Tramadol. And I want you gone by the time I get back: Susanne's coming round.'

'Nnnng ... fnnn brrkn...'

'And would it kill you to tidy up now and then? Place is a shitehole.' I grabbed my car keys and leather jacket. Dug the phone from my pocket. The name, 'MICHELLE', sat in the middle of the screen.

Great.

Because today wasn't screwed up enough.

I hit the green button. 'Michelle.'

Her Highlands-and-Islands accent was clipped and pointed. *'Put that down!'*

'You phoned me!'

'What? No, not you: Katie.' A muffled pause. *'I don't care, put it down. You'll be late!'* Then back to me. *'Ash, will you* please *tell your daughter to stop acting like a spoiled little brat?'*

'Hi, Daddy.' Katie: putting on her butter-wouldn't-melt little-girl voice.

I blinked. Shifted my grip on the cigar box. Tried to force a smile.

'Be nice to your mother. It's not her fault she's a bitch in the mornings. And *don't* tell her I said that!'

'Bye, Daddy.'

And Michelle was back. *'Now get in that car, or I swear to God...'* The sound of the door clunking shut. *'It's Katie's birthday next week.'*

'It's Rebecca's birthday today.'

'No.'

'Michelle, she's—'

'I'm not talking about this, Ash. You promised to sort out the venue and—'

'Five years.'

'She didn't even leave a note! What kind of ungrateful little…' A pause, the sound of breath hissing between gritted teeth. *'Why do we have to do this every single year? Rebecca doesn't care, Ash: five years and not so much as a phone call. Now, have you got a venue for Katie's party or haven't you?'*

'It's in hand, OK? All booked and paid for.' Well, almost…

'Monday, Ash: her birthday's on Monday. *A week today.'*

'I said it's *booked*.' I checked my watch. 'You're going to be late.'

'Monday.' She hung up without saying goodbye.

I slipped the phone back in my pocket.

Would it really be so bad to just *talk* about Rebecca? Remember what she was like before… Before the birthday cards started.

Upstairs, I slipped the cigar box back in its hiding place – under a loose floorboard in the bedroom – then clumped down to the lounge and nudged the useless lump of gristle lying on the couch. 'Two Tramadol every four hours, *maximum*. I come home and find your overdosed corpse mouldering on my sofa, I'll bloody kill you.'

'…sources close to the investigation confirm that Oldcastle Police have uncovered the body of a second young woman. Local news now, and Tayside Police are refusing to comment on claims that parents of missing teenager Helen McMillan have received a card from a serial killer known as "The Birthday Boy"…'

'What? No, you'll have to speak up.' I pinned the phone between my ear and shoulder, and coaxed the ancient Renault around the roundabout. Dundee was a mass of grey, scowling beneath a clay-coloured sky. Rain spattered the windscreen, rising in twin streams of spray from the Audi in front. 'Hello?'

'Hello?' DCI Weber was barely audible over the engine, squealing windscreen wipers, and crackly radio. *'I said, how long?'*

'…where Assistant Chief Constable Eric Montgomery issued the following statement.'

Dundee's ACC sounded as if he had both thumbs wedged in his nostrils. *'We want anyone who remembers seeing Helen, when she went missing in November last year, to get in touch with their nearest police station…'*

I turned the radio down to a dull buzz. 'How should I know?' The dual carriageway was a ribbon of red taillights, stretching all the way to the Kingsway junction. An illuminated sign flashed, 'ROADWORKS ~ EXPECT DELAYS'. No shit. I hit the brakes. Drummed my fingers on the steering wheel. 'Could take weeks.'

'Oh for… What am I going to tell the Chief?'

'The usual: we're pursuing several lines of enquiry, and—'

'Do I look like I floated up the Kings River on a mealie pudding? We need a suspect, we need a result, and we need it now. *I've got half of Scotland's media camped out in reception wanting a comment, and the other half laying siege to McDermid Avenue—'*

Traffic was barely moving, crawling along, then stopping, then crawling again. Why could no bastard drive any more?

'—are you even listening to me?'

'What?' I blinked. 'Yeah … not a lot we can do about it, though, is there?' A hole opened up in the other lane, and I put my foot down, but the rusty old Renault barely noticed. Should have held out for one of the pool cars. 'Come on you little sod…'

A Tesco eighteen-wheeler thundered past into the gap, dirty spray turning the Renault's windscreen opaque until the wipers scraped it into twin khaki-coloured rainbows. 'Bastard!'

'Where are you?'

'Just coming into Dundee – by the Toyota garage. Traffic's awful.'

'Right, let's try this again: remember I told you to play nice with Sergeant Smith? Well, it's not a request any more, it's an order. Turns out the slimy tosser was PSD in Grampian before we got him.'

Professional Standards? Sodding hell...

Actually, that made sense – DS Smith looked the type who'd clype on his colleagues, then get a hard-on while he stitched them up.

The traffic lurched forwards another couple of car-lengths. 'Why have *we* got him then?'

'Exactly.'

'Might be an idea if everyone kept their heads down for a while.'

'You think?' Silence on the other end. And then Weber was back. *'Professional Standards. From Aberdeen.'*

'I know.'

'Means they don't trust us to police ourselves. Which – to be honest – is fair enough, but still, there's the principle of the thing. We need a result, sharpish.' A clunk and Weber was gone.

Yeah, we'd get a result sharpish, because that's how it worked. Didn't matter that the official task force had been after the bastard for eight years: Weber needed a result to keep Grampian and Tayside from finding out that all the rumours about Oldcastle CID were true, so one would *miraculously* appear.

I turned the radio back up, and some sort of boy-band crap droned out of the speakers.

'Ooh, baby, swear you love me,

don't say maybe.

Ooh-ooh – say we – can make it right...'

The phone went again, its old-fashioned ringing noise a lot more tuneful than the garbage on the radio. I stabbed the button and wedged the mobile back between my ear and shoulder. 'Forget something?'

A small pause, then an Irish accent, female: *'I think it's yerself that's forgotten somethin', don't ye?'*

Oh God… I swallowed. Wrapped my hands tighter around the steering wheel. Mrs Kerrigan. Sod. Why did I answer the bloody phone? *Always* check the display before picking up.

'Baby, let's not fight tonight,

let's do it, do it, do it right…'

I cleared my throat. 'I was … going to call you.'

'Aye, I'll bet ye were. Yez are late. Mr Inglis is very disappointed.'

'Let's do it right, tonight!' Instrumental break.

'I need a little time to—'

'Do ye not think five years is enough? 'Cos I'm startin' to think ye're takin' the piss here. I'm wantin' three thousand bills by Tuesday lunch, OK? Or I'll have yer feckin' hole in flitters.'

Three grand by tomorrow lunchtime? Where was I supposed to get *three grand* by tomorrow lunchtime? It wasn't possible. They were going to break my legs…

'No problem. Three thousand. Tomorrow.'

'That'd be bleedin' deadly, ta.' And she hung up.

I folded forwards, resting my forehead against the steering wheel. The plastic surface was rough, as if someone had been chewing at it.

Should just keep on going. Drive right through Dundee and sod off down south. Birmingham maybe, or Newcastle: stay with Brett and his boyfriend. After all, what were brothers for? As long as they didn't make me help plan the wedding. Which they would. Bloody seating arrangements, floral centrepieces, and vol-au-vents…

Bugger that.

'Let's do it right, Baby,

let's do it tonight!' Big finish.

A horn blared out somewhere behind me. I looked up and saw the gap in front of the Renault's bonnet, goosed the accelerator and coasted in behind the Audi again.

'You're listening to Tay FM, and that was Mr Bones, with "Tonight

Baby". We've got the Great Overgate Giveaway coming up, but first Nicole Gifford wants to wish her fiancé Dave good luck in his new job. Here's Celine Dion singing "Just Walk Away"...'

Or better yet: run like buggery. I switched off the radio.

Three grand by tomorrow. Never mind the other sixteen...

There was always extortion: go back to Oldcastle and lean on a few people. Pay Willie McNaughton a visit – see if he was still flogging GHB to school kids. That should be worth at least a couple of hundred. Karen Turner had that brothel on Shepard Lane. And Fat Jimmy Campbell was probably still growing weed in his loft... Throw in another dozen 'house calls' and I could pull in a grand and a half, maybe two tops.

Over a thousand pounds short, and nothing left to sell.

Maybe Mrs Kerrigan would go easy on me and they'd only break *one* of my legs. And next week the compound interest would set in, along with the compound fractures.

The car park was nearly empty, just a handful of silver rep-mobiles and hire cars clustered around the hotel entrance. I pulled into a space, killed the engine, then sat there, staring off into the middle distance as the rain drummed on the car roof.

Maybe Newcastle wasn't such a bad idea after—

Clunk, clunk, clunk.

I turned in my seat. A chubby face was peering in through the passenger window: narrow mouth, stubble-covered jowls, bald head dripping and shiny, dark bags under the eyes, blueish grey skin. Big round shoulders hunched up around his ears. The accent was pure Liverpool: 'You coming in, or wha?'

I closed my eyes, counted to five, then climbed out into the rain.

Those teeny little lips turned down at the edges. 'Jesus, look at the state of you. Be frightenin' old ladies, face like that.' He had a brown paper bag clutched in one hand, the Burger King logo smeared with something red.

'Thought the Met would've beaten the Scouse out of you by now.'

'You kidding? Like a stick of Blackpool rock me: cut us in half and it's "Sabir loves Merseyside" all the way down.' He pointed a chunky finger at my face. 'What's the other bloke look like?'

'Almost as ugly as you.'

A smile. 'Well your mam never complains when I'm givin' *her* one.'

'To be fair, she's got a lot less fussy since she died.' I locked the car, rain pattering on the shoulders of my leather jacket. 'The McMillans here?'

'Nah: home. We're keepin' our end low key, didn't think they'd want a Crown Office task force camped out on their doorstep, like.' Sabir turned and lumbered towards the hotel entrance, wide hips rolling from side to side, feet out at ten-to-two, like a duck. 'The father's just about holdin' it together, but the mother's in pieces. How 'bout your lot?'

I followed him through the automatic doors into a bland lobby. The receptionist was slumped over her phone, doodling on a day planner. 'I know... Yeah... Well, it's only 'cos she's jealous...'

Sabir led the way to the lifts and mashed the button with his thumb. 'We're on the fifth floor. Great view: Tesco car park on one side, dual carriageway on the other. Like Venice in spring, that.' The numbers counted their way down from nine. 'So: you here on a social, or you after a favour?'

I handed him a photograph. The doors slid open, but Sabir didn't move. He stared at the picture, mouth hanging open.

A snort from the reception desk. 'No... I swear I never... No... Told you: she's *jealous*.'

The doors slid shut again.

Sabir breathed out. 'Holy crap...'

3

The bitter smell of percolating coffee filled the fifth-floor conference room. One wall was solid glass – patio doors at the far end opening out onto a balcony – the others festooned with scribble-covered flip charts and whiteboards.

Sabir unfurled the top of his Burger King bag and pulled out a handful of fries as he lumbered across the beige carpet. I followed him.

Two men and two women were clustered at the far end of the room, perching on the edge of tables, gathered around a stocky man with salt-and-ginger hair and a face gouged deep with creases and wrinkles. Detective Chief Superintendent Dickie. He hooked a thumb at the nearest whiteboard. 'Aye, and make sure you pull *all* the CCTV footage they've got, this time, Maggie. Don't let the buggers fob you off; should all still be on file.'

One of the women nodded – no-nonsense pageboy haircut bobbing around her long, thin face. 'Yes, Chief.' She scribbled something down in a notebook.

DCS Dickie settled back in his seat and smiled at a lump of muscle with no chin. 'Byron?'

'Yes, right...' The huge sergeant straightened his wire-rimmed glasses. 'When Helen went missing last year, Tayside

Police talked to all of her friends, classmates, and everyone at the hairdressers she worked in on Saturdays. No one saw anything. Stable enough home life, wanted to go to university to study law. No boyfriend. Liked gerbils, Lady Gaga, and reading.' He turned and pointed at a corkboard covered in about thirty head-and-shoulder shots of young girls, all reported missing within the last twelve months: just before their thirteenth birthday.

Rebecca's photograph used to be up there...

One of the pictures had a red border around it – ribbon held in place with brass thumbtacks. That would be Helen McMillan: hair like polished copper, grinning, wearing a white shirt and what looked like a school tie.

A frown crossed Byron's face. 'According to Bremner, she was only a twenty-five per cent match with the victim profile.'

Sitting on the other side of the group, DS Gillis ran a hand down his chest-length Viking beard, long blond curls tied in a ponytail at the back of his head. When he spoke, it was in a Morningside-sixty-Benson-&-Hedges-a-day growl. 'Far as we know, Helen's never kept a diary, so we've no idea if she was planning to meet anyone the day she was abducted. Told her mother she was going window shopping after the hairdressers shut on Saturday – wanted a new phone for her birthday. Last sighting we have is her leaving the Vodaphone shop in the Overgate Centre at five thirty-seven. After that: nothing.'

Dickie made a note on the whiteboard. 'Our boy seems to have a thing for shopping centres. What about social networking?'

Sabir cleared his throat. 'Goin' through everything again: got this new pattern-recognition software that spiders her friends too. So far it's all about who's gorra crush on who, and aren't Five Star Six *dreeeemy*.' He clapped a hand down on my shoulder. It smelled of chips. 'In other news.'

Everyone looked, and nodded – well, except for that hairy tosser, DS Gillis – a couple even waved.

A smile deepened the wrinkles around the chief superintendent's mouth. 'Detective Constable Ash Henderson, as I live and wheeze. To what do we owe…' Then quickly faded. 'Something's happened, hasn't it?'

'At two thirty yesterday afternoon, a team of council workers were repairing a sewage main in Castleview.' I pulled out the photograph I'd shown Sabir and handed it to Dickie. It was an eight-by-ten big glossy blow-up of a trench. The earth was dark, almost black, in sharp contrast to the bright yellow council digger in the background. A tattered fringe of black plastic surrounded a scattered mess of pale bone, ribs and femurs and tibia all scraped into a jumble by the digger's back hoe. The skull lay on its side, the right temple crushed and gouged. 'We got a match on the dental records last night. It's Hannah Kelly.'

'Holy, crap…' DS Gillis tugged at his Viking beard, grinning. 'We got one! We *finally* got one.'

'Bloody brilliant.' Dickie stood and grabbed my hand, pumping it up and down. '*Finally* some forensic evidence. Real, proper, physical evidence. Not half-remembered interviews, or grainy security camera footage showing sod all: actual evidence.' He let go of my hand and for a moment it looked as if he was moving in for a hug.

I backed up a step. 'We found another body at three this morning. Same area.'

Sabir flipped a laptop open with one hand, the other clutching a half-eaten burger. 'Where?' The fingers of his left hand danced across the keyboard and a ceiling-mounted projector whirred into life, turning the wall by the door into one big screen: Google Earth booting up.

I settled on the edge of a desk. 'McDermid Avenue.'

'McDermid Avenue…' A rattle of keys and the map swooped in on the north-east of Scotland, then Oldcastle: the glittering curl of the Kings River cutting it in half. Then closer, until

Castle Hill covered the whole wall – the twisted cobbled streets surrounding the castle, the green expanse of King's Park, the rectangular Sixties bulk of the hospital. Closer – streets lined with trees, terraced sandstone houses with slate roofs and long back gardens. McDermid Avenue appeared dead centre, growing until it was big enough to make out individual cars. The houses backed onto a rectangle of scrub, bushes, and trees – an overgrown park criss-crossed with paths.

DCS Dickie walked over, until he was close enough to throw a shadow across the projected street. 'Where's the burial site?' He shifted from foot to foot, rubbing his fingertips together.

Probably thought this was it: all we needed to do was ID the house where the bodies were buried, find out who lived there nine years ago, arrest them, and everyone could go home. Poor sod.

I nudged Sabir to the side, brushed sesame seeds off the laptop's keyboard, then swirled the mouse pointer over the parkland behind the houses. Double clicked about an inch away from the ruins of a bandstand, deep inside a patch of brambles. The screen lurched in again, but this time the satellite photo resolution wasn't high enough, so everything turned into large fuzzy pixels.

Dickie's shoulders slumped a little. 'Oh...'

Not quite so easy.

I zoomed out, until McDermid Avenue was joined on the screen by another cluster of streets: Jordan Place, Hill Terrace, and Gordon Street, all of them backing onto the park.

The woman with the bowl haircut whistled. 'Got be, what, sixty ... eighty houses there?'

I shook my head. 'A lot of these places got subdivided up into flats in the seventies, you're looking at about three hundred households with access to the park.'

'Shite.'

A small pause, then Byron jerked his chin up. 'Yes, but we've got somewhere to start now, don't we? We've got three hundred possible leads instead of none at all. This is still a result.'

I rolled the lump of Blu-Tack in my palms until it was sticky, then tore it into four bits and stuck the sheet of paper on the wall, completing the set. Eight homemade birthday cards, blown up to A3 on the hotel photocopier. I'd laid them out in two rows of four, the oldest top left, the latest one bottom right. All the Polaroids had a number scratched into the top-left corner of the picture: 1, 2, 3, 4, 5, 6, 7, 8. One every year, for eight years.

The first card showed Hannah Kelly strapped to a chair in a filthy room, eyes wide, tears shining on her cheeks, a rectangle of silver duct tape covering her mouth. She was fully dressed in this one, wearing the same clothes she'd had on the day she'd gone missing: tan-leather cropped jacket, strappy pink top with some sort of logo on it, a pink tartan miniskirt, black tights, and biker boots. Cable-ties were just visible against the dark leather around her ankles, both hands behind her back.

She still had all her hair – long, midnight black, poker straight.

She'd been missing for twelve months and four days by the time the card arrived in the post.

Hannah wasn't naked until number five. Not fully anyway. And by then she was a mass of cuts and bruises, little circular burns angry-red on her pale skin.

That familiar cold weight settled in my chest.

Eight cards. This was what the future was going to look like: Rebecca's photo, year after year, getting worse. Making sure I knew what he'd done to her. Making sure I saw every—

'Ash, are you OK?' Dickie was staring at me.

I cleared my throat. 'Yeah, just ... long night last night, waiting for those dental results.' I went and helped myself to the stewed coffee in the conference-room percolator, leaving everyone else to stare at the time-lapse torture session. Then one by one they drifted away, until there was no one left but DCS Dickie and the only member of the team I didn't recognize. The other woman – the one who'd sat quietly, taking notes while everyone else had celebrated the discovery of Hannah Kelly's body. The only one who didn't look like a police officer.

She was peering up at the cards through a pair of heavy-framed glasses, one hand fidgeting with a long strand of curly brown hair. Her other arm was wrapped around herself, as if she was trying to hold something in. Stripy grey top, blue jeans, and red Converse Hi-tops, a tan leather satchel slung over one shoulder. Standing next to Dickie, she made it look like bring-your-daughter-to-work-day.

Maybe granddaughter – she couldn't have been a day over twenty-two.

I joined them. Heat leached out of the coffee mug and into my fingers, soothing grating joints. 'Hannah's parents don't know yet.'

Dickie stared at the last photograph in the set, the one that arrived two months ago on Hannah's birthday. She was slumped in the chair, her long black hair shaved off, her scalp a mess of cuts and bruises, the word 'BITCH' carved into her forehead, eyes screwed shut, tears making glistening trails through the blood on her cheeks. Dickie sniffed. 'Do you want me to tell them?'

I sighed. Shook my head. 'I'll do it when I get back to Oldcastle. They know me.'

'Hmm…' A pause. 'Speaking of which…' Dickie nodded at the young woman in the stripy top. 'You two met?'

'Hi.' She stopped playing with her hair. 'Dr McDonald. Well, Alice really. I mean you can call me Alice if you like, or Dr McDonald, I suppose, or sometimes people call me "Doc", but I don't really like that very much, Alice is OK though…'

'Ash.' I held my hand out for shaking. She just looked at it.

'Right, great, thanks for the offer, but I don't really do

physical contact with people I barely know. I mean there's all sorts of bacterial and hygiene issues involved – are you the sort of person who washes his hands when he goes to the toilet, do you pick your nose, are you one of those men who scratch and sniff – not to mention the whole personal space thing.'

Complete. And utter. Freakshow.

She cleared her throat. 'Sorry. I get a little flustered with unfamiliar social interactions, but I'm working on it, I mean I'm fine with Detective Chief Superintendent Dickie, aren't I, Chief Superintendent, I don't gabble with you at all, do I, tell him I don't gabble.'

Dickie smiled. 'As of yesterday, Dr McDonald's our new forensic psychologist.'

'Ah.' Set a freak to catch a freak... 'What happened to the last one?'

She wrapped her arm tighter around herself. 'I really think we need to visit the burial site. The Birthday Boy didn't pick this spot at random, he must have known it was going to be safe, that they wouldn't be discovered for years, and if it was me killing girls and burying them I'd want to keep them close so I knew they were safe. Wouldn't you? I mean it's all about power and possession, isn't it?' Dr McDonald stared at the white toes of her red Converse Hi-tops.

I glanced over her head at Dickie. 'And she doesn't talk like this when it's just the two of you?'

'Hardly ever.' He raised his hand, as if he was about to pat her on the shoulder.

She flinched. Backed up a step.

Dickie sighed. 'I'll ... em ... leave you to it then.' He put his hand in his pocket, out of harm's way. 'Ash? You hurrying back to Oldcastle, or have you got a minute?'

Hurrying back? Still hadn't decided if I was pointing the Rustmobile towards Newcastle and putting my foot down. 'Long as you need.'

* * *

'So,' I slid the glass door shut, and leaned on the safety rail, 'does she provide her own straitjacket, or does that come out of your budget?'

The view from the balcony outside the meeting room was every bit as dismal as Sabir had promised: overlooking the dual carriageway and the Kingsway Retail Park. Huge glass and metal sheds bordering a lopsided triangle of parking spaces. Up above, the sky was solid grey, the light cold and thin through the pouring rain. At least it was relatively dry here – the balcony for the room above kept the worst of the weather off.

Cigarette butts made soggy drifts in the corners, little orange cylinders swelling on the damp tiles. DS Gillis was down the other end, puffing away – the smoke clinging to his beard as if it was smouldering – grumbling into a mobile phone, pacing back and forth.

DCS Dickie sparked up a cigarette, took a long, deep drag, then rested his elbows on the safety rail, one hand rubbing at the bags under his eyes. 'How's the arthritis?'

I flexed my hands, the joints ached. 'Been worse. How's the ulcer?'

'You know, when I took on this bloody investigation, I was untouchable. Top of my game, going places... Remember the Pearson murders?' Another puff. 'Now look at me.'

'So what *did* happen to your last profiler?'

Dickie made a gun of his thumb and forefingers, stuck it to his temple, and pulled the trigger. 'All over a hotel bedroom in Bristol, three weeks ago.' He glanced over his shoulder, towards the meeting room. 'Dr McDonald might be a nut-job, but at least we won't be sponging her brains off the walls anytime soon. Well ... touch wood.'

I turned, looking back through the glass doors. She was still standing in front of the blown-up birthday cards, fiddling with her hair. Staring up at Hannah Kelly's bleeding body. I forced a smile into my voice, laid it on thick. 'Not really your fault though, is it? The Birthday Boy was always going to be a bastard to catch.'

'By the time we know he's got them, it's a year too late. The trail's cold. No witnesses, or they can't remember, or they make shit up because they watch too much telly and think it's what we want to hear.' Dickie flicked the ash from the end of his cigarette, then stared at the glowing tip. 'I'm up for retirement in four months. Eight years working the same bloody case and not one single sodding clue... Until now.' His eyes narrowed, wreathed in smoke. 'Two bodies, probably more on the way. We'll get DNA, fibres, and we'll catch the bastard. And I'll take my gold watch and march off home to Lossiemouth with my head held high, while the Birthday Boy rots in a shite-smeared cell for the rest of his unnatural little life.'

'You coming to help with the door-to-doors?'

A pause. 'Any chance you could take Dr McDonald back to Oldcastle with you? Show her the body recovery site, let her get a feel for the place?'

Yeah, because babysitting a mentally unstable psychologist was right up there on my list of life goals. 'You're not coming?'

Dickie pulled a face, curling the corners of his mouth down. 'Do you know why I'm still here, Ash? Why they didn't boot me off the case and get someone else in?'

'No other bugger wants the job?'

A nod. 'Career suicide. Speaking of which ... I need another favour.' He stood up straight, one hand rubbing at the small of his back. 'Our last psychologist, Bremner, didn't just top himself, he took his notes with him. Burned the lot in the hotel bin: disabled the smoke detector, set fire to everything, then bang.'

I tucked my hands in my pockets. It was getting colder. 'Always thought he was a bit of a prick.'

'Managed to screw something up on the servers too. Every psychological document we had – poof, up in smoke. Sabir tried recovering the data, but Bremner cocked up so long ago all the backups were shagged too.' Dickie took one last draw on his cigarette, then sent its glowing corpse sailing out into the rain. 'Not wanting to speak ill of the dead, or anything, but still...'

'What's the favour?'

'Well, you're still friends with Henry, aren't you?'

'Henry who?' Frown. 'What, *Forrester*? The occasional Christmas card maybe, but I've not seen him for years.'

'Thing is, Dr McDonald has to start again from scratch; be a big help if she could discuss the case with him. Maybe see if he's got any of his original files?'

'So give him a call. Get him to courier everything over.'

Down the other end of the balcony, Gillis snapped his phone shut, then ground his cigarette out against the wall and let it fall to the tiles at his feet.

Dickie stared out across the retail park. 'She says she needs to see him. Face to face.'

Gillis lumbered over. 'You tell him yet?'

'"Tell him" what?'

A smile cracked the space between the cigarette-stained moustache and bristling beard. 'Shetland. You're taking the Doc up to see your old mate, Forrester.'

I pulled my shoulders back, chin up. 'Take her yourself. You're the one looks like a bloody Viking.'

'The old git doesn't want anything to do with the case. We need his help. You're his friend. Go up there and talk him round.'

Dickie sighed. 'Come on, Ash, you *know* what Henry's like: once he digs his heels in...'

I scowled at them. 'Shetland?'

Gillis squinted back. 'You don't want to help us catch the bastard? *Really*? What kind of cop are you?'

'It's only a couple of days, Ash: three or four tops. I'll square it with your boss.'

Dr McDonald wasn't the only mental one. 'I'm not going to Shetland! We just turned up two bodies and—'

'It's going to be nothing but hanging around waiting for lab reports in Oldcastle now anyway. That and processing three hundred door-to-doors.' Dickie nodded towards the meeting room, where Dr McDonald was gazing up at the birthday cards. 'When we catch the Birthday Boy we'll need her up to speed for the interviews. I want a full confession, in stone, not something he can wriggle out of in court six months later thanks to some slimy defence lawyer.'

'I'm not your bloody childminder! Get someone else to—'

'Ash, *please*.'

I stared out into the rain... Four days about as far away from Oldcastle as it was possible to get and still be in the UK. Four days where Mrs Kerrigan's thugs couldn't find me. And maybe, once Henry had seen how much of a disaster Dickie's new criminal psychologist was, he'd drag his wrinkly arse out of retirement and help me catch the bastard who'd murdered Rebecca. Four days to convince the old sod that four *years* in Shetland was penance enough for what happened to Philip Skinner. It was time to get back to work.

I nodded. 'OK. Flying from Aberdeen or Edinburgh?'

Gillis's smile grew wider. 'Funny you should ask that...'

4

'Can you slow down, please?' Dr McDonald tightened her grip on the grab handle above the passenger door, knuckles white. Eyes screwed tightly shut.

I changed down, burying the accelerator pedal into the Renault's carpet. Yes, it was childish, but she'd started it. Outside the car windows, a residential road blurred past, skeletal trees raking the grey sky. Drizzle misted the glass. 'Thought you were supposed to be a psychologist.'

'I *am*, and it's not my fault air travel terrifies me, I know it might *seem* illogical, statistically you're more likely to be killed by an electric toaster than die in a plane crash in the UK – that's why I never make toast – but I can't…' She gave a little squeal as I swung the car around onto Strathmore Avenue. 'Please! Can you slow—'

'You've no idea how fast we're going: you've got your eyes closed.'

'I can *feel* it!'

My phone rang. 'Hold on…' I pulled the thing from my pocket and thumbed the green button. 'What?'

A man's voice: '*We've got another one—*'

Dr McDonald snatched the phone out of my hand. 'No, no, no!' She held it to her ear, listening for a moment. 'No, I will *not* put him on: he's driving, are you trying to cause an accident, I don't want to die, why do you want me to die, are you some sort of psychopath that you want random passengers to die in car crashes, is that your idea of *fun*?'

I stuck my hand out. 'Give me the phone back.'

She switched the thing to her other ear, out of reach. 'No, I told you: he's *driving*.'

'Give me the bloody phone!'

She slapped my hand away. 'Uh-huh... Hold on.' She looked across from the passenger seat. 'It's someone called Matt, he says to tell you you're a "rotten bastard".' Back to the phone again. 'Yes, I told him... Uh-huh... Uh-huh... I don't know.'

'Matt who?'

'When are we going to be back in Oldcastle?'

'Who the hell is Matt?'

'He says, while you've been "poofing about" in Dundee, the ground-penetrating radar's turned up what looks like a third set of remains...' She tilted her head to one side, frowning as she listened. 'No, I'm not telling Constable Henderson that... Because it's unnecessarily rude, that's why.'

Well, at least that explained who Matt was: the head of Oldcastle's Scenes Examination Branch always did have a mouth like a sewer.

Another body.

Don't let it be Rebecca. Let her lie quiet and safe in the ground until I get my hands on the bastard who tortured her to death. *Please.*

I threw the car into a right. 'Ask him if they've ID'd the second body yet.'

'Constable Henderson wants to know if you've ID'd... Uh-huh... No... I'll tell him.' She looked at me. 'He says you owe him twenty pounds, and—'

'For God's sake: did they get a bloody ID or not?'

Left onto another street of prison-block tenements.

'He says they're still excavating the remains.' She held a hand over the mouthpiece. 'Apparently the Procurator Fiscal insisted on putting some forensic archaeologist in charge of the dig, and he's turning everything into a big production.'

I took the next left, then left again into a cul-de-sac with three-storey blocks of flats on one side and grey bungalows on the other. Just after ten on a wintery Monday morning and most of the homes were in darkness. Here and there the occasional window glowed in the drizzly gloom.

Sodding hell. 'We've got company.'

A grey Transit van, with the SKY News Logo emblazoned down the side, sat at the kerb, its roof bristling with antennae and a satellite dish. It was the only outside broadcast unit in sight, the other vehicles were the usual crappy assortment of Fiats, Vauxhalls, and Fords beloved of tabloid and broadsheet reporters.

I parked in front of the L-shaped block at the end of the road – the one with a uniformed PC standing outside in the rain, crossed arms resting on her swollen belly. A light above the main door made her fluorescent-yellow jacket glisten.

I hauled on the handbrake, then killed the engine. Stuck out my hand. 'Phone.'

Dr McDonald dropped the mobile into my palm, as if she didn't want to risk her fingers actually touching me.

'Matt: tell Archaeology Boy to get his finger out. This is a murder investigation, not a fucking slumber party.'

'But—'

I hung up and slipped the phone back in my pocket. 'How can you be afraid of flying?'

'It's not natural. And I'm not afraid of flying.' She undid her seatbelt and followed me out into the drizzle. 'I'm afraid of *crashing*. Which is completely logical, when you think about it, it's a survival mechanism, perfectly rational, everyone should be afraid of crashing, what's strange is *not* being afraid, you: you're the one who's strange.'

I stared at her. 'Yeah, *I'm* the one who's strange.'

We had to show our IDs to the rain-soaked lump standing guard outside the small block of flats. A dark fringe poked out from underneath her bowler, plastered to her forehead by the drizzle, her chubby face stretched into a permafrost frown.

I nodded back towards the clump of journalists. None of them had bothered to get out of their nice warm cars. One *had* rolled down their window to stick a telephoto lens out, but other than that it was a hotbed of apathy. 'Giving you any trouble?'

The constable bared her top teeth. 'Like you wouldnae believe. You going up?'

No, we were going to stand out here in the drizzle, bonding. I looked up at the redbrick building. 'The McMillans in?'

'Yeah. But watch yourself, they've got a journo up there.' She stood to one side. 'And we're no' exactly flavour of the day.'

'When are we ever?' I held the door open and ushered Dr McDonald inside.

She just stared at me. 'Erm...'

'This was your idea, remember? I wanted to go back to Oldcastle, but *no*, you said—'

'Can't you go first?'

'Fine.' The stairwell smelled of musky perfume and frying onions. A collection of pot plants was expiring on the first landing, the carpet beginning to go bald at the edge of each tread. The sound of a television turned up too loud.

My shoes scrunched on the steps, as if someone had put sand down to stop the carpet getting too slippery. The second landing was a lot like the first – more dying pot plants, a couple of plain doors painted reddish-brown, a stack of unopened Yellow Pages sitting on the windowsill still in their clear plastic wrappers.

Dr McDonald's voice echoed through the stairwell from somewhere below. 'Is it safe to come up?'

'Safe?' I looked around at the mouldy pot plants. 'No, the whole place is full of rabid Ninjas.' Pause. 'Of course it's bloody safe!' I grabbed the balustrade and hauled myself up to the top floor.

A pair of doors led off to separate flats: a welcome mat sat outside one of them, a grubby brown rectangle on the gritty carpet. The word 'McMillan' was hand-painted in wobbly childish lettering on a wooden plaque above the bell.

I leaned against the wall and waited.

Three minutes later, Dr McDonald poked her head around the corner, looking up at me. 'You don't have to be so sarcastic, you know, it's not like I'm *trying* to annoy you, I just have certain ... concerns with unfamiliar enclosed spaces.'

It was a miracle she was allowed out unsupervised.

I knocked on the door.

It was opened by a police officer wearing the white shirt-and-tie outfit that every beat cop had abandoned years ago in favour of Darth-Vader-black. His long nose was speckled with spider-veins, his dark eyes spaced wide on a narrow forehead. A set of silver sergeant's bars shone on his black epaulettes as he had a good look at Dr McDonald, then turned and sniffed at me. 'You Henderson? Let's see some ID.'

Officious little prick. I flashed my warrant card again. 'You Family Liaison?'

A nod. 'Cool: thanks. Sorry, but the amount of bloody journos trying to wangle their way up here – kidding on they live in the flats, or they're relatives, friends of the family...' He hooked a thumb over his shoulder. 'Parents are in the lounge with some tabloid gimp.'

'How'd *he* get in?'

'She: they invited her up. And her chequebook. Going to let her publish the birthday card.'

'Oh for... That's evidence in an ongoing investigation! Why haven't you thrown her out? Do I really need to—'

'We can't stop the victim's family inviting people up to their house: it's *their* house.' The FLO stuck his chest out. 'And by the way, *Detective Constable,* I don't care if you are one of Dickie's "Party Crashers",' he patted himself on one shoulder, making the black epaulette with its silver bars wobble, 'see these? These say *"Sergeant"*, so watch the lip. You bloody special-task-force dicks are all the same. Well, you know what: if you're so damn special, why haven't you caught the Birthday Boy yet? Party Crashers? You bastards couldn't crash a wobbly shopping trolley.'

Silence.

I clenched my fists – the knuckles grumbled and creaked. Punch the bastard. So what if he was a sergeant: wouldn't be the first time—

Dr McDonald stepped into the doorway, right between us. 'This *is* a pickle, isn't it, well, not literally, that would be silly, but figuratively, I mean we're all working towards the same ends, but we've got different pressures and expectations.' She smiled up at the sergeant as he backed away. 'Being a Family Liaison officer must be incredibly high pressure, my name's Dr Alice McDonald, I'm a criminal psychologist, well, I don't mean I'm a psychologist who commits crimes – that kind of thing only ever happens in the movies, and in books and things I suppose, but not in real life – is it OK if we come in?'

And all the time the sergeant was retreating down the hallway, his eyes flicking from left to right, as if looking for somewhere safe to hide from the tsunami of crazy advancing across the beige-coloured carpet.

His back bumped into a door. Nowhere left to run. No option but to drown... He turned and wrenched it open.

The living room was full of shelves and units, all covered with vases, postcards, decorative glassware, stacks of envelopes, bits of polished rock... The furniture looked as if it came from Ikea, but the clutter was car-boot-sale chic. Three people: one man, two women.

It wasn't difficult to tell which one was the journalist – she was the middle-aged go-getter in the moderately priced suit, eyebrows furrowed, mouth set in a grim line. I feel your pain, it's all so terrible, a tragedy... But the corners of her lips twitched, as if she was trying *really* hard not to grin. An exclusive like this wouldn't come along every day.

The sergeant stepped into the lounge and cleared his throat. 'Ian, Jane, this is Dr McDonald, she's a ... *psychologist.* She wants to talk to you about ... er...' He looked back at her.

She walked right in. 'I'm so sorry about Helen. I know this is difficult, but I need to ask you a few questions about her – try to get a feeling for what she's like.'

What happened to the rambling?

The father, Ian, scowled at Dr McDonald, his thick eyebrows drawing together like the doors on a battleship. Trackie-bottoms in Dundee United orange, a Mr Men T-shirt, close-cropped hair, arms folded across his chest.

His wife was ... huge. Not just wide, but tall: a floral-print behemoth with long brown hair and puffy pink eyes. She cleared her throat. 'I was about to make some tea, would you—'

'They're no' staying.' Ian plonked down on the sofa and stared at Dr McDonald. 'You want to know what Helen's like? Helen's dead. *That's* what she's like.'

Jane tugged at a handkerchief in her lap. 'Ian, *please,* we don't know for—'

'Of course she's bloody deid.' He jerked his chin in our direction. 'Ask them. Go on, ask them what happened to the other poor cows.'

She licked her lips. 'I... I'm sorry, he's upset, it's been a horrible shock. And—'

'They're dead. He grabs them, he tortures them, he kills them.' Ian twisted his hands together so tightly the fingertips turned pale. 'End of story.'

Dr McDonald looked at the carpet for a moment. 'Ian, I won't lie to you, it's—'

'Actually...' I squeezed into the room, keeping my eyes fixed on the reporter. 'Perhaps we could talk about this in private?'

Ian shook his head. 'Anything you say to us we're gonnae tell her anyway. She's gonnae tell the world what it's really like, no' that press-release pish you dole out. The *truth*.'

The reporter stood, held out her hand. 'Jean Buchanan, freelance. I want you to know that I've got the *utmost* respect for the police in this difficult—'

'Mr McMillan, this is an ongoing investigation and if we're going to catch the person responsible for abducting—'

'—in the public interest to report—'

'—stop this happening again; and we can't do that if these parasites are reporting everything we—'

'Parasites?' The professional voice slipped. She jabbed a finger at me. 'Listen up, Sunshine: Jane and Ian are *entitled* to compensation for their stories, you can't censor—'

'—surely want to stop other families having to go through this!'

Ian glowered at me. 'Fuck them. Fuck the lot of them, it's not gonnae bring Helen back, is it? She's dead; he killed her a year ago. There's bugger all we can do to change that.' He bit his lip, stared at the window blinds. 'Doesn't matter what we want: papers are gonnae write about it anyway. Least this way we get... Why should we give our pain away for free?'

His wife sat down next to him, reached out and held his hand. They stayed like that, in silence.

Maybe he was right: why should he let the jackals pick over his daughter's life for nothing? Money wasn't going to bring Helen back, but at least it would be something. Show they weren't powerless. Stop them wrenching awake in the middle of the night, drenched with sweat, shivering... But I doubted it.

The reporter cleared her throat, jerked her chin in the air, then settled back into her seat and scribbled in a notebook.

Dr McDonald hunkered down in front of the couch, then placed a hand on Ian's knee. 'It's OK. Everyone deals with things in their own way. If this is what's best for you ... well, we'll do what we can to help. Now, tell me about Helen...'

I backed out of the room.

5

Helen McMillan had the same kind of posters on the wall as Katie. OK, so the bands were from the insipid-plastic-*X-Factor* school of music instead of the pretentious-angsty-emo-rock Katie liked, but other than that the sentiment was the same. These are the things that I like, this defines who I am.

With Rebecca it was Nickelback and the Pussycat Dolls... She always was a strange kid.

'Find anything?'

'Hmm?' I looked up from the cluttered desk in the corner of the bedroom.

Dr McDonald was standing in the doorway. 'Did you find anything?'

'Still looking...'

A big pink fuzzy unicorn sat in the middle of the single bed, surrounded by brightly coloured teddy bears, all neatly arranged. The duvet cover and pillow slips were smooth and crisp, as if they were still changed regularly – probably no point searching under the mattress for hidden secrets, if they *were* still making Helen's bed a year after she went missing anything would have been uncovered ages ago. But I checked anyway. Just wooden slats, and the plastic under-bed storage boxes I'd already been through.

'Ash, are you OK?'

The mattress thumped back down on its wooden frame. 'They say anything useful?'

'You don't mind if I call you Ash, do you, because we're going to be working together and calling you Detective Constable Henderson seems awfully formal and you look worried, or maybe concerned, and a bit depressed actually, was it the argument with the journalist, because I think she came on too strong, don't you, it's really not—'

'That'll be a "no" then.' I tucked the sheet back in and straightened the duvet. So it would look a little less like I'd violated their daughter's bedroom. 'The first card's the worst… Well, they're all fucking horrible, but that first card – that's when you know your daughter hasn't run away, that what's happening is…' I cleared my throat. 'It must be horrible.'

'They said Helen was a quiet girl who liked her books and her gerbils and going to see her nan on a Sunday for lunch. She wasn't a wild child, she wasn't into drinking or drugs or boys, don't you think it's sad that we live in a time when people have to ask if a twelve-year-old is getting hammered and doing drugs, and you said, "That's when *you* know *your* daughter—"'

'Figure of speech.' I scanned the room again. No sign of a cage. 'What happened to the gerbils?'

'They died. Ian's body language got very defensive when he talked about it… He probably looked after them for three or four months after she went missing, starts off as a duty, turns into a bargain – if I keep the gerbils alive she'll come back to us – and the longer it goes on the more desperate they get, the gerbils become symbolic of Helen's disappearance, then they become *responsible* for it, and gradually Ian stops feeding them and they die.'

'What a lovely—'

'Or perhaps one night he got drunk and battered them all to death with a hammer…' She fiddled with her glasses.

'Detective Chief Superintendent Dickie tells me you're still in touch with Hannah Kelly's parents?'

'Hannah didn't have any gerbils.'

'Is her house like this, have they kept it like a shrine to her memory, do they expect her to just turn up one day like nothing ever happened?'

The pink unicorn had fallen on the floor while I'd been shifting the mattress. I picked it up. Fuzzy. Soft. Warm. 'Her parents don't live there any more. Must've moved about five times in the last eight years, and he *still* finds them. Every sixteenth of September: another card.'

Dr McDonald wrapped an arm around herself, head on one side, frowning at the bookshelves on the wall above the desk. They were full of hardbacks: a couple with leather bindings – Dickens, C. S. Lewis – others in faded dust jackets – Ian Fleming, Jilly Cooper, Harper Lee – some that looked as if they'd been wrapped in clear plastic sheeting – Anthony Horowitz, Gabriel King, a couple of Harry Potters, some vampire bollocks. She pulled *Moonraker* from the shelf and flicked through it, the creases between her eyebrows getting deeper. Then she did the same with *The Lion, the Witch and the Wardrobe*, chewing on her bottom lip.

'I've been through them, no hidden messages tucked in between the pages.' I checked my watch. 'Time to make a move.'

Nothing. She was still squinting at the book.

'Hello? You in?'

A blink. 'Yes, right, time…' Dr McDonald slid the book back onto the shelf, then picked up a framed photograph from the chest of drawers. It was a little girl in a pink princess party dress complete with tiara, magic wand, and a pair of fairy wings. Big grin. Two missing teeth. Bright ginger hair swept up in a sort of bun. She was holding a turnip lantern, a candle glowing inside its jagged mouth. 'When I was eight Aunty Jan made me this all-in-one suit for Halloween: black, with a white tummy and paws, a swishy tail, and a three-foot-tall stripy red-and-white hat. All my friends wanted to be Disney princesses.'

'Rebecca was a zombie. Katie went as Hannibal Lecter. We got her an orange jumpsuit and Michelle made this little straitjacket from an old blanket.' A smile broke free. 'I got her a restraint mask, and we pushed her about on one of those two-wheeled trolley things, Rebecca shambling along behind us, growling "Brainssssss" at everyone... Tell you, they ate so many Sherbet Fountains and little Mars Bars they were sick for days.' I ran a hand through the unicorn's soft pink fur. 'Was the best Halloween we ever had.' And the last. Before the bastard took Rebecca and everything went to shit. I put the fuzzy unicorn back on the bed and arranged the Multicoloured Bear Gang around it, then dug my hands into my pockets. Shrugged. 'Anyway...'

Dr McDonald put the photo frame back on the chest of drawers.

Silence.

I cleared my throat. 'We'd better get going.'

The windscreen wipers sounded like someone rubbing a balloon along a window, back and forth, leaving one greasy arc across the glass where the rain refused to shift. Squeak, squeal, squeak, squeal.

Dr McDonald wriggled in her seat. 'Of course it was never *his* fault – you know what some pathologists are like, kings of their own little kingdom and anyone who shows the slightest backbone, or contradicts them in *any* way, has to get this huge lecture about how things are done in the "real world", and I mean how can they even say that—'

On and on, all the way from Dundee – the rain, and the squealing wipers, and the roar of tyres on the road, and the grumbling engine, building up into a headache that must have registered on seismographs on the other side of the bloody world.

A green road sign loomed out of the rain: Oldcastle 5.

Thank Christ.

'—so when I turned around and showed him the injection site hidden in the bite marks on her breast I thought he was actually going to explode, boom, right then and there—'

A huge Asda eighteen-wheeler roared past in the outside lane, and the crappy little Renault rocked on its springs, caught in the backdraught. The windscreen disappeared under a wall of spray.

'—I mean psychologically it was the obvious place to look, given the indicators, but try telling *him* that—'

On and on.

I tightened my grip on the steering wheel: imagine it's her neck and *squeeze*...

'Ash?'

Keep squeezing.

Silence – nothing but the engine and the road and the radio and the rain.

She coughed. 'You don't really like me, do you? Every time you look at me, there's this little pause, like you're trying not to beat me to death. Do I threaten you, or am I just really annoying? I bet it's annoying, I annoy people when I'm nervous and new people make me nervous, especially when they're all covered in bruises.'

'Maybe... Maybe we could listen to the radio for a little bit.'

More silence, then a little, 'OK.' She reached out and turned the volume up. A song by one of those emo bands Katie liked crackled out of the speakers, all guitars and angsty vocals.

I glanced over at the passenger seat. Dr McDonald was staring out of the side window, both arms wrapped around herself, as if she might split down the middle and this was the only way to hold both halves together. Probably sulking.

As long as she did it quietly it was OK with me.

The road climbed up Pearl Hill, past the huge Costco, then down again. The valley opened out in front of the car as the dual carriageway dipped towards Oldcastle. Amber streetlights mapped out the city, even though it had only just gone twelve. Up on Castle Hill, floodlights caught a squall of rain as it hammered the crumbling ramparts. On the other side of the river, warning lights blinked red on top of the Blackwall transmitter. The high-rise blocks and grimy council houses of Kingsmeath loomed up the side of the hill, as if a tidal wave of concrete was about to crash down and sweep everything away. The sky looked like a battered wife.

Welcome home.

I pulled the crumbling Renault into the kerb and killed the engine. McDermid Avenue was a dirty-beige terrace of four-storey buildings with railings to keep the pavement at bay and steps up to the front door. Satellite dishes pimpled the sandstone walls like blackheads on a teenager. Bay windows, fanlights, gnarled oak and beech trees lined the road, their naked branches dripping in the rain.

The twin chimneys of Castle Hill Infirmary's incinerator poked up in the background, trailing plumes of white steam into the bruised sky.

Dr McDonald peered out through the windscreen. 'Oh dear…'

A pair of outside broadcast vans, the battered BBC Scotland Volvo, and a collection of crappy hatchbacks were parked in front of a patrol car – blocking the road about a third of the way down. Most of the journos were still in their cars, staying out of the rain, but the TV crews had set up on the pavement with the barricade in the background, doing serious-faced pieces for the next news bulletin, clutching umbrellas and microphones, trying not to look as if they were creaming themselves with excitement.

Bastards.

I opened the door and climbed out. Icy rain stinging my ears and forehead. 'Just keep your head down, and your mouth shut.'

She clambered out after me, pulling on her leather satchel – the strap diagonally across her chest, like her own private seatbelt – following as I marched towards the line of blue-and-white 'Police' tape. With any luck we'd get through into the scene before anyone noticed us.

PC Duguid stood on the other side of the cordon, in front of the patrol car; glaring out from beneath the peak of an oversized cap. His fluorescent-yellow high-vis jacket was all slick and shiny. Like his face. Only not as ugly.

Duguid jerked his chin up and tapped two fingers against his nose. A car door clunked shut behind me. Then another one. Then an English accent, all marbles and plums, at my shoulder: 'Officer Henderson? Hello?'

I kept walking.

A duffle-coated woman waddled alongside, thrusting a microphone under my nose. 'Is it true you've uncovered a second set of remains?'

Someone else: 'Have you identified the first body?'

'Any comment on the new Dundee victim, Helen McMillan? Will Douglas Kelly be speaking to her parents?'

'Your own daughter went missing, does that give you special insight into how the victims' families are feeling?'

I kept going: just three more feet till the safety of the police tape. 'We're pursuing several avenues of enquiry.' Never give the bastards anything they can quote.

A squat man barged in front, ears like knots of gristle, broken nose, little digital recorder in hand. 'How do you respond to criticism that your botched investigation into Hannah Kelly's abduction eight years ago left the Birthday Boy free to kill— Hey!'

I shoved him to one side and ducked under the cordon, holding it up so Dr McDonald could follow. PC Duguid leaned back against the bonnet of the patrol car, grinning. Gave a wee salute. 'Morning, Guv. Like the bruises: very fashionable.'

'You tipped the bastards off, didn't you?'

The grin grew wider, pulling his chubby cheeks with it. 'Bottle of Macallan, Guv. What's a boy to do?'

I marched past, didn't give him the satisfaction. Or a knee in the balls.

Dr McDonald trotted up beside me. 'Did he really tip off those reporters for a bottle of whisky, what kind of police officer takes bribes like that, I mean it's not right, is it, we should report him...'

Yeah, see how much good that'd do.

A dirt track led away from the road, grass growing down the middle, disappearing into the gap between two sandstone buildings.

Cameron Park must have been impressive once – back when this was an exclusive neighbourhood. A manicured landscape of oak, elder and ash; rhododendron bushes with their gleaming leaves; beds of flowers and shrubs; a duck pond; and a bandstand with a paved area around it for dancing... Now it was a rest home for weeds and litter. A shopping trolley stuck out of the long grass, nose up, one wheel missing, empty crisp packets caught in its metal grille. The rhododendrons were huge sprawling masses, their leaves trembling in the rain, the ground beneath them thick with shadow.

Three blue plastic marquees had been erected in the undergrowth, one – the largest – next to a dirty-yellow digger and a long trench gouged through a barbwire patch of brambles. The second was beside the crumbling bandstand, the third just visible behind one of those massive rhododendrons.

Flickering light came from inside two of the tents – crime scene photography casting the silhouettes of kneeling figures against the plastic walls.

A voice boomed through the rain: 'I don't care – get it bloody sorted!'

Dr McDonald flinched.

A prick in a grey Markie's suit with matching overcoat

marched out of the tent by the bandstand, carrying a brolly and a stack of forms. High forehead, close-cropped hair like a Kiwi fruit, long nose, not much going on in the chin department. 'Amateurs…'

A uniformed PC scurried out after him.

The prick slapped the wodge of paper against the PC's chest, then turned his back on the poor sod, leaving her in the rain while he pulled out a phone and made a call.

She stared at the back of his head for a moment, stuck up two fingers, then stomped off down the path towards us. Muttering all the way.

I nodded at her. 'Julie.'

'Guv.' PC Wilson jerked her chin in my direction. Rain drummed on the rim of her bowler, a blonde ponytail drooping and damp at the back. Her eyes were two tiny slits, mouth working on something nasty. She didn't stop. 'I swear to God, I'm going to *swing* for that sheep-shagging bastard.'

'The boss about?'

She jerked a thumb over her shoulder, in the direction of the bandstand, as she passed us. 'Comes down here acting like we all fell off the fucking Thick Wagon.'

'Thanks.'

'Swing for him!'

Dr McDonald peered at me through her rain-speckled glasses. 'Is it always like this, I mean I enjoy a bit of team-based horseplay as much as the next psychologist, but it does feel as if… Ash?'

I set off again, making for the bandstand. It looked ancient: the woodwork crumbling and saggy – boards missing in the cladding, half the roof gone. Swirly bits of cast iron formed decorative flourishes between the bloated pillars, the metal pitted and stained with rust.

'Ash?' She was back again, doing a weird hop-skip thing until her feet were in step with mine. Left, right, left, right. 'Is there anything I should know about before we interact with your team, I mean I've never met any of them and it's going to be in an enclosed space and you know I'm not good under social pressure and you're the only one here I know, so—'

'Why don't you let me do the talking, then? Just until you feel more comfortable joining in.' Which would have the added bonus of shutting her up for a bit.

The blue plastic marquee next to the bandstand was about the size of a double garage, with 'PROPERTY OF SPSA SCENES EXAMINATION BRANCH – OLDCASTLE – TENT C' stencilled in white along the side.

The prick was still on the phone, wandering up and down, kicking at tufts of yellowed grass. But as we got within spitting distance he looked up, narrowed his eyes. 'Hold on...' He stuck the mobile against his chest. 'Where the hell have you been? Shift started three hours ago.'

Yeah, because God forbid he went for more than thirty seconds without making sure everyone knew what a cock he was.

I left it a couple of beats, letting the silence get nice and uncomfortable. Then flared my nostrils, as if I could smell something shitty. 'Dr McDonald, this is Sergeant Smith. He's new.'

'I asked you a question, *Constable*.'

'Hmmm...' A pair of Transit vans were parked beside the tent, a police minibus – complete with riot shielding – sitting behind them. A couple of liveried Land Rovers. No sign of a big black Porsche Cayenne. 'Fiscal been?'

A finger jabbed into my chest.

'I don't care how you used to do things before I got here, *Constable*, but right here, right now, you answer your superior officer when he asks you a question.'

Dr McDonald cleared her throat, but kept her mouth shut. For a change.

I stared at the finger, then up at the prick. 'You've got till I count to three.'

Smith flinched back a couple of steps. 'Are you *threatening* me?' Then he squared his shoulders, brought his chin up. 'Are you that desperate to get hauled up on a charge, *Constable*?'

I smiled. Why not? It'd be five, maybe six minutes before someone bothered to pull us apart. Probably all stand around placing bets. Fight! Fight! Fight! Five minutes: plenty of time to batter the living shite out of the stuck-up little bastard. I clenched my fists. The knuckles groaned in protest. But it'd be worth it.

He stepped forwards—

A voice behind me: 'Guv?' An Oldcastle accent that sounded as if it was being squeezed down a blocked nose: Rhona. She shuffled round, into view.

The bags under her eyes were the only colour on her face. She had her jacket draped over one shoulder, even though it was pouring down and cold enough to make her breath steam. Ancient sweat stains had bleached her navy shirt light blue around the armpits. Straw-blonde hair pulled back in a frizzy ponytail. She curled her top lip in a sort of twitchy grimace, exposing a set of beige teeth in an expanse of pale gum. 'Sorry to interrupt, Guv. You got a minute?'

DS Smith hung his head, one hand massaging his temples. '*What*?'

But Rhona wasn't looking at him, she was looking at me. 'The boss needs you.'

Smith squared his shoulders. 'I'll be there in—'

'Oh, sorry, Sergeant Smith, didn't see you there.' Rhona flashed her pale gums again, then pointed at me. 'I was talking to...'

Smith's chin came up, grinding the words out between his teeth. 'In a *professional* police force we do *not* refer to detective constables as "Guv", do I make myself clear?'

Rhona just smiled at him for a minute. Then back to me. 'Anyway, Guv, if you can pop inside, that'd be great.'

6

The SOC tent trembled, rain turning the blue plastic into a million little drums. Inside it was almost loud enough to drown out the diesel generator in the corner – powering the lighting rigs spread around the scene on thick-legged tripods. The large tent had been split into three areas: the first was for suiting-up-and-signing-in, with a line of standard blue-and-white 'POLICE' tape separating it from everything else. The rest of the space was grass and weeds, with the burial site secured within a cordon of bright-yellow 'CRIME SCENE DO NOT CROSS' tape towards the back wall.

It was an open trench, about the size of a double bed, surrounded by kneeling figures – all dressed in white oversuits – carefully trowelling mud and stones into plastic crates as the flicker and whine of the photographer's digital camera captured everything for posterity.

Bones poked up through the dark earth.

Please don't be Rebecca. Be anyone else but her…

'…and gross insubordination.' DS Smith pulled his shoulders back, nose stuck in the air, one arm out – pointing at me with a trembling finger. 'DCI Weber, I must insist—'

'Veeber, it's pronounced, Veeber. *Veeee*-Ber. Sandy, we've been over this.' Detective Chief Inspector Weber tugged at the ends of his stripy scarf. He must have run the clippers over himself that morning, because there was a faint dusting of short brown hairs on the shoulders of his tweed jacket – trying to hide the fact there wasn't much left on his head. Just a fringe around the sides and a single island in the middle, surrounded by a moat of shiny skin. His beard was the same length, as if he'd started at the top of his head and forgotten to stop. He straightened a pair of black-rimmed NHS-style glasses. Then sighed. 'Well, I suppose with any transfer there's always going to be a period of adjustment; you're bound to settle in sooner or later.'

Pink bloomed on Smith's cheekbones. 'But, sir, I—'

'No,' DCI Weber held up a hand, 'don't blame yourself. I'm sure once the team gets to know you, you'll get on like my grandmother in a bratwurst factory.'

I tried not to smile, I really did.

Smith folded his arms. 'I see. That's the way it is, is it? Fine.'

Poor baby.

Weber looked past Smith's shoulder. 'What have you got, Matt?'

A figure in full SOC suit was lumbering across the car park towards us, carrying a plastic crate with a mound of evidence bags in it. 'Mmmphnn-fmmmmnnnn-nnnmmph.'

He plonked the crate on the damp grass and stretched, making grunting noises, one hand in the small of his back. Then hauled off his facemask, exposing a round sweaty slab of flesh with a little cupid's bow of a mouth. 'Fuck me, it's hot in these things.' He nodded towards the trench. 'Our forensic archaeologist's sodded off for lunch, so we've *finally* got the poor cow uncovered. You want to take a look before we cart her off to Teaboy's lair? Indian Jones'll be back in twenty minutes – if she's not out of here by then we'll still be pissing about at bloody midnight.'

Weber raised an eyebrow. 'I don't think Professor Twining would really appreciate being called—'

'Fuckim.' Matt sniffed. 'You coming or what?'

Someone tugged at my sleeve.

It was Dr McDonald, her voice so quiet I had to bend down to hear it. 'Ask them if I can see the body.'

It was like having a six-year-old again. I turned my back on Smith. 'Can we tag along?'

Weber fiddled with his scarf. 'I don't see why not. Just...' He frowned at the psychologist. 'Sorry, who is this?'

I did the introductions. Dr McDonald only managed a sickly smile and a little wave.

Weber nodded. 'Ah, good. For a minute there I thought your Katie had grown a bit since last time I saw her. That probably wouldn't have been appropriate. Right, suit up everyone.' He paused, then patted Rhona on the shoulder. 'Do me a favour and find out how they're getting on in Tent B, would you?'

'Oh...' She drooped a little. 'Yes, Boss.' Rhona slouched to the exit, paused on the threshold to stare back at Dr McDonald struggling her way into a SOC oversuit that looked two sizes too big, then slipped out into the rain.

Suited and booted, we followed Matt back to the open trench. It was about three feet deep, the soil dark as tar, streaked through with veins of milky coffee. They'd set up a grid of yellow string, segmenting the burial site into fourteen-inch squares.

A skeleton lay in the middle of the grid, bones the colour of dried blood.

Something fizzed at the base of my throat, then down my aching chest and gravel-filled stomach, making my knees lock. Mouth bone dry. A high-pitched whine swirling in my ears.

Please don't be Rebecca...

Inside the SOC suit, my shirt clung to my clammy back like a cold wet hand.

Please don't be Rebecca...

The remains lay on their side, left arm draped across the

ribcage, knees bent double so the feet were under the pelvis. The spine ended in a ragged-edged vertebrae, just above the collarbone – the smooth dome of the skull poked out of the dark earth in the gap between the ribcage and the pelvis.

Dr McDonald put a hand on my arm, and I flinched. Turned it into a cough. Nothing to see here. Everything's fine.

She leaned forwards – standing on the lip of the trench, peering in at the remains. Then back up at me. She'd put the safety goggles on over her own glasses, the lenses already starting to mist up. Dr McDonald stepped away from the edge and tugged at my sleeve again, keeping her voice almost too low to hear. 'It's Lauren Burges, she was abducted seven years ago.'

Thank God. I closed my eyes. Let my breath hiss out into the facemask. Not Rebecca. Thank you, God.

I passed on the information. Everyone stared at me.

DS Smith snorted. 'What, are you psychic now? I think we *might* just wait for the DNA results before we go flying off on—'

'Don't speak shite.' Matt hopped down into the trench, moving his blue plastic bootees through the yellow-string grid like an overweight ballet dancer. 'DNA? Be sod all left. See that?' He pointed at a scrap of black plastic sticking out of the soil by the body. 'He wrapped her in bin-bags.'

Smith stiffened. 'What's that got to do with—'

'Mr DNA likes it cool and dry. Stick your dead girl in a bin-bag, and she'll rot away, making lots of nasty heat and lots of icky moisture: all trapped inside. Mr DNA hates that: goes through him like a paedo in a nursery.' Matt knelt by the side of the body and gently eased the skull out of the ground, then lowered it into a clear plastic evidence bag. 'We might scrape some DNA from the tooth pulp cavity, but after seven years I doubt it. Got more chance getting a blowjob off the pope.'

'I don't appreciate your—'

'Course, on the *plus* side: he wrapped her in bin-bags.'

'You just said—'

'Like little hoovers made of static electricity, they are. Should get some fibres if we're lucky.' Matt cradled the skull in the hollow of his elbow, filling in the form printed on the evidence bag. 'And before you ask, our wee skeleton's that colour 'cause of iron and aluminium elemental staining. This whole area's hoaching with old red sandstone mudstones.' He popped the top back on his pen. 'Any other basic science lessons you're needing while I'm here?'

Smith actually trembled. 'You – don't – *ever* – speak – to me – like – that!'

A shrug. 'Not my fault you're thick.'

'THICK?' The word bellowed out from behind the facemask.

'Oh, for God's sake.' Weber stared up at the rain-drummed roof.

'How *dare* you call—'

'ENOUGH!' Weber's hands were claws, turned to the sky. '*Both* of you.'

Silence.

'Sorry, Boss.' Matt went back to the remains.

Smith stared after him. 'I was only—'

'Sergeant, why don't you just...' Deep breath. 'Why don't you go check up on the door-to-doors? I need to speak with DC Henderson here.'

'But...'

'Off you go. And remember: Veeber – "*Veeeeee*-Ber".'

Smith didn't move for a moment, then his shoulders went back, head up. 'Sir.' He turned and marched towards the changing area, arms swinging as if he was on parade.

I cranked the heating up full and treadled the accelerator. The minibus was parked beside Tent C, its diesel engine rattling away as the interior slowly got up to a reasonable temperature.

Filthy carpet, stained upholstery, and the smell of stale chips and cheesy feet. Sitting in the passenger seat, Dr McDonald fiddled with the air vent, doing her best not to make eye contact with Weber.

He was in the next row back, leaning forwards, arms draped over the seat. 'I told you to play nice with the new boy.' He took his glasses off and polished them on a hanky, before blowing his nose. 'What happened to your face?'

I shrugged, tried for a smile. 'Can we not just get rid of him? Palm him off on Traffic, or something?'

'Dr McDonald, I want to assure you that my team isn't normally quite this…' He wiggled a hand.

'Dysfunctional?' A blush spread across her cheeks. She'd finally plucked up the nerve to say something loud enough to hear.

'Actually, I was going to say, "high spirited", but I suppose either works.' Weber blew his nose again, a honking snork that ended with a sniff and a wipe. 'What makes you think the remains are Lauren Burges?'

Dr McDonald popped open her satchel and rummaged inside – it looked as if the thing was full of files, folders, and a big silver laptop. She pulled out a red plastic sleeve with Lauren's name written on a white sticker in careful block capitals, then flipped through the contents before producing an A4 blow-up of a homemade birthday card. The number five was scratched into the top-left corner. She handed it to Weber and he made a little hissing noise.

'What?'

He passed it over and I couldn't breathe. The girl in the photo … every inch of skin was smeared with blood, head shaved, a gaping hole torn in her belly, coils of glistening grey draped between her slashed thighs like vile bunting. Her mouth hung open, the duct-tape gag gone, gaps where the front teeth had been torn out.

This was two years before the bastard took Rebecca.

And just like that the minibus was too hot.

'Ash?'

I looked up. Weber was handing me another blow-up: number six. The girl's neck ended in a jagged stump. The Birthday Boy had stuffed her head inside her abdomen – her dead eyes gazed out at the camera. 'I don't...' I coughed, swallowed it down, tasting the bile: rancid and bitter in my throat. I gave the copies back to Dr McDonald.

She frowned down at the most recent card. 'Lauren was abducted on the twentieth of October, seven years ago, from the Kings Mall shopping centre in Hammersmith, London. Security camera footage puts her in the car park at three fifteen.' Dr McDonald returned everything to her bag. 'The Metropolitan Police went through every piece of CCTV footage for a mile around the shopping centre, did the usual appeals... Nothing. She was recorded as a missing person until the card arrived a year later. Of course seven years ago there was no proof he'd actually killed Amber O'Neil or Hannah Kelly: just tied them to a chair and taken a couple of photographs. He wasn't even *called* the Birthday Boy till the *Daily Mail* came up with the name a year later.'

'Right, yes.' Weber gave his nose another seeing to. 'Well, while I'm sure you're right, we're going to have to hold off issuing any identification until we've checked Lauren Burges's dental records... Assuming we find enough teeth.' He folded his hanky into a neat square. 'Speaking of which: Hannah Kelly.'

I went back to staring out of the window. Not picturing Lauren with her stomach torn open and her head stuffed inside. Not hearing her scream as he ripped out her front teeth. Not seeing the look in her eyes when she realized no one was coming to save her. She was going to die.

At least he couldn't hurt her any more.

Lauren was dead by the fifth card – but Rebecca... How long would ... how long *did* she hold out for, before giving up hope?

The bile burned my throat.

Weber shifted in his seat. 'Our beloved Assistant Chief Constable wants to issue a statement saying we've ID'd Hannah Kelly.'

I swallowed, but it wouldn't go away. 'So? Drummond always did like the spotlight.'

'Yes, well, *unfortunately* we can't really do that until someone's informed the parents…?'

Silence.

I closed my eyes. Should've done it before going to Dundee. Should've done it as soon as I got back. But I didn't. I put it off. 'It's next on the list.'

'Ash, I can always send—'

'I said I'll do it. They don't deserve to get the news from some spotty stranger in a uniform.'

Silence.

Dr McDonald put her hand up. 'Can I go with him, I mean if that's OK – I need to talk to them about their daughter to get some context on the victimology, did Ash tell you that we've had a problem with the psychology data on our servers and I have to start again from scratch and I only joined the investigation yesterday, but I want to assure you this isn't the first case I've handled and I'm sure Ash will vouch for me, won't you, Ash?'

Great, so now whatever happened would be all *my* fault.

7

Douglas Kelly peered around the door. His cheekbones stuck out more than they used to, so did his forehead, nose, and chin, as if he were slowly disappearing from the inside out. His freckled scalp stood out through a crown of thin grey hair. Wasn't even forty yet, and he already looked the other side of sixty.

It was a nice house, about a third of the way down a small Georgian terrace – one of four that enclosed a little private park. But where the one behind McDermid Avenue was sprawling and overgrown, this one was trimmed and tidy, closed off from the road by a set of four-foot-high railings. Nice neighbourhood too: mullioned windows, no litter, every car an Audi, a Porsche, or a Range Rover.

Couldn't have been further from my crappy little Kingsmeath council house if it was in Australia.

Douglas Kelly blinked at me.

I stood on the top step, hands behind my back. 'Douglas, can we come in, please?'

He opened and closed his mouth a couple of times, as if he was tasting the air, then turned and stalked back into the house. Not so much as a word.

We followed him into the lounge.

Douglas slumped into the leather couch and reached for a china mug. He peered up at the carriage clock ticking away on the mantelpiece, the noise jarring in the cluttered room. Cardboard boxes made a cubist city on the polished floorboards, each one printed with a red squirrel in dungarees, carrying a huge acorn: 'SAMMY'S MIDNIGHT FLIT ~ YOU'D BE NUTS TO TRUST ANYONE ELSE!!!'

A standard lamp cast a yellow glow in the gloomy room.

I licked my lips. Took a deep breath. 'Douglas, you'll have seen—' My phone rang. 'Fuck...' I dragged the thing from my pocket, dropped it, grabbed it before it hit the deck. A name sat in the middle of the screen: 'KERRIGAN, MRS'. No thanks. I switched the phone off, then stuck it back in my pocket again. 'Sorry.'

Tick. Tick. Tick. Tick.

A car drove by on the street outside.

Try again: 'Douglas, it's—'

'I'm sorry about the mess. We should really get round to unpacking, but...' He blinked, biting his bottom lip, deep breaths hissing in through his nose. His pale blue eyes shimmered. He scrubbed a hand across them. Stared down into his tea. 'I'm sorry. It's been...'

Tick. Tick. Tick. Tick.

'Douglas, we've found—'

'All these years you've come out and sat with us: every sixteenth of September, even when Angela had her breakdown... You didn't have to do that.'

'Douglas, I'm so sorry, we—'

'Don't say it. *Please.*' The china mug trembled in his hands. 'Please...'

Tick. Tick. Tick. Tick.

Dr McDonald picked her way between the boxes, squatted down in front of Douglas Kelly and put a hand on his knee. Just like she'd done with Helen McMillan's parents. 'It's OK. You can let go.'

'It's...' Douglas screwed his eyes closed, biting his lips.

'It happened a long, long time ago. She's not suffering any more, he can't hurt her. It's over.'

'Who...' A tear ran down the side of his nose. 'Who...' When he opened his eyes they were pink and swollen. Lips quivering.

'It's OK, Douglas, it's OK. It's over. She's—'

Douglas Kelly slammed the mug into Dr McDonald's face. It shattered, shards of delicate white bursting open in slow motion like a flower blooming, tea spraying out. She grunted, toppled backwards, glasses clattering into the fireplace. He let go of the remaining bits of mug and clenched his hand into a fist – launched himself off the couch, swinging for her.

I dipped my knees and lunged. And then everything snapped back to normal speed.

Slam: I barrelled into his side, pinning him against the couch as he struggled and kicked and screamed.

'WHO THE *FUCK* ARE YOU?'

I grabbed his arm – twisted it around behind his back. 'Calm down!'

'IT'S NOT OK! IT'LL NEVER BE OK!'

His leg jerked out, and Dr McDonald grunted again.

'DOUGLAS: CALM DOWN!' I twisted harder, shoving his face into the leather upholstery and keeping it there. 'Come on, stop it...'

He bucked, and writhed, and swore, and after what seemed like hours, finally went slack. Shoulders quivering, sobbing.

Dr McDonald huddled by the fireplace, staring at the palm of her left hand. Scarlet trickled down her pale face from a gash in her eyebrow. 'I'm bleeding...'

I let go of Douglas and backed away from the couch. He didn't even move, just lay there crying, so I helped Dr McDonald to her feet.

She wobbled in her bright-red Converse Hi-tops. 'I'm *bleeding...*' She frowned. 'Where's my glasses?'

I picked them out of the fireplace and handed them to her. One leg was bent and twisted.

On the couch, Douglas drew his knees up to his chest, curling into a ball, arms wrapped around his head. 'Hannah…' He rocked back and forth. 'Oh, thank God, it's *over*…'

'Ow…' Dr McDonald held onto the wall outside with one hand, the other clutching a wad of bloodstained kitchen paper against her eyebrow.

The rain was on again. Getting darker too. The Dickensian streetlights flickered on as the gloom tripped their automatic sensors.

'He's not normally like that.' I looked back towards the house, where Douglas Kelly was finally getting to mourn his daughter. He was wrong though – it wasn't over. Because next year, on the sixteenth of September, another homemade birthday card would slither through his mailbox and bring it all back again. And the year after that, and the one after that too… 'Sure you don't want some painkillers?'

'Can we just get to the hospital, please?'

High overhead, a plane roared across the dark-grey sky, navigation lights blinking red and green. Lucky bastards getting away from… Shite.

On the other side of the road a woman leaned against the park railings, the smoke from her cigarette curling around beneath the dome of her black umbrella: long camel-hair coat and black suit, auburn hair tied back in a ponytail. Thin rectangular glasses. Jennifer.

Shite and buggery.

I dug out the car keys and slipped them into Dr McDonald's hand. 'Why don't you go wait for me in the car. I'll only be a minute.'

'But I don't—'

'Two minutes tops.' I put a hand in the small of her back and steered her down the stairs, onto the pavement, then gave her a nudge in the direction of my decrepit Renault. She stumbled a bit, but kept on going.

Jennifer dropped the cigarette, ground it out with a black high-heeled boot, then crossed the road, hands in her pockets. Smiled like the sun coming out. 'Ash: long time, no see. You're looking…' A pause as she frowned up at my face, and then the smile was back. 'Good.' Lying cow. 'How've you been?'

I nodded. 'Jennifer.'

She stepped closer so the umbrella covered us both. Rain pattered on the black fabric. Up close, she smelled musky and peppery with a hint of lemon – probably something French and expensive. 'It's been too long.' She wrinkled her upturned little nose. Crow's feet spread out from the corners of her eyes. They were new. 'I've been thinking about you.'

'Forget it.'

'Oh, come on: lunch, my treat. Well, technically it's on Uncle Rupert, but what's the point of having an expense account if you can't treat an old flame now and then?' She nodded towards Dr McDonald – staring out at us through the Renault's windscreen. 'You can bring Katie, if you like? She's gotten *big*, hasn't she?' Jennifer slipped her arm through mine. '*Actually* … might be better if you gave her a couple of quid to go to the pictures, then it'd be just you and me. Like old times.'

I stopped, pulled my arm away from her. 'How did you find him?'

Jennifer's eyes flicked towards a scarlet Alfa Romeo parked opposite Douglas Kelly's house. The driver's window was down, a telephoto lens poked out into the cold morning. Staring straight at me.

She brushed something off my shoulder. 'You used to love that little bistro on Castle Hill, remember?'

'How – did – you – find – him?'

She shrugged, pursed those perfect lips of hers. 'All that digging in Cameron Park… You found Hannah's body, didn't you? That's why you're here.'

'He's ex-directory, the house isn't even in his name… What did you do, follow me?'

A pout. 'Ash, I'm hurt. But it's OK: if you don't want to speak to me, I can go ring the bell and ask him. "How does it feel to finally get your daughter back?" The public *love* that kind of thing.'

I leaned in close. 'Pin back your pretty little lugs, Jennifer. If you so much as *breathe* in Douglas Kelly's direction—'

'What? You'll put me over your knee and give me a good spanking?' She ran her hand down my chest. 'Have you still got those handcuffs?'

I stepped back. Glowering. 'Leave him alone.'

'I'll do that *thing* you like…?' She closed the gap, pressing her breasts against me, looking up into my eyes. 'And after – if I've been a *very* good girl – you can give me a wee exclusive on the Birthday Boy, off the record. You know you want to…'

'Want to?' I pushed her away. 'There's not enough Dettol in the world.'

Streetlight glinted off the camera lens. *Click, click, click.* Photos for the late edition.

'Oh, come on, Ash. You knew what you were getting into. We're both adults.'

Click, click, click.

She licked her lips. 'It *is* her, isn't it? Hannah Kelly. And you've got other bodies too.'

Click, click, click.

'Go away, Jennifer.'

'You've found the Birthday Boy's body dump. Who is he? You've got DNA or something, don't you? If you know who he is, you have to tell me.'

Click, click, click.

'We're pursuing several lines of investigation.' I stepped off the kerb and marched towards the Alfa Romeo. Rain soaked into my hair.

The sound of high-heeled boots clattered along behind me. 'Who else have you found? I want an exclusive, Ash. You *owe* me!'

'Owe you?' I kept going. 'For *what,* Jennifer? What do I fucking owe you?'

Click, click... The photographer looked up from his viewfinder. Too slow. I smacked the flat of my hand against the end of the lens, driving the whole camera into the hairy little shit's face. Crack – his head jerked back, a bead of scarlet glistening in one nostril. Weak chin, pointy nose, hairy hands, hairy head. Like someone had cross-bred a rat with a chimp and given it a top-of-the-range Canon digital camera.

'Frank!'

'Gagh...' Frank blinked, hairy paws smearing red across his face.

I grabbed the lens and pulled; the camera strap yanked his head forwards, clunking it into the window frame. I twisted the Canon through ninety degrees – turning the strap into a noose. Pulled harder. Knuckles like burning gravel, fingers aching.

'Ash! Don't be a dick, let him go!'

Frank gurgled.

Another twist and there it was – a small hatch marked 'SD Card', set into the camera body. I flipped it open, pushed on the plastic edge, and the SD card popped up. About the same size as the end of my thumb, but rectangular, with one corner cut off. I gritted my teeth and pulled it out. Stuck it in my pocket. Let go.

'Gaahhhhh...' Frank scrabbled away, clambering over the gearstick and the handbrake, camera clunking against the steering wheel.

Jennifer grabbed my sleeve. 'What's *wrong* with you?'

I jerked my arm away, leaned on the window ledge and glared inside. The car smelled of stale digestive biscuits, cigarettes, and cold coffee. 'Listen up, you little fuck: I see you anywhere near here again, I see you *at all*, I'm going to turn that telephoto lens of yours into an endoscope. Understand?'

Frank just coughed and spluttered.

'Ash!' She grabbed me again.

I spun around and shoved. Jennifer staggered back against a Porsche – the car alarm blared, the lights flashing on and off. 'Get this into your thick little skull: it's over. I don't owe you a damn thing.'

Her eyes were two cold slits, wrinkles creasing either side of her narrowed lips. Teeth bared. 'Who the *hell* do you think you are?' She spat at me: a gobbet of frothy white that spattered against my chest.

I turned and walked away.

'This *isn't* over, Ash, you hear me? This isn't over!'

8

I pulled the curtain back. 'Feeling any better?'

Dr McDonald perched on the edge of a hospital gurney, her left eye partially closed, a square of white wadding taped to her forehead and cheek. 'No.'

'Doctor says it could've been a lot worse. Just superficial really.'

She scowled at me. 'It's sore.'

'I offered you painkillers.'

'I'm not taking pills from a man I barely know, I mean they could be anything: roofies, GHB, Rohypnol, Ketamine—'

'Roofies and Rohypnol are the same thing. And trust me: you're not my type.'

Her bottom lip protruded a little, then she sniffed and hopped down from the gurney. 'The body deposition sites were stupid, I don't mean the park: the park isn't stupid, but burying a dead body there *is*. Only a set number of people have easy access, and what if someone looks out of their window and sees you with your shovel and a big black-plastic bundle. Who's Jennifer?'

None of your sodding business, that's who.

I dropped my vending-machine coffee in the bin. 'Far as we can tell, Cameron Park's been a wilderness for the last twelve years. Council cut the maintenance budget, told the residents it was their responsibility, so it all went feral.' The sounds of an afternoon in A&E echoed through the corridors – muffled swearing, a young man sobbing, some drunken singing. 'Door-to-doors spoke to an old biddie been living there for sixty years. She says people dump their garden waste in the park all the time.'

'Well, that's not very public spirited of them…' Dr McDonald frowned down at the floor. A series of lines were painted on the cracked linoleum: yellow, blue, red, purple, white, and black. She placed one foot on the black line, then the other, both arms held out sideways as if she was walking on a tightrope. Teetering along.

I pointed in the opposite direction. 'Exit's that way.'

She kept going. 'This goes to the morgue, doesn't it?'

'No, it goes to the mortuary. You watch too much American TV.'

'Sounds a lot more genteel, doesn't it: "mortuary", a morgue is full of serial-killer victims, a mortuary is somewhere you go to see Great Aunty Morag who's passed away at the ripe old age of ninety-two.'

'You're still going the wrong way.'

'Follow the little black line.' She grabbed my arm and gave a skip. 'Like Dorothy in the *Wizard of Oz*.'

Around the corner and deeper into the hospital. The paintwork was cracked and grubby, the gurney bumpers scuffed and dented, the floor patched with strips of silver duct tape. Paintings broke up the magnolia monotony, landscapes and portraits mostly, all done by school children.

Dr McDonald didn't even look at them. 'Detective Chief Inspector Veeeber – that's German, isn't it, but shouldn't the pronunciation be "Veber", or "Veyber", I mean I'm sure he knows how to pronounce his own name, but—'

'Weber will let Smith get comfortable saying "Veeber" for a couple of weeks, then change the pronunciation on him. Give him a hard time for getting it wrong, and go right back to the start.' I smiled. 'I've seen Weber keep it up for *months*. Be surprised how quickly little things like that can break somebody.'

She shrugged. 'Seems a bit cruel...'

'Serves him right: he's a prick.'

We walked along in silence for a while, enjoying the twin reeks of disinfectant and stewed cauliflower.

Dr McDonald stopped. 'There's something significant about the deposition site – not only *where* it is but the nature of the burials themselves. I mean did you see Lauren Burges's body? He didn't even bother to put her head back in the right place, just wrapped the whole lot up, dragged it out to the middle of the park and dumped it in a shallow grave.'

A voice behind us: 'Beep, beep!'

We flattened to the wall, and a hospital bed trundled past, pushed by a balding porter with a squint smile. A pair of chunky nurses brought up the rear, gossiping about some doctor caught taking a female patient's temperature the naughty way. The guy in the bed looked as if he'd been hollowed out, leaving waxy skin draped over a framework of brittle bones, wheezing into an oxygen mask.

'Don't you think that's strange?' As soon as they were past, Dr McDonald hopped back onto the black line. 'I'd expect someone like the Birthday Boy would want to keep them as trophies, Fred and Rosemary West only started burying their victims in the garden when they ran out of room in the house, they wanted to keep them near, but the Birthday Boy dumps them like a wheelbarrow full of lawn clippings.'

'Well, maybe he's—' My phone rang. I dug the thing out and checked the display: 'MICHELLE'. Arseholes... I grimaced at Dr McDonald. 'I'll catch up.'

She shrugged and wobbled away, through a set of double doors, still following the black line.

I hit the button. 'Michelle.'

Twice in one day.

Lucky me.

'I saw you on the news.' Her voice was even more clipped than usual. *'I thought Susanne was a blonde, have you traded her in for someone younger already? Is this one a stripper too?'*

'I told you: Susanne isn't a stripper, she's a dancer.'

'She dances round a pole: it's the same thing.'

'Bye, Michelle.'

But before I could hang up: *'We need to talk about Katie.'*

Oh God. 'What's she done now?'

'Why do you always *have to think the worst?'*

'Because you only ever call when you want someone to read her the riot act.'

A grey-haired woman in a flowery nightie shuffled down the corridor, wheeling a drip-on-a-stand along beside her.

'That's not...' A pause – about long enough for someone to count to ten – and when Michelle came back, her voice was groaning with forced cheer. *'So, how are you settling in?'*

The old dear scuffed past, glowering at me. 'You're no' allowed on your mobile phone!'

'Police business.'

She flipped me the Vs, then wandered off. 'No' supposed to be on your phone in a hospital...'

'Ash? I said how—'

'It's been three years, Michelle: think it's maybe time to stop asking?'

'I was only—'

'It's a shitty little council house in Kingsmeath: the drains stink; someone keeps flicking dog shit into my back garden, which is a jungle, by the way; and that useless bastard Parker is still crashing on my couch. I'm settling in just *great*.'

Silence from the other end of the phone.

Typical. She started it, but I was the one who ended up in trouble. 'Sorry, it's... Didn't mean to snap.' I cleared my throat. 'How's your dad?'

'I thought we weren't going to do this any more.'

'I said, I'm sorry, OK?' Every damn time. 'So, Katie: can I speak to her?'

'It's twenty to four on a Monday afternoon: what do you think?'

'Don't tell me she's—'

'Yes, she's at school.'

'Who died?'

'She wants to go to France for a month.'

Frown. 'What?'

'I said she wants—'

'How can she go to France for a month?' I took two steps across the corridor, turned, and paced back the other way, the phone clenched in my fist. 'What about school? She's barely there as it is! For God's sake, Michelle, why do I always have to be the bad cop? Why can't—'

'It's the school doing *it: an exchange thing – staying with a French family in Toulouse. They think it'll be good for her. Help her focus.'* And the clipped voice was back. *'I thought you'd be more supportive.'*

'They want to pack her off for a month, where we can't keep an eye on her, and you're OK with this?'

'I…' A sigh. *'We've tried everything else, Ash. You know what she's like.'*

I ground my fingertips into gritty eyes. It didn't really help. 'She's not a bad kid, Michelle.'

'Oh for God's sake: grow up, Ash. She's not your sweet little girl any more. Not since Rebecca abandoned us.'

Because that's when everything went wrong.

I pushed through a set of double doors, into a quiet corridor. Dr McDonald stood at the far end, leaning on a radiator and staring out of the window. Outside, two wings of Castle Hill Infirmary formed a six-storey canyon of dirty concrete. The sky was a violent splash of blood and fire, low clouds catching the light of the dying sun. But Dr McDonald wasn't looking up, she was looking down, into the darkness.

She pressed the fingertips of her left hand against the wadding on her face. 'Did you know that Oldcastle has one of the highest instances of mental health problems in the whole UK, even more than London ... well, on a percentage basis. Fifteen confirmed serial killers in the last thirty years. *Fifteen*, and that's just the ones we've heard of. A lot of people blame inbreeding, but it's probably because of the chlorine factories, I mean inbreeding isn't rampant here, is it?'

She'd obviously never been to Kingsmeath. 'I'll introduce you to Shifty Dave Morrow, if you like. He's got webbed toes.'

'Do you remember anything odd about the books Helen McMillan had in her bedroom?'

'Harry Potter, vampire love stories, stuff like that? Katie's got Stephen King and Dean Koontz and Clive Barker, so my idea of what's normal for a twelve-year-old might be a bit off.'

'Kind of ironic, don't you think, I mean there's Oldcastle churning out all that chlorine gas to help with the war effort: everyone thinks they're helping win World War One and all the time the factories are dumping tons of mercury into the environment, guaranteeing generations and generations of mental illness...' She stood on her tiptoes, cupped her hands against the glass, and stuck her head in the makeshift porthole.

I joined her, peering down into the depths.

A pair of headlights swept the road at the bottom of the concrete canyon, followed by a silver Mercedes van. The words, 'McCrae And McCrae, Funeral Services' were printed along the side. It slowed to a crawl below the window, then disappeared down a ramp into the hospital basement.

Dr McDonald shifted her feet, Hi-Tops squeaking on the linoleum. 'Is that her, do you think: Lauren Burges?'

I checked my watch. 'Might be.' Assuming Matt got her out of the ground before the forensic archaeologist returned from lunch.

'By 1916 Oldcastle was producing more chlorine than anywhere else in Europe, and now there isn't a single factory left.' She backed away from the window. 'When will they do the autopsy?'

'Post mortem. Not "autopsy".'

She started to sing: a little girly voice, not much more than a whisper.

'I say morgue, you say mor-tu-ary.

You say post mortem, I say au-topsy…'

She backed away from the window and followed the black line to where it disappeared under the dented metal doors of a lift. A sign next to it was marked, 'AUTHORISED PERSONNEL ONLY, NO PATIENTS OR VISITORS'.

'Tomorrow morning. Professor Twining always starts at nine, on the dot.'

Dr McDonald prodded at the wadding on her head again. 'You know there's probably enough mercury left in the soil around here to keep driving people loopy right into the next millennium?'

'Look on the bright side,' I turned and walked back towards the exit, 'at least you and I will never be out of a job.'

'Thanks.' Dr McDonald clunked the car door closed, then turned and limped across the gravel driveway to a house that had to be worth *millions*. Like everything else on Fletcher Road it was a big Victorian home, complete with turrets, set in a large garden and shut off from the outside world behind eight-foot-high walls.

Strings of white lights glowed in the naked branches of ancient oak trees – this wasn't the kind of neighbourhood where you put up neon reindeer and inflatable Santas.

I popped open the Renault's hatchback and hauled out her luggage – two bright-red suitcases, one huge, one medium-sized. Their wheels dragged and growled through the damp gravel, resisting all the way.

A woman was standing under the portico, mid-to-late-forties, bathed in the light from a pair of carriage lanterns. Her bobbed blonde hair was jelled into spikes on one side, but not on the other; a diamond stud glinted in her nose; ripped blue jeans and a leather waistcoat – no shirt. As if she was auditioning for a heavy metal video. She'd gone the whole hog and got tattoos to go with the outfit – some sort of floral thing poking out over one shoulder; swallow on one foot, anchor on the other.

She flicked the ash off her cigarette and sipped clear liquid from a crystal tumbler full of ice. Didn't sound local, more like something off *The Archers*: 'All right, Alice love?' She opened her arms and gave Dr McDonald a hug, then stepped back and frowned. 'Here, what have you done to your head? Is it sore? Looks sore. You come inside and get yourself a drink. Got a nice bottle o' Belvedere in the freezer and some tonic.'

An elderly Jack Russell wheezed out through the open front door, and Dr McDonald beamed. 'Where's Uncle Phil?'

'Taking Ellie and Colin to see that boy band, Mr Bones, in Glasgow. Still ... no accounting for taste I suppose.' She took another puff, stared at me through a cloud of smoke for a moment, then back to Dr McDonald: 'He the knobber smacked you one? Want me to set the dogs on him?'

'Don't be silly. Jessie would have his throat out.' She smiled down at the geriatric terrier. 'Wouldn't you, Jessie?'

The dog didn't really sit, it was more like its back end collapsed – puff, pant, tongue lolling out the side of its mouth.

Dr McDonald swept a hand out towards me, as if she was introducing a magic trick. 'Aunty Jan, this is Detective Constable Ash Henderson. Aunty Jan's a vet.'

Aunty Jan sniffed. 'You her bit of rough then? Kinda old for our Alice, aren't you?'

Cheeky cow.

'Dr McDonald's assisting us on a case.'

'Hmm…' Another stare, this one accompanied by a swig of whatever was in the glass. Then she stuck out her hand. 'Janice Russell. We're getting a Chinese for tea; bet you're partial to a bit of chicken chow mein, big lad like you.'

And pass up the chance to get the hell away from Dr McFruitLoop?

I pulled on a pained smile. 'I'd love to, but I've got a ton of paperwork to catch up on.'

And more importantly: an appointment with a lap-dancing bar.

9

Whatever song was pounding through the place faded out and there was silence.

A mirror stretched the length of the bar – behind the optics and bottles of whisky. I watched the reflection of a chunky blonde scoop up her cowgirl costume and bra, then wobble off the stage in too-high heels, biting her bottom lip, cheeks streaked with mascara tears. An Aberdeen accent crackled out of the speakers. *'That wis Tina. Big round of applause fir Tina! Come on, big round of applause…'* Nothing. *'Next we've got a real treat for you: Naughty Nikita the Polish Princess!'*

The music cranked up again.

That was the trouble with early evening slots at the Silver Lady: the handful of after-work-let's-go-to-a-titty-bar-isn't-that-cool-and-or-ironic? brigade weren't worth putting on the best talent for. So management put on newbies like Tina – out of her clothes and out of her depth, trying to prove she had what it takes to keep the punters aroused and drinking.

A lanky bloke in a black waistcoat and bow tie sidled up behind the bar, wiping the wooden surface with a cloth. He smiled. 'Another?' Enough gel in his hair to keep him looking like a prick, even in a force ten gale.

'Thanks, Steve.'

He was back a minute later with a fresh glass of sparkling mineral water. The ice cubes clinked as I raised it to my lips.

Steve leaned on the bar. 'Hear your brother got him a spanking from three of Big Johnny Simpson's boys last night.'

I put it down again. 'Oh yeah?'

'Seriously: chattin' up Big Johnny's sister? Like that was ever gonnae end well.'

But then Parker never was the brightest.

Steve glanced up and down the bar. Inched closer, voice barely audible over the thumping music. 'I heard you waded in and battered the crap out them. All *three* of them.' He licked his lips. 'It true you're gettin' back in the game?' Steve threw a couple of messy punches in the air. 'Man, I'd love to see that – Ash Henderson, Comeback King of the Bare-Knuckle Ring! How legendary would that be?'

I took a sip. 'Someone's been pulling your leg.'

'Oh…' His face fell, and so did his shoulders. Then he snapped on a grin as a chubby man in a wrinkled grey suit with matching comb-over lurched up to the bar. 'Same again, sir?'

A booming laugh. 'She's after *champagne*, Steveyboy. Mak' it a bottle, eh? And none of your foreign pish – French. And twa glasses.'

'Coming right up, sir.'

Mr Champagne shuffled his feet, shoogling his bum in time to the music. 'Do you no' love this place?' A network of parallel brown streaks scarred his trouser leg from knee to groin. Skidmarks, the sign of a classy lap dance.

A hand landed on my shoulder. 'What's this I hear about you getting back in the bare-knuckle game?'

I didn't look around. 'Evening, Shifty.'

In the mirror, DI Shifty Dave Morrow gave me a wink. His neck had disappeared years ago taking his hair with it. He wrapped an arm around Mr Champagne. 'Do's a favour and bugger off before I twat you one, eh?'

The dance came to a sudden stop and Mr Champagne stood there with his mouth open for a moment, then shuffled down to the other end of the bar.

Shifty Dave levered his huge arse up on the stool next to me. 'How's the titties? Anyone good been on yet?'

'The new girl, Tina, fell off again.'

'Oooooh...' He pursed his lips, pulling in a whistling breath. 'How many times?'

'Twice.'

A nod. 'Well, at least it's an improvement on last night.' He unbuttoned his suit jacket, showing off a straining blue shirt and a spatter-stained tie. 'Any chance of a drink here, I'm parched.'

Right on cue, Steve the barman reappeared with an ice bucket. An open bottle of Moët & Chandon stuck out of the top.

Oldest trick in the book. Management buys one case of the stuff, drinks it, then fills the empty bottles with the cheapest supermarket sparkling wine they can find. All the girls are told: some punter wants to buy you a drink? Got to be champagne. So the punter buys the 'champagne'. Then the staff collect the empties, fill them with Asda's discount cava, and round we go again. The Happy Hedgehog in Cowskillin doesn't even bother with the cheap fizzy – they get a crate of bargain-basement Liebfraumilch and stick it through a SodaStream.

Shifty watched Mr Champagne hand over a credit card. 'Look at this tosser.' Not bothering to keep his voice down. 'Buying fizzy plonk 'cos he thinks it'll impress the halfwits he works with if he can clamber inside some stripper's G-string. Like *that's* ever going to happen.' A little louder: 'You're fucking dreaming!'

The wee man in the rumpled grey suit took his bottle of expensive cava and marched back to his booth, head held high. Noble in the face of rudeness. With someone else's skidmarks on his trousers.

I took another sip of sparkling water. 'Any idea where I can get somewhere to hold a kid's birthday party?'

Shifty licked his lips as Steve pulled a pint of Tennent's. 'Could do it here? There's that function suite upstairs. Sure Dillon would give you a decent rate.'

Up on stage, a woman with space-hopper breasts twirled herself around a shiny pole, dark hair trailing behind her like a banner.

Yeah, maybe not.

Steve plonked the pint down in front of Shifty. 'Don't pick on the punters – it screws up my tips.'

'Cheers, Steve.' Shifty didn't even bother pretending to get his wallet out any more. On the house was on the house. He resurfaced after downing half the glass in one. 'Ahhhh...' A small belch. 'Shitter of a day, Ash, complete shitter. You'd think that wanker Smith was the Chief Bloody Constable, way he's ordering everyone about. Only a DS, for Christ's sake.'

'Word is he's PSD from Aberdeen.'

Shifty's whole face pinched in around his bared teeth. 'Rubber-heeling little bastard.' The rest of his pint disappeared, then he held out the glass. 'Put another one in there, Steve.'

Steve did as he was told, then wandered off to serve someone else.

This time Shifty savoured it. 'You really fighting again? Seriously, with *your* hands?'

'I'm not – it's all bollocks.' I went back to my water. 'You get anything from the door-to-doors?'

'Early days yet. Got a team pulling an all-nighter down the Land Registry, finding out who owned what house when the poor cows went missing. No point interviewing buggers who only moved in a couple years ago, is it?'

I shrugged. Up on the glittering stage, Naughty Nikita ground her way along the floor.

'How far back you going?'

'Nine years: when Amber O'Neil got snatched…' He frowned at me. 'What's *that* look for?'

'Did you know Oldcastle produced more chlorine gas for World War One than anywhere else in the UK?'

'Come on – surely *nine years* is enough.'

'Apparently the ground's all contaminated with mercury, that's why we get so many nutters.'

'We're talking about three hundred houses here.'

'That prick Forbes sacks the place, the wanker Montrose burns it down, and the arch fucker Huntly—'

'Salts the earth, "so nane croppes shall growe on the accursd haven of evill and wicked Covenanters", yeah: went to school, I know. So come on: Land Registry.'

I hunkered down over my glass, resting my aching knuckles against its cool surface. 'Remember that guy we caught three years ago: Martin Floyd? Where did he dump those prostitutes' bodies?'

'Can we not stick to the one topic for five minutes?'

'He strangled them, raped them, then dumped them in Moncuir Wood. Why?'

'Because he was a fucking nut-job, that's why. Now can—'

'He dumped them there, because when he was a wee boy he used to go camping in Moncuir Wood with the scouts. He knew the area.'

'That thump in the head must've loosened your…' Shifty stood there with his mouth hanging open.

I took another sip of fizzy water. 'Penny just dropped, has it?'

'Eight o'clock.'

I looked into the mirror. The place was getting busy, the after-work suits joined by stag nights and leaving dos: blokes up for a night on the batter with a little gratuitous nudity thrown in. Kicking off an evening that'd end with kebab vomit all down their front and a bollocking from the wife.

'Come on, gents, let's hear it for Naughty Nikita! Yeah, OK, whoo!'

No one joined in with the idiot on the PA system. '*Now, the girls are going to take a little break, but we'll be back in five minutes with the one, the only, the wonderful* Kayleigh! *Yeah!*'

Eight o'clock… I scanned the crowd's reflection. Suits; stag night; that tosser 'Sensational Steve' off the morning drive-time show, plus hangers on; one of the council's last remaining Liberal Democrats, sitting all on his own; a couple of local hoods sharing a joint. But no sign of anything… Fuck.

Fuck!

The man standing by the club's entrance had barn-door ears, a sloping forehead, jutting chin, and a haircut so short you could see every inch of scar tissue criss-crossing his misshapen head. He couldn't have been an inch over five-three. He ran a hand across his open mouth as he scanned the crowd. A DIY swallow tattoo perched on his wrist, blue ink spidering out into the surrounding skin.

I hunched my shoulders up to my ears and slouched down, making myself as small as possible.

Fuck.

Shifty groaned. 'Are you hiding from—'

'I'm not hiding, I'm—'

'Oh, you stupid *prick*. I told you to steer clear of—'

'Shut up, OK?' I glanced in the mirror again. 'What's he doing?'

'Looking for someone.'

See, that's what happens when you have a local: people can find you. I downed the last of my water in one. The bubbles made my stomach churn. The bubbles. Nothing else.

And then a voice came from right behind me, high-pitched and breathy. 'Well, well, well, Detective Constable Ash Henderson, how fortuitous.'

Too late to do a runner.

I swivelled around on my seat, still holding the empty glass. Not the most elegant of weapons, but it would make one hell of a mess. 'Joseph.' I had a quick look behind him. 'Where's your boyfriend?'

'Homophobia, Constable Henderson? I expected more from a man of your standing in the community.' A small shake of the head. 'If you must know, Francis is parking the BMW. But don't worry, he'll be joining us presently.' Joseph pulled on a breadknife smile. 'And Detective Inspector Morrow, how's life treating yourself?'

Shifty shrugged. 'Did you know Oldcastle made heaps of poison gas for killing Nazis in World War One?'

Joseph raised a scarred eyebrow. 'Fascinating.' Then back to me. 'Constable Henderson: do you, by chance, have something for me?'

A figure appeared at Joseph's shoulder. Tall and broad, curly ginger hair tied back in a ponytail, broken nose, huge moustache with matching tuft below the bottom lip. He took off a pair of John Lennon sunglasses and slipped them inside his leather jacket. Small pink eyes. He gave me a stiff little nod. ''Spector.'

I nodded back. 'Francis.'

Joseph took a pair of black leather gloves from his pocket and pulled them on. 'Tell me, Francis, is our friend Constable Henderson on our list for today?'

The big man produced a notebook and flicked through the pages, his forehead all creased up, tip of his tongue poking out the corner of his mouth. 'Nah.'

'Oh…' Joseph frowned. 'Are you sure?'

'Yeah.'

Thank Christ for that.

'Oh well, perhaps tomorrow.' He winked at me. 'It seems Lady Fortune is smiling upon you this evening, Constable Henderson. Perhaps you should consider paying off your debt to Mr Inglis, before it becomes necessary to arrange a late-night home visit from our fiscal management services?'

Francis sniffed. 'Our boy's off tae the bogs.'

A thin man with a rectangular bald-spot was lurching his way towards the toilets. The door swung shut behind him with a thump. Francis set off after him.

Joseph stuck his hands in his pockets and rocked on his heels. 'Actually, the Nazi Party didn't come into being until 1920, so they can't have been the recipients of Oldcastle's gaseous emissions... Ah. Francis has liaised with our friend. Excellent.'

Francis hauled the balding bloke out of the toilets.

The guy was fumbling with his trousers, still doing up his flies. 'Please, I can explain, I didn't think it was due till next week, I mean I've got the money, I never said I didn't have the money, did I?'

Francis dragged him past, making for the entrance.

'I can get it tomorrow, when the banks open, that'll be OK, won't it?' Out onto the cobbled street. 'Really, I've got the money, it's not a problem, we can—'

The door clunked shut.

'And now, the girl you've all been waiting for, the one, the only, the incredibly sexy: Kayleigh!' The lights dimmed and 'Bad to the Bone' thumped out of the speakers. Amateur hour was over.

Joseph flashed his teeth again. 'Well, if you gentlemen will excuse me, I have business to attend to. Do enjoy the show.'

Shifty waited until Joseph joined Francis outside, before turning to stare at me. 'How much do you owe Andy Inglis?'

I turned back to the bar, pulse pounding in my ears almost as loud as the music. Christ, that was close. I signalled Steve for another water. 'The Birthday Boy might have lived near Cameron Park when he was a wee boy. You're going to have to go back a lot further than nine years.'

'Ash?'

Up on stage Kayleigh showed everyone how it was done, hanging upside down, thighs wrapped around the pole, spotlights glittering off her sequined bra.

'Enough. Too much.' I ran my tongue over the two loose molars. 'More than I've got.'

Retching noises echoed out from one of the toilet cubicles. I splashed water on my face, took a deep breath, and stared at myself in the mirror. Fucking halfwit. Another splash of water, scrubbed away with a handful of green paper towels that smelled like sour milk. It went with the rank perfume of piss-soaked floors and bitter vomit.

I checked my watch – half ten. Susanna would do her last set soon, then we could get the hell out of here. Before Joseph and Francis came back.

Time for some fresh air.

The fire exit had one of those, 'THIS DOOR IS ALARMED', signs on it, but it was open anyway – a brick stuck in the gap to keep it that way, so the staff could nip out for a sneaky cigarette. I pushed through into a gloomy alley. The security light bolted to the wall above the loading bay didn't come on, just fizzed and crackled, never quite getting there.

A siren wailed in the distance, the rumble of a late-night bus, a singing drunk, two women fighting, the thump-thump-thump bassline of whatever song was playing inside. The fumbling moans of a couple going at it, hidden in the shadows of a recessed doorway on the other side of the alley.

I took a deep breath, hauling in cold air, letting out a cloud of white.

Should have kept on driving to Newcastle.

More moaning from the snoggers.

Still could. Car was parked outside the club: get in and bugger off before they dump my mangled body in a shallow grave somewhere. Like Rebecca.

'Fuck...' I scrubbed a hand over my face.

I wasn't going anywhere. What was the point of struggling through the last four years, only to give up and run away before we'd caught the bastard?

I pulled out my phone and called Rhona. She picked up on the third ring. A diesel generator rumbled somewhere in the background. *'Guv?'*

'Any news?'

A yawn drowned out everything else. *'Yeah, sorry... I was about to call you: ground-penetrating radar think they've got a fourth burial site. No way he's getting away this time, right? Four bodies down, seven to go.'*

Eight. But the only people who knew that were: Henry Forrester, me, Rebecca, and the bastard who killed her.

'Any ID on the other girl?'

'Hold on, I'll check...'

From the doorway opposite came the sound of a zip being undone. A knee-trembler in the alley behind a lap-dancing bar. Talk about romantic.

I stuck the phone against my chest. 'Hoy, you two: get a room.'

'Fuck!' Frantic scrabbling, and one of the figures lurched out of the shadows. Andrew: the Silver Lady's head doorman, hauling up his flies. 'I was... We...' He cleared his throat. Flexed his shoulders. Chin jutting out like a slab of freshly shaved granite. 'You tell anyone about this and I'll snap your bloody neck. Understand?'

He grabbed a bottle from one of the recycling bins. A sharp tap against the wall turned it into a multi-bladed weapon. 'I'm no' kidding, you hear me? One *fucking* word!' Jabbing the broken bottle in my direction. Trembling.

I backed off a couple of steps, palms out. 'OK, Andrew, I hear you. Our little secret.'

He licked his lips, glanced across at the shadowy doorway, then dropped the bottle and charged through the door, back into the club.

What the hell was that all about? Doormen got hand jobs from star-struck women every evening. Friend of mine once told me it's the bow tie that does it: reminds the ladies of James Bond. But then he always was a bit of a prick.

Back to the phone. 'Rhona?'

'I was about to give up on you.' She sniffed. *'It's not confirmed or anything, but we think number two might be Sophie Elphinstone, went missing from Inverness four years ago.'*

'They doing a dental chart match?'

A small pause. *'Can't. He tore all her teeth out.'* Another yawn.

'Go home and get some rest. You're no good to anyone knackered.'

I hung up, scrolled through my contacts list, and picked the number Dickie had texted me for Dr McDonald. Listened to it ring and ring...

On the other side of the alley, Andrew's bit of stuff was getting restless. Feet shuffling in the darkness. Waiting for me to bugger off so she could slip back into the club unnoticed.

Tough. She could wait.

I let the phone ring through to voicemail, then tried again.

'Mmmph? Lo?' Not quite words, mumbled and fuzzy.

'Dr McDonald, sorry to wake you, but—'

'Ash... No it's fine, I'm awake.' A yawn. *'Urgh... What time is it?'*

'We've found another body. Might be Sophie Elphinstone. We'll talk about it in the morning. Sorry to bother—'

'Sophie Elphinstone?' Dr McDonald sounded a lot more awake. *'Is she... Did he decapitate her?'*

More shuffling from the doorway opposite.

'He ripped all her teeth out instead.'

'Isn't that interesting: he decapitates his third victim, Lauren Burges, but he doesn't decapitate his second or his sixth. Hannah Kelly and Sophie Elphinstone get to keep their heads...'

'Maybe he goes through phases, and—'

'It's almost as if he's experimenting. The normal pattern is to keep doing the same thing over and over, getting better at it every time, refining it, building up the fantasy, but it's...' A pause. *'It's as if he doesn't really* like *what he does – he cuts Lauren Burges's head off, but he can't bring himself to do it again.'* A strange clicking

sound came from the earpiece, as if she was banging the phone off her teeth. '*When they examine the remains tomorrow, we need to get them to look for patterns of wounding – map the correlation points, see what else he's tried and discarded.*'

'Yeah ... OK.' I hung up, slipped the phone back into my pocket and stood there watching a rat rip a hole in a bin-bag. *He doesn't really like what he does.* Bollocks – if he didn't like it, he wouldn't keep doing it.

More shuffling from the other side of the alley.

'Oh, grow up.' I turned my back on them and hauled the door open. 'I don't care, OK? Shag who you want, where you want.'

Whoever it was cleared their throat behind me. 'How long have you known?'

I stopped, one hand on the door, the music from inside getting louder. Licked my lips. Didn't say anything.

'Ash?' Footsteps on the tarmac. 'How long have you known?'

I glanced over my shoulder and there he was: DI Shifty Dave Morrow, sausage fingers fidgeting with his jacket buttons.

Tuesday 15th November

10

'What? No, I can't hear you…' I peered into the gap between the bread and the glowing orange elements – the toaster hadn't burnt it yet – my mobile pinned between my shoulder and ear, while I dumped teabags into mugs with my other hand. The kettle rumbled and rattled on the working surface.

Cold this morning. The window was a fogged-up slab of dark grey.

On the other end of the phone, Rhona yawned again. *'I said, there's been a complaint down the station.'*

'What time did you clock off yesterday?'

'Didn't pass my sergeant's exams so I could be DC my whole life. Got to put in the hours or you don't get the promotion. You told me that.'

True, on both counts. The kettle clicked, then went silent. 'Yeah, but if you fall asleep on the job, or screw something up because you're knackered, you can kiss three stripes goodbye.'

Boiling water into the mugs. Two slices of slightly overdone toast on a plate.

'It was that cow Jennifer Prentice: said you beat up her photographer yesterday.'

'Surprised she waited that long.' A scrape of butter, followed by raspberry jam.

'I told Dougie I'd take a look. You know, do some prelim before Professional Standards get hold of it?'

Two sugars in one of the mugs, then a good splosh of milk in both.

'Where does she get off making accusations like that? So what if you thumped some paparazzi dickhead, sure you had a good reason, right?'

'Something like that.' Out in the hall, the sound of muffled snoring rattled the living room door. So much for Parker making himself scarce. The steps creaked under my socks as I climbed upstairs.

'Yeah, well don't worry: I'll have a word with him. Make sure he has another go remembering what happened.'

The bedroom was dark, the smell of musk and spice with a faint tinge of bleach. I put breakfast on the chest of drawers, then hauled the curtains open. Condensation made dewy spider webs in the corners of the window. Pale blue fringed the horizon, but Oldcastle was a mass of darkness sprinkled with pinpricks of yellow and white.

'Guv?'

Susanne's policewoman costume hung on the back of the wardrobe door. Not the utilitarian workaday UK bobby's uniform, but a sort of fantasy New York Police Department job, with ra-ra-style skirt and leather corset; a hat, handcuffs, and knee-high black PVC kinky boots finishing off the look.

'Guv? You there?'

'Do me a favour: tell Weber you're off following-up on the door-to-doors this morning, park the car somewhere quiet, and grab a couple hours' sleep. Don't let that prick Smith saddle you with anything.'

I could hear the smile in her voice. *'Thanks, Guv. And don't worry about Photography Boy, I'll sort it.'* She hung up.

The mattress groaned as I sat on the edge. 'Susanne?'

'Nnnnnngh...' She was flat on her back with one arm

draped over her eyes, bleached blonde curls draped across the pillows – tumbling over the side of the bed. A small bruise on the fake-tan flesh of her wrist.

'Susanne!'

The arm twitched, then she peered out at me, one side of her face scrunched up. 'Time is it?'

'You getting up?'

One hand fumbled about on the bedside cabinet, grabbed her iPhone and took it back for a good squinting at. 'Urgh… It's seven in the *morning*!'

'Tea and toast?'

The phone went back on the cabinet and she burrowed under the duvet until nothing was visible but that mass of golden curls. 'Fuck tea. Fuck toast. Seven in the morning…'

'Raspberry jam, your favourite?'

'Fuck raspberries. Come back to bed.' She curled up, on her side, back turned towards me. 'Bad enough I had to spend the night in this craphole.'

I stared at the ceiling for a couple of breaths. Susanne was Page Three pretty, with … *phenomenal* breasts, thighs of steel, and an arse you could crack walnuts with. Energetic and flexible. Insatiable and pneumatic. Doesn't understand what I'm talking about half the time. Because she's twenty-one and I'm forty-five – more than halfway to a single room with satin lining and a screw-down lid.

By now I should be living in a nice house in Blackwall Hill, with a lovely lawyer wife and two gorgeous daughters who worship me, not having to sweet-talk my stripper girlfriend into staying the night in the tiny mouldering council house I get for free because it's not fit to rent out.

I put a hand on the shape beneath the duvet. 'I've got to go. Work.' Trying to sound enthusiastic. 'See you tonight?'

'Mmmph…' A twitch, then nothing.

I grabbed my jacket, checked that Rebecca's cigar box was safely tucked away, then stomped back down the stairs.

My phone rang as I got to the front door. The display read 'DR MCFRUITLOOP'. 'Hello?'

'I think we should meet up before the post mortems this morning, it's going to be really odd, isn't it, I mean normally it's all about finding out how the victim died, but we've already got photos of it happening, don't you think that's odd?'

I closed my eyes. Rested my forehead against the cool front door. 'Actually, I've got a couple of things on this morning.' Also known as visiting some dodgy bastards and squeezing as much cash out of them as possible to pay off Mrs Kerrigan before she breaks my legs at lunchtime.

'It's all right, I cleared it with DCI Weber, we're a team now, isn't that great? I thought we should maybe get some breakfast or something first, because I'm guessing it's going to be a pretty long day, I mean with three bodies to post mortem, though I suppose it might be a bit quicker as they're all just bones.'

A team... Oh joy. 'You start the day with a double espresso, don't you.' I unsnibbed the heavy Yale lock. 'Going to take me at least an hour, hour and a half to get to you, so why don't we meet up at the hospital?' That should be enough time for a little light extortion. 'PMs don't start till nine anyway, so...' I hauled the door open.

There was a patrol car sitting outside my house, headlights gleaming in the dark. Dr McDonald stood in front of it, bundled up in a duffle coat, a woolly hat pulled down over her ears with an explosion of brown curls sticking out from underneath. She waved, still holding the mobile phone to her ear. 'I got a lift.'

The smell of sizzling bacon and hot chip fat filled the air.

'*...warn that the following report contains disturbing images and flash photography.*' The TV mounted above the counter glowed through a thin film of fluff and grease. The picture jumped to a press conference: DCS Dickie shared the stage with Helen McMillan's parents and a senior officer in full dress uniform.

Jane McMillan clasped her husband's hand, blinking in the media strobelight. She was wearing the same floral frock she'd had on yesterday, her eyes red, nose shiny, bottom lip wobbling. She looked as if someone had taken away her innards and replaced them with broken glass. *'I ... I want you to know that our Helen was a special girl. If anyone knows who took her: you have to go to the police. You* have *to.'*

I clunked two huge mugs of tea down on the red Formica tabletop.

The Tartan Bunnet wasn't that busy for a Tuesday morning – normally the little café would be full of nightshift CID and uniform, but everyone was on overtime: searching Cameron Park, or going door-to-door, or trying to track down whoever lived in the area nine years ago.

Dr McDonald took a sip of tea, made smacking noises with her lips. She had the café's copy of the *Daily Mail* laid out on the table: 'HELEN'S BIRTHDAY HORROR' was stretched across the front page, above a close-up of the birthday card. Helen McMillan, tied to a chair, cheeks streaked with tears.

'Please, we just want our Helen back...'

'I know they have to put out an appeal and they have to believe it's going to make a difference, but it really isn't, Helen's father was right: she's already dead, she's been dead for a year.'

'What else can they do?' I settled into the seat opposite, facing the window. The sun was crawling over the horizon making the rooftops glisten. A pair of white chimneys poked up above the surrounding streets – Castle Hill Infirmary's incinerator, twin trails of steam glowing against the heavy purple clouds.

'And it's not like someone's going to come forward and say, "Hey, I know who the Birthday Boy is," because *no one* knows who he is, he's clever and he's careful and he's been doing this for at least nine years, he's good at blending in with the normal people, that's why he's got away with it for so long.'

A man's voice replaced Jane McMillan's, not Dickie or the father so it had to be the guy in the dress uniform. *'I want to assure the public that Tayside Police are following several lines of enquiry. But we need your help: if you saw Helen the day she disappeared...'*

Dr McDonald produced a black Sharpie and sketched a map of Britain on the newspaper, adding two squares roughly where Oldcastle would be, one over Dundee, Inverness, Bristol, Newcastle, Cardiff, and Glasgow, and two for London. 'Five girls taken from Scotland, four from England, one from Wales. All mainland UK.'

Almost right.

'Meanwhile, in Oldcastle, police continue to excavate Cameron Park...'

She scrawled a rough approximation of the motorway network on her map, joining the squares. Then looked up at me. 'You don't have a red pen or something, do you, only if I keep adding stuff in black it's going to get a bit confusing.'

There was a clatter from the counter behind us, then a gravelly voice. 'One poached egg on toast. One coronary classic.'

I turned and put a hand up. A baggy-faced woman in a chequered apron shuffled over, carrying two plates. She stood over the table, thin grey hair plastered to her shiny forehead. 'Who's gettin' the coronary?'

Dr McDonald bounced up and down in her seat. 'Ooh, that's me, thanks.'

The plate was about the size of a hubcap, heaped with toast, sausages, grilled tomato, streaky bacon, mushrooms, two fried eggs, two slices of black pudding floating on a sea of baked beans, and a mound of golden chips.

I took the other plate. 'Thanks, Effie.'

'Sure you don't want me to do you some chips, son?'

'Honestly, I'm fine.'

'Hmmph.' She hoisted up her bosoms. 'Well, don't blame me when you waste away.' She shuffled off.

Dr McDonald hacked off a chunk of sausage, dipped it in yolk, then stuffed it into her mouth. Talking as she chewed. 'The interesting thing is when you overlay the abduction dates on the map – I did it last night with noodles and prawns – he's taking most of them in the latter third of the year: both Oldcastle ones are in September, the London ones in October, so there's probably an external stressor operating around then, maybe job-related.'

'A four-month seasonal stressor?' I popped my egg yolk with my knife; golden yellow oozed out onto the toast.

She grabbed the tomato sauce from the garrison of condiments at the end of the table and liberally decorated her plate with it. 'I'd say he definitely has to travel for work, and maybe spends pretty big chunks of time away from home, so it's worth looking at lorry drivers, perhaps long-distance bus drivers too.' She wolfed down bacon. Mushroom. Toast. Beans. It was like watching bin men hurling black bags into a skip. 'And that leaves us with the puzzle of Amber O'Neil, victim number one, she was grabbed in May, does that not seem odd to you, that she's the only one grabbed in the summer, when everyone else is taken September to December?'

'Maybe.'

Chew, munch, shovel, mumble. 'When we finish with the post mortems today I want to go through everything they've got on Amber O'Neil's disappearance, actually I'd like everything they've got on everyone, do you think Detective Chief Superintendent Dickie would let me take it to Shetland, could he burn it all onto a disk or something?'

I looked at her, bean juice dribbling down her chin, and fought the impulse to spit into a napkin and wipe it off. 'Do you have any idea how much paper there is on a single Birthday Boy victim? We've got three boxes on Hannah Kelly alone. We'd need to head up the road in a Transit van.'

'Oh…' A shrug, then back to the sausages.

'What about the locations? Five in Scotland, five not. Might be a local lad?'

'Mmmm...' More chewing. 'Do you really visit Hannah's parents every year, so they won't have to deal with the birthday card on their own?'

I mopped up the last of my egg with the final chunk of toast. 'You've got bean juice on your chin.'

Silence from the other side of the table.

Outside the window, the Number 14 rumbled past, ferrying bleary-eyed suits-and-ties to work.

Dr McDonald wiped a hand across her chin, then licked the palm. 'In case you're wondering, this is the bit where we share things about ourselves and bond over communal experiences.'

No thanks.

More silence.

She sliced a circle of black pudding in two, then stuffed it in. 'I'll go first. My name isn't really Alice, it's Charlotte, but I hate it because it's the same as that spider in the book about the pig; I came top of my class at Edinburgh University, my thesis was in aberrant psycho-sexual behaviour in repeat offenders; I've helped catch three rapists, a paedophile ring, and a woman who killed her four children and two in-laws; I like raspberries, but I'm allergic to them; I have a fiancé who's a systems analyst, but I'm pretty sure he's having an affair, I mean that cow Nigella from his office was all over him at the last Christmas party like I wasn't even there; I was born in Peebles; and I've never been to France.'

OK...

She piled beans onto toast into mouth. 'Your turn.'

'I'd rather not.'

'I'll do it for you, if you like?' She actually put her knife and fork down. Then wrapped an arm around herself, the other hand twiddling with her hair. 'Let's see... You were married, but the job got in the way, your wife resented always having to come second; you tried to fix it by having children, and it almost worked, but then your first daughter ran away from home and the marriage fell apart, and you didn't get custody of the other girl and now she's growing away from you; you're living in a crummy house in a crummy neighbourhood and you drive a crummy car, so you've got money worries... Gambling?'

'Do we really have to—'

'You're obviously used to people doing what you say, which is pretty unusual for a detective constable, so you used to have a much higher rank, but something happened and they demoted you, and you wanted to quit, but you need the money; life hasn't turned out anything like you'd hoped, so you're trying to recapture your lost youth by sleeping your way through a string of younger women, because you can't afford a sports car or a motorbike.' She paused for breath. 'How did I do?'

I kept my eyes on the window. 'You must be a big hit at parties.'

'Top of my class, remember?'

'A: I can see my daughter, Katie, whenever I like – and for your information we get on fine. B: I kicked the living shit out of a detective inspector called Cunningham. And C: I'm not "sleeping my way through a string of younger women", it's *one* woman and her name's Susanne.'

Dr McDonald nodded, picked up her cutlery again and went back to work. 'There we go, we're bonding, isn't it nice?'

Fruitloop.

Mushrooms, egg, chips. 'So ... this Susanne: is she old enough to vote?'

'OK, this bonding session is now officially over.'

She just grinned and chewed.

11

The corridors under Castle Hill Infirmary stretch for miles, a tangled maze lined with pipes and cables. It smelled of damp, disinfectant, and something floral and cloying. When I was wee, Jane Moir's dad worked maintenance for the council and he swore blind the tunnels went all the way out to the river, so medical students could buy dead bodies from smugglers to dissect. But then he was done for fiddling with girl guides eight years later, so I wouldn't put too much faith in it.

'It's creepy down here, what happens if we get lost and end up wandering the corridors for days in the dark?' Dr McDonald inched closer until she bumped against me with every other step. Sticking close.

The hospital throbbed above us, distant clanks and bangs echoing back from the concrete walls.

She slipped her arm through mine. 'Lost forever in the dark…'

The corridor split up ahead. On the right, the black line disappeared under a set of dark-green doors marked 'MORTUARY', the metal bumper plates scuffed and dented by the passage of the dead. But Dr McDonald was staring the other way.

Her grip on my arm tightened.

The corridor on the left stretched away into patchy gloom – half the bulbs were blown, plunging sections into thick shadow, others were stuck in the process of warming up, never getting beyond the blinking stage.

Someone stood in one of the dark spots, about fifteen feet away. That cloying floral air-freshener smell was even stronger.

Whoever it was stared at us, eyes glinting in the shadows. Big, hunched shoulders, a wheeled cart... The light directly above them flickered and buzzed. It was a woman in a slate-grey boilersuit and scabby trainers. Face like a slab of meat, deep creases around her mouth and eyes. Her cart looked like a hostess trolley. Only instead of the box to keep food in, there was a large metal cage. Something furry moved inside: pointed noses, long pink tails. Rats. The bottom of the cart was piled with traps and a big bag with 'BAIT' written on it.

Another buzz, and the light died again.

Singing echoed down the corridor from somewhere behind us. A man's voice, getting louder, accompanied by the grinding squeak-squeak-squeak of a dodgy wheel.

'Ooh, baby, swear you love me,
doo-dee-doo, oooh-ooh,
something la-la ... right...'

The rat catcher didn't move.

'Baby, let's not fight, da-dada, night...
let's do it, do it, do it...'

The singing drifted to a halt. 'Ah, there you are.'

I turned. Alf: hair scraped back in a ponytail, high forehead gleaming in the flickering light, beard neatly trimmed, wearing pale blue scrubs, and hauling a hospital gurney behind him. Its occupant was covered in a white plastic sheet. Alf popped an earbud out and smiled. 'Was about to send a search party for you guys. You know what the Prof's like if he can't start bang on nine.'

Alf nodded towards the mortuary. 'Can you get the door for us? Bloody gurney's like a wonky shopping trolley today.'

And when I turned back, the rat catcher was gone.

'Break on the left tibia and fibula show approximately eight years of bone growth…' Professor Mervin Twining, AKA: Teaboy, ran a gloved finger along the stained bone. His dark floppy hair hung over his forehead – with the square jaw, dimple, and little wire-rim glasses he looked like an extra from a period spy drama.

The skeleton laid out on the dissecting table in front of him had been cleaned of dirt and mud, but it was still the reddish-brown colour of stewed tea. They'd put the head back where it belonged.

Alf looked up from a set of notes, earbuds dangling loose from the neck of his scrubs. 'Lauren Burges fell off her bike when she was five, treated for broken left leg.'

Castle Hill mortuary was a Victorian monstrosity. Cracked black tiles on the floor, grout turned grey by generations' worth of bleach, formaldehyde, and disinfectant. Drainage channels leading to wire-mesh grilles and the sewers beyond. The walls had probably been white once, but their tiles had aged to a dirty ivory. Harsh overhead lighting glittered off stainless-steel work surfaces, a wall of refrigerated drawers, and the dissecting tables.

Three of them, each with an inch-high lip, a drain, a tap, a hose, and a blood-coloured set of bones.

Half a dozen flip charts were arranged around the room in pairs, one of each set was covered with copies of the victim's birthday cards – the other with medical notes, X-Rays, and dental charts.

It was cold too, almost as cold as it was outside. Dr McDonald's nose was going pink, the woolly hat still pulled down over her ears, duffle coat toggled up to her chin, shoulders hunched, hands in her pockets. 'Shouldn't we be wearing masks and safety goggles and things?'

Professor Twining looked up from the remains. 'Not a huge amount of point, I'm afraid: no soft tissue, no DNA, just bones. And they've been cleaned by the soil science people, so there's nothing left for us to contaminate. Can I have the corresponding X-ray, please, Alf? ... Thank you.'

Twining worked his way through Lauren Burges's skeletal remains, comparing the damage to her medical records and the photos on the birthday cards. Confirming her identity.

Three sets of bones on three separate cutting tables. It wouldn't be long before the SEB turned up the other victims. Only they'd get one more than they were expecting: Rebecca, laid out on a cold metal slab. My little girl, reduced to a collection of mud-stained bones. Chipped and scarred where he slashed and stabbed and broke...

The mortuary air was like cold treacle, sticking in my throat.

I thrust my hands in my pockets. Clenched my jaw.

No one knew: there was still time to find the bastard.

So why couldn't I breathe?

Think about something else. *Anything* else. Anything but Rebecca.

Money. Think about the money. About how utterly and completely screwed I was.

That was better...

OK, so I didn't get the chance to squeeze money out of anyone *before* the post mortems, but there was still time, wasn't there? Slip out for a couple of hours while they were examining the other remains. Plenty of time.

Yeah, plenty of time...

'...median damage and periosteal hematoma evident on the left humerus, anterior...'

There was no way in hell I'd ever get enough money. Turn up at the Westing with a fistful of fivers and Mrs Kerrigan's goons would send me home in a wheelchair.

'...compound fracture of the right radius and ulna, seven centimetres from the wrist joint...'

So don't. Don't turn up at all. As long as I kept my head down till the ferry left Aberdeen at seven tonight, I'd be fine.

'...striated scarring on the fourth and fifth ribs consistent with a serrated blade...'

Well, maybe not *fine*, but it'd buy some time.

And all this would still be waiting for me when I got back.

The hands on the mortuary clock clicked around to eleven thirty: two and a half hours of watching Professor Twining pick his way through a murdered girl's bones.

'...and one tea: milk, no sugar.' Alf handed me a mug with 'WORLD'S GREATEST PROCTOLOGIST!' printed on the side.

'Thanks.' One thing you can say about Anatomical Pathology Technicians: they make a decent cup of tea.

Twining stretched out his arms, hands locked together, as if he was about to crack a safe. 'Well, I think we can confirm that the remains belong to Lauren Burges.'

I settled back against the working surface. 'And it only took you two and a half hours. Dr McDonald did it in thirty-five seconds.'

Pink bloomed on her cheeks. 'Well, the position of the head was a bit of a giveaway, I mean there might be other victims he's decapitated that we don't know about. We don't have a complete collection of birthday cards, and most haven't got to the bit where he kills them yet...' She cleared her throat, shuffled her feet. 'It was an educated guess.'

Twining brushed a hand through his floppy hair. 'Unfortunately, I have to make *my* identification stand up in a court of law.' He took his tea across to the two flip charts with Lauren Burges's details on them, and pointed at the second-last photo in the series of birthday cards. 'She was almost certainly dead by the time this one was taken. Difficult to tell with no internal organs left to examine, but working from the photographs I'd say heart failure triggered by blood loss and shock.'

Maybe she was lucky – maybe she was dead when he hacked her open and pulled out her insides. Maybe Rebecca was lucky too...

That fizzing sensation burned at the base of my throat again.

Twining tapped the first card. 'Given the size and colour variation of the bruises between this picture and when she was killed – I'd say Lauren was probably tortured over a period of six or seven hours. Nine at most.'

Dr McDonald looked up at me. 'She went missing four days before her birthday.'

'Yes...' Twining squinted at the first card again. 'That would be consistent with her appearance in this photograph. As if she's been living in those clothes for a couple of days.'

Eight or nine hours screaming into a duct-tape gag while he carved names into Rebecca's skin, burned her head with bleach, ripped out her teeth with pliers...

I put my tea down, worked hard to keep my voice level. 'So...' Try again. 'So he doesn't kill them till it's their actual birthday. He grabs them, he ties them to a chair and leaves them sitting there till it's time. Waiting.'

Dr McDonald crossed to the dissecting table, with its collection of red-brown bones. 'Can I hold Lauren's skull?'

Twining shrugged. 'Well, I don't see why not. As long as you don't drop it.'

I stepped out into the corridor and let the mortuary door swing shut behind me. 'Are you OK?'

Dr McDonald sniffed, then rubbed a hand across her eyes. She did the same with the shiny trails beneath her nose. 'Felt like some fresh air...'

In a subterranean corridor, in the bowels of a hospital.

She turned, so I couldn't see her face. 'Perhaps I'm allergic to formaldehyde or something.'

Yes. That was it. 'We're breaking for lunch. The food's pretty dreadful, but there's a private canteen for senior staff Twining can sneak us into.'

'Right. Great.'

'That was your first post mortem, wasn't it?' I moved around so I could look at her... And stopped. A pair of eyes glittered in the shadow of a missing bulb about thirty feet away. The Rat Catcher was back: just standing there, watching Dr McDonald.

'Poor Lauren... He makes you sit there till it's your birthday, three days tied to a chair, waiting for the pain to begin, can you imagine how lonely, how terrified you'd be, and she was only twelve...' A sniff, and another wipe. 'Well, thirteen, at the end.'

Of course I could. Every bloody day.

The Rat Catcher was like a statue. Standing. Watching. Staring. Not moving.

I took a couple of steps towards her, put a bit of gravel into my voice. 'What the fuck are you looking at?'

Dr McDonald flinched, then turned to see who I was shouting at.

The Rat Catcher didn't even flinch.

'Go on, fuck off!'

Nothing.

And then, finally, she turned and walked away, no rush, her trolley squeaking and groaning in the darkness. A sudden flare of light as she passed beneath a working bulb, her greying hair glowed around her head like a grubby halo. And then she was gone.

'Freak.' I put a hand on Dr McDonald's shoulder. 'You sure you're OK?'

A small nod. 'Sorry.' She wiped her eyes again. 'Just being stupid.'

'If we're going to make the ferry we have to be out of here by about ... half four? Five at the latest.'

'I mean I've been to post mortems before, but it's always the same: I spend so much time trying to empathize with killers... I have to stand there and pretend I'm him, imagining what it'd be like, how *good* it would feel to do all those horrible things.' Another sniff. 'And then it's over and I can't help...' She stared at the ground.

'You don't have to be here for the rest of this. Go back to your aunt's house, put your feet up. Crack open a bottle of wine. I'll catch you up when we're done.'

Dr McDonald shook her head, dark brown curls bouncing around her puffy face. 'I'm not abandoning them.'

'Far as we can tell anyway.' I sat back in the creaky plastic chair.

Dickie's image nodded on the laptop's screen. *'Fair enough. We're packing up here tomorrow, so we should be in town mid-afternoon-ish.'*

DCI Weber drummed his fingertips on the desk. 'You're going to march in and take over my investigation?'

Weber's office was one of the nicer ones in the building – a proper corner job with big windows looking out on the boarded-up cinema opposite.

Dr McDonald's laptop was perched on Weber's desk, where everyone could see the screen, and the webcam could see us. But she was gazing out of the window, one arm wrapped around her chest, the other hand fiddling with her hair.

Dickie sighed. *'Don't be like that Gregor, you know how this works. I'm carrying the can for everything the Birthday Boy does, whether I like it or not.'* He frowned. *'Did I tell you about my ulcer?'*

'I don't care about your ulcer, I've got—'

'How about this: if we get anything, you sit next to me at the press conference. We both make the announcement: you get half the credit,

twelve-year-old girls get to grow up without some sick bastard torturing them to death, and I get to retire and put the whole bloody mess behind me.'

Weber took off his glasses and polished them on his hanky. 'Well, in the interests of interagency cooperation, I suppose we could come to some operational understanding.'

Dickie didn't even bother trying to smile. *'Dr McDonald?'*

Gaze, twiddle.

'Dr McDonald, do you have anything to add? Hello? ... Someone give her a poke, for Christ's sake.'

I did and she jumped, eyes wide. 'Aagh. What was that for?'

'DCS Dickie wants to know if you've got anything to add.'

'Oh, right, yes, well...' She scooted her chair forwards, closer to the laptop. 'Did Helen McMillan's parents say anything about where she got her books from?'

On the little screen, Dickie opened his mouth, then shut it again. Frowning. *'Books?'*

'Did they say where she got them, I mean did she have a rich relative who collected them, and then died and left them to Helen, or something?'

OK, Dr McDonald had been on fairly shaky mental ground to begin with, but it looked as if that bash on the head yesterday had knocked something loose.

'Books?'

Weber sat back in his chair. 'Is this really relevant to—'

'Do you still have that Family Liaison officer at her house, because if you do, can you get him to check the books in Helen's room? The ones on the shelf.'

The frown got deeper. *'Dr McDonald... Alice, I know this has all been very stressful for you, and you're doing your best, but maybe it'd be better if we found someone more suited—'*

'I mean when we were in her room I remember thinking it was a strange collection for a twelve-year-old girl, and I think they were first editions.' She turned to me. 'They were, weren't they, you looked at them too, and—'

'No idea. They were just books.'

'Signed first editions. Do you have any idea how much they're worth? *The Chamber of Secrets* is about one and a half thousand, *The Prisoner of Azkaban*: two to three thousand, depending on which version it is, and God knows what a *Lion the Witch and the Wardrobe* or the Dickens would cost.'

Dickie's face went an alarming magenta colour, but that might have been the screen. 'Ah... I see.'

Dr McDonald wrapped her arm back around herself again, the fingers of her other hand making tight little curls through her hair. 'What's a twelve-year-old girl doing with twenty or thirty thousand pounds' worth of books?'

12

'If we don't go now we're going to be late. What if we can't get there in time and miss the ferry, what are we going to do then, you said we had to leave at half past four!'

I pulled the next statement from the pile. 'You moaning about it doesn't make this go any faster. Read a magazine or something.'

The room was jammed with a dozen tatty Formica desks and towers of paperwork. Magnolia walls, carpet tiles curling at the edges and covered in suspicious stains, bulging in-and-out trays, the bitter-leather fug of BO. Someone had patched the sagging ceiling tiles with diarrhoea-brown parcel tape.

A handful of uniform had clumped in the far corner – by the kettle and fridge – hammering data into ancient beige computers, everyone else was in plainclothes.

DS Smith marched up and down, hands behind his back, playing general. 'This simply isn't good enough!' He turned to face the huge whiteboard that stretched the length of the CID office. 'Do I *really* have to tell you people how important the first twenty-four hours are in a murder enquiry?'

As if this was the first time we'd dealt with a body dumpsite.

Dr McDonald fidgeted with her leather satchel. 'I mean

it's nearly half four now, what if we miss the ferry and have to stay in Aberdeen, what if we can't get a hotel at short notice, I had a friend who left it too late and had to sleep in her car, I don't want to sleep in a car, what if someone comes?'

DS Smith pulled a marker pen from his pocket and scrawled something up on the whiteboard. Strips of black electrical tape divided the surface into columns headed with things like 'Body Recovery', 'Victimology', 'Loci Of Offence', and 'Psychological Indicators', with bullet points listed underneath. The new boy, making his mark. Teaching the parochial thickies how *Grampian Police* did things.

He tapped the whiteboard with a marker pen. 'The question you need to be asking yourself is, "Where were they held prior to being buried?"'

No shit.

Rhona looked up from her computer monitor and saw me. She curled her top lip, then nodded over her shoulder at DS Smith, mouthed the word 'wanker' and made the accompanying hand gesture. Then stood and worked her way between the crowded desks, until she'd reached mine. 'What a dick-head.' Keeping her voice low. 'Lording it over the rest of us like he's God's bloody gift.'

She settled on the edge of the desk, close enough to Dr McDonald to make the psychologist shuffle her chair back a good six inches.

'We heard back from Tayside, Guv: the books in Helen McMillan's bedroom are all signed first editions. Soon as he found out they were worth something, the dad checked online. The older stuff isn't exactly mint, but all together you're looking at about thirty-two thousand quid's worth.'

'Thirty-two—'

'Yeah, I know,' Rhona's eyes widened, 'just sitting there on a kid's bookshelf.'

If she'd lived in Oldcastle, instead of Dundee, someone from

CID would have lifted them by now. Like me. Thirty-two grand would make a whole load of shite go away.

Dr McDonald undid her seatbelt. 'We're going to be late…'

'Not if you get your finger out.'

The house on Fletcher Road was in semi-darkness. The wind had picked up, making the oak trees groan as their bony fingers scratched at the clouds. Fairy lights twinkling. Quarter to five – plenty of time.

She pulled the woolly hat tight over her head and clambered out, scurrying across the gravel drive, the tails of her duffle coat billowing out behind her.

I waited until she was inside before digging out my phone and turning it back on again. It bleeped and chirped at me: text messages, missed calls, voicemail – all from Mrs Kerrigan. All wanting to know why I hadn't turned up with three grand to save my kneecaps.

And I could have walked off with thirty-two thousand pounds' worth of books…

Fuck.

I scrolled through the contacts list, looking for Henry Forrester's number.

Thirty-two grand. What kind of man steals books from a dead girl?

Found it, pressed the button, and sat back listening to the phone ring.

Well, it wasn't as if she was going to miss them, was it?

Not as much as I was going to miss my legs.

Click. *'I'm sorry: I'm not answering the phone at the moment, but if you want to leave a message … well, it's up to you.'*

'Henry? It's Ash: Ash Henderson. Look, I wanted to tell you I'm going to be up in Shetland tomorrow, so do you fancy getting a drink or something? Been too long…' I hung up.

Dr McDonald struggled her massive red suitcase out of the house and across the gravel – her rock-chick aunty following with the two smaller ones. I got out and popped the hatchback.

'Are you *sure* we've got time to—'

'I'll only be a minute.' I hauled the Renault up to the kerb and killed the engine. 'We'll be fine.'

She picked at the dashboard, staring out through the windscreen at Kingsmeath in all its grey, boxy, housing-estate glory. That prick from number fourteen had let his Alsatian loose to wander the streets again, its ribs clearly visible through its fur as it stopped beneath a streetlight to eat something from the gutter.

Dr McDonald licked her lips. 'I don't have to come in, do I? Only I don't do so well with—'

'Unfamiliar enclosed spaces: I know. Stay here. Lock the doors if you like.' I climbed out into the cold. Soon as I closed the driver's door she reached across and pressed down on the little locking nipple, then did the same on her side.

The Alsatian raised its head from the gutter and growled.

I stared at it. 'Fuck – off.'

It went quiet, dropped its head, then slunk away into the darkness.

The front garden was a rectangle of paving slabs, yellowing weeds poking up through the joins, bordered by a knee-high concrete wall. I checked my watch again on the way to the front door: five to five. Fifteen minutes to pack, hour, hour and a half to Aberdeen – depending on traffic…

Going to be tight. The ferry sailed at seven whether you were on it or not.

I let myself in, snapped on the light, shut the door behind me, then stuck my head into the lounge. No sign of Parker, for once. Maybe the shiftless bastard had finally buggered off and got a job?

As if I could be that lucky.

Upstairs.

A wheelie case sat on top of the wardrobe. I took it down and chucked a few pairs of socks inside, some pants, the washing kit from the bathroom, a pair of jeans from the pile in the corner, all the Naproxen, Diclofenac, and Tramadol from the bedside cabinet, and a random dust-furred paperback from the windowsill.

Anything else? Shetland in November: jumpers. There was that cable-knit monstrosity Michelle's mum gave me for Christmas.

It wasn't in the chest of drawers. Where the hell did I—

A noise behind me. I froze.

'Goin' somewhere, like?' A man's voice: low-pitched, coming from the little landing at the top of the stairs.

I pulled the zip on the wheelie case, shutting everything inside. 'Your mum never teach you to knock?'

''Cos it looks to me like yer plannin' on doin' a runner there.'

I turned, nice and slow, keeping my hands in plain sight. 'You got a name?'

The man on the landing smiled, showing off a set of yellowed teeth. His face was lopsided, angular, lumpy and twisted; covered with pockmarks and scar tissue. He was bloody huge too. 'Ye can call us, "Mr Pain".'

Seriously? Mr Pain?

The corners of my mouth twitched, but I got them under control. 'So tell me, *Mr Pain*, this a social call, or an antisocial one?'

He took one hand from behind his back. There was a two-foot length of metal pipe in it, the end swollen with washers – nuts and bolts stuck out at random angles. The modern equivalent of hammering a couple of nails into a baseball bat: a plumber's mace.

Definitely not a social call.

'Been a naughty boy, haven't ye? Missed another payment.'

'You're wasting your time.' I shifted my weight, moving

closer to the bed. 'Going to take me a while to get the money together.'

'No' my problem, is it?' The length of pipe flashed through the air, spines quivering.

I dropped one knee, pitching sideways. Something tugged at my left shoulder, then the bedside lamp exploded into ceramic shrapnel. I snapped my foot out, but Mr Pain wasn't there.

I hit the bed and kept going, rolling right over it as the mace whomped down on the mattress, making the springs sing. I dropped onto the floor on the other side, looked up—

The pipe whistled towards my face.

I flinched, the back of my head slamming into the wall as the mace swept past, its spines ripping the air less than an inch in front of my nose.

Jesus, the bastard was *fast.*

A backhand swing. Splinters flew from the windowsill – the mace carved straight through the wood and into the plaster where my head would've been if I hadn't moved.

Fast and strong.

Another swing and the collection of paperback books burst into flight, paper wings fluttering as they spiralled to the floor.

I dived left, grabbed a handful of clothes from the pile of dirty washing in the corner and hurled it at Mr Pain. Socks and pants, a T-shirt, not exactly deadly weapons, but if they distracted the big bastard even for a couple of seconds...

The T-shirt snagged on the mace's spines, the fabric crackling like a fire as the thing smashed down on the bed frame.

I was on my feet like a sprinter, charging straight into Mr Pain's stomach, sending him battering back into the wardrobe. The pipe would be useless at this distance. Ha, not so clever now, was he? Dancing about at arm's length from the bastard was going to get my head caved in, but up close? Different matter.

That was where experience trumped a big dod of metal.

I grabbed Mr Pain by the throat and slammed him back into the cracked MDF again. He stank of garlic and raw onions, breath like curdled shite. Left fist – uppercut to the floating ribs, putting my shoulder into it, driving hard, ignoring the broken-glass scream of my swollen knuckles. Once, twice, three times. The satisfying soggy-feeling as his ribs cracked and bucked. With any luck a sharp end would puncture the bastard's lung.

A knee slammed into my thigh – probably going for the balls, but this wasn't exactly my first bare-knuckle fight.

Mr Pain jerked his head back, then forwards. Shite. I ducked my chin into my chest and a dull thunk reverberated around my skull, a harsh ringing in the ears. The carpet lurched and buckled like the deck of a ship.

I let go of his throat, staggered back a couple of steps.

Blood bubbled from the flattened mess of Mr Pain's nose, little scarlet droplets flying from swollen lips. 'Fucker!' The mace flashed up for another blow.

What the hell was he *made* of?

Sod this. I turned and ran, leaping the wheelie suitcase, out the bedroom door – pulling it shut behind me. Hauling on the handle to keep it that way.

Get to the bathroom. Rip the front panel off the bath, grab the gun… And then what? It wasn't loaded, the bullets were in a separate box. Was it even in one bit, or did I take it apart for cleaning? Shite – I *did*. It was in half a dozen pieces, each stored in a separate zip-lock freezer bag for extra freshness.

Fuck.

OK, think, think, think, think—

BANG. The jagged end of the pipe carved through the bedroom door, chunks of fibreboard and cardboard insulation burst out into the little landing. Cheaply built shitey council houses…

I grabbed the pipe, below the nut-and-bolt spines, and yanked.

Something large and ugly slammed into the other side of the door. Then the hinges gave way, tearing out of the frame as the whole thing cracked down the middle and Mr Pain toppled out. Eyes wide. Blood dripping from his chin. Hands grabbing at thin air as he kept on going.

He blundered straight into me, shoving me back into the handrail. The wood bent, cracked, snapped with a BANG.

We clattered into the stairwell, a second of freefall and then THUD. It was like being kicked between the shoulder blades by an angry horse. All the breath rushed out of my lungs, taking a groan with it. Then I was tumbling down the stairs, arms and legs tangled with the big smelly bastard. Grunting and swearing.

CRUNCH.

The floor slammed into my chest. As if it wasn't *already* hard enough to breathe...

Jesus, that hurt.

Get up. Get up before he starts swinging that bloody pipe again.

GET UP!

I dragged in a breath, coughed, gritted my teeth, and shoved till I was on my knees.

The hallway was a mess, the carpet littered with bits of door and snapped balusters, a smear of blood on the curling wallpaper. Mr Pain was lying on his back by the front door, groaning, his left arm twisted and bent the wrong way at the elbow.

Looked sore.

Good.

I dragged myself up the wall, swayed on the seasick carpet for two deep breaths, then staggered over and stamped on the joint.

The big man didn't scream. He lay there, eyes wide, mouth working up and down, then grabbed the arm and clutched it to his chest. 'Agghghhhhh...'

Served him right. He could—

The kick came from nowhere, pistoning up into my stomach, lifting me off my feet and sending me smashing back into the wall. The plasterboard cracked, a faint dusting of powdery white drifting out into the air.

My knees buckled, fire blazing through my guts as I scrabbled to stay upright.

Mr Pain grunted his way to his feet and stood there, swaying back and forwards, blood and spittle dripping from his open mouth. And then he started to laugh.

I grabbed what was left of the stairs for support. 'What... What the fuck ... are you ... are you *on*?'

The big man cricked his neck from side to side, voice all bunged up and soggy. 'You've been a naughty boy. Gotta take yer spankin'.' The left arm dangled limp at his side, but the right ended in a huge fist.

He lowered his head and charged.

13

His right shoulder caught me in the chest – his head jammed underneath my arm as we slammed backwards into the wall. The plasterboard erupted in jagged shards, dust swirling out in a cloud.

A fist hammered into my stomach.

Breath hissed out between my teeth, taking a little spray of spit with it.

Of course the bright thing to do, the *safe* thing, would be to wrap my arms around the big bastard's neck. Ride out the blows and keep squeezing until there was no oxygen getting to his warped Neanderthal brain... Unless the spiky-pipe wasn't the only weapon Mr Pain had brought to the party. It was a lot more difficult to ride out a knife in the guts.

Another punch, same place, twice as hard.

Go for the arm.

I grabbed his left bicep and forced the arm back and up – reached across that broad, stinking back with my other hand, caught hold of his forearm and hauled. A grating, popping noise sounded somewhere inside.

The next punch was barely a pat. Mr Pain dragged in a huge breath, but there wasn't a scream to follow it. Instead he dropped to his knees, panting, right arm held out horizontally to his body, the fingers splayed, as if he was waving to the devil all the way down there in hell.

I kneed him in the face.

A grunt and he rocked back. I let go of the buggered arm and took a handful of hair at the back of Mr Pain's head, then introduced the front of it to the third step from the bottom.

Thunk.

'One's a wish...'

I pulled him back up, and did it again, putting all my weight behind it.

Thunk.

'Two's a kiss...'

Blood spattered across the stairs.

'Three's a disappointment.'

THUNK.

He went limp.

I let go and staggered back a couple of steps, panting. 'Should've done ... done your homework, you thick ... bastard, and brought ... a few friends... I was kicking ... kicking the shit out of ... arseholes like you back when ... back when...'

Ah fuck it. I slumped against the wall.

The hall was completely trashed, the staircase ruined, the carpet covered with bits of shattered wood and blood, the air reeking of plaster dust, copper, and rancid-oniony sweat.

His plumber's mace glinted in the corner, by the coat rack.

I wobbled over, bent down, and grabbed it. The world waltzed when I straightened up again, something pounding inside my skull, threatening to pop my brain out through my ears.

Lean on the kitchen door for a bit. Get my breath back. Try not to throw up.

OK.

Any minute now.

Deep breaths.

Ow... Adrenalin was a great anaesthetic, but see when it started to wear off? The knuckles of my left hand pulsed and throbbed, my shoulders felt as if they'd been wrapped in hot barbed-wire, the small of my back stung, my stomach burned, and everything else *ached*.

Getting too old for this kind of thing.

Right. Time to take care of my visitor.

I turned, the length of spiky-pipe swinging loose at my side.

He was lying at the foot of the stairs, curled up in a ball, shuddering, clutching his twisted left arm, face a ruptured mess. For someone calling himself 'Mr Pain', he didn't seem to enjoy it very much.

I grabbed him by the collar and dragged him through into the kitchen – leaving a slick of dark red on the dirty linoleum – then out the back door into the garden.

Dark out here. A sickly glow bounced back from the low clouds, just enough to make out vague shapes and turn everything monochrome. Steam rose from the big man's body, breath fogging the air as I dumped him by the hole where a whirly washing drier would have stood, if some thieving Jakey bastard hadn't nicked it.

The drizzle had started up again, soothing and cool. I turned my face to the sky and let it soak into my skin.

Got to take pleasure in the little things.

I rested the spiky end of the pipe on Mr Pain's ankle. Tapped the spines against the joint. 'You know how this is going to go, don't you?'

The big man gurgled and twitched.

'Yeah.' I swung the mace overhead. 'That's about right.'

I hauled the boot open and threw the wheelie suitcase in next to Dr McDonald's posh red luggage.

She turned and stared at me between the seats. 'I thought you said you'd only be five minutes, it's been quarter of an hour, what if something happened, that dog's been sniffing around the car...' She pulled her head back, eyebrows furrowed, top lip curling. 'What happened to your face?'

I slammed the hatchback shut again, then turned and limped back into the house, grabbed one of the cardboard boxes from the spare room. Put it in the boot, then did the same twice more, until there wasn't room in there for anything else. That was the only good thing about living in a shithole – it wasn't worth unpacking after Michelle threw me out.

One last trip inside. I dragged out my phone on the way up the knackered staircase and called Parker. Seemed to take forever, but eventually he picked up, voice all muggy and slurred. *'Embers! How they hangin'?'*

Already pissed. Or high. 'I need you to stay away from the house for a bit.'

'You're no' shaggin' her again tonight, are you, Embers? God, man, you're a randy—'

'It's not safe, OK? Someone wrecked the place.' I pulled back the bedroom carpet and prised up the loose floorboard. Reached inside, pulled out Rebecca's cigar box, cradled it against my chest.

'Fuck... Wasn't Big Johnny Simpson, was it? Man, I swear I didn't know she was his sister, she—'

'Find somewhere else to crash for a while: go see Mum or something.' Through to the bathroom. The front panel came off the bath easily enough. I grabbed the collection of zip-lock bags hidden under the tub and stuffed them in my pockets. Back down the stairs.

'Embers, I'm sorry, OK? I didn't mean—'

'I'll call you when I get back.' I hung up, slammed the front door behind me, and hobbled over to the Renault.

Dr McDonald peered at me from the passenger seat, eyes wide, chewing on her bottom lip.

I popped the boot, unzipped the wheelie suitcase and tucked the wooden cigar case inside. Unlocked the driver's door, and climbed in behind the wheel. Sat there for a moment with my eyes closed, letting the seat take my weight, muscles settling into new and painful configurations.

She cleared her throat. 'I think it might be a good idea to just drop me off somewhere, doesn't matter where, I mean I don't want to take you out of your way, and I can probably—'

'Going to be tight, but we'll make it.' I turned the key, and the Renault spluttered into life. 'The trick is to only brake when you see the speed cameras.'

'You've got blood on your face.'

The steering wheel was set in concrete, but I dragged it all the way over, the bearings groaning as the car bumped up onto the opposite kerb, then down again onto the road, facing the right way. I snapped on the lights, cranked up the blower to clear the foggy windscreen, switched on the radio. Identikit pop music buzzed and crackled out of the speakers.

'Constable Henderson…' Dr McDonald turned to look out the back window. 'Ash? What happened?'

'An hour to Aberdeen. Hour and a half with rush hour.' I put my foot down, weaving the car through the sodium-lit streets. 'You got your seatbelt on?'

'Are you sure you're all right to drive?'

Not really.

The song faded away and what sounded like a kids' TV presenter, or coke addict, burbled from the speakers. *'Yeah, wasn't that great? Really sets you up for: midweek madness!'* Sirens and trombones made roaring farting noises. *'Ha, ha. You're listening to Crazy Colin's* Rush-Hour Drive-Time Club*, and we've got the sports news coming up in a minute…'*

'If something's happened, perhaps it would help to talk about it? That's what I do after all. Usually it's not till people have been arrested, but that's not important right now.'

Mr Pain. What kind of name was 'Mr Pain' for a grown man? Had to be on meth. Or crack. The big bastard had to be taking *something* to keep on coming like that.

Two missed payments and they send someone round to cripple me. How was that fair?

My head pounded, blades digging into my eye, every oncoming headlight turned into a rusty knife.

Dr McDonald grabbed the handle above the door as the Renault screeched around the roundabout and I floored it, heading north. 'Is it... Do we really have to go this fast, I mean, what if something happens, like a tyre bursts, or we hit something, or there's diesel on the road and—'

'Please ... shut up. For a minute. OK? Just *one* minute.' I ground the heel of my hand into the socket of my left eye. It felt as if I'd been battered with sledgehammers. Should pull over and pop some of the Tramadol in my suitcase. Only take five minutes. And then we'd probably miss the boat.

Probably miss it anyway, thanks to Mr Pain-in-the-Arse.

There was silence from the other side of the car.

She had her arms folded, legs crossed, head turned to the window. Didn't have to be an expert in body language to know what that meant.

Well, you know what? Sod her. See how chatty *she'd* be if some junkie bastard tried to cripple her.

The lights on the Oldcastle bypass flickered through the rain ahead.

OK, so maybe I *had* been planning on doing a runner for a couple of days, but it wasn't as if I had any choice, was it? Police business – escort the lunatic psychologist up to Shetland, make sure she didn't fall into the sea, or get hit by a bus, or mauled by a sheep, or whatever other disaster she had up her stripy sleeve. OK, so I missed a couple of payments; there was no need to send a coked-up nut-job after me with a plumber's mace.

Bloody lucky for Mr Pain I'm a reasonable man.

The slip road swept down to the left, dipping below the level of the motorway, then up again, joining onto the A90 north to Aberdeen. The speedometer crept past eighty.

She was still sulking.

Just because I'd asked her nicely to shut up for a minute.

Well, maybe not asked...

OK, so I was wrong, happy now? It was all my fault. As usual.

'I'm sorry. It's...' Deep breath. 'Didn't meant to snap.'

She shrugged one shoulder, bringing it all the way up to her ear.

Oh, for God's sake.

'Really: I'm sorry.'

She turned in her seat and looked me up and down, then smiled. 'Fifteen minutes, I'm impressed, I thought you'd take at least half an hour to apologize, there might be hope for you yet, Ash. Ash ... Ash ... it's a strange name, isn't it? I mean your parents probably named you after the tree, but I bet most people think of fire and burning and running and screaming...'

14

'Well, how was I supposed to know they'd be digging up half the bloody road?' The Renault juddered across the dual carriage-way and into the harbour entrance. 'Still got fifteen minutes…'

Aberdeen's ferry terminal was a long covered walkway bolted onto the side of an ugly slab-faced building. A red-and-white barrier arm blocked the entrance to the vehicle-loading area. I buzzed the window down, letting in the screech of seagulls and the mingling odours of diesel and fish.

A wee man peered out of the security booth. Droopy face, bags under his eyes. 'Sorry, mate. You're too late.'

'No!' Dr McDonald gripped the edges of her seat. 'Ash, I told you I'm not sleeping in the car, what if someone comes, it's—'

'Will you calm down?' I flashed my warrant card through the open window. 'Police.'

'Nothing I can do – they're closing the bow. Car deck's locked down.'

'Shite…' I stared up at the huge blue-and-white bulk of the MV *Hrossey*. 'Fine, we'll leave the car here. Dr McDonald – out.'

'Ah.' The security guy sucked at his teeth. 'Last boarding's half an hour before sailing. You're fifteen minutes late.'

'Come on, we're on official business, we have to—'

'Actually...' Dr McDonald clambered out into the drizzly night, marched around to the security booth's window, and smiled up at him, 'Sorry, I don't know your name, I'm Alice.'

'Archie.'

And then she started talking at him.

I pulled out my phone. Better give Dickie a call, let him know the trip was going to take a bit longer than anticipated. See if we could get the ferry booking shifted to tomorrow evening before we headed back to Oldcastle... Where Mrs Kerrigan would be waiting.

Might be better to find somewhere to stay up here. Which was easier said than done in Aberdeen. Might find a B&B somewhere further out—

Someone thumped on the car roof. Dr McDonald bent down and smiled in at me. Then pointed back towards the terminal building.

'Grab the bags, and give Archie your car keys.'

Oh God that *hurt*... I lumbered up the covered walkway, following Dr McDonald and her fancy red luggage. Every step was like being pummelled with breeze blocks. And my crappy wheelie suitcase was re-enacting some sort of rodeo fantasy – bucking and twisting every time I dragged it from one section of the walkway to the next.

Dr McDonald stopped and stared back at me, shifting from foot to foot. 'Come on, going to be late, going to be late...' All she needed were big floppy ears and a pocket-watch.

Should have taken a Tramadol when I'd had the chance.

'What did you say to him? Archie, the security guy?'

She marched off. 'Top of my class, remember?'

How come her luggage behaved itself? She had twice as much as I did.

The gangway came to an abrupt end at the ferry's hull. A pair of thick metal doors lay wide open. Inside, the ship's reception area looked like a hotel lobby – lined in polished wood with chrome handrails, a big shiny desk, some sort of leaping salmon sculpture, and a pair of stairs leading up to the next deck.

A grey-haired woman in a black waistcoat raised a radio handset to her lips. 'Right, that's them onboard, close the outer doors.'

A clang and a clunk as the doors swung shut, then the deck beneath my feet started to vibrate – a deep rumbling that worked its way up through my knees until it made my lungs tremble.

The woman came forward and held out a hand for Dr McDonald. 'Archie told me all about it. Anything we can do to help, you let me know.' Was that a tear in her eye?

'Thanks, I *really* appreciate it.'

Bizarre.

I limped over to the reception desk, trundling the Buckaroo suitcase behind me. 'You've got a reservation for McDonald, and Henderson?'

The man poked at a keyboard. 'Let's see...' He looked up and nodded, his mouth pinched together, lips slightly puckered. 'Ah, here we go. Your cabin is down there on the left, and you've got a restaurant booking for half seven.'

'Thanks.' I took the little white tickets. Frowned. 'What about the other cabin?'

'Other cabin?' He went back to the hidden keyboard. 'Nope: just the one, and we're fully booked. Are you two not...' He tilted his head to one side.

'Oh for... Perfect.' Sod it. Too tired and sore to care. 'Thanks.'

I slumped along the corridor to the left of the reception desk, found cabin 16A and slid the paper ticket into the hotel-style lock.

The door opened on a small beige cabin with two single beds facing each other; a walled-off section – that would be the toilet – a space for hanging coats; somewhere to make tea and coffee; and a porthole. The lights of Aberdeen harbour slid past, massive orange supply boats, mud tanks, cranes, pipes, containers.

I dumped my wheelie case in the middle of the little room and collapsed onto one of the bunks. Groaned. And then my phone rang. 'Go away.'

It went through to voicemail.

Everything. Hurt.

I lay on my back staring up at the ceiling tiles. Get up and take a pill... Sod that, it meant moving. I pulled out the phone, ignored the 'missed call' icon, and picked a number from the address book instead.

It was answered on the fifth ring. *'DI Morrow.'* Shifty Dave's voice was barely audible over the sounds of a crowded pub.

'Thought you guys had a murder enquiry to run?'

Pause. *'Ash...'*

'I need a favour.'

Nothing but the burble of bandits and general pub hubbub. Then a clunk, and a sort of roaring whoosh. Drunken singing. A car horn. *'Look ... about last night with Andrew, I—'*

'Does Charlie know?'

'Of course Charlie doesn't know! What am I supposed to tell her, "Hey, darling, how was your day? Oh, by the way, I'm a big poof now; what's for dinner?" How's that going to go down?'

Like a bouncer in an alleyway. 'So don't tell her.'

'You can't say anything, OK? If this gets out I'm—'

'Oh, like I give a toss. My big brother Brett's getting married next month, to an electrical engineer called Gareth.' I closed my eyes, ran a hand across them, trying to scrub away the headache. 'Now shut up – I need a favour.'

'You're not going to tell anyone?'

'I need you to go round to my place and ... tidy up a little.'

A pause. On the other end of the phone someone was singing in the background, an ambulance siren getting closer. *'Why? What did you do?'*

'Had an uninvited visitor.'

'I see.' A deep breath. *'Is he…?'*

'No. He wasn't looking very well when I left, but he'll live.' And they could probably save his leg.

A long, hissing sigh. *'OK, OK, I'll see what I can do.'*

'Thanks, Dave.'

'And you promise *you won't tell anyone?'*

'Bye, Dave.' I hung up. According to the phone's screen there were another two missed calls waiting for me. Well they could go on waiting.

The cabin rocked from left to right. Must be leaving the harbour, giving up its protective arms for the North Sea's cold embrace. Then the room started going forward and backwards as well. Pitch and yaw getting stronger the further out we got, the ship's engines getting deeper.

Kind of comforting…

I closed my eyes. Let it wash over me. Yawned.

Could drift off for a—

Three loud knocks at the door. 'Hello? Ash? Constable Henderson? Hello? It's me, Alice…' Dr McDonald. Wonderful. 'Hello? Are you in there?'

I gritted my teeth, rolled off the bunk up to my feet, and stood there like a dose of brewer's droop – back bent, arms dangling.

'Hello?' Knock, knock, knock.

I opened the door.

She was standing in the narrow corridor, both arms wrapped around herself, eyes darting from side to side. 'They said there's been a mistake with the cabins, the team admin officer only booked the one, and the other cabins are all full, and obviously we can't *share* a cabin. It wouldn't be right: we work together, and you're a man and I'm a woman and what if something happened, it wouldn't—'

'Don't flatter yourself.' I slouched back to the rumpled bunk and collapsed face-down onto it. 'Ow…' It was like being battered all over again.

'But we can't share a cabin it's ridiculous, I mean it's—'

'Trust me,' words muffled by the pillow, 'you're not that irresistible.'

There was a pause, then the creak of someone sitting on the other bed. 'Can't you sleep somewhere else?'

'I think I *might* be able to control my sexual ardour if… buggering hell.' Bloody phone was ringing again. I fumbled it out, stuck it against my ear. 'What?'

An Irish accent, female, clipped. *'Officer Henderson, have yez forgotten yer manners along with everythin' else?'*

'Mrs Kerrigan.' As if today couldn't have got any worse.

'They've got these seats upstairs you can recline almost all the way, I'm sure they're comfortable, you could get one of those—'

'I've got a message for yez, Officer Henderson—'

'Oh, I got your bloody message all right. Well, you know what: I know where *you* live too.'

'—and you can probably hire one for a couple of pounds—'

'Yez've got a hard neck, talkin' to me like—'

'You tried to have me crippled! You really think I'm going to let that *go*?'

'—I can't sleep in the open, surrounded by strange people, anything could happen, I mean I couldn't sleep at all, it would be—'

'Where's our money, Officer Henderson? We had a deal.'

'You should've thought of that before you sent "Mr Pain" to my house.' My knuckles ached, the phone's casing creaked in my fist. 'Deal's off. I so much as see one of your dogs near me, I'm coming after you, understand?'

There was silence on the other end of the line.

'—and what would happen then, it would be horrible, I can't have people watching me sleep, Richard has to go into the spare room when he stays over—'

'Listen up, ye little bollox, if ye ever *eat the head off me again*

I'll feckin' come round meself, *understand? Then we'll see how gobby ye are. Deal's not off till* I *say so: four grand by Thursday lunch.'* And then she hung up.

'—it's not that I don't value you as a colleague, obviously I do, but I really don't think we should be sleeping in the same room—'

Oh fuck... I dumped the phone on the bed and folded my arms over my head. Fuck. Fuck. Shitting fuck. Why? Why couldn't I keep my big gob shut? Threatening Andy Inglis's right-hand woman, what a *great* idea that was. No way that was going to come back and bite me on the balls. Fuck...

'—I mean we only met yesterday... Ash? Hello?'

I rolled over onto my side: it hurt slightly less than being hit by a car. 'I'm going to have a shower. You can stay and watch if you like, but I wouldn't recommend it.'

The ferry thrummed and throbbed beneath my feet, rocking and rolling as I hauled myself upstairs to the main deck level – all pale wooden floors and shiny chrome. A shop, two bars, a cinema, lifeboats... Who could ask for more? It was busy: families; groups of friends; couples; people on their own; what looked like a rugby team, wearing matching red tops, downing pints of lager and singing some sort of folk song.

'Roond da boat da tide-lumps makkin,
Sunlicht trowe da cloods is brakkin.'

A wall-mounted TV played the news, but no one was watching it.

I stopped for a minute. On screen was a shot of Oldcastle Police Headquarters in all its mouldy Victorian glory. A woman with wind-blown hair and a blue umbrella stood in front of the entrance, talking at the camera. It was impossible to make out what she was saying over the singing, but the ticker along the bottom of the screen read, 'SERIAL KILLER – BODIES FOUND – OLDCASTLE POLICE CONFIRM REMAINS ARE "BIRTHDAY BOY" VICTIMS.'

'We maan geng whaar fish is takkin,

Rowin Foula doon...'

The picture jumped to ACC Drummond at some sort of media briefing. Busy grabbing the credit before Dickie's team of Party Crashers turned up tomorrow.

The ferry had two eating areas: a canteen at the back of the ship, and a fancy sit-down place with tablecloths and wine – closed off from the common areas with a glass wall. So the people outside could see what a good time the people inside were having.

I hauled the door open and joined the chosen few. There were only half a dozen tables, and they were all taken. Dr McDonald had the one in the far corner, sitting with her back to the wall hunched over a menu.

I wandered over and pulled out the chair opposite. 'Our Assistant Chief Constable's on the telly right now, marking his territory before Dickie turns up.'

She didn't look up. Sulking.

A man appeared, carrying a tray. 'The large Glenmorangie?'

Dr McDonald stuck up her hand. 'Mine. And can I get a bottle of the Pinot Grigio too.'

'Of course. Sir?'

I turned in my seat... Grimaced as burning needles jabbed up and down my back and stomach. 'Sparkling mineral water: big bottle.'

'Are you ready to order, or would you like a couple more minutes?'

Dr McDonald snapped her menu shut. 'I'll have the herring followed by the pork and black pudding.'

'Excellent choice; sir?'

'Er... Can you give me a minute, I—'

'He'll have the smoked salmon, and the fillet steak: rare.' She threw back her whisky and dumped the empty glass on the table. Shuddered. 'And I'll have another one of these.'

'Coming right up.' The waiter put the tumbler on his tray, collected the menus and melted away.

As soon as he was gone, Dr McDonald picked her satchel up from the floor and took out a red plastic folder. She laid the contents out on the table: copies of every card Hannah Kelly's parents had received from the Birthday Boy.

'You sure you should be doing that in here?'

'That's why I'm sitting in the corner. No one can see over my shoulder.' She arranged them in chronological order, oldest top left, newest bottom right. Then wrapped one arm around herself, the other hand fiddling with her hair as she stared. 'Everything he does has a meaning, we just don't know what it is yet. He dyed Hannah's hair – right here in card number three – he didn't do that with Amber O'Neil. He's turning Hannah into someone else, it's all about projection…'

'Didn't think you were a whisky drinker.'

'And in number seven he shaves it all off, everything, even the eyebrows, he's not punishing her, he's punishing whoever it is she represents…'

Dr McDonald stared and twiddled, and stared some more.

'How do you know I'm not a vegetarian?'

'Hmm?'

'You ordered me a steak, how do you know I'm not—'

'Your hands.'

I held them up. They looked like hands. Bruised and swollen around the knuckles, but other than that…? 'How can you—'

'He doesn't have a physical type: the girls are all different shapes and sizes, straight hair, curly, long hair, short hair; blonde, brunette, ginger – I suppose it doesn't really matter if he's going to dye it anyway; some are pretty, some not so pretty, he doesn't really see them, he sees what he wants them to be…' Dr McDonald unfurled her napkin and draped it over the table, covering the cards. Then smiled – the waiter was back.

'Large Glenmorangie?'

15

She spanked the second whisky down in one, screwed up her face and stuck out her elbows, hissed a juddery breath.

I sat back, helped myself to some fizzy water. 'Why do I get the feeling you're not a drinker?'

'Would you call the Birthday Boy normal, because I wouldn't, but I have to try to think like him if I'm going to figure out what he wants, and what he needs, and why torturing young girls makes sense to him, and that's a bit of a stretch, because he's *not* normal and I am.' She put the glass back on the table. 'Luckily alcohol's a great depressor of inhibitions.'

'You're *normal*?' I could feel the smile spreading. 'You sure?'

Pink rushed up her cheeks and she broke eye contact, staring down at the photos of Hannah Kelly instead. 'He's been active for ten years, he abducts one girl a year for the first six – except for one twelve-month gap – then three years ago he takes two victims within three weeks, then the same again last year—'

'You really think you're normal?'

'—and by now he's probably abducted another two.' She glugged Pinot Grigio into her wine glass, then gulped down a mouthful. 'That brings his total to twelve girls, snatched just before their thirteenth birthday, next one will be number thirteen... Thirteen thirteen-year-olds: that might be significant ...' Another swig. 'Or it might not, I mean there was always going to come a time when he'd have killed thirteen girls, as long as he keeps doing what he's doing and we keep not catching him, eventually he's going to have nineteen victims, then twenty-one, then...'

The bread rolls were warm, I slathered one with butter. 'Unless he's escalating. Last year it was two victims, but this year it might be three, or four. Maybe he'll go on a spree – wind up dead in a ditch with a shotgun in his mouth?'

Dr McDonald rubbed a hand up and down the sleeve of her stripy top. 'The number is definitely significant, you don't randomly pick a girl's thirteenth birthday as the trigger-point for your abduction and torture fantasies for no reason, something must have happened to him when he was thirteen...' This time, when she picked up the wine glass she drained it.

'You're going to be sick, you know that, don't you?'

She peered at the bottle, licked her lips, then filled the glass up again. 'Why isn't it working?'

'Oh ... give it time.'

A lump of marinated herring wobbled on the end of her fork. 'Or perhaps whatever happened ... happened when someone *else* was thirteen and he was mush younger, which is more likely, I mean to develop a pathology like this you need to be in the early stages of sexual development, when your sense of right an' wrong an' good an' bad an' normal annn' weird are still ... still mall ... malleable—' The last word rumbled out on a belch that wafted alcohol and vinegared fish across the table. 'Ooh, pardon.' She reached for the wine and topped her glass up again. There wasn't much left in the bottle. Her cheeks were a rosy pink, and so was the point of her chin.

I picked at my smoked salmon. 'You *might* want to think about pacing yourself.'

* * *

'I think … I think we're looking for someone who was traumatized by a thirteen … thirteen-year-old-girl.' Dr McDonald closed one eye and glugged Shiraz into my glass. Almost all of it went in, the rest making blood spatters on the white tablecloth. 'Then again, who hasssn't been traumatized by a thirteen-year-old girl at some … at some point. There was this horrible cow at Gordons called Clarissa an' she used to say horridible things behind my back.'

I pushed the glass away. 'Let me guess: you stood up to her, she realized she was just as scared as you, and you became bestest friends.'

'No, she … she beat the crap out of me behind the bins at break time.' Dr McDonald skewered a lump of black pudding with her fork, held it up and squinted at it. 'Perhaps she sexually abused him, or he wan … he wanted her to and she wouldn't but … but he *loved* her and it was all doomed… Dooooomed. You're not dringing your wine, why are you not … dringing your wine?'

'Yeah, sorry about that.' I took my card out of the chip-and-pin thing, then dug out a twenty and handed it over too. A pretty generous tip, but then again, given the way Dr McDonald had behaved…

She was slumped forwards in her seat, arms folded in her Orkney fudge cheesecake, head on her arms, brown curly hair dangling in a puddle of spilled brandy. Singing quietly to herself.

That was the trouble with psychologists – too much time spent grubbing about in the minds of nutters, rapists, killers, and paedophiles, tended to rub the 'sane' off a bit.

I jammed the red plastic folder back in her satchel, hooked it over her head, then hoisted her up by the armpits.

She stopped singing. Frowned. 'He wasss hurt by a blonde … thirteen-year-old girl. She broke … she broke his heart… An' maybe his arm. Or a leg or something.'

'You've got cheesecake all over your cheek.' I let go and Dr McDonald wobbled a bit, took a step back – looked as if she was going to keep on going into the other table. I grabbed her again. 'Top of your class, eh?'

'Have you ... you been ... has a thirteen-year-old-girl ever broke ... broken your heart?'

Oh, she had no idea.

'Can you walk?'

'I bet she did. Bet she snapped it in two and ... and stomped on it, like a ... like a bug.'

The sound of vomiting echoed out of the cabin bathroom. I lay back on my bunk, pillows folded behind my head, bare feet on the duvet, flicking through the photos in Dr McDonald's folder. Tramadol and Naproxen wrapped their warm arms around me, more soothing than the ferry's gentle rocking.

Another round of splattering heaves. Then a voice. 'Ash ... Ash ... hold my hair back...'

'No.'

McDonald's printouts didn't seem to be in any sort of order. The Hannah Kelly birthday cards were at the top, but right after those were Helen McMillan's: the twelve-year-old from Dundee with thirty-two grand's worth of signed first editions on her bedroom shelf.

She didn't look much like the photo we'd found on her chest of drawers. The fairy princess outfit and the gap-toothed smile were gone; now her Irn-Bru hair hung in lank curls around a heart-shaped face and long, bruised neck. Freckles covered her nose and cheeks, a thin line of blood running from her nose. Too much eye makeup, the mascara smudged and tear-streaked.

The collar of Helen's bright-green coat was torn on one side, the stuffing sticking out. Both arms behind her back, both ankles strapped to the chair legs, jeans dark around the crotch and thighs. A number '1' was scratched into the top-left corner.

The photograph wasn't a Polaroid like the ones on Rebecca's cards, or any of the earlier victims. The Birthday Boy had finally moved with the times and got himself a digital camera. Well, it wasn't as if he could take conventional film into the supermarkets and get them to process it for him.

I stared into Helen's eyes. They were grey-green, surrounded by pink, shining where the flash bounced off her tears. The card only arrived yesterday, but she'd already been dead for a year.

'Ash... Ash, I'm dying...' More retching. 'Oh no... There's ... there's black pudding in my *hair*...'

Thank God the bathroom had an extractor fan that came on with the light: wheeching away the stench of a three-course meal, two whiskies, a brandy, and two bottles of wine. She'd better be getting it all in the toilet, because if not she could clean it up herself.

I put Helen McMillan's card to one side and pulled out the next set: the girl from Cardiff. Then the one from Bristol. Aberdeen. Newcastle. Inverness. London. London again. Oldcastle, Glasgow... Ten victims – not counting Rebecca – going back nine years. Forty-two cards in total.

Amber O'Neil's cards sat at the back of the pile. Abducted from the Princes Square shopping centre in Glasgow ten years ago, she was the first girl to catch the Birthday Boy's dark little eye.

A mousy blonde, tear streaming down her pale face, nose a bit too big, lips drawn back showing off bloodied teeth. No gag. Not in the first couple of photographs anyway. He wanted to hear her scream, then changed his mind. Maybe it wasn't quite as much *fun* with her roaring her throat raw as he carved shapes into her naked skin.

Blonde to start with: so no need to dye her hair. Abducted in Glasgow. Never seen again.

Lauren died between card four and five; Hannah between seven and eight. Amber lasted till number six, eyes wide and pleading, Stanley-knife graffiti scrawled across her naked body. And a year later, card number seven arrived. The left side of her head was caved in, the mousy blonde hair matted with blood. The next card was worse, but at least by then Amber couldn't feel it any more. Now it was her parents' turn to suffer.

I unzipped my wheelie suitcase and pulled out the cigar box, opened the lid and took Rebecca out. Five cards and she was still alive, still struggling and screaming and bleeding…

The sound of a toilet flushing, then a couple of groans, then the shower running. Washing off the chunks.

I was staring at Rebecca's last birthday card when the toilet door clunked open and Dr McDonald lurched out, wrapped in a towel, clutching her clothes to her chest. Wet hair hung in straggly curls around her face – one eye scrunched shut, the other all bloodshot. She opened and closed her mouth, making sticky clicking noises.

'Urgh…'

I pulled one of Amber O'Neil's cards on top of Rebecca's. 'Well, what did you expect?'

Her voice was still slurred. 'I'm dead. I've died, and this is hell…' She slumped down on the other bunk, rocking back and forwards with her knees clamped together. 'Do we have any water? The stuff in the tap tastes like dog pee.'

Not so rambly now, was she?

'Bottle beside your bed, got it from the little shop while you were spewing your ring.'

'I'm never – drinking – again.' She dumped her clothes on the floor and helped herself to the two-litre bottle, drinking deep. Then surfaced with a burp. 'Urgh… Tastes of sick.'

'Stop whinging and drink it. You'll feel better tomorrow.'

'*Why* did you let me drink all that wine?'

'You're supposed to be a grown-up, remember?'

'Urgh…' She collapsed back, lying half on, half off the bed, one arm thrown across her face. 'You're doing it wrong.'

I frowned at her. 'I'm looking for—'

'That's Amber, right? You have to … you have to look at them all at once, or it's… All her birthday cards, all at once…'

'What difference does that—'

'See, for us they arrive a year apart, it's like … it's like paintings on a cave wall, something that happened long time ago. Slow motion, but for … for him it's quick, it's visceral, it's … it's happening all in a whoooooosh…' Another belch. 'Urgh…' More sticky clicking noises. 'It's all *now* and *bright* and *bloody* and *sharp*. You've got … you've got to appreciate it like he does, you've got … got to *be* in the moment like him. Got to beeeee. A busy, busy little bee…' Getting quieter all the time. Then silence.

'Dr McDonald?' Nothing. 'Alice? Hello, Alice?' Silence.

She'd conked out.

I slipped Rebecca's birthday cards back into the cigar box, stuck everything else on the little table bolted to the bulkhead, and clambered off the bunk. Rolled Dr McDonald onto her side, pulled out the duvet, then rolled her back again so she was covered up. Might be an idea to put her in the recovery position so she didn't choke on her own vomit. Assuming she had any chunks left to choke on.

After that, I got the cabin's bin out from under the tea-and-coffee bit and placed it next to her head. Then stood and looked down at her, lying there with her mouth open a crack, dribble slowly glistening its way down her cheek.

Just like Katie after her first proper party. First week in secondary school and there she was: white sweatshirt stained the colour of clay, flecked with little chunks of sausage roll, reeking of sick and sticky cider-and-blackcurrant. Eleven years old, and she didn't want to be daddy's little girl any more.

Ah, the good old days.

I tucked the duvet under Dr McDonald's chin. 'Sleep tight, you complete and utter rambling lunatic…'

Something rumbled under the covers, followed by a waft of mouldering cauliflower.

'Oh, Jesus! Ack…' It was followed by three aftershocks, sounding like someone was kicking a duck down a length of metal pipe. And the *smell*! I opened the toilet door and flicked on the light, setting the extractor fan going.

There were lopsided letters scrawled across the mirror above the sink in plum-coloured lipstick: 'WHOSE HE REELY TORCHERING?'

She'd come top of her class? What the hell were the rest of them like?

Wednesday 16th November

16

'There you are, I've been looking all over for you, you want breakfast, I want breakfast, I mean I'm ravenous this morning, no idea why: had a *huge* dinner, actually are you OK, because you look a bit rough…'

I twisted my head to the side. Pops and cracks rippled down my spine; someone jabbed a rusty compass right between my shoulder blades.

The forward bar was full of bleary-eyed people and the smell of stale breath and stale beer. The metal grille was still down, locking away the row of taps and glinting optics, but the place was alive with stretching and yawning. A collection of booths and horseshoe-shaped sofa-style benches surrounded little round tables heaped with personal possessions. Like a refugee camp the morning after a booze-up.

Dr McDonald fiddled with her glasses. 'Thanks for not … you know, thanks for letting me have the cabin, I know it probably seems silly, but I really get uncomfortable if—'

'I didn't.' I swung my feet onto the blue-and-green carpet and sat there, blinking, rubbing the grit out of my eyes. A cough ripped through me, making my ribs ache. 'You *snore.*'

She pulled her head back, giving herself a double chin. 'I do *not* snore, it's—'

'Thought the farting was bad, but Jesus – you're like someone hacking up a metal dustbin with a chainsaw.' One. Two. Three… I pulled myself upright, then slowly straightened. Twinges, aches, and pains.

'You were *there*? In the room while I was *sleeping*?' Her eyes widened, then pink rushed up her cheeks. She wrapped both arms around herself. 'I was naked, I woke up and I was naked, and I'd been drinking, and I was naked in bed when I woke up! What did … did you … it wasn't … oh no, no, no, tell me we didn't actually—'

'Like rabbits. All night. Couldn't keep your hands off me.' Why wouldn't my shoes fit properly? Like trying to squeeze a Labrador into a letterbox.

'Oh God…' The pink got a shade darker. 'I didn't … it was a mistake and I really don't think…'

And then she slapped me. Not hard enough to do any real damage, but it still stung like a bastard.

'How *could* you? How could you take advantage of me like that, I was drunk, what kind of a man are you, you're old enough to be my *father*, you slimy, lowlife, exploitative—'

'Don't be stupid; nothing happened. You spent half the night throwing up, and the rest of it snoring from both ends.'

'Ah.' She bit her top lip, looked away. 'I see, you were being humorous, joking that I was promiscuous and predatory, when in fact I was revolting and disgusting…'

'Believe it or not: you're not irresistible, and not all men are potential rapists.' I rubbed a hand across my throbbing cheek. 'And if you hit me again, I'm hitting you back.'

A pale blue glow edged the horizon, the sky a deep indigo twinkling with stars. Most of Lerwick lay in darkness, just the sulphur ribbons of streetlights and the occasional car's headlights breaking the gloom, but the Holmsgarth ferry terminal was lit up like a football stadium.

My badly behaved wheelie case jinked and skittered as I

limped down the covered walkway after Dr McDonald. Her breath streamed out behind her in the fluorescent lighting.

Cold leached through the soles of my shoes, making my feet ache.

Shetland in November – I had to be mad.

The ferry terminal looked like a massive corrugated-iron pig sty, its grey curved roof trimmed in red.

She stomped down the stairs into the reception area. A ZetTrans bus idled outside, its blue-and-white livery spattered with pale brown. 'How are we getting there?'

It speaks! 'Thought you weren't talking to me.'

She stuck her nose in the air. 'That wasn't nice.'

'Yeah, well, it wasn't nice getting hammered, sticking me with the bill, then puking all over the bathroom, was it?'

Headlights swept across the ferry terminal as a little white Ford Fiesta pulled in beside the bus. It had the distinctive blue-and-yellow checked stripe down the side and blues-and-twos fixed to the roof. The world's smallest patrol car. A uniformed constable unfolded himself from the driver's seat, then stood there, checking his watch.

I dragged my wheelie case out into the cold dark morning.

The PC looked up. He had a thin pale face, a long nose, and a short-back-and-sides haircut with a gelled fringe at the front. 'You Henderson?' A north-east accent, so he wasn't a local lad.

'Thanks for the lift, Constable…?'

'Clark. Royce Clark. Like James Bond only without the gadgets.'

'OK…' I went around to the boot, but there was sod all space for luggage in there – it was jammed full of safety gear and black holdalls.

'Sorry.' He shrugged. 'Everything bigger is out at that double murder on Unst.'

Dr McDonald peered into the back seat. 'Oh dear…' More safety gear.

'Well, you're not going that far.' Royce pulled open the back door, grabbed the smaller of her cases and jammed it in behind the driver's seat. 'Maybe fit the big one on your lap?'

She swallowed, shuffled her feet on the frosty tarmac. 'Right, yes, that'll be fine, it's not like we're going to be stuck in there for ages, is it, it's more of an adventure this way, and—'

I took the big case off her. 'It's bloody freezing: stop faffing about and get in.'

'You know I don't like enclosed—'

'You're the one wants to go and see Henry.'

Royce blew into his cupped hands. 'No offence, guys, but I've got a load on today and we're short staffed, so...?'

'Yes, we're fine, perfect, it's all good, no problem here at all, I'll get in the back...' She rubbed her fingers together, then took two deep breaths and climbed in.

I lumped the big case onto her lap; it took up all the remaining space, leaving her peering over the top like a wee kid at a sweet-shop counter. Clunked the door shut. Then squeezed in the front, wheelie case stuffed down at my feet.

Royce stuck the blower on full and pulled out of the car park, heading north out of town. Some sort of live Queen concert blared out of the car stereo – Freddie Mercury singing about not wanting to live forever.

Be careful what you wish for.

I turned it down.

'So,' Royce looked in the rear-view mirror, 'you're a criminal psychologist then?'

'Can you keep your eyes on the road, please, only I get nervous in cars, well, any enclosed space really, I mean it's nothing personal, but—'

'Yes, she's a criminal psychologist.'

'Great.' He nodded, shifting down as we turned the corner and headed up a steep hill. The last remnants of Lerwick disappeared behind us. 'You here about the murder? Bizarre, right? Married couple hacked to death with an axe. Word is they were *swingers*.'

'Actually—'

'Can you believe that? On a wee island like Unst? Not like everyone doesn't know everyone else's business up here, is it? Break wind in Valsgarth and everyone in Sumburgh knows what it smells like before you're halfway home.'

'We're not really—'

'Tell you: it was quite the culture shock, coming up here from Lossiemouth. You know most of them are related? Well, except for the incomers. Our victims – you know, the swingers – they were from Guildford originally. That kind of thing's probably quite normal down there...'

Scrubby heathland drifted by in the dark, pale yellow and green in the patrol car's headlights.

I pulled out my mobile. 'We're not here for your murders.'

'No?'

'Birthday Boy.'

Another nod. 'Right.' The road swept around to the left, and the bleak landscape opened up into a valley. Pre-dawn light turned a sea loch into a pewter slab, nestling between dark hills. 'Want to know what I think?'

Not really.

My phone bleeped and pinged: fifteen missed calls. Eight from DC Rhona Massie – probably wanting another moan about Sergeant Smith from Aberdeen – the rest from Michelle. Three new text messages as well, all sent while the ferry was out of mobile range.

Royce held up a finger. 'I think your Birthday Boy's a paedophile: he's torturing them 'cos it's the only way he can get off, so he's probably impotent. The photos help him relive the experience when he's masturbating. Probably got a big house in the country somewhere, so no one can hear them screaming. How am I doing, Doc?'

A plastic creak came from the back seat. 'Can we slow down, please?'

'Bet he's a single white male, twenty-four ... twenty-five, menial job, but his parents were loaded: that's how he can afford his place in the country.'

'Hmm...' I clicked on the first message – Shifty Dave Morrow:

Holy FUCK! You owe me big time!

The next was from Michelle:

WTF were you thinking?
Wre suppsed 2 b past all this!!!

What the hell was *that* supposed to mean? The third one was from her as well, sent at eleven fifty-five:

Yr suppsed 2 b a grown up!
Fkn act like 1
U cant just have kt stay ovr & not tell me!

Shit. I jabbed the call button. 'Pull over.'

'We're only going to be another five—'

'Stop the fucking car!'

'Answer the bloody—'

'*Ash?*' Michelle's voice boomed in my ear. '*What the hell are you playing at? We had a deal!*'

I took another couple of steps away from the patrol car. PC Clark had parked on a crescent of tarmac by the side of the road, at the top of a steep hill overlooking Scalloway. The little town curled at the join between two fingers of land reaching out for the Atlantic Ocean – street and harbour lights glittering back from the dawn-blued water.

'I have no idea what you're on about, OK? Can we discuss it like adults for a—'

'*Don't you dare talk to me like* I'm *the one being unreasonable! We had a deal, Ash Henderson!*'

'What am I supposed to have—'

'I'm her mother, *for Christ's sake! Why can't you ever think about anyone but yourself? At least you could've called me and let me know everything was OK!'*

'It—'

'Do you have any *idea how worried I was?'*

The morning was getting lighter, gold rippling across the water. 'I don't understand what you're—'

'You can't have Katie stay the night without telling me! I was worried sick!'

Stay the night?

'It... I don't—'

'You're impossible.' Michelle hung up.

Stay the night? How the hell could she stay the night, I wasn't even there!

Katie's number was on speed-dial. It rang, and rang, and—

'Daddy, I was just thinking about you!'

'Your mother's been on the phone.' Dealing with kids is exactly the same as dealing with criminals: never let on how much you do or don't know.

A pause. *'Has she? Is she OK, I was—'*

'Why does your mother think you stayed at my house last night?'

'Does she? Wow, how weird is that?' Another pause, as if Katie was giving it some serious thought. Then she was back, every sentence sounding as if it was a question. *'Oh, you know what happened: she must've misheard me? I told her I was staying with my friend Ashley and* her *dad? And Mum must've thought I meant—'*

'You do know I'm a police officer, right, Katie? It's my job to spot when someone's lying their arse off.'

'Ah...' Deep breath. *'I really* was *round Ashley's house, but Mum hates Ashley's parents 'cos they're Tories, and sometimes they let us stay up late watching horror films and drinking Red Bull and you* know *what Mum's like about Tories and horror films. Ashley's mum and dad were in the house the whole time, so we were always*

safe and looked after and it was only a little teensy-weensy *white lie… I didn't want Mum getting all upset.'*

'I don't—'

'You can ask Ashley's dad if you like? He's really nice, not as cool as you, but he's OK, and he'll tell you we did our homework first and everything*! Hold on, he's right here…'*

Some rustling, then a smoker's voice: Oldcastle accent, trying hard to sound posh. What Michelle would call a typical Tennent's Lager Tory. *'Hello?'*

'You Ashley's father?'

'Is something wrong?'

'I'm Katie Henderson's dad.'

'Ah, right, lovely kid. Good as gold last night: pizza and a Freddy Krueger marathon. Sweet.'

'Just wanted to check she'd behaved herself. Can you put her back on?'

'Here we go…'

'See, Daddy? You won't tell Mum, will you? She'll freak*, you know what she's like.'*

So the choice was: land Katie in it, or say nothing and pretend I'm a complete tosser who couldn't be arsed telling her mother she wasn't going to be home last night.

Well, it wasn't as if Michelle could actually hate me any more than she already did.

'OK, but only on the condition that you're nicer to your mum. I know she can be a bit…' There was no way to end that sentence well. 'Be good, all right? For me?'

'I promise.' The little girl voice again. *'Daddy, can we go pony trekking for my birthday?'*

Pony trekking? How the hell was I supposed to organize that?

'We'll see.'

'Oops: got to go, Daddy, Ashley's dad's giving us a lift to school. Love you!'

'Be nice to your mother.'

I jammed the phone in my pocket and turned back to the tiny patrol car. Dr McDonald was peering out over the top of her big red suitcase. Her glasses were on squint, it made her head look lopsided.

Why did every woman in my life have to be a card-carrying nutcase?

I got back in the car.

We stopped at the Scalloway Hotel to drop off our suitcases and check in, then it was a five-minute drive through the dark streets to a house on the outskirts of town, overlooking the bay. The garden was a mix of overgrown bushes and stunted trees, their bare branches clawing at each other, fighting for space. Moss had colonized the pantile roof, lichen speckled the walls, and both front windows were jagged holes fringed with broken glass.

PC Clark hauled on the handbrake. 'Not *again*...'

I climbed out into the cold morning.

A sign was bolted to the garden wall: 'FREIBERG TOWERS'. I pushed through into the garden and marched up the path as Royce called it in.

'Sarge? Lima One Six: we're out at the Forrester place... Yeah, looks like Burges has been at it again.'

The doorbell sounded a dismal two-tone chime from somewhere deep inside. I cupped my hands and blew into them, shifting from foot to foot. Then tried again.

'...both windows panned in... Uh-huh... Uh-huh... Don't know...'

I forced my way through the grabbing skeleton of a rose bush and peered into the lounge. A chunk of breeze block lay in the wreckage of a coffee table, carpet covered in glittering cubes of glass. 'Henry?'

It was dark inside – no sign of life.

'...has he not called it in? ... Ah, OK. Well, I've got the camera in the car anyway. You want me to dust for prints too?'

I fought my way back to the front door – locked – then around the side of the house. The damp fingers of an ancient leylandii pawed at me as I waded through knee-high weeds to a tall wooden gate. The hinges squealed as I shouldered it open.

The back garden was a riot of thistles, docken, and grass. It followed the slope of the hill, the top corner just catching the first rays of dawn. A small pond choked with reeds, a greenhouse with no glass left in it, and an outbuilding that needed a coat of paint and a new roof.

I took the path along the back of the building to the bedroom window. Dark. Probably had the curtains drawn. The kitchen door was locked like the front one, but...

Up on my tiptoes, fingers spidering along the top of the architrave. Bingo: a little ceramic puffin, the black and white paint flaking and brittle. A Yale key was wedged inside. I pulled it out and unlocked the kitchen door.

'Henry? Henry, it's Ash. Ash Henderson? You in? You awake? You sober?' Nothing but silence from the dead house. 'Henry? You still alive, or have you pickled yourself to death, you daft old bugger...?'

No answer.

The kitchen was disappearing under a layer of dust. Piles of newspapers and unopened letters covered a small breakfast bar, four stools tucked beneath the worktop.

'Henry?'

Through into the hallway, breath streaming out in a thin grey fog. It was colder in here than outside.

'Henry?'

The stairs led up to a small landing, but I went for the back bedroom instead. Knocked, waited, then eased the door open. Darkness. The smell of rancid garlic and stale booze underpinned something foul and rotting. 'Henry?'

I felt for the light switch and flicked it on.

Henry was lying on the bed, flat on his back, dressed in a

black suit, white shirt and black tie. Grey hair made a rumpled tonsure around a bald crown speckled with liver spots. His face was slack, like a sock-puppet without a hand, his features too big for that little head. A bottle of Bells lay beside one thin hand, only a third of it left.

A small plastic bottle of pills sat on the bedside cabinet.

The silly old git… He'd finally done it.

17

I stared at the ceiling for a minute, then settled down on the stool in front of the vanity unit.

So much for getting Henry's help catching the Birthday Boy: looked as if Dr McDonald was on her own...

Which wasn't exactly fair. The poor old sod deserved better than this, rotting away in a cold and lonely house, until the booze, an aneurism, or hypothermia finished the job.

Let's be honest, the end probably came as a bit of a relief.

'Henry, could you not have waited till—'

A dry squeak came from the corpse, followed by the smell of death. Or rotten eggs. Or a mouldering otter... Not dead, just farting.

'Agh, not you too!' What was it with psychologists?

I stuck a hand over my mouth, marched over to the curtains and threw them open, then did the same with the window, letting the cold air in and the smell of whatever was festering in Henry's bum out.

'Henry!'

'Mmmmmph... Nrm slppn...' Pale gums in a slack mouth.

'Henry, you manky-arsed bugger: up! You've got visitors.'

He cracked an eye open and blinked at the ceiling. 'Sodding hell...' His voice sounded like a handful of walnuts being slowly crushed, the Aberdeen accent twisting the vowels out of shape. 'Fit time is it?'

'Nearly eight.'

'Tuesday?'

'Wednesday.'

'Near enough.' He looked as if he was trying to sit up, then flopped back on top of the duvet. 'Am I dead?'

'You smell like it.'

'Oh... In that case, give us a hand?'

I hauled him out of bed, and propped him up against the wardrobe, trying not to breathe through my nose. 'God almighty, when did you last have a bath?'

'You look like a punch bag.' A long, rattling cough. 'Where did I leave my teeth?'

The little plastic bottle of pills rattled when I shook it. A printed label on the side: 'FLUVOXAMINE 50MG. TWO PILLS TWICE A DAY TO BE TAKEN WITH FOOD. AVOID ALCOHOL.'

'You shouldn't be drinking with these.'

'Ah, there they are.' Henry picked a tumbler off the windowsill – a set of dentures were floating in what looked like old urine. He fished his teeth out and popped them in, then drank the rest of the liquid, and sighed. The unmistakable reek of whisky. 'Ash, much though I've missed you like an amputated limb, I'm guessing you want something...' His eyes narrowed. Then closed completely. His shoulders slumped. 'Of course, I'm sorry. Rebecca's birthday was Monday, wasn't it? I meant to call, but...'

'It's OK.'

'No, it's not.' He clicked his false teeth together a couple of times. 'I used to be a psychologist, not an idiot.' He snatched the bottle of Bells from the bed and slouched through to the kitchen. 'Put the kettle on, I need to wrestle my prostate into a decent morning piss for a change...'

By the time he came back from the toilet, I had four mugs of coffee sitting on the dusty kitchen worktop, the big ring on the gas stove turned up full to take the chill out of the air.

Henry froze in the doorway, frowning at Dr McDonald. 'Who's this? I thought you...' A sniff. 'And what's that bloody racket?'

The strains of *Bohemian Rhapsody* came through the kitchen wall – Royce, whistling away to himself in the lounge. I didn't have the heart to tell him to knock it off.

'Dr Forrester, this is Dr McDonald, she has a tendency to babble and her hangover farts smell even worse than yours.'

Pink bloomed on her cheeks. 'He's not exactly ... it's ... this isn't really the first impression I wanted to make, I mean we've come all the way up here and now you think I'm some sort of drunkard, when really I was trying to dis-inhibit my normal thinking patterns so I could examine the case from the offender's perspective.'

Henry raised an eyebrow. 'Well, aren't you ... delightfully quirky.' He settled onto one of the breakfast-bar stools. 'What makes you think *I'm* hungover?'

I clunked a mug of black coffee down in front of him. 'You've no milk.'

His hands shook as he picked it up and slurped. Then topped it off with Bells, the neck of the bottle clattering around the mug's rim. 'Before you say anything: it's the Fluvoxamine – stops your body breaking down caffeine properly, gives you the tremors. And you're not my mother. I'm seventy-two, I can drink what I want, when I want.'

Another slurp, then more whisky.

'What happened to your windows?'

Henry peered over the rim of his mug. 'Tell me, Dr McDonald, do you always binge drink when you're working on a profile?'

She pulled out a stool and sat opposite him. 'Actually, we call it "behavioural evidence analysis" now, everyone was watching all those television shows where the FBI come in and give a profile and it's bang on and they catch the serial killer every time, and—'

'Do you drink, or don't you?'

She swallowed. 'Sometimes ... it helps loosen things up.'

He nodded, then tipped half the remaining Bells into her mug. 'This isn't a social visit: you're here about a case. And as you're here with DI Henderson, I'm going to assume it's the Birthday Boy. We worked a couple of rapes together, but ... I think they both died in prison?'

Heat leached through my mug into my aching fingers. 'Crouch got shanked in Barlinnie, Chambers drank a whole thing of bleach.'

'So it's the Birthday Boy.' Another slurp, and this time when the whisky bottle went back on the breakfast bar it was empty. 'Can't help you.'

A knock at the door and Royce stuck his head in from the hall. 'I've photoed and fingerprinted everything, so you can clean up if you like. Watch yourself though, there's glass and dog shit all over the place...' He grinned at me. 'Any chance of a coffee? I'm freezing.'

Henry's mouth turned down at the edges. 'Lucky me.' He clapped his hands against his legs. 'Sheba? Sheeeeeee-ba?'

I handed the last mug to Royce. Frowned. 'You said: "Burges has been at it again." Not, *Arnold* Burges?'

'Yeah, that's him: tall, fat, bald, big beard like he's eating a badger? Works one of the fish farms out by Calders Lea, he's been—'

'Constable Clark,' Henry pointed at a door in the corner of the room, 'if you want to make yourself useful there's a dustpan and brush in the cupboard. Some bin-bags too. And no more bloody whistling!'

A wobbly dog shuffled into the kitchen, moving one leg at a time, its claws clicking and clacking on the floor. It bumped its head against Henry's leg and he reached down to rub a greying ear. The dog groaned.

'Sheba, what did I tell you about crapping in the house?'

More groans; one back leg twitched.

'Crap in the kitchen, it's easier to clean up...' He stopped rubbing and looked at me. 'Well, she's old, what do you expect?'

Dr McDonald sniffed her coffee, as if there was something sinister lurking at the bottom. 'Fluvoxamine's an antidepressant. Mixing it with alcohol can cause ... problems.'

Henry shrugged. 'Still better than Paroxetine: side effects include diarrhoea and erectile dysfunction. Talk about putting the kybosh on your sex life. And don't get me started on Escitalopram.'

Royce slouched out of the room, taking the dustpan and brush, bin-bags, and his coffee with him. Muttering.

She tilted her head to one side, and stared at Henry. 'If you're depressed, it might help to talk to someone, I mean, you're dressed in funereal black, you're mixing your medication with whisky, but it's nothing to be ashamed of: we all have times when it feels like we can't cope, and I'm—'

'You remember Detective Inspector Pearson, Ash?'

'Strathclyde, wasn't it? Retired to Aviemore; lives with his granddaughter.'

'Not any more.' Henry dug something out of his jacket pocket and handed it over.

It was an order of service, folded in half lengthways: 'In Loving Memory Of Albert Pearson' in gothic script above a photograph of a beady-eyed grey-haired man in full dress uniform.

'Buried him Monday in Clydebank. Nice service, very upbeat. Horrible sausage rolls at the reception.' Henry tugged at the lapels of his black suit. 'Hence the...?'

Dr McDonald fidgeted with the newspapers covering the breakfast bar. 'You weren't trying to kill yourself?'

'Oh, I've thought about it. After Ellie passed I thought about little else. But maybe not quite yet.' He gave the ancient dog's ears another rub. 'Sheba would miss me, wouldn't you, girl? Couldn't do that to her, she's all I've got left.'

Sheba's back end lowered to the floor, and she sat there with her chin on his knee, gazing up at him with milky eyes, dribbling onto his trousers.

Henry swished a mouthful of coffee back and forwards through his false teeth. Swallowed. 'Albert and I used to meet up a couple of times a year and chew over the cases we never managed to solve, trying to work out what we missed. A six-year-old girl strangled and dumped at the side of the road when her parents couldn't pay the ransom. The accountant who died in the Royal after someone cut off his hands. The family of four on holiday in Dingwall, battered to death in their caravan. The eighteen-year-old receptionist strung up by her ankles in Knapdale Forest and gutted...' He sighed, then threw back the rest of his coffee. 'Licking old wounds, then rubbing salt into them.'

I laid the order of service on the worktop. 'The Party Crashers' last psychologist screwed up all the notes, then topped himself.'

'All of them?' Henry raised an eyebrow. 'How did he—'

'Buggered the server too: nine years' worth of interviews, assessments, profiles, the whole lot. There's nothing left.'

A nod. Then Henry reached into the nearest kitchen cupboard and pulled out a fresh bottle. Grouse this time. 'Then you're in luck, Dr McDonald, you get to start with a clean slate. None of that legacy thinking from useless old farts like me to get in your way.' He twisted the top off and threw it over his shoulder. 'You're not drinking your coffee.'

Silly old bugger. 'Is this about Denis Chakrabarti?'

'I don't do profiling any more. I retired.' Henry pointed at the draining board, where half a dozen cut-glass tumblers were lined up on the stainless steel. 'Pass me three of those, will you?'

I placed three glasses on the breakfast bar. 'Denis Chakrabarti wasn't your fault.'

'Yes he was. You know it, I know it, and the six little boys he raped and dismembered know it. Philip Skinner's widow knows it too.' Henry slugged a generous measure into each tumbler, then held one up. 'A toast: to new beginnings. May Dr McDonald not make the same mistakes I did.'

She stared at the glass in front of her. 'It's not even eight o'clock yet, I mean it's a lovely offer, but I don't know if—'

'If you're going to climb inside the mind of the monster, you should really go prepared, don't you think?' A smile pulled at his cheeks; the glass trembled in his hand.

I put a hand on his shoulder, it was hard and knobbly beneath the jacket. Just bones and whisky in a funeral suit. 'Look ... talk it over with Dr McDonald, OK? Be a sounding board – you don't have to *do* anything.'

'I don't—'

'We need your *help*, Henry. If you're still blaming yourself for Chakrabarti, maybe this is your chance to redeem yourself.'

'He doesn't want to help, he doesn't want to have anything to do with the case, what am I supposed to do, I mean I can't—'

'Talk to him. Work whatever freaky mojo you did on the ferry crew.' Outside, through the shattered lounge window, Scalloway harbour glittered in the sunshine – a bright-red fishing boat chugged out to sea, stalked by a cloud of whirling seagulls. 'Look, we don't have time to dick about up here, OK? Flirt with him, flatter him, dazzle him with your brilliance, I don't care: get him to help.'

'But he doesn't *want* to—'

'Top of your class, remember?' I pulled on my jacket. 'I'll be back in a couple of hours.'

She sagged, stripy arms hanging by her sides. 'But, Ash—'

'God's sake: you're worse than Katie, and she's *twelve*.' I grabbed Dr McDonald's shoulders and spun her around, so she was facing the kitchen. Gave her a push. 'Now go.'

She scuffed her Hi-tops across the carpet.

When she'd closed the door behind her, I headed outside. Royce was waiting in the patrol car with the engine running. I squeezed into the passenger seat – at least it was nice and warm in here. 'Tell me about Arnold Burges.'

The constable pursed his lips, leaned forward, voice turned down to a whisper. 'Came up here from London four years ago: been hassling Dr Forrester ever since. We've got him … God, what, about twenty, thirty times for public nuisance and destruction of private property. But the Doc never wants to press charges. Daft, eh? I think he feels sorry for him, you know, after what happened to his daughter.'

I pulled on my seatbelt. 'Drive.'

18

'...and the time before that, he took a sledgehammer to Dr Forrester's wife's headstone. Smashed it to bits... Here we go.' Royce pulled the Fiesta into the side of the road. Mountains surrounded a slash of water, glowing green and blue in the early morning sun. A handful of white cottages dotted the landscape, looking out across the sea loch to the village of Calders Lea. 'That's the cages there.' He pointed at a collection of three wide, wheel-like things lying in the middle of the water, made from a framework of black pipes. Some sort of large floating shed was moored between them.

'You sure Burges is there?'

A shrug. 'It's Wednesday, so he should be... Less he's got a day off, or something.'

Royce drove on another couple of hundred yards, then took a narrow road on the left, down the hill towards a collection of bus-shelter-sized offshore containers in various shades of rust-flecked blue with a logo painted in white on the side – three salmon swimming in a circle around the words 'CALDERS LEA AQUACULTURE LTD ~ DA FASH FOR DU!'

A wooden hut sat next to a concrete slipway that disappeared into the water. Royce parked alongside it. 'How's your sea legs?'

'He going to have friends?'

'Depends how drunk Benny got last night.' Royce squinted, held a hand over his eyes – shading out the morning sun. 'Talk of the devil...'

A wide boat with a small wheelhouse was *brrrrring* its way through the sapphire blue water, making for the slipway. Two minutes later it bumped against the concrete and a stick-figure of a man in blue overalls and black wellington boots hopped out, holding one end of a thick rope. His eyes were sunken and pink, underlined with heavy purple bags, a threadbare woollen hat perched on top of his head. Long arms, short legs, big ears and a wild mess of ginger hair.

Royce held up a hand. 'Benny.'

'Constable Clark!' A lopsided grin and an almost impenetrable Shetland accent. 'Whatever it was, me darlin', I didn't do it. Was home all night with ma sister.'

'Yeah, I bet. You busy?'

'Never aff o' da go, you know?'

'Arnold about?'

'On da barge.' He tilted his head to one side, contorted his eyebrows. 'He do it again?'

'Yeah.'

Sigh. 'Less an dule... Give us a minute to load some feed, and I'll give du a hurl.' He clomped over to one of the containers and unlocked the padlock, then creaked the door open. It was stacked full of paper sacks – like the ones tatties came in. A smell, like cat biscuits, wafted out of the container.

Benny hefted a bag onto his shoulder and shuffled back to the boat, hauling up the droopy backside of his overalls. 'Du can lend a hand if du want.'

The boat clunked against the floating platform. It was about the size of a boxing ring with a big wooden shed taking up almost all of the available surface area, barely enough room around the edge for a walkway and handrail.

Benny switched off the engine, then threw a line around a cleat in front of the shed doors, wrapping it tight. 'I lichtit til him: leave the poor auld fart alone, but dis he listen til me? Course he doesn't.' Benny dragged a sack of feed from the bottom of the boat and thumped it down on the walkway. 'Arnie? ARNIE, DU GOT VISITORS!' Benny hefted another sack. 'ARNIE?'

Nothing.

It was still and silent out here in the middle of the sea loch; sunlight glinted off the water all around us.

I clambered up onto the walkway. The shed door was lying wide open. A metal hopper took up nearly half of the building, attached to some sort of engine and a length of pipe that disappeared out through the wall. A small table and a couple of folding chairs. A wee diesel generator, portable TV, kettle, mugs, microwave, and other assorted bits and bobs. Not exactly luxurious. Half the shed was empty, the area fenced off with chicken wire and wooden slats, a couple of bags of fish feed stacked against the wall. The smell of cat biscuits was nearly overpowering. No sign of Burges. 'Thought you said he was out here.'

'He is.' Benny dumped another sack on the walkway.

'What, he's invisible?'

A shrug.

I squinted out at the shining water. 'Maybe he saw the patrol car and ran for it?'

'Swum for it, du means.' Another sack. 'We've only got the one boat.'

The diesel generator spluttered into silence. Royce appeared at my shoulder carrying two mugs. He held one out. 'No biscuits. But if you're hungry there's plenty of fish food?'

'Arnold Burges going to be long?'

'Depends.' I took a sip: it was coffee, but only just.

Something broke the surface of the water – over by the

furthest of the three cages. It was a bald head, the shiny pink crown surrounded by a fringe of soggy black hair. Big diving goggles, breathing apparatus for an aqualung. And then it was gone again.

I leaned against the handrail, following the trail of bubbles. 'When Burges gets here, make yourself scarce. You and the little orang-utan.'

'How?' Royce pursed his lips and looked around. 'Not exactly a lot of places to—'

'Get in the boat, go fishing, I don't care.'

'Hmmm...' A sip of coffee. 'You're kinda ... *pushy* for a detective constable.'

Cheeky bastard. 'I'm only asking for ten minutes. Fifteen tops.'

'Yeah, well, you remember *I'm* the one who's got to keep the peace here after you've buggered off back to the real world... Here we go.'

The bald head resurfaced a good twenty feet closer, making for the barge. Something bobbed along behind it: looked like a fluorescent orange buoy. Two minutes later, a huge man hauled himself out of the water and up onto the platform.

He'd been squeezed into a tatty old drysuit. The arms, legs and neck looked as if they'd been black once, the chest and stomach ancient yellow. Water dribbled from a bushy brown beard.

Arnold Burges.

He pulled off the diving goggles and narrowed his eyes at Royce. 'The old bastard's lying. I was here all night with Benny. After that frigging seal.' He turned his back, squatted at the edge of the walkway, and reached into the water.

Royce sighed. 'Benny's already told us he was round his sister's all night. How many times do we have to go over this? You've got to stay away from Dr Forrester.'

The big man flexed his shoulders and hauled on a length of blue plastic rope – the buoy cut through the water until it was close enough for him to grab. 'Another seven hundred fish last night. Seven *hundred*.' He looped the rope around a metal contraption, then cranked the handle.

'I mean it, Arnold: leave him alone.'

A foot of black net rose from the loch, the rest of it still submerged. Silver shapes glistened inside. Burges pulled one of them out. It was a salmon, nearly as long as his arm, scales glistening pink, silver and grey, its distinctive jutting jaw hanging open. A single, ragged-edged chunk was missing from its belly. 'See that?'

'Arnold—'

'One bite. Sticks his nose through the net, tears out the liver and leaves them to die. Seven hundred frigging fish in one night.' Burges curled his top lip, then tossed the salmon into a plastic barrel, sending water splashing up the side of the shed. 'Been picking dead fish out the cages all week.'

'Arnold, this is Detective Constable Henderson, he wants a word.'

Burges went back to the winch, lifting more net out of the water. 'Benny? You get that feed?'

Benny nodded towards the pile in the barge. 'Twenty bags.'

'That's no bloody good, how's twenty bags going to last us—'

'Don't draa doon der broos at me, Arnie Burges. A'm hed me some passengers, didn't I?'

Draa doon der…? What the hell was that supposed to mean? It was as if he was making up words.

Benny hopped back in the boat. 'Wis just aff to get the balance.'

I stared at Royce, jerked my head towards the shore.

A pause, then the constable nodded. Not as daft as he looked. 'Yes, right, well, why don't I give you a hand, Benny? Less of a job for two. This pair can stay here and … have that word.'

* * *

The boat's engine faded to a grumble, then a whisper, then nothing.

I leaned back against the rusty metal handrail. 'Stay the hell away from Henry Forrester.'

Burges hurled another dead fish into the barrel. 'Fertilizer. That's all these are good for now.'

'It's not his fault.'

'Waste of good fish.'

'Look, Mr Burges, I know you've been through a lot, but—'

'You *know* what I've been through?' THUMP. The next salmon didn't go in the barrel, it battered into the wooden platform at my feet. 'You fucking *know*?'

Yes, I fucking did.

'It isn't—'

'My Lauren's dead, *Constable* Henderson. Oh yeah, I *know* who you are. I remember you from the frigging press conferences. Calling yourself the "Party Crashers": like this was some sort of *game*. Tell you what, how about we all throw a party, because some twisted bastard killed my Lauren?'

'Henry Forrester did his best to—'

'We'll all have jelly and ice cream, because someone pulled out her teeth, cut her, tore out her fingernails, hacked off her head, and gutted her like a fish? Yeah, let's have a frigging party!' The big man's face was getting darker, red spreading across his round cheeks. The veins in his neck throbbed where the skin met the drysuit's rubber collar.

I stared out across the water. Took a deep, slow breath. At least he knew; he wasn't waiting for the next card to turn up to find out what the bastard had done. Lauren was dead, the Birthday Boy couldn't hurt her any more. But Rebecca...

There was something in my throat. 'You're not the only one who lost a daughter.'

'She wasn't even thirteen!' Spittle flew from his lips, sparkling in the sunshine.

'Then take it out on the Birthday Boy, not the poor old bastard who—'

'If you useless wankers had done your jobs and caught him, Lauren would still be here!' He squared his shoulders, bearded chin jutting out. 'Two years. TWO FUCKING YEARS you had before he took her!' Burges took a step forwards.

Here we go.

I pushed myself off the handrail, coiling my aching hands into fists. 'You need to calm down, before you get hurt.'

'You got any idea what it's like? The waiting? Every birthday, waiting for the next card, waiting to see what he's done to her?'

All the time.

I closed my eyes, counted to five. Had another go: 'Henry Forrester tried to help you.'

Burges threw his arms wide, the drysuit creaking as it stretched. A balding bear in a rubber romper suit, beard jutting out like wire wool. 'Why should *he* get to forget? Eh? Why should *he* get to put it all behind him? Every year we get another card. Every *frigging* year. We moved up here and he still found us! He's out there with his camera and his knives and other people's daughters, because you FUCKERS can't do your—'

'What the hell are we supposed to do: magic the bastard up out of thin air?' Getting louder. 'You think this is *easy*? You think you're the only one fucking suffering? At least we've found Lauren's body, at least you get to...'

Burges's eyes went wide, mouth hanging open, face drained to a pale grey.

'Are you OK?'

He took a step back, then thump, he was sitting on the platform's wooden surface. Staring up at me.

'Mr Burges?' Shite, he was having a heart attack. 'Mr Burges?'

'You...' He blinked, rubbed a huge hand across his face.

Then looked out across the water, eyes glistening. 'You found my Lauren…?'

'No one told you?' For fuck's sake – surely *someone* should have told him. One of Dickie's team, or Weber, or—

'You little bastard…' He scrambled to his feet, neoprene drysuit squeaking and groaning. Backed up to the open doorway. 'You're fucking for it now!'

Great. If I'd known I was going to be delivering the sodding death message I wouldn't have opened with, '*Stay the hell away from Henry Forrester.*'

Idiots. How could they not tell him? How could they be so bloody…

Burges was back on the walkway, clutching a rifle. Big wooden stock, black metal barrel – a two-twenty-two, more than capable of blowing a massive hole in anyone daft enough to stand in front of it.

Oh. Shit.

The big man racked the bolt up and back, then forward again. Putting a bullet in the breech.

SHIT.

Where the hell was Royce? I glanced over my shoulder – the little boat was still tied up on the shore by the containers. They'd hear the shot … but by then I'd be dead.

Then *do* something. Rush him. Grab the gun. Move.

Burges raised the rifle to his shoulder, took aim, and pulled the trigger.

Too late.

19

Missed. The bastard missed! Everything was crystal clear, each detail rendered in glowing HD Technicolor, with Dolby surround: the slap of the water against the platform, the grain of the wood on the walkway, the flecks of rust on the handrail, the golden flash as the brass cartridge spun through the air, the ping as it bounced off the shed wall.

MOVE!

I rushed the fat bastard, head down like a battering ram.

Nothing hurt any more. Like being reborn.

I slammed into Burges's swollen stomach, sending him crashing back into the door frame. He wasn't just big, he was solid too – it was like rugby-tackling a sofa. The two-twenty-two went flying, clattered against the wooden platform.

'Get off me!'

I did: coiled a fist back, ready for the fat bastard's face, but he was faster than he looked – barging past, making for the railing where I'd been standing, feet thumping on the walkway, making it judder.

I grabbed the rifle, hauled it up and round until it was pointing right in the middle of Burges's huge back.

He stood there, at the railing, staring out at the water.

Why didn't he go after the gun?

I racked another bullet into the chamber.

Burges jabbed a finger at the loch. 'There! Got you, you little shit!'

A grey shape floated past, about eight-foot from the barge – skin like freckled neoprene, a ragged scarlet hole in its side. The body rolled and twitched, one flipper making eddies in the bloody water. The thing had to be at least five feet long. Jesus...

Burges turned and grinned at me, like a crack-head with a chainsaw. 'The boathook – give me the boathook. Quickly!'

'On your knees. Hands behind your head.'

The boat puttered towards the platform, PC Clark in the prow – holding a coil of rope at the ready – while Benny peered out through the wheelhouse window.

The constable's mouth worked up and down, but no sound came out, his eyes wide, staring at the thick smear of blood that went from the open shed doors to the edge of the walkway. Then he stared at me instead: sitting there on a folding chair in the sunshine, the rifle across my knees.

Finally Royce found his voice again. 'Oh God...'

The boat bumped against the platform and he fumbled the rope around the cleat. 'We heard a shot; where's Arnold Burges?' The constable scrambled onto the walkway, one hand over his mouth, staring down at the blood. 'What did you *do*? I *told* you! What am I going... How am I supposed to explain this?'

Benny nodded. 'Yokkit horns, did dey? What did I tell du: rile Arnie and he's laek ta glaep du.'

Royce took a couple of deep breaths, hands fluttering at his sides. 'Got to call it in. Get on the radio and call it in. Not your fault, Royce, nothing you could do. Oh God...'

Benny picked up a sack of fish food and thumped it down on the walkway. 'There's no point being aff a leg an on a leg, Royce ma darlin', Arnie's Arnie, du knows that.'

The constable shifted from foot to foot. 'Oh God, we'll have to drag the loch: what if the body drifts out to sea? They're going to blame me!'

Arnold Burges walked out of the shed, drysuit peeled down to his waist, the arms knotted around his massive stomach. His white T-shirt was stained red across the chest, blood smeared up to his elbows. He wiped his hands on a towel. 'You got the rest of that feed, Benny?'

'You're alive…' Royce grabbed the handrail with both hands and closed his eyes, then bent forward until his forehead rested on the rusty metal. 'Oh thank God…'

'Where du been, Arnie? Poor Constable Clark was worried: thought du'd gien da lang gaet.'

Burges grinned. 'I got him.'

'No.' Benny's mouth fell open, showing off more fillings than teeth. 'Du got the greedy bugger?'

A nod towards the shed. 'Inside.'

'Ha, ha!' Benny did a little dance, then scampered in to see for himself.

Royce straightened up, wiped a hand across his forehead, then turned and peered into the shed. 'Bloody hell…'

The seal's body hung, head down, over a sheet of tarpaulin, split from tail-flippers to throat, innards piled beneath it – steaming in the chill morning air. The smell of rancid fish was strong enough to make Royce gag a little. Couldn't blame him.

He cleared his throat. 'You shot it…'

'Big bastard, isn't he?' Burges squatted by the pile of offal and cut free a slab of purple, about the size of a large hot-water bottle. He slapped the liver onto a chopping board. 'Guess what's for lunch.'

'Ha!' Benny loped out through the doors. 'I'll get the beer.'

Royce stuck his chest out. 'Arnold Burges, I'm arresting you for violation of the Marine Scotland Act, 2011, making it illegal to shoot seals without—'

'It's OK.' I put a hand on the constable's shoulder. 'I've already done this bit: he's got a licence.'

Burges pointed at an official-looking letter pinned to the shed wall, beside the feed cage. 'We've tried exclusion nets, tensioners, sonic scarers and the greedy bastard kept coming. Had about three thousand fish off us.' He squatted back down and hacked out what looked like a kidney. 'Got what he deserved.'

Burges and I sat on the walkway with our backs against the shed, out of the wind, bathed in sunshine. The view on this side of the barge was spectacular: mountains on both sides, sweeping down to the sparkling water, islands in the middle distance like emeralds on blue silk, the Atlantic Ocean a line of hazy sapphires beyond.

A rattling whoosh came from inside – Benny and Royce tipping bags of fish feed into the metal hopper. It was warm, in the sun. And the smell of cat biscuits wasn't that bad once you got used to it. Better than disembowelled seal at any rate.

Burges looked out at the rippling water, his eyes swollen and pink. 'Can you believe we *actually* thought the cards would stop when we moved?'

'I'm sorry you had to find out like this. Someone should have told you yesterday when we ... identified Lauren.'

He drained his can of Stella, scrunched it in his car-crusher hand and dumped it on the wood beside him. Cracked open another one. 'Been out here since yesterday morning, trying to catch that frigging seal...' He bent forwards, head hanging over his gut. 'Does Danielle know? Did someone tell her?'

'I don't—'

'Can't get a mobile signal out here. Should phone her. See if she's OK...'

We sat in silence.

Burges knocked back a mouthful of lager. Wiped a hand

across his eyes. 'How? How does he find us? How are we supposed to…' A sniff. Another drink. 'Can we bury her? Our Lauren: do we get her back, can we bury her?'

'They'll release the remains soon as they can. You'll get her back.'

He nodded and a tear plopped onto his bloodstained T-shirt. 'We thought she'd run away from home. Thought we'd *done* something. Danielle still blames herself. Spent months searching every street in Edinburgh, London, Glasgow – posters in shop windows, pestering the papers to print her photo, talking to every homeless bastard and junkie we could find.' He gave a little laugh, then bit his bottom lip. 'Thought she'd just come back one day. Then that first card arrives: happy fucking birthday…'

'Yeah.' I stared out over the water. 'My daughter, Rebecca, went missing five years ago. She was nearly thirteen… Never heard from her again.'

Burges nodded. 'Hurts, doesn't it? Wondering if it was your fault.' He stared at the tin in his hand. 'At least you still get to hope.'

No. That died four years ago with card number one.

I took another mouthful of luke-warm coffee. 'I meant what I said: Henry Forrester did everything he could. We all did. Still are.'

The diesel generator chugged and rumbled into life, then a clunk came from inside the shed, followed by a deep rattling sound. A pipe jutted out of the shed wall, connected to a thick plastic hose that disappeared into the loch. It shivered and shook, then out in the middle of one of the salmon cages a spray of food leapt into the air, then pattered down on the water. The surface boiled with fish.

Burges finished his second can and cracked open a third. 'She was our little girl…'

'Henry did his best, he really did. Lauren was missing for over a year before we even found out she was a victim. Twelve months for everyone to get hazy on the details. Even the CCTV footage gets erased eventually. It's not his fault.'

Burges rested his arms on his knees. 'Every year we get another card, and it's like a knife: gouging... How are we supposed to deal with that?' He drank, chugging back at least half the can in one go. 'Henry Forrester doesn't deserve to forget. And neither do you.'

20

A dirty blue van sat outside Henry's house, the legend 'DAVIE'S DA JOINER!' painted down the side in Gothic script. A little man was hammering a large sheet of plywood over the lounge window, whistling as he battered in the nails.

I let myself in, not bothering to wave goodbye to Royce, and followed the sound of voices into the kitchen.

Henry leaned back on his stool, sleeves rolled up, one hand resting on top of his little pot belly, the other wrapped around a tumbler. Sheba wheezed and twitched on the floor by the oven, dreaming old dog dreams.

Dr McDonald was hunched over her glass, elbows on the table, fingers drumming a random beat on the wooden surface, curls hiding her face. Her glasses were sitting beside an open bottle of Isle of Jura, the lenses almost opaque with fingerprints. 'I think ... I think Amber O'Neil's the moss important, he picked ... picked her because she looked like *Her*, I mean whoever it was hurted him ... have ... have you ever been hurted by a thirteen-year-old girl?' Then a belch. 'Oops...'

Henry took a sip and smacked his lips. 'Yes, but have you considered the possibility that she was a cipher?'

'Ooh.' McDonald's head snapped up. 'I han ... han thought

of that, a cipher...' A little crease formed between her eyebrows. 'Nah, that makes no ... makes no senses... Why would she be a cipher?' A laugh. 'You're *silly*.'

I closed the door. 'See the two of you are getting along.'

Henry pointed at the bottle. 'It's hard to say no to a lady who brings a single malt for an old man.' Then a small frown. 'Where have you been?'

'Anyone want tea?'

'I don ... I don think she's a cipher, I think ... I think she's a massage...'

I filled the kettle and stuck it on to boil. 'No more whisky for you.'

'Nooo!' Dr McDonald grabbed her tumbler and clutched it to her chest; Isle of Jura sloshed onto the stripy top. 'You know what I ... what I wonner, Henry, I wonner...' One eyebrow dipped. 'I wonner... Em...'

'Who's he really torturing?' Wild guess, but it was what she'd written on the mirror above the sink in the cabin's toilet.

Dr McDonald banged a hand on the table top and looked at me as if I'd invented bacon. 'God, that's ... that's *brilliant*, who's he really torchering, that's right ... that's ... you're a *genius* ... isn't ... isn't he a genius, Henry?'

The four mugs from this morning sat on the working surface, their bottoms crusted and stained with brown. I rinsed one out under the hot tap.

'Oh, our friend Ash is a man of many talents.' Henry put his glass down on the table. 'You went to see him, didn't you? Burges. That's where you've been.'

'No, he's a *genius* ... I mean, Ash, Ash, Henry tol ... tol me all bout you and what ... what...?' She downed a gulp of whisky. 'Who's he really torchering? Is ... is not juss the girls, is it, he's torchering the parents too, torchering them for years an years an years an years.'

'We identified Arnold Burges's daughter's remains

yesterday.' Teabag in the mug, followed by boiling water. 'Someone had to tell him.'

'I don't need you to fight my battles for me, Ash.'

'Yeah, because you're doing such a *great* job of sorting him out on your own.'

'You're not a genius, you're an idiot.'

'Prhaps ... prhaps thass the point, I mean, is ... is *horrible* for the girls, but ... but prhaps they're the means to ... to the ends, an that ... that's why he keeps them gagged while he ... while he does it?'

I fished the bag out with a spoon and dumped it in the sink. 'I'm not the piss-head sitting in a freezing house with shattered windows and dog shit on the carpet, drinking myself to death.'

Henry poured himself another measure of whisky. 'Do I look pished to you?'

No he didn't. He looked more sober than he had when we'd arrived. And the 'caffeine' tremors seemed to have vanished as well.

'He doesn't ... doesn't want to hear them scream cos ... because he's not innit for ... for *their* pain, he wans ... he wans the parents to feel it, ooh I needa pee...' Dr McDonald lurched up from the table and grabbed the working surface. 'Oops... Floor's all ... slippy ... like Switzerland...'

The teaspoon rattled against the stainless-steel draining board. I sploshed some milk into the mug. 'What, I'm not supposed to worry about you now? Thought we were friends.'

'I don't want you interfering.'

Interfering? For God's sake. 'He took a sledgehammer to Ellie's headstone!'

'Back inna ... inna bit, you got any crisps, I like crisps...' And she was gone, leaving the door open behind her. 'Crisps, crisps, crisps, crisps, crisps...'

Henry drank, rolling the whisky around his mouth. 'Arnold Burges is *entitled* to feel bitter. I screwed up the profile, if I'd been a better psychologist his daughter would still be alive.' He stared at his gnarled hands, the skin peppered with liver spots. 'And Rebecca would be too.'

Maybe he was right.

There was a little patio in the top corner of the garden: a suntrap with a wooden table and some folding chairs, looking out over the harbour, the mountains, the boats, and the sea. Good view. Certainly a hell of a lot better than the one from my kitchen window.

I pulled out my phone and scrolled through the messages, deleting all the ones where Michelle ranted and raved about what a thoughtless prick I was. OK, so she could be a pain in the arse, but that didn't mean it was OK for Katie to lie to her. Even if Michelle was being unreasonable.

Mind you, Ashley's dad *did* sound like a bit of a tosser...

A grunt from the bottom of the garden. It was Henry, labouring his way up the weed-strewn path to the patio, puffing and panting all the way. Sheba wobbled along behind him, tongue lolling out.

Henry collapsed into one of the folding chairs. 'She's stopped throwing up.'

'You OK?'

He shrugged, then clunked the bottle of whisky down on the table, followed by a single tumbler. 'When did you stop drinking?'

'Pills. Unlike you I actually read the instructions.'

'She's curled up on the kitchen worktop, snoring like a drain and making the most *appalling* smells.'

'That's what you get for leading her astray.'

'True.' He poured himself a stiff measure. The Isle of Jura was about halfway done already, and it was barely noon. 'Just because I don't want you interfering with Arnold Burges, doesn't mean I'm not happy to see you. And I'm sorry I didn't call. The funeral was on Monday and I—'

'It's OK. It doesn't matter.'

He wrapped his hands around the tumbler. 'You got another card.'

'Number five.'

A nod. 'Ash, if you tell Dickie, or Weber, or McDonald, they can—'

'Shouldn't even have told you.'

He fiddled with the glass, not looking at me. 'No, probably not.'

Because if I hadn't, Philip Skinner might still be alive. And Detective Superintendent Len Murray wouldn't be serving eighteen years in Glenochil Prison.

'Do you know what Dickie and his Party Crashers have achieved in the four years since you quit? Sod all. If we hadn't found Helen Kelly's remains they'd still be poking about in Dundee, waiting for the next girl to go missing. They're treading water, Henry, and he's still out there.'

Henry took a sip, pursed his lips. The stubble on his chin glowed in the sunlight. 'I'll help Dr McDonald with her "behavioural evidence analysis", try and stop her from making the same mistakes I did, but there's one condition: it's all off the record. Unofficial. You keep me out of the investigation.'

'Deal.'

Sheba gave up halfway up the path and groaned down onto her side in the middle of a sunny patch.

'And I'm not coming back to Oldcastle with you. If I help, it's got to be from here.'

'Oh... Well, maybe we can—'

My phone buzzed on the tabletop, skittering as the ringing got louder. DC Massie's name flashed on the screen. I picked it up and jabbed the button. 'Rhona.'

A pause. Then, *'Oh thank God, you're OK... You are OK, aren't you? I've been trying to get hold of you for* hours.'

'Of course, I'm OK. Why wouldn't I be?' Pause. 'Look,

Rhona, is this important, only I'm in the middle of something.'

Silence.

'Rhona?'

'I... I wanted to check you were OK. No one knew where you were, and your house was trashed, and the Fire Brigade said it was—'

'Fire Brigade?' I nearly dropped the phone. What the hell were the Fire Brigade... Bloody Shifty Dave: I asked him to tidy up, not burn the place down!

Henry sat forward in his seat. 'Everything all right?'

'I was worried when you didn't call me back, so I went by your house this morning and there was a fire engine sitting outside, and council vans, and the bastards wouldn't let me in, but there was water everywhere and the whole place was trashed. I mean completely *fucked. And no one knew where you were...'*

'What the hell did you do to my fucking house?'

A large woman with a pushchair full of screaming toddler gave me the evil eye, then hurried past. Well, screw her. How would *she* like it if someone set fire to *her* bloody house?

Main Street was relatively busy for a small town on the east coast of Shetland. Parked cars lined one side of the road outside the Scalloway Meat Company shop, its frontage plastered with signs about 'FANCY GOODS, TOYS, AND SOUVENIRS'. The flat-fronted houses opposite were painted in various pastel shades. All very quaint.

Shifty Dave Morrow grumbled on the other end of the phone. *'You're bloody welcome. You any idea what kind of mess that big bastard made in my car?'*

'Dave, I swear to God—'

'I didn't do anything to it, OK? The place was like that when I got there. And you could've bloody warned me! Water pishing down the stairs, the walls, all the furniture wrecked, ceiling caving in... How was I supposed to tidy that up? What am I, Kim and fucking Aggie?'

Water?

Main Street ended at a little make-believe roundabout. I took a right, into a car park overlooking the harbour.

'The house wasn't wrecked when I left it! Well, maybe the hall and the stairs, but that's it. So don't—'

'Nah: whole place was smashed up. Don't know how your visitor managed it with his ankle fucked like that, but your house was a bombsite when I got there.' A sniff, then a honking snork as Shifty blew his nose. *'He got a bit rowdy: had to hit him with a spade a couple of times. Dumped him outside A&E, so he's either OK by now, or he's dead.'*

'How could he... My sodding house?' A pair of seagulls stopped pecking at a fishing net draped over a couple of bin-bags, and stared at me, heads tilted on one side. I aimed a kick in their direction. 'And you can fuck off as well!'

They scrambled into the air, screeching abuse.

'Should be thanking me: put my back out, dragging that big bastard in from the garden. Bloody suit's ruined. And *he puked in the boot.'*

I slumped back against a big Toyota flatbed. It was stacked with creels, the smell of stale fish and seaweed wafting out into the cold air. 'Is the whole place really wrecked?'

'Total bombsite. ... Hold on.' Muffled crunches came from the phone, as if Shifty had stuck a hand over the mouthpiece. Then he was back. *'Got to go: three-line-whip briefing in the canteen. Party Crashers have turned up and the ACC's going mental.'* The connection went dead. He'd hung up.

I jammed the phone in my pocket, then let my head fall back until it clunked against the truck's roof and stared up at the gathering clouds. 'It was my house...'

Even if it was a shithole.

The seagulls were back, swooping and jeering around a fishing boat as it chugged into harbour. Must be nice to be a seagull. You eat, you sleep, you shag, and if you're having a bad day you can shite on everyone from a great height.

Doesn't even have to be a bad day, you can do it just for fun.

I leaned against the low stone wall and scowled out at the birds.

The whole house: wrecked.

How the hell could Mr Pain wreck the place on one leg? What did he do – hop from room to room, smashing things like a demented Heather Mills?

Maybe it was local neds...? Then again, maybe not. After the last thieving git got out of Castle Hill Infirmary the little sods tended to steer clear of my place.

Unless Shifty Dave Morrow was a lying fat bastard and *he* was the one who'd trashed my house? But why go to all that effort? Not as if I couldn't tell his wife about him and Andrew the Barman...

Definitely getting colder.

Let's be honest: it was probably more of Mrs Kerrigan's goons, sent to teach me a lesson after I threatened to come after her. What a great idea *that* had been. Really smooth.

I stuck my hands in my pockets and did the grand tour of Scalloway: all the way back down Main Street, past the various boathouses and halls and shortbread-box terraces, until the buildings ran out and I was walking along with water on one side and a scrubby hill on the other.

Two rows of small boats were tied to a floating walkway about twenty yards from shore. Someone had hauled an upturned fibreglass dinghy onto the grass at the side of the road – I perched on the edge. Looked out across the glittering water to the grey-green hills speckled with tiny white houses.

Cold leached into my bones, nipping my ears and nose.

Arnold Burges had a point – how *did* the Birthday Boy find them all the way up here? And how did he manage to track down Hannah Kelly's parents even though they'd moved house again and again and again...

It was different for us – we'd stayed put. Well, Michelle

had. She got the house and I got a kicking from her divorce lawyer. But all the other parents…

I gave Sabir a call and asked.

His Scouse accent was muffled, as if he had a mouthful of something. *'Dunno.'*

'Oh, come on: don't tell me you guys haven't looked into it. Hannah Kelly's parents couldn't be more difficult to track down if they were in witness protection and they still get a birthday card every year. That doesn't seem a bit suspicious to you?'

The sound of slow chewing came from the earpiece.

I waited.

'Sabir?'

'Are youse finished?'

'I was just—'

'Treatin' us like we're a bunch of bell ends. Course we thought about it, you divvie. We gorra big list of jobs our lad could be doing that'd let him find out where the victims' families live. Might work for the Inland Revenue, or the DMV, or maybe he's a doctor, orra journalist, or he's in the Post Office, or with a telecoms provider, or he's a bizzie—'

'A police officer?'

'Maybe. Or maybe he's someone who knows how to use the internet, you think about that? I want to find out 'bout a suspect I don't even bother with the PNC these days, I look them up on Facebook, LinkedIn, Google Plus, electoral register… Internet's a goldmine: everyone's gorra digital footprint, if you know where to look.'

Yeah, right: because Donald Kelly would be updating his status to 'WE'VE MOVED HOUSE TO 36 DUNROSS STREET, OLDCASTLE, OC23 9WP. DON'T TELL THE BIRTHDAY BOY! LOL!!!!'

'Point is, if our lad's computer savvy, it's not gonna take him long…' The rattle of fat fingers on a keyboard. *'Ash Henderson: Forty-Two Fletcher Avenue; Royal Bank of Scotland … overdrawn by a grand and a bit; mobile number: oh seven eight four two—'*

'OK, OK, I get the—'

'Divorced, two children: Rebecca... ran away when she was twelve, Katie...' More keystrokes. *'Katie lives at Nineteen Rowan Drive, Blackwall Hill, Oldcastle; she goes to Johnston Academy; and is "in a relationship" with someone called Noah. Apparently it's "complicated", but—'*

'Enough. I get it.' And who the hell was Noah?

'How long did that take us?'

'Donald Kelly isn't on Facebook.'

'Doesn't have to be. If we're all seven steps of separation from Kevin Bacon, how many steps do you think it takes to find someone posting photos to Flickr, blogging, tweeting, sticking stuff up on any one of a million social networking sites? Might never have touched a computer in your life and youse'll still have a digital footprint.'

Sod.

The clouds were getting darker, spreading like cancer across the pale-blue sky.

'How's Dundee going?'

'Nothing more we can do there, so we've all upped sticks to your neck of the woods. Helpin' your divvie mates – see if we can narrow the search down a bit. You wanna talk to the guvnor?'

'Nah, I'm good.' A tiny fleck of white drifted through the cold air, followed by a second and a third. Not really snowing, but definitely thinking about it. 'Do me a favour: find out who's been searching for Donald Kelly, or any of the other parents.'

'On the internet? I'm good, but I'm not that good.' More munching noises. *'No one's* that *good. Youse are talkin' about millions of servers all over the world and—'*

'Well, can't you... Erm...'

What? If it was impossible it was impossible. I stood, stamped my feet to get some feeling back into them. Maybe we should start small. 'What systems *could* you do it for?'

'Seriously?'

'Just because it's a pain in the arse, doesn't mean it's not worth trying.'

'You're the pain in the arse.' A sigh. *'I'll see what I can do, but I'm promisin' bugger all.'* And he was gone.

I headed back along the harbour. The flakes were still tiny, but there were more of them – settling on the cold pavements, making it look as if they'd been dusted with icing sugar.

On the other end of the phone, DCI Weber sighed. *'You're a silly bugger, Ash.'*

I pushed my empty plate away: macaroni cheese and chips – lunch of champions. 'Thanks, Gregor, that helps.'

'Ash, Ash, Ash, what did I tell you about pissing off Mrs Kerrigan? It doesn't matter if Andy Inglis likes you, she'll still have your—'

'I know, OK? I know.' I dropped a tenner on the table, drained the last of my mineral water, and pushed out onto the street. My breath plumed around my head. 'Who told you?'

'They didn't put me in charge of CID because I'm pretty. I do work things out from time to time.'

I took a right, heading back along Main Street towards Henry's house, one hand stuffed deep in my pocket, the other nipping in the frigid air. 'It's not—'

'Ash, we've talked about this: while Sergeant Smith is with us we have to be extremely *discreet. I don't think getting your house trashed by the local hoodlums is very discreet, do you? What if she decides to have you killed? Do you have any idea how awkward a position that would put me in?'*

'Yeah, how thoughtless of me. What *was* I thinking?'

Wind whipped down an alley, swirling the tiny white flakes into a vortex. There was some sort of bookshop on the other side. I stopped.

'You know what I mean. Obviously your loss would be tragic, but it'd be the rest of us getting a screwing from Professional Standards.' A pause. *'How much do you owe?'*

There was a fluffy stuffed puffin in the window. Katie would love that. She might dress like something out of the Addams Family, but she still had every fluffy toy I'd ever bought her.

'Got to go. Bird-related emergency.'

'Ash—'

'I'll sort it, OK?' Though Christ knew how...

21

The lounge bar at the Scalloway Hotel was busy that evening. I picked my way around a clump of men in overalls, then through a swarm of girlies – dressed in pink Stetsons and 'L' plates – to where Henry and Dr McDonald were sitting.

Her face had developed a pale-grey tint, like unpainted wood-chip wallpaper, the bags under her eyes a greenish-purple. I put a pint glass full of milk and another of water on the table in front of her. A thin smile, then she puffed out her cheeks and gulped at the milk.

Sitting opposite, Henry took his double Grouse with a nod. 'Sally came, so we ordered for you.'

I pulled out a chair and parked myself next to Dr McDonald. At least this way if she puked it'd be all over Henry and not me. 'I was only gone five minutes.'

Dr McDonald wiped a hand across her mouth, then put the empty glass back on the table. 'You're having the lamb.'

'OK...' I probably would have picked that anyway, but it would have been nice to get the choice. That was the problem with psychologists: they always had to know best. 'And did you two achieve anything today? Cirrhosis? Alcohol poisoning?'

Henry took another sip of whisky.

She picked up her water. 'What: you don't like lamb?'

'Do we have a profile? Vague pointers? Something for the door-to-door teams to look out for?'

'What's wrong with lamb?'

'There's nothing...' For God's sake. 'Look, do we have *any* idea what the Birthday Boy wants, or don't we?'

She glanced across the table at Henry.

He lifted his whisky as if he was toasting her. 'In your own time.'

Dr McDonald nodded, then toasted him back with the water. 'There's something deeply wrong about the way he deals with the victims: when he snatches them he should be all excited and wound up and desperate to relive the fantasy again, but he leaves them tied to a chair for two or three days until it's their birthday, I mean I could see a couple of hours' delayed gratification, but three days is too much.'

Deep breath. 'Then there's the disposal, there's no ritual to it, no meaning, just getting rid of bodies, I wondered if there was something significant about them being naked...'

I shook my head. 'He buries them naked because it's a pain in the arse to dress a dead body. You should try it sometime: worse than undressing a drunk. He strips them when he tortures them, why would he want to dress them again?'

She smiled at me, as if I was a small child who'd managed to tie his own shoelaces for the first time. 'Exactly: it's like they don't matter to him at all, you know I think he'd put them out for the bin men if he thought he could get away with it, they're irrelevant.'

I settled back in my seat and raised an eyebrow at Henry.

He shook his head. 'It's Alice's show.'

'If they don't matter, why abduct them at all?'

She opened her mouth to say something, but a large grey-haired woman got there first: 'Two Cullen Skinks and a smoked salmon starter?'

* * *

Inside, the music swelled – the crowd joining in with the three-piece band. Guitar, violin and an accordion doing a Scottish country dance version of 'Johnny B. Goode', with the occasional 'Heuch!' thrown in for good measure.

Outside it was freezing.

I put a finger in my ear to block out the noise and hunched my back against the cold. 'What do you mean: he's watching you? Where?'

Michelle's voice trembled. *'We're in Tesco – the changing rooms. Ash, he's right outside!'*

'You're sure?'

'Of course I'm bloody sure!' A clunk and some rustling, a pause, and then Michelle was back. *'He's watching the changing rooms. What am I supposed to do? Katie's here – we're trying to get something nice for her party, and Ethan's standing right outside waiting for us!'*

The wee shite. 'OK: does the changing room have an assistant? Get them to call store security.'

Silence. Snow drifted down from the dark sky, shining in the streetlights, thick and quiet. *'Ash, what if he comes to the house? What if he—'*

'I'll sort it. Don't worry, it'll be—'

'When? When will you sort it? Tonight?' Her voice was getting higher, the words faster. *'Can you do it tonight?'*

'I said I'll sort it. Won't be till tomorrow though, maybe we can—'

'Tomorrow? You know what Ethan's like: if he's—'

'I'm in Shetland, Michelle, I can't click my heels together three times and magically—'

'You're in Shetland?' A pause. *'I thought you said Katie stayed with you last night!'*

Bugger.

'Yes, well ... I flew up this morning. Part of the investigation.' Silence. 'Look, I'll make some calls. Meantime: tell store security he's stalking you.'

More silence. *'Fine.'* And she was gone.

Bloody Ethan Baxter. Couldn't take a bloody telling, could he?

I scrolled through my contacts list. Maybe get Shifty Dave to pay him a visit with a crowbar? ... No. *That* pleasure was going to be all mine. I scrolled down and clicked another number.

It rang, and rang, and rang, and then a recorded voice came on the line: *'Hi, this is Rhona. Leave a message.'* Beeeep.

'Rhona, it's Ash. Listen, I need you to do me a—'

'Hello?' Scrambling, clicking noises. *'Hello? Guv?'* Voice a little slurred around the edges.

'Ethan Baxter: not sure where he's living now, but he used to have a house on Lochview Road. He's been hassling Michelle and Katie.'

'Right, Jesus, OK... You want him picked up? I'll get Norm and we'll give him a tour of the station stairs.'

She would too. 'Just get someone to keep an eye on Michelle, drive by the house now and then, make sure Baxter's behaving himself. I'll deal with him when I get back from Shetland.'

'Cool. I'll come with you and—'

'I don't really think that's a good idea, it's—'

'Guv, you'll need someone to watch your back: make sure you're covered in case the wee shite makes a complaint, or there's an investigation... That kind of thing.'

A Range Rover growled past, windscreen wipers going full pelt, headlights making the snow flare brilliant white in the darkness.

'I'll be fine. Make sure whoever's doing the drive-bys lets Michelle know they're there, OK?'

'You can count on me, Guv: she'll know you're looking out for her.'

'And if the bastard goes anywhere near them, pick him up and stick him somewhere till I get back.'

'Somewhere quiet and out of the way. No witnesses. Got you.'

'Thanks, Rhona.'

We spent a few minutes moaning about the Warriors' chances against Aberdeen Football Club on Saturday, what a cock Sergeant Smith was, and the weekend's weather forecast; then she caught me up on the Cameron Park investigation. Which didn't seem to be achieving much more than producing a small rainforest's worth of paperwork.

The band's Jimmy-Shand-style interpretation of 'Smells Like Teen Spirit' got louder for a couple of seconds, then a door clunked and Henry's voice cut through the snow's feathery silence. 'Wondered where you'd got to.'

I hung up and slid the phone back into my pocket. 'Checking in with the station.'

Henry turned up his collar and squinted out into the slow-motion blizzard. He didn't look that great – even for someone slowly pickling themselves into oblivion. Sunken cheeks, sunken eyes, skin the colour of parchment. He sniffed. Held out his arms, voice a gravelly monotone.

'Then winter's icy claws dig deep into the hearts of men
pulling forth the long dark nights, the pale bone touch of death again…'

'Poetry? God, you're a cheery bastard.'

A shrug. 'My clown suit's been in the wash since Ellie passed.' He wiped a finger under his nose – catching a drip. 'You know the funny thing about Albert Pearson's funeral? The only person I knew there was dead. What was the point? We're all dead now, even me. I just haven't stopped moving yet.'

Thursday 17th November

22

The kitchen clock ticked quietly on the wall, Sheba groaned and twitched on a hairy tartan beanbag, and the muffled sound of snoring came from the master and spare bedrooms. I sat at the breakfast bar, looking out at the back garden. All the sharp edges were gone, softened by eight inches of snow, more of it drifting down from the pale sky. A puffed-up robin perched on top of the washing line, shouting territorial abuse at anyone within listening distance.

No sign of Henry or Dr McDonald, so I'd let myself in and taken over the kitchen. Flicking through the case files, brooding about Michelle, Katie, and Rebecca, listening to the clock carving the day into thin sharp slices.

And my coffee was cold.

What to do about Ethan Baxter? The vicious little bastard never learned... Well, tomorrow morning he was going to get a telling he wouldn't forget.

Maybe it was time for Ethan to have an accident? Drag him out into the middle of nowhere and put a bullet through his head. Put an end to his crap once and for all...

Well, it was worth thinking about.

And once I'd taken care of Ethan Baxter, there'd be Mrs Kerrigan to deal with. Four grand by lunchtime today. Even if I had four grand, which I *didn't*, there was no way I could get it to her – not from here. Never mind the other fifteen.

Where the hell was I supposed to get *nineteen thousand* pounds from?

It was like a weight, sitting on my chest, forcing me back into the chair.

Focus on the do-able first, then worry about the rest.

Four grand by today was impossible: the ferry wouldn't get back to Aberdeen till seven tomorrow morning. OK, I could blag a flight from Sumburgh Airport – flash my warrant card and pretend it was urgent police business – but what would be the point? Rush home so I could be in time to get my legs broken? Bugger that.

The house was a wreck, my car wasn't worth the duct tape holding the rear bumper on, and I had nothing left to sell. Nothing: it was all gone. And shaking a few perverts and drug dealers by the ankles would only net a couple of grand tops, so how the hell was I going to get my hands on nineteen thousand pounds…?

A smile tugged at the corners of my mouth. Ethan Baxter wasn't exactly scraping along the poverty line, was he? No: Ethan drove a Mercedes; Ethan lived in a nice big house in Castleview; Ethan was due a battering anyway, why not throw in a bit of demanding money with menaces too?

Wasn't as if the bastard didn't deserve it. And I'm sure – given the choice of a shallow grave or making a *donation* – he'd jump at the chance to help out an old friend.

I'd be doing him a favour really.

Rationalization that good deserved a fresh cup of coffee.

I got as far as filling the kettle when someone banged on the front door.

'OK, OK, I'm coming.'

More banging.

I hauled the door open.

Winter had claimed Scalloway. The rooftops were laden

with thick crusts of white, the gardens nearly buried. Arnold Burges stood on the path, scuffed yellow wellingtons ankle-deep in snow, dressed in a scabby pair of orange overalls with a quilted jacket over the top and a woolly hat. His eyes were thin and dark, beard bristling.

I blocked the doorway. 'Arnold.'

He bit his top lip, flexed his hands into fists. 'She was alive.' His breath hung in the cold air around his head. It stank of stale booze.

'Did you drive here? Because—'

'She was our little girl, and we loved her.'

'Mr Burges, I know it's—'

'But Lauren's never going to be a person in her own right, is she? She's always going to be "Lauren Burges: the Birthday Boy's third victim". Like her whole childhood, all the time we had together, we were only killing time till the bastard grabbed her.' Burges reached into his padded jacket and pulled out a red-top tabloid.

Lauren's photo was on the front page – grinning away with a party hat perched on top of her spiky pink hair – beneath the headline, 'BIRTHDAY BOY VICTIM'S BODY DUG UP IN OLDCASTLE.'

Bloody Oldcastle CID couldn't keep its mouth shut if it fell in a septic tank.

'I'm sorry. I really am.'

Burges looked away, blinking, then went back into his jacket and produced a bulging folder. He held it out. Thick snowflakes settled on the blue surface. I took it from him, put it under my arm.

'You read that.' He squared his shoulders, stuck his chin out. 'You read that and you know our Lauren was *real*. She wasn't just a frigging victim.'

'You have to let the police do their job, Mr Burges. We're going to find him, and we're going to stop him. We're going to make him pay for what he did to Lauren and... And the others.' And no matter what else happened: he'd live to stand trial. The bastard would be hauled up in front of everyone, found guilty, and sent down for life. Six months tops, before someone carved his eyes out and cut off his balls in the prison laundry. Then we'd all throw a huge party.

Burges stared at me, then took a step back, nodding. 'They sent someone round the house while I was at work yesterday, stuck a camera in Danielle's face, wanted to know what it feels like to find out they've dug up your dead daughter...'

Before anyone official had even bothered to tell Burges and his wife that we'd found Lauren's remains. 'I'm sorry.'

'You should be.' Burges turned, and lurched back down the path, scuffing his wellies through the snow. A scarred Berlingo van sat by the kerb, 'CALDERS LEA AQUACULTURE LTD.' written along the side. Benny waved at me from the driver's seat.

I waited until Burges reached the gate. 'I meant what I said yesterday: Henry Forrester did everything he could. It's not his fault.'

The big man paused for a moment, then clambered into the van without a word.

It slithered away from the pavement and off into the snow.

I shuffled my chair closer to the open oven door. Not the most ecologically responsible way of heating a room, but at least now the kitchen was warm enough to sit in without getting frostbite.

Sheba creaked up from her bed in the corner and collapsed beside my chair, rolled onto her side and exposed her stomach to the warmth.

'Dear God, when did Henry last give you a *bath*?'

She sighed.

I unpacked the folder Burges had given me. It was full of reports from private investigators; interview transcripts; Freedom of Information requests; statements from Lauren's friends and family trying to piece together the last time they'd seen her alive; photos of Lauren at the beach, parties, playing in the back garden. It painted a very different picture from the official file. That one was all about facts and evidence, this one was all about Lauren Burges.

She was like Rebecca in so many ways: a nice girl, from a nice home, who got snatched from her family and tortured to death.

'Urgh…' A voice from the doorway.

I turned, and there was Dr McDonald: shuffling, swollen-eyed, brown curls hanging lank and greasy around her pale face.

'You look awful.'

She winced, held up a finger. 'Shhhh…'

'Hungover?'

'If you make too much noise you'll wake him, and then I'll have to start drinking again, and I really don't want to start drinking again, can we not just sit in silence for a bit and then maybe it'll all be OK and I won't feel like throwing myself under a bus or something?' She lowered herself onto one of the stools at the breakfast bar, then folded over until her head rested on the working surface. 'Urgh…'

'Hungry?'

'Urgh…'

'Trust me: get something in your stomach now, before Henry wakes up and cracks open that litre of Bells.'

'Do I have to?' She peered at me, head still resting on the countertop. 'OK. I'll have eggs and toast and bacon and sausages and tomato and mushrooms and chips and black pudding, and—'

'Then you should've stayed at the hotel last night, instead of staggering back here with Henry to polish off the Isle of Jura, shouldn't you?' I stood and pulled a greasy paper bag out of the bread bin. 'Bought a couple of sausage rolls on the way over this morning. You want them warmed in the microwave, or the oven?'

'I want to go *home*.' Music blared out of her jeans. 'Noooo…'

She pulled a smartphone from a pocket and jabbed a finger at the display. It kept on singing. Jab, jab, jab. Dr McDonald dumped the thing on the breakfast bar and wrapped her arms around her head. 'Make it stop...'

I picked the phone up. A photo of Detective Chief Superintendent Dickie flashed on the screen.

I went to press the green button, but the music stopped before I got there. He'd rung off.

Then my phone started ringing: 'DCS DICKIE'. I answered it. 'What: I'm not your first choice?'

'Hello? Hello, I can barely hear you...' A siren blared in the background, nearly drowning out everything Dickie said, even though he was almost shouting. *'Look, I can't get through to Dr McDonald – can you tell her Sabir's discovered an encrypted file on Helen McMillan's computer. It's a diary: we know where the signed first editions came from.'*

'Where?'

'Hello? ... Ash? We're hot-footing it down to Dundee now: speciality bookshop on Forrest Park Road, near the university... Hello? ... Hello? ... Can't hear a bloody—'

And that was it: the connection was gone.

I tipped the sausage rolls out of the bag and onto a plate, stuck it in the microwave for a couple of minutes on full. Then passed on Dickie's message while the thing groaned and buzzed.

Ding.

I clunked the plate down in front of Dr McDonald. 'Eat.'

She hauled her head off the worktop. 'Don't suppose Henry's got any brown sauce, does he?'

'You think our bookseller could be the Birthday Boy?' I nudged the plate. 'Eat: before the pastry turns to linoleum.'

'I wouldn't have put running a specialist bookshop at the top of my list for Birthday Boy occupations. I mean how's he going to track the families so he can deliver the card every year?' She took a bite, then huffed and puffed with her mouth wide open. 'Ooh: hot, hot, hot.'

'Sabir says he could be using the internet to find them. Or maybe they all bought books from him?'

Another bite. No puffing this time. 'Did Hannah Kelly collect rare signed first editions?'

'No.' And neither did Rebecca.

'Exactly.' Bite, chew, munch.

I put the kettle on again, gritting my teeth as the joints of my fingers grated together. Always was worse when the weather changed. The bruises across the knuckles were starting to fade to yellows and greens. I rinsed out a mug for her. 'You said you knew I wasn't a vegetarian because of my face and hands – when we were on the boat, you ordered that steak. And the lamb last night.'

'The Birthday Boy doesn't sell books, don't get me wrong: I've known a few people who work in bookshops and they can be really weird, but not torture-porn weird, and that seems to be what he's making, only not for himself to enjoy – he's making it for someone else.'

'What's wrong with my hands and face?'

'I think he's making it for the parents. I think that's why he's so squeamish about the girls screaming, why he just dumps the bodies afterwards, why it takes him three days to work up the courage to torture his victims: he's not really interested in *them*, he's interested in their mums and dads.'

I poured hot water into the mugs. '"Who's he really torturing."'

'Exactly.' She crunched into the other sausage roll. 'I know you're not a vegetarian, because you've got bruises on your fists and your face, then there's the way you talk to people – the alpha male strut – and I have the deepest respect for you as a police officer, so please don't take this the wrong way, but you're a man of violence, it ... *oozes* out of your pores. That doesn't really go with being a vegetarian.'

'I *strut*?' A small laugh broke free and I smiled. 'Ever seen a G-Twenty anti-capitalist riot? Half those buggers are vegetablists. You wouldn't think they'd have the energy.'

She cleared her throat. 'Yes, well ... sometimes men of violence are what's needed.'

Twenty past ten and Henry still hadn't surfaced, but Dr McDonald had figured out how to work the central heating and now the kitchen was positively balmy. She'd perked up a bit too – three mugs of coffee, a pair of sausage rolls, and all was right with the world.

She hunched over the laptop she'd taken out of her leather satchel. 'He's signing in...'

The speakers gave a jangly ringing noise, a hiss, a click, and then Sabir's huge grey face filled the screen. He squinted, and leaned forwards. *'Mornin' everyone... Bleedin' heck: you look like crap, Doc.'*

I shifted around behind Dr McDonald, until I could see myself in the little window inset into Sabir's video feed. 'Any news on the bookseller?'

'They've got him in an interview room, acting all indignant and "I've never done nothin' to no one". Dozy Get.'

I leaned in. 'What about my searches?'

'Ah, right...' He grimaced. *'I might owe you a bit of an apology on that one. Went and did a search on all twelve families and four of them didn't come up with nothin' recent enough to find out where they were. Nowhere Joey Public gets access to. Not without some serious IT skills, anyway.'* Sabir's fingers clacked over the keyboard. *'Even then: there was bugger all on Hannah Kelly's ma and da. So I went and did a bit of a hack on the Police National Computer – told it to gizza list of everyone who's entered search criteria for any Birthday Boy families for the last four years.'*

A dialogue box popped up on Dr McDonald's screen: 'SABIR4TEHPOOL WANTS TO SEND YOU A FILE. ACCEPT – DECLINE.'

She clicked accept and a spreadsheet opened up in another window. A long list of names and dates.

'I've sorted it by family, year, who's done the search, and from where.'

I frowned at the names. 'And?'

'If youse were hoping for one person who'd done the lot, you're stuffed. We got about sixty-two searches spread out over forty individuals, no one's searched for all twelve families. Well, 'cept for me trying it out, and that. Otherwise the record's eight.'

'So no Birthday Boy.'

'Not unless he's about ten different people, no.'

I got Dr McDonald to scroll through the list. Most of them were from Oldcastle – Rhona's name was on there, so was Weber, Shifty Dave, along with a chunk of CID and nearly every uniform in the place. And of the lot, Rhona was the one who'd done the most searches: a whole three. Sod.

'Sorry, Sabir: wasted your time.'

'Nah, don't worry about it. We did the same thing four, five years ago when we thought the Birthday Boy might be a bizzie. Even thought we had him once – this sergeant up in Inverness – but turned out he was just a dirty paedo got his rocks off on the Birthday Boy photos. Was worth checking again.'

Henry knocked on the doorframe. 'Ah, Alice, you're up. Good.' He'd changed out of his funeral suit, into a pair of flannels and a beige cardigan going bald at the elbows. He placed a litre bottle of Bells whisky on the breakfast bar. 'Ready to get back to it?'

Dr McDonald swallowed. Pulled on a smile. 'Super...'

'Sabir?' I turned the laptop around so the screen was pointing at Henry. 'You remember Dr Forrester?'

Sabir's face broke into a grin. *'Doc, how you been? You're looking—'*

Henry reached forwards and closed the laptop lid, shutting him off. 'I told you, I'm not getting involved: I'm simply helping you and Alice out. If you do that again, I'm out.'

OK... 'Thought you might like to say hello.'

'Hmmph.' He opened the whisky and plucked two glasses

from the draining board. Put one in front of Dr McDonald and glugged in a generous measure. 'Now, if you'll excuse us, we really need to get back to work.'

23

The smell of frying garlic filled the kitchen, steam from the boiling pasta turning the window opaque as the extractor fan struggled to cope.

Henry plonked himself down on one of the stools by the breakfast bar, the litre of Bells clutched in both hands. 'You know, I rather like Alice: she's a trooper.'

'Still throwing up?' I scraped langoustine tails and chunks of smoked haddock into the frying pan, gave it all a shake. My phone vibrated in my pocket – not an incoming call, a text message. The kitchen clock was pointing out ten to two. That would be Mrs Kerrigan then, wanting to know where her money was and which kneecap I'd like shattered first.

Well screw her. I left it where it was, unread.

Henry made a little harrumphing noise. 'I'm sorry about earlier. It was… After what happened last time…' Sigh. 'Maybe my delightful daughter is right: I'm just a bitter selfish old man.' A shrug. 'Tell Sabir I'm sorry, but I can't face it any more.'

I shredded some fresh parsley and spring onions, chucked them in, then added the double cream. 'Did you know there's bugger all in your cupboards, other than bottles of whisky, empties, and a packet of stale Bran Flakes?'

'I have Bran Flakes?'

'Had to go shopping.' It wasn't as if I'd had anything else to do while the pair of them banged on about stressor events and psychological trigger-points.

He unscrewed the top off the whisky and poured himself a stiff measure. 'Didn't know you were a domestic goddess.'

'Used to cook with Rebecca and Katie all the time. Never really saw the point when I'm on my own...' I tested the spaghetti. Not quite there yet. 'So who was this policeman you lot were looking at?'

'For the Birthday Boy? Pffffff... Now you're asking.' He raised the glass to his lips. 'Glen Sinclair, I think. Or was it Strachan? Struthers? Something like that. He was a sergeant with Northern Constabulary, kept doing PNC searches on the families, so we picked him up and questioned him. Got a couple of Party Crashers to keep tabs on where he went and who he saw. Two days later he jumped off the Kessock bridge.' A sip. 'Long way down.'

'It wasn't him then.'

Henry hunched his shoulders. 'Yet another of my spectacular failures. I'd done a revised profile and he fit perfectly, right down to volunteering to work with children.'

'Scouts?'

'Junior league football. After he died we went through his home computer: it was stuffed full of naked little boys. Wasn't the Birthday Boy at all.'

I drained the spaghetti in the sink, sending a huge cloud of steam billowing up into the room. 'Only you could make catching a paedophile sound like a bad thing.'

'We didn't catch him though, did we? We thought he was someone else, and he killed himself before we knew anything about his photo collection. Probably part of a ring, and we missed the chance to do something about it.'

'Go shout on Dr McDonald: if she's finished throwing up, it's lunchtime.'

Henry stared at his hands. 'I meant what I said, Ash: you need to tell her about Rebecca.'

I dumped the spaghetti into the frying pan, swirled it around in the sauce. 'No.'

'You can't expect her to draw up an accurate profile when she doesn't have all the information, you *know* that. She'll make assumptions based on what she has, and it isn't going to—'

'Then steer her in the right direction. Prod her. Guide her. Make her get it right.' The pan thumped back down on the cooker. 'If I tell her, she'll tell Dickie and they'll kick me off the case. Compassionate leave, grief counselling; I'll have to sit at home and watch them fuck everything up while the Birthday Boy keeps on going.'

'Perhaps grief counselling wouldn't be a bad—'

'I'm not telling her, Henry, and neither are you. Understand?' I switched off the gas. 'Now go get her before it's ruined.'

Snow drifted down outside my hotel-room window, shining as it passed through the streetlights. Henry's dent-covered Volvo estate sat by the kerb, the word 'WANKER' scratched in big letters along the side, engine running, exhaust curling out into the darkness. I wrapped Rebecca's cigar box in two T-shirts and that ugly jumper Michelle's mum gave me, wedging socks and pants and jeans in around it. Keeping it safe. Then went through to the en-suite for my toilet bag.

My mobile rang, echoing back from the pristine tiles: Dickie again.

I jammed the thing between my ear and shoulder. 'Let me guess, she's not answering her phone.' Gathered up my things: toothbrush, toothpaste, razor, shaving foam...

'Sometimes it's better to talk to the monkey than the organ grinder.'

'Cheeky bastard.' Pills, pills, more pills...

'We've got a confession out of the bookshop owner.'

I stopped. Stared in the mirror, pulse thumping in my ears. After all this time... 'He's the Birthday Boy.'

'No, he's not. I couldn't be that bloody lucky. But he does have a collection of explicit videos of him sexually abusing Helen McMillan. She was only twelve...' Dickie made a sort of rubbery flapping sound with his lips, like an underwater sigh. *'Apparently they had an arrangement – she'd do whatever he wanted, on camera, as long as he paid her in signed first editions. Told him she was going to sell them when she was eighteen so she could afford to go to Edinburgh University. Study law.'*

I closed my eyes, leant on the sink, breathed again. It wasn't him... The Birthday Boy was still out there. I stuffed the Naproxen in the toilet bag.

'That's very ... *pragmatic* for a twelve-year-old.' I nicked the complimentary soap, shower cap, cotton buds, then the little bottles of body lotion and conditioner. Zipped the toilet bag shut.

'When I was twelve I got a paper round. What the hell happened to Scotland?'

'Same thing that happened everywhere else.'

A car horn blared outside. I peered through the window. Dr McDonald was in the passenger seat of Henry's Volvo, staring up at me, pointing at her watch and grimacing, even though we still had a whole hour to catch the ferry.

I dumped the bag in the suitcase and took one last tour through the chest of drawers, wardrobe, and bedside cabinet: making sure I hadn't missed anything.

'You remember when this used to be a good job? Something you could be proud of?'

'No.' The only thing left was the Gideon Bible, and let's face it: it was far too late for that. I zipped the wheelie case shut and hauled it off the bed onto the floor.

'Me neither.' Another rubbery sigh. *'Right, I'd better go – have to inform Helen McMillan's parents that she was being sexually abused for two years. Two years getting molested by a greasy old man, then the Birthday Boy grabs her... What sort of a life is that?'*

* * *

Snow battered down from a dark sky, a billowing curtain of white and grey that hid half of Lerwick as we stood in the forward bar of the MV *Hjaltland*.

The deck beneath my feet throbbed and purred, the street-lights sliding past as we headed out towards the harbour exit.

Dr McDonald appeared beside me, holding a glass of something that fizzed and frothed. She knocked it back, shuddered, then topped the glass up with bottled water. 'Thank you.'

'What for?'

'Introducing me to Henry, I mean he's a *committed* alcoholic, and he's got some very hidebound ideas about psychological indicators, but he really cares, even after all this time.' She swirled the liquid in the glass, making a vortex of little white flecks, then swigged the lot down. 'But if I never have to look another whisky in the eye I'll be very, very happy.'

'Can you catch him?'

She tilted her head to one side, eyes fixed on the ferry's starboard windows. Lerwick was a little knot of yellow and white lights, twinkling through the snow, getting smaller all the time. 'Do you want to hear the profile?'

'Thought you called it "behavioural evidence analysis" these days.'

'He's a white male, mid to late forties – which is pretty unusual, normally they're in their early twenties – he lives on his own or with an elderly relative, someone housebound who can't see what he's up to, he drives a large car or van, something he can transport his victims in, and he probably works in the media.' Another mouthful of water. 'Nothing that high-profile, just enough to make him look showbiz to a twelve-year-old girl. Make her think he can take her places, make her famous...' A shrug. 'Or he might be a bricklayer from Falkirk: it's not an exact science.'

Lerwick disappeared into the blizzard as the ferry began to pitch and yaw. 'Should narrow the field.'

'I'll put it into proper, woolly, percentage-based,

science-speak before I present it. We can't say outright "this what you're looking for", because ... well ... you know.'

My phone vibrated in my pocket – another text message. I pulled it out and pressed the button. Unknown number:

We're coming to get you.

Join the queue.

Friday 18th November

24

'...for the next couple of days as that cold front sweeps down across the north-east of Scotland, bringing snow and sleet with it. Steve?'

'Thanks, Davie. You're listening to Sensational Steve's Breakfast Drive-Time Bonanza, *and we'll be back with another* bonkers *wind-up call right after these words from our sponsors.'* Grating honk, cheesy trombone noise, and then the adverts.

'Have you had an accident in the last five years, and it wasn't your fault?...'

I turned the rusty Renault onto Lochview Road, the steering wheel juddering on full lock. A screeching noise came from somewhere inside, even though I can't have been doing more than five miles an hour.

Lochview Road wasn't bad – a tree-lined street of sandstone buildings, iron railings, bay windows, Mercs and Beamers parked outside. Small front gardens with a flight of steps up to the front doors. Classy. The kind of place that hid behind the curtains when Jehovah's Witnesses came round, instead of telling them to fuck off.

'...think I'm crazy, but there's an additional twenty percent *off this weekend when you buy a new sofa!'*

Ethan's house was down at the far end. I parked as close as I could. Checked my watch: five past eight. Should have got here twenty minutes ago, but the Renault wasn't exactly in rally-fit condition. And having to drop Dr McDonald off at her aunt's place hadn't helped.

With any luck Ethan would still be bumbling about inside: where's my keys, is the toast burnt; have I got everything; don't want to be late for work; hurry, scurry, hippity hop. Not quite as good as three in the morning for catching someone off guard, but it would have to do.

'*...and nothing to pay for eight months! That's right,* nothing *to pay—*'

I killed the engine and climbed out of the car.

Wind ripped through the street, shivering the trees' naked branches, slamming into my chest like a cold fist. I gritted my teeth, stuck my hands in my pockets, and marched down the road towards Ethan's house.

There was a clunk behind me and Rhona's voice cut through the groaning wind. 'Guv?'

Shite.

I stopped, turned, the tails of my jacket flapping around my waist. 'Thought I told you—'

'Don't worry.' She didn't even bother trying to cover her mouth, just yawned like a hippo, showing off those large beige teeth. 'He got home at half seven yesterday evening: hasn't moved since.'

'You've been here all night?'

'Said I'd keep an eye on things for you, didn't I?' She produced a pair of black leather gloves from her pocket and pulled them on. 'Besides, you're going to need someone to hold him down.'

I closed my eyes, rubbed at my forehead. 'Rhona, you can't—'

'What, he's going to open the door for you? Guv, soon as he sees you through the peephole he'll barricade himself in and call the cops. You need a nice approachable female face to put him at his ease, make sure the place is wide open for you.'

She had a point. 'Well...'

'And anyway, I read the wee bugger's file. He deserves whatever he's got coming.'

A smile pulled at my cheeks. 'OK, you're in.'

Rhona grinned back at me. 'You ready?'

She rang the doorbell again, leaning on it for a good five or six seconds – long enough to be really annoying. Then turned and gave me the thumbs up.

I ducked back down behind the silver Mercedes parked outside the house – kidding on I was tying my shoelace, in case any nosey neighbour was looking.

Clunk.

Rhona put on her official police officer voice: 'Mr Baxter?'

A man's voice, slightly bunged up and jowly. 'Look, is this important, because—'

'Mr *Ethan* Baxter? Oldcastle Police, can I come in, please?'

'I haven't got time for— Hey, stop pushing! You can't—'

Clunk.

I popped my head over the bonnet. The front door was closed, no sign of a struggle. Say what you like about Rhona, she did a good forced entry. I pulled on my own leather gloves, then strolled around the car, up the stairs and in through the front door. Closed it behind me, shutting out the groaning wind.

The hall was full of polished wood and things in frames.

Muffled struggling noises came from the other side of a half-glazed door at the end of the hall. It opened on a huge kitchen – the kind with a range cooker, prints of farmyard animals, and a wall packed with cookery books.

Ethan was sitting in a wooden dining chair, gagged with a tea towel, his hands cuffed behind his back. Soon as I walked in his eyes went huge above that squint nose of his. 'Mmmmmmmmph. Mmmmmmphngn mmmphn!'

He'd let himself go: chubby cheeks flushed and shiny, a pot

belly hanging over the waistband of his suit trousers. His hairline was quite a bit higher too, but for some reason he'd decided that the best way to compensate was to grow it long. Not a good look on an overweight, middle-aged man.

Rhona stood with her back against the range, smiling. 'Nice house, eh, Guv? These architect bastards must be raking it in.'

I settled into the seat on the other side of the table. Flexed my black-leather fingers. Stared.

He blinked a couple of times, then looked away.

Silence: I let it thicken.

'Mmphhmnnngh...'

'You've been a naughty boy again, haven't you, Ethan?'

He kept his eyes on the kitchen floor.

'You were in Tesco on Wednesday night, the big one in Logansferry: clothes department, remember?'

A pause ... then he nodded.

I leaned forwards. Up close he smelled of aftershave and old garlic. 'Michelle was there too.'

His eyes widened. 'Mmmmmph! Mmmmnnghph!'

'She says you were watching her. Says she was in the changing rooms with Katie and when they came out, there was good old Ethan Baxter: lurking.'

'Mmmphnnghmm...'

Rhona whistled. 'They hand out restraining orders for a reason, Baxter. Did you *really* think you could sneak up on a woman you beat the shit out of for six months, and she's not gonna recognize you? You're even thicker than you look.'

'Mmmgn mnnnph!'

I gave him a big theatrical sigh. 'Ethan, Ethan, Ethan... Rhona's right: you're not a very quick learner, are you? Thought you'd *actually* got it last time, but obviously I was wrong. You need a refresher.'

He clamped his eyes shut, head bowed, shoulders shivering.

She leant over and spoke straight into his ear. 'Nah: I know what he needs, he needs taking out and—'

'Rhona, do me a favour and go keep an eye on the road. Don't want someone popping past unannounced, disturbing Ethan from his lesson.'

'You sure I shouldn't—'

'*Now*, Rhona.'

She pursed her lips for a moment, then nodded and wandered out, hands in her pockets, whistling a jaunty tune.

I stood, closed the kitchen door, then went around all the units, opening the drawers and rummaging about inside. Tea towels. Coasters and mats. Assorted bits and bobs. 'Nice place you've got here, Ethan. Very swish.' Cutlery… I pulled out a steak knife and a fork. Next drawer: cooking implements. Helped myself to a heavy wooden rolling pin. There was a little blowtorch in the last drawer, perfect for making crème brûlée.

'Ever heard of DIY Dave? Killed about eight people so far. Tortures them.' I arranged everything on the table in front of Ethan. 'We call him "DIY" because he never brings anything to the scene, just uses whatever his victims have lying about the house.'

I picked up the steak knife and stabbed it into the table top; when I let go it stayed upright, quivering.

'Mmmmmmphmmmph!'

'Yeah, thought you'd say that.' I took out my own set of handcuffs: shiny stainless-steel hoops with a rigid plastic hand-hold in the middle. I fastened Ethan's right arm to the chair, then unlocked Rhona's cuffs on one side, so they dangled from his left wrist.

I grabbed the rigid plastic bar and hauled his arm up onto the table.

'Mmmmmph nnnph!' His fingers spidered on the wooden surface, as if his hand was trying to get away. Which wasn't a bad idea.

The rolling pin was nice and weighty. I tapped it against his wrist. 'You're a southpaw, that right, Ethan? A lefty?'

'Mmmnngh...' His eyes darted from the rolling pin to me then back again. Little drops of sweat beaded his forehead, making it shine. The smell of old garlic got stronger.

'So, when you're fantasizing about how you used to beat up my *wife*, this is the hand you wank with.' I raised the rolling pin. 'What did I tell you last time?'

He stared up at me, eyes glistening with tears. 'Mmmn gnndnnn nnnnngh mnnngnnng!'

I slammed the pin down on the back of his hand. The jolt radiated all the way up my arm to my shoulder. The bang echoed around the kitchen.

A small pause.

Then Ethan screamed behind the gag, jerking back and forwards in the chair – unable to go anywhere.

Didn't blame him: must have broken a few bones.

'You promised last time, didn't you? You *promised* me you'd never go anywhere near Michelle and Katie again.' Another go with the rolling pin.

Another scream.

'Curl your fingers up. Now.'

'Mmmmmph! Mmmmmph!'

'CURL YOUR FUCKING FINGERS!'

His hand trembled, the fingers fluttering and twitching, then he dragged them into a loose fist.

'Bastards like you are all the same: you think women are gagging for it, don't you? Think you can do whatever you like and it's OK, because you're so *big* and *special*. Think they'll love you for it. Right?'

I smashed the rolling pin down on his raised knuckles, hard enough to knock the fork and blowtorch off the table.

'MMMMMMMMMMPHNNNN!' Tears streamed down his face. The scuffing sound of feet scrabbling on the tiled floor. 'MMMMMMMMMMPHNNNN!'

'You know what, Ethan? Looks to me like *you're* gagging for it.' One more go, putting my weight behind it.

'MMMMMMMMMMPHNNNN!'

I dropped the rolling pin, let it clatter on the table top. His hand was already starting to swell, the skin a deep angry red, blood oozing out from what was left of his knuckles.

'Mmmmmmmmmmmnnph... Mmmmmmmmmmmnnph...' Head back, eyes screwed shut, tears running down the sides of his face, breath whistling through his broken nose.

I let go of the handcuffs, and he curled his shattered hand against his chest, rocking back and forwards.

I filled the kettle and put it on the range to boil. Waited for Ethan to stop sobbing.

'Michelle's still got the scars, did you know that?' Three mugs from the cupboard, one tea, two coffees. Boiling water made a plume of steam in each. 'I saw the photos in the case file. What was it, a cigar? Too big to be a cigarette.'

'Mmmnnph...' Voice small and low, as if he wasn't really trying any more.

'The only reason you're not mouldering away in a shallow grave right now is Michelle *begged* me not to do it. Can you imagine that? Didn't want your blood on her hands, even after everything you'd done.' The fridge was one of those fancy American double-door ones – I sloshed milk in the tea and one of the coffees.

'I wanted to carve you up like a Sunday roast. I mean, it was bad enough you moved into my fucking house, you had to pull *that* shit too? And I don't give a toss who your dad is: if I thought you'd laid a hand on Katie, all the begging in the world wouldn't save you. Understand?'

I pulled out the chair opposite and sat back down. Two coffees, one tea. I lined them up on the table, not bothering with coasters. Knew Ethan wouldn't mind.

'You're going to give me your car, Ethan. You're going to tell me where the registration documents are, and you're going to sign the Merc over. Then you're going to tell me where you keep your cash. You've got cash here, don't you Ethan?'

He slumped forwards in the chair, folded around his hand. 'Mmnnnph...'

'Yeah, I'll bet you do. Jewellery too. You're going to throw that in too, and you're going to be grateful I took it off your hands. Well ... *hand*.'

Ethan's eyes narrowed above the gag, pink flushing his cheeks.

'And in case you're thinking, "Why should I give this bastard anything? Why shouldn't I call the police?"' I reached into my jacket and pulled out the gun. Surprisingly heavy for something so small. Only took a couple of minutes to put it back together last night. 'Doesn't look like much does it?'

The hissing sound stopped – he was holding his breath.

I hauled back the slide, racking a round into the chamber. Click, *clack*.

Ethan's eyes went very wide.

'Beretta ninety-two G. It's French.' I pointed it at his face. 'You want to see how it works?'

'Mnngh, mnnnghmmmphnng!'

'You're going to hand over everything, aren't you?'

A nod, quick, jagged, never taking his eyes off the gun.

'And you're never, ever, *ever* going to bother Michelle and Katie again.'

He shook his head. 'Mnngh!'

'And if I think you've breached the terms of our little agreement, you know what's going to happen, don't you?'

His Adam's apple bobbed up and down. 'Mmmnph.'

Good boy.

25

I parked Ethan's Mercedes behind a grey-and-yellow Transit van with the Oldcastle City Council logo on the side. The back doors were secured with welded metal straps and a big brass padlock: not taking any chances in Kingsmeath.

I climbed out and plipped the Merc's locks. I wasn't taking any chances either.

My place had always looked like every other shitty council house on the street – harled walls streaked with dirt, ancient single-glazing with wasp-eaten wooden frames, grass growing in the guttering, but now that all the windows were boarded up too it actually managed to lower the tone. In *Kingsmeath.*

The council had replaced the front door with a slab of solid chipboard. A wee man in orange overalls was nailing a notice to it. 'WARNING: THESE PREMISES ARE CONSIDERED DANGEROUS AND UNFIT FOR HUMAN HABITATION. AUTHORISED PERSONNEL ONLY.' The sound of his hammer echoed around the street.

He bashed in the last nail, took a step back to admire his handiwork, then turned and squealed. 'Fuck's sake...' A hand on his chest, breathing hard. 'Scared the crap out of me.'

I flashed my warrant card. 'I need in.'

'Nah, sorry, mate – she's all locked up till they can get a renovation crew down here. Besides: place is a shitehole, you don't want in there, trust us.' He picked up his toolkit and hobbled back to the van, unlocked the driver's door and climbed inside. Wound down his window. 'You can give the Housing Department a bell if you like, see if they'll let you in?'

He gave me a smile, a wave, then gunned the engine and drove off.

Officious little prick.

The new front door was hefty, solid. Looked like a Yale deadbolt set into it.

I took two steps back then slammed my foot into the wood beside the lock. CRACK. The sound of squealing wood. One more for luck... BOOM, the whole thing burst inwards in a shower of splinters.

Gloom and darkness inside. They hadn't just boarded up the windows around the front: they'd done the back too. I reached for the switch, flicked it on. Then off. Then on again. Nothing. They'd killed the power.

I pulled the torch from my pocket and swung the beam across the hallway.

'Holy shite...'

Shifty Dave hadn't been exaggerating. The whole place reeked of mould and damp, the wallpaper peeling off the grey plaster. The ceiling sagged like a pregnant cat's stomach. Both doors off the hallway were hanging off their hinges.

I went through into the kitchen. The linoleum curled under my feet. Whoever it was had ripped the doors off the units, hauled out the drawers; cutlery and tins and jars lay amongst the debris of shrapnelled plates, glittering in the torchlight.

A big patch of the ceiling had caved in, the support beams for the floor above exposed like skeletal ribs, chunks of swollen plasterboard piled up in the sink.

Lounge: the sofa torn up, everything else trashed.

Upstairs, the bathroom was a disaster area – broken toilet, sink stuffed with towels, a pile of sodden clothes and blankets shoved to one side in the bath. Medicine cabinet looked as if it had exploded.

Bedroom: every drawer pulled out, wardrobe tipped over onto the bed, mattress slashed. All the paperbacks from the windowsill were bloated on the damp carpet. Clothes everywhere.

Spare room.

Fuck...

All the cardboard boxes were torn open, their contents strewn around the room. Everything Michelle had hurled out of the bedroom window when she found out about me and Jennifer – everything I hadn't sold or pawned – was sodden and broken.

The carpet squelched as I bent down and picked up a little wooden plaque with a tiny gold-coloured truncheon mounted on it. Someone had stamped on it, breaking the plastic shape in two – the dirty imprint of the boot clearly visible on the wood.

There was no way this could have been Mr Pain. OK, *maybe* he could have hauled himself through the house smashing things, but it's pretty difficult to stamp on something when you've only got one working leg. I dropped the plaque. It hit the soggy carpet sending up a little splash.

It was all ruined. All of it. Books, newspaper clippings – the announcement of Rebecca's birth, the article on her when she won silver at the Oldcastle Highland Games when she was six, the little piece about Katie and some other kids appearing in the school panto... Nothing more than grimy papier-mâché.

The council were right: *not fit for human habitation*.

The fat man behind the counter smiled. White shirt fraying at the cuffs, maroon waistcoat stained with dollops of brown and red, small round glasses, comb-over greased flat across a wide shiny scalp. 'Ah, Mr Henderson, and what brings you to my emporium of delight this fine day?'

Little Mike's Pawnshop smelled of dust and mildew, with a lingering undercurrent of stale cigar smoke. The walls were lined with shelves packed with other people's possessions: everything from electric guitars to vacuum cleaners, with a line of washing machines and flat-screen TVs down the middle. The counter was glass-fronted, full of rings and watches that sparkled in the dim lighting.

An old-fashioned glory hole in both senses of the word: it was full of random crap, and you knew you were going to get screwed.

I dumped the Waitrose carrier-bag on the countertop. 'How much?'

He shook his head. 'And there was me thinking you'd come in to redeem one of your priceless family heirlooms.'

'How much?'

A sigh. He reached into the bag and pulled out Ethan's watches, rings, necklaces, and a couple of iPods. 'Ah… Not your usual items, Mr Henderson…' He wiped his chubby fingers on his waistcoat. 'Tell me, how warm *are* these? Will one of your colleagues be paying me a visit in the not too distant future, miraculously find these items, and infer some wrongdoing on my part?'

'They're not hot. I just don't need them any more.'

'You don't need a steel Rolex?'

'How much?'

'"How much", "How much", like a broken record.' He pulled out a jeweller's eyeglass and popped it in, scrunching his face around it as he peered at each item in turn.

'Well?'

'Patience is a virtue, Mr Henderson.' More scrunching and peering.

I settled against the counter, looking down at the array of engagement rings. Big sparkly ones, little sparkly ones, all with a price tag attached. Probably came from Argos. All those hopes and dreams for the future, ruined and up for sale in a manky little shop in a manky little shopping centre, in manky old Kingsmeath.

Mike settled back in his creaky chair. 'Two thousand.'

'Four.'

'Two.'

'... Three and a half.'

'Mr Henderson, much though I trust you *implicitly*, I have my reputation to consider. My livelihood depends on my clients seeing me as an honest and upright man. These items make me nervous.'

'Three then. The Rolex is worth that on its own.'

He puffed out his cheeks and frowned up at the ceiling. 'Two and a half, and that's my final offer. But I'm not a heartless man, Mr Henderson...' He swivelled his seat around and hunched over, muttering to himself. Click, click, click, click, whirrrrrrrr – an old-fashioned safe tumbler being spun back and forth – then a clunk, and then more muttering.

When Mike turned back he was holding a wad of notes and a small purple velvet box. He counted out two thousand five hundred pounds in twenties on the countertop, then placed the little box carefully on top of it. 'With my compliments.'

I parked Ethan's Merc in the 'RESIDENTS ONLY' section. Be a shame to sell it. Been years since I'd driven something that wasn't falling apart... But needs must.

I popped the boot and hauled out the three heavy black plastic bin-bags. My fingers ached as I carried them to the building's entrance. Before the development boom in Logansferry it was a warehouse for machine parts. Now it was luxury apartments with onsite shopping.

Through the double doors and out of the rain. The atrium was big enough to boast its own patch of manicured woodland, yellow-brick trails winding across it, surrounded by empty shopping units with dusty 'To Let!' signs in the windows. Half the apartments were still up for sale too: 'FREE CARPETS AND WHITE GOODS!', '£20,000 OFF YOUR NEW HOME!', 'PART EXCHANGE AVAILABLE!'

My phone rang. I let it.

Dumped the bin-bags on the floor of the lift, then pressed the button for the fourth floor.

No reply, so I rang the bell again. Checked my watch: coming up to twenty past ten. She'd be awake by now, *surely*. A muffled rattle and a clunk.

'Who is it?' A woman's voice, slightly high-pitched, trembling.

'Kimberly? It's Ash.'

Pause. Some mumbling.

'Go away.'

'No.'

Another pause. More mumbling.

'She doesn't want to see you.'

'Kimberly, stop dicking about and open the door, OK? I'm having a crappy day already, I don't need this.'

A clunk, then the door swung open, and there was Susanne in a pink fluffy dressing gown, one hand on her hip, the other waving a finger in my face. 'You've got a lot of bloody nerve!' She was wearing sunglasses, a stain of purple and blue spreading out from behind the dark lenses. Another bruise on her chin, lips swollen and cracked on one side.

I dropped my bin-bags. 'What happened?'

'What happened? *You* happened.' The finger stopped wagging and started poking. 'You and your bloody debts!'

I stared at her. 'Who was it?'

'I don't know. Some ugly little troll and his big ginger sidekick. They said I had to give you a message.'

'Did the wee one sound like he'd swallowed a dictionary?' Joseph and Francis. 'I'll bloody kill him.'

Susanne hauled open the front of her dressing gown. Bruises covered most of her stomach, disappearing into her fleecy pyjama bottoms and crop top. 'How am I supposed to dance like this?'

I curled my hands into fists. 'What was the message?'

She howched and spat in my face, then slammed the door in it too. Her voice boomed from inside. 'And you're fucking dumped!'

'And you're *sure* we can't put you in a new car today?' The salesman pulled on a shark's tooth smile. It went with the shiny grey suit.

'Positive.' I pocketed the envelope with the cash in it and walked off the car lot, taking my heavy bin-bags with me.

Rhona leaned back against the bonnet of her Vauxhall, waiting for me. 'You want to throw those in the boot?'

She popped it open and I dumped the bags inside.

'Let me guess – body parts?'

'Sodden clothes. Everything else in the house is ruined.'

'Ooh.' She clunked the boot shut again. 'Susanne not wash them for you?'

'We're not... No.'

Rhona sucked her teeth for a moment, then got in behind the wheel. 'Meh, you were always too good for her. That mean you've got nowhere to crash tonight?'

Well, there was no way I'd be going back home. 'Yeah.'

She started the engine as I climbed into the passenger seat. 'Then you're staying at mine. I've got the spare room, and we can chuck your stuff through the washing machine. You like cats, right?'

My phone went again – DCI Weber.

'Where are you?'

'Out and about. You?'

'In the office, where you *should be. The ACC's giving some sort of motivational speech at half past and I want you here.'*

K&B Motors disappeared in the rear-view mirror. 'I don't need motivated.'

'Tough. We've lost another girl.'

26

I'd expected a motivational speech to be a bit less of a rant. The Assistant Chief Constable paced up and down at the front of the crowded briefing room – a thin man with a hunched-over walk, wearing dress-uniform black. 'And while we're on the subject of unprofessional conduct, I clearly need to spell this out again: you will *not* speak to the media!' He stopped, turned, and glared out at the crowded room. 'Never. Not so much as a word. As far as those bastards are concerned, you are bloody mute!'

No one said anything.

'Do you understand me, ladies and gentlemen? M – U – T – E.' The ACC straightened up for a moment, before hunching over again and stalking from the room, slamming the door behind him.

Weber shook his head, then stood, held up his hands for silence. 'Now that you're all feeling perky and loved, it's update time. We've discovered a fifth body at the dump site, Matt and his team are recovering it at the moment, no ID as yet.'

Please don't be Rebecca, please don't be Rebecca…

'Slightly more pressing: Dickie's team of Party Crashers have a system they use to identify possible Birthday Boy victims.

Most of the time they're simply runaways who turn up eventually, but other times…'

Sabir heaved himself out of a small plastic chair and lumbered to the projection screen. He pointed something at the back of the room and a mosaic of girls' faces appeared on the screen. 'We're tracking nineteen girls this year, all gone missin' three or four days before their thirteenth birthday. They're all up and down the country, but we got a new one last night.' He pointed the thing again and the screen changed to a head-and-shoulders shot of a young girl trying desperately to look older. Far too much makeup, broad face stretched wider by a smile that looked practised, hair the colour of wet straw scraped back from her face in a Kingsmeath facelift.

Sabir nodded at the screen. 'Megan Taylor: she'll be thirteen on Monday. Bunked off school on Thursday to hang about the shops with her mates. They say she was acting all secret-like, you know, thought she was going to meet someone special. We've got her on CCTV at the Templers Vale shoppin' centre at three-fifteen yesterday afternoon, after that – nothin'.'

He pointed the remote again and Megan's face was replaced by grainy security camera footage with a timestamp flickering away in the bottom right-hand corner. Six kids, none of them wearing school uniforms, all of them with backpacks.

Two girls were sitting on the edge of a large square planter at the centre of the group. One was a bit on the chunky side with a low-cut top, the other was Megan. She was smoking a cigarette: making a big production of it, as if she was in a film. Look at me: look how sophisticated and grown up I am. Slurping at a large wax-paper cup of something fizzy from a fast-food outlet – probably the KFC on the ground floor – working the straw like a pro.

The big girl stomped away, out of the picture.

Then the group froze, looked left.

A wee man in a security guard's uniform appeared onscreen, pointing his finger as if it was a gun.

Megan took one last draw on her cigarette, dropped it, then ground the butt out with her trainer. She stood, said something. Her mates all laughed.

Mr Security Guard marched closer.

She flipped the drink at him. The wax-paper cup spun through the air then exploded on the marble floor – ice and fizzy sugared water going everywhere.

He danced back a couple of steps, and she was off, running and laughing, giving him the finger as she disappeared off screen.

Nice girl. Her mum and dad must be *so* proud.

The picture froze, then jumped back to Megan's face.

Sabir sniffed. 'Course, we don't really know if she's a victim yet. Won't get confirmation one way or the other till the parents gerra birthday card next year. But given you lot've found all them bodies, and she's gone missin' from Oldcastle, chances are...?' A shrug. And then he sat down again.

'Thank you, Constable.' Weber picked up a clipboard from the nearest desk and flicked through the attached sheets. 'In light of this I'm pulling Gilbert, McTavish, and Urpeth off the door-to-doors: you're seconded to DCS Dickie's task force, try not to embarrass anyone. DI Morrow will hand out the rest of the assignments.'

Shifty Dave went through the list, rearranging the teams while I scanned the room. Dr McDonald was sitting at the back, on her own. She was even paler than yesterday, face glistening, hair lank, bags under her eyes, glasses in one hand as she rubbed at her forehead. She'd seemed fine when I'd dropped her off this morning...

She put her glasses back on, glanced up, saw me watching her, and pulled on a thin smile. Gave a little wave.

When Shifty had finished dishing out the crap, everyone

stood and shuffled towards the exit. I went to join them, but DCI Weber got to me first.

'Ash…' He looked around, then dropped his voice to a whisper. 'Have you sorted your problem with Mrs Kerrigan yet?'

'Give me a chance: only been back a couple of hours.'

'Look, if you need a hand I know someone who's in the market for a little after-hours security – no questions asked – and… Dr McDonald!' Weber threw his arms open. 'How are you feeling? Any better?'

She was standing right behind me.

Pink rushed up her cheeks. 'I'm so sorry about earlier, I didn't mean to, and certainly not in your office, I'm really, really, *really* sorry.'

'Don't worry about it, you're not the first person to lose their breakfast in my office, you probably won't be the last either. And if you leave the windows open for a couple of hours the smell soon goes away.'

She nodded and stared at her feet. 'Sorry.'

'Anyway, Ash: have a think and let me know if you want that guy's number, OK? In the meantime…' Weber flipped through his clipboard again. 'I've got you down to accompany Dr McDonald today. She wants to do some follow-ups on the door-to-doors.'

Great. A day dicking about outside in the cold. 'Are you sure someone else wouldn't be—'

'Absolutely positive. Dr McDonald tells me you're the man for the job, and apparently everyone else scares her, so…'

She coughed. 'I'm standing right here.'

Weber patted me on the shoulder. 'Off you go.'

The patrol car dropped us off on Lochview Road. Down at the far end of the street, Ethan's house was all lit up. Must have decided not to take his shattered hand into work today. Couldn't blame him.

I unlocked the rusty Renault and climbed in. Put on my seatbelt. Sighed. After driving his nearly new Merc it really wasn't the same.

Dr McDonald got into the passenger seat. She reeked of extra-strong mints and stale booze, a happy-hour sweat shining on her forehead and top lip as the alcohol oozed out of her.

'What happened to you?'

'Henry phoned at nine this morning, wanting to go over the profile again before I presented it. I'm really glad he's decided to help out, but I can't do this any more.' She leaned forwards until her head rested on the dusty dashboard. 'Urgh...'

A taxi pulled up outside Ethan's house. Beeped its horn twice.

Sod it, why not? 'I'll be back in a minute.' I climbed out and marched down the street.

Ethan's front door opened and there he was, his left arm encased in plaster from the tips of his fingers all the way to the elbow. He turned on the top step and fumbled with his keys, then stomped down the stairs and froze – staring at me. 'I didn't do anything! I was up at the hospital: I haven't been anywhere near them!'

Good. I unfolded the ticket from Little Mike's Pawn Shop. Held it out.

Ethan flinched back.

'It's the receipt for your things. Pawnbroker's name and address is on there. You can redeem them.'

He picked at the cast on his smashed hand. 'Why?'

'Because you *know* what'll happen if you fuck with my family again. I've won. Don't need to rub your nose in it.'

Ethan didn't move.

I pinned the ticket under the windscreen wiper of a Porsche parked at the kerb. 'Your car's at K&B Motors in Cowskillin. Probably haven't sold it on yet.' I turned and walked back towards the Renault. 'Do yourself a favour and think about leaving town. Next time you don't get another chance.'

I climbed in behind the wheel again.

He was still standing there, staring after me. Then he crept over to the Porsche, grabbed the pawn ticket, and got in the taxi.

As it drove past he kept his gaze fixed out the other window.

Maybe this time the little shite would take a telling.

Dr McDonald hadn't moved since I'd left – head resting on the dashboard, arms dangling by her sides. 'Urgh…'

'You ready?'

'Can you go really fast and crash into something, please?'

I eased out of the parking space, bearings making that wonky squealing noise every time I put the wheel on full lock. 'Get your seatbelt on.'

'I want to curl up and die…'

'You're the one who wanted to go traipsing round town in the cold. Now get your bloody seatbelt on.'

Groan. She did, then slumped back in her seat as if someone had removed all her bones. 'He keeps making me drink whisky, I don't even *like* whisky…'

'You're a grown-up. If you don't like it, don't drink it.' Elegant Georgian houses slid past as we headed for Dundas Bridge.

'But then he won't like me, and he won't *help* me, and—'

'Henry was on the *phone*. You could've been drinking camomile tea: how would he know?'

She put her hands over her face. 'He'd know.'

'You can't let people pressure you into doing things, just so they'll like you. It…' For fuck's sake, it was like talking to an eight-year-old. Not my responsibility – if she wanted to rot her liver with Henry it was her problem, not mine.

Dundas Bridge stretched over Kings River in a gentle arc of white-painted steel held up by two sets of pylons and thick black suspension cables.

Dr McDonald grabbed the dashboard. 'Pull over.'

'What? Did you see something—'

'Oh God, pull over, pull over right now!'

I stomped on the brakes and she fumbled open the passenger door, then retched. And heaved. Her back hunched and convulsed, arse rising out of the seat with each contraction.

Then she sagged, one hand holding on to the door handle as she spat into the gutter. 'Urgh…'

'You *sure* you want to go door-to-door?'

'Urgh, bile…'

'What did I tell you about not having breakfast?'

More spitting. Then she hauled herself back into the car. 'Had a big fry-up on the boat. Stayed down till about half eight.'

I pulled out again, taking us up onto the bridge. The Kings River was a gunmetal ribbon below us. 'Do you really need a lecture about matching drink for drink with an alcoholic?'

'I don't feel well…'

There's a bloody shock.

The granite blade of Castle Hill loomed above us, like the bow of a submarine breaching through the valley floor, casting everything around it into shadow. On the other side of the bridge, I took a left, skirting the twisted cobbled streets and heading for the post-war beige-and-grey sprawl of Cowskillin.

'Where are we—'

'I'm not letting you interview anyone like that: you'll scare the serial killers.' Up ahead the City Stadium dominated the surrounding housing estate like a big metal BDSM mistress. 'Trust me, I know what'll sort you out.'

The Renault bumped over the rutted dirt of the parking lot. About half a dozen morons were marching in a little circle outside the main entrance to the Westing, each one carrying placards with things like 'GAMBLING IS SATAN'S PATH!', 'HE THAT HASTETH TO BE RICH HATH AN EVIL EYE!', and 'JESUS

Will Save Us From Our Sins!!!' Breath streaming out behind them.

From the front, the Westing had all the bland grey-and-blue-painted-corrugated-iron charm of a cash-and-carry on a rundown industrial estate. Six-foot-high plastic letters were mounted above a little recessed opening: 'The Westing', and the silhouette of a sprinting greyhound, bordered with blue and red neon. As if anyone didn't know what this place was. Or who owned it.

I parked next to a dented minibus with 'PaedoPopeMobile' in spray-paint graffiti along the side, then climbed out into the cold afternoon.

The greyhound track sat on the edge of a sprawling Fifties housing development. A couple of pubs lurked on the other side of the road along with a minicab office, and a newsagents, the shiny modern bulk of the City Stadium looming in the background.

A stray beam of sunshine carved its way through the heavy clouds, glittering off Bad Bill's Burger Bar – a jury-rigged Transit van that scented the air with the dark, savoury smell of frying onions and mystery meat.

The man himself lounged in a folding chair in front of the van, sunbathing and smoking a cigarette and scratching himself. His pale hairy stomach bulged out between a pair of fraying jeans and a pink short-sleeved shirt. Arms thick as cabers, tattoos snaking about beneath the fur.

He looked around, squinted at me, then jerked his chin in the air, setting everything wobbling. Nodded towards his van. He pinged his cigarette butt off into the shadows, levered himself out of the chair, stomped to the back doors, and clambered inside. The Transit rocked on its springs.

Dr McDonald shifted her feet. 'Are you ... it's not exactly the most hygienic-looking of places. I'm sure it's got its own rustic charm, but I can't... Ash?'

I was already walking.

'Great, now I get alcohol poisoning *and* food poisoning.'

By the time we'd reached the serving hatch Bill was tying an apron around his swollen middle, the rumble of a kettle filling the van's interior with steam. A radio burbled out mass-produced plastic pop, fighting against the hiss and crackle of onions on a flat greasy griddle.

'You believe these pricks?' Bill jerked a thumb at the protesters. 'Like that's going to make a pube's worth of difference.'

I sniffed at the menu chalked up on the side of the van – where the paint was matt, like a blackboard. 'Two teas: white, sausage buttie, and a hangover special.'

Dr McDonald tugged at my sleeve. 'But I don't—'

'Like I said: trust me.'

Bill took the stainless-steel lid off a deep-fat fryer and dumped six sausages into the hot oil. A handful of streaky bacon rashers went in after them, popping and crackling. He scratched himself with a pair of tongs. 'These religious types get right on my moobs.'

The song faded out on an autotuned harmony. *'And we'll be playing the other three semi-finalists' songs after the break, but first here's Doug with the news and weather. What do you think, Doug, who you backing?'*

'Sophie for Britain's Next Big Star, definitely, Mike. Anyway, here's the headlines at half-past twelve this morning. The head of Oldcastle City Council says he won't *be resigning after allegations surfaced earlier this week…'*

The little circle of protesters started singing: a ragged sound that favoured volume over talent. 'ROCK OF AGES, CLEFT FOR ME, LET ME HIDE MYSELF IN THEE!' Pumping their placards up and down like the world's dreariest merry-go-round.

'Holier-than-thou bawbags.' Bill curled his lip. 'People go to the Westing, they're no' looking for spiritual awakening, are they?' He produced two floury white rolls from beneath the counter, tore them open, and slathered both sides with butter. 'Nah, folks are looking for a wee thrill. Want to escape the grinding shite of the old day-to-day.'

'BE OF SIN THE DOUBLE CURE, SAVE FROM WRATH AND MAKE ME PURE!'

'*...unavailable for comment. Oldcastle Police have refused to confirm or deny that local girl Megan Taylor – missing since last night – has been snatched by the serial killer known as "The Birthday Boy". We spoke to Assistant Chief Constable Gary Drummond...*'

So much for the *'you're all mute'* talk.

Bill oiled the griddle and cracked two eggs onto it. 'I heard he eats their livers, like that bloke in the films.' Another scratch. 'Got a special on muesli bars, if you're interested?'

ACC Drummond sounded as if he'd trod in something. '*... pointless media speculation isn't helping. We're taking Megan's disappearance very seriously, but that does* not *automatically mean she's been abducted...*'

'COULD MY ZEAL NO RESPITE KNOW, COULD MY TEARS FOREVER FLOW!'

I looked back towards the Westing. There was a light on in the little row of windows, two floors up. 'Mrs Kerrigan about?'

'Got a job lot off this Dutch bloke. No fucker wants them.' Styrofoam cups, teabags, water from the steaming kettle. 'Do us a favour, eh? Steer clear of Mrs Kerrigan.' Milk – sploshed in straight from the carton, turning the contents anaemic beige, the teabags bobbing about like little brown islands. 'There you go, Katie...' He handed one of the polystyrene cups to Dr McDonald. 'Haven't seen you for years: how's your mum keeping?'

'Actually, I'm not—'

'Red or brown?'

'Er ... tomato?'

I helped myself to the other tea. 'Is she here or not?'

'*...assure the public, we* will *catch him.*'

'*And we'll be keeping you updated on that story as it develops.*

Sport now, and Oldcastle Warriors are at home to Aberdeen in the third round of the Scottish Cup tomorrow...'

'NOTHING IN MY HAND I BRING, SIMPLY TO THE CROSS I CLING!'

A good squirt of red on one roll, then Bill hauled the wire basket out of the fryer. 'Come on, Ash, your luck's for shite, I wouldn't want—'

'Every bastard thinks they're my mother...' I fished the teabag out of my cup and dumped it on the hard-packed mud. Splatch.

'Just saying.' He stuck one fried egg on the sauce-covered roll, then arranged three sausages on it, added the bacon, and topped it with the second egg. Another squirt of tomato sauce, then Bill squeezed the lid back on. 'Don't want to see you go the same way as your old boss.' He wrapped the buttie in a paper napkin and stuck it in front of Dr McDonald. 'There you go, Katie darling, get that down you and you'll feel much better.'

'Ah, right, erm, great, thanks...' She stared at the thing. Took a deep breath, then bit into it, crunching and chewing, bright-yellow yolk dripping down her chin.

'WHILE I DRAW THIS FLEETING BREATH, WHEN MINE EYES SHALL CLOSE IN DEATH!'

'...struggling to avoid relegation for the second year in a row, and with Hallet still off with a groin injury, chances are: that's set to continue...'

Bill piled the remaining sausages on the other roll, and passed it to me. 'Speaking of Len: you ever see him these days?'

I added a liberal squeeze of brown sauce. 'What do I owe you?'

'On the house, like the advice.'

'Thanks.' The deep-fried sausages were napalm-hot, but tasty. I pointed at Dr McDonald, talking with my mouth full. 'Do me a favour and look after this one for a couple of minutes?'

'...and if you're heading out this afternoon, make sure you wrap up – temperatures are set to plummet as low pressure settles in...'

'Deal.'

She shuffled her feet, red sauce and egg all over her chin and cheeks. 'Who's Mrs Kerrigan, why do you have to see her, is she some sort of—'

'Don't wander off or speak to strangers. I won't be long.' I turned and walked towards the Westing.

'ROCK OF AGES, CLEFT FOR ME, LET ME HIDE MYSELF IN THEE!'

Bill's voice boomed out across the car park. 'Don't say I didn't warn you!'

27

The little recess in the front of the Westing hid a set of turnstiles and a gloomy tunnel. A hairy golem was perched behind a waist-high partition, locked away behind a metal grille. She looked up from her *Twilight* novel as I knocked on her cage. Neither of her thick eyebrows moved.

'Morning, Arabella, I need to see Mrs Kerrigan.'

She sniffed, marked her place in the book with a callused thumb. 'Oh aye?'

'Aye.'

'Mmph.' She picked up a mobile phone and jabbed at the buttons in silence. Thirty seconds later it buzzed and chirruped on the countertop. Arabella squinted at it, then grunted and flicked a switch. The turnstile clunked, the bars dipping a couple of centimetres. She went back to her book.

I pushed through into a long dark corridor with a little square of daylight at the end.

A soft, Irish voice broke through the gloom. 'Detective Constable Henderson?'

I froze, balled my hands into fists. 'Mrs Kerrigan.'

A light clicked on above a featureless doorway and there she was: black suit with a red silk shirt, golden crucifix resting in the wrinkled crease of her freckled cleavage. Her greying hair was piled up in a loose bun, curls escaping its grasp, waving in the breeze. Mrs Kerrigan smiled, baring sharp little teeth. 'Mr Inglis would like a word with yez.'

Click and the light went off again.

Here it comes...

I reached into my inside pocket...

But no one jumped out at me. Instead, Mrs Kerrigan closed the door and marched away down the tunnel towards the Westing's interior. The whub-wheek of her wellington boots echoed off the concrete walls. 'If ye'd like to follow me?'

OK...

I closed the distance, keeping my hand inside my jacket – feeling the comforting weight of the Beretta. March right up to her, stick the gun in her ear and Artex the corridor with her brains. But then I'd have to go back and do the same to Arabella: get rid of the witness.

And as I didn't have a silencer, everyone in the car park would have to go – they'd seen me walk in here. I'd have to shoot Dr McDonald too.

For some reason that wasn't quite as appealing as it would've been a couple of days ago.

The tunnel opened out at the foot of the new stands – a sweeping block of concrete steps broken up into sections by lines of white railings. All the tout booths were shuttered, and an old man with a broom was waging war against drifts of damp ticket stubs. It didn't look as if he was winning.

The Westing's track was a flat-sided oval of sandy brown, with a big swathe of grass in the middle. Crumbling wooden stands wrapped around the rest of the course, gaping holes in their corrugated metal roofs, chains blocking them off from the main building.

Andy Inglis's Range Rover was parked in the middle of the grass, glistening deep-blue in the low sunlight.

I stopped. 'You sent someone round to my house.'

Mrs Kerrigan walked on a couple of steps, then turned,

smiled. 'And let me guess, yez are wantin' to apologize for lettin' yer foul mouth run away with yez on the phone the other night?'

'You sent someone round to cripple me.'

'Did I now?'

'You wrecked my house.'

'There's a reason a man pays his debts, Constable Henderson.'

'You got Joseph and Francis to beat the crap out of Susanne.'

'A man pays his debts so he can keep himself and his loved ones free from reprisals.'

I pulled my hand from my jacket.

Her eyes darted down to what I was holding, then back up again. She licked her lips. 'That what I think it is?'

I gave her the envelope. 'Fifteen grand. You'll get the other four in a couple of weeks.'

She ripped it open and flicked through the bills. Two and a half thousand from Little Mike's pawn shop, twelve from flogging Ethan's Mercedes, and five hundred from the grand and a bit he'd had hidden under the desk in his study. Leaving six hundred for me. Enough to pay for Katie's birthday party, pony trekking, and a nice present.

Mrs Kerrigan stuffed the notes back into the envelope, then the envelope into her pocket. 'You mean the other *six*.'

'Four. It was nineteen grand, not—'

'Dry yer arse, Constable Henderson: that was *before* ye decided to miss yer repayments. Now it's twenty-one thousand, all in, with interest.'

Do it. Walk right up to her *right* now and blow a hole in her head big enough to shit through. Take out the gun and fucking do it.

I took a step closer.

She smiled. 'Last time we had a wee chat with yer girlfriend. Want us to have one with yer missus and kid?'

'Listen up, *Mrs* Kerrigan, and pin your lugs back because this is the only warning you're getting—'

'Who the feck do yez think yer talkin'...'

Her mouth fell open, eyes wide.

I rested the barrel of the Beretta against her forehead. 'In case you're wondering: it's French, there's no safety.'

She shut her mouth, licked her teeth.

'Your one and only warning. You ever go anywhere near Katie ... or Michelle, I'm coming after you. There won't be any sirens, there won't be any uniforms – there'll be me, and you, and a shallow grave in Moncuir Wood. And it'll take a long, *long* time. Do you understand?'

A pause. 'Yes.'

'Fuck with my family and I'll make you beg for it.'

'I *said* I understand. Now put that thing away before you get hurt.' She backed up, turned, and whub-wheeked towards Andy Inglis's Range Rover. 'And it's still six thousand.'

The big double gates on the other side of the racetrack swung open and an ancient-looking Ford Capri rattled and banged to a halt just inside. A big man in a parka jacket followed it in, then hauled the gates shut again with a muffled clang. He dragged a figure out of the car's boot: a young man, dressed in blue jeans and a black T-shirt, hands behind his back, as if they were tied together.

T-Shirt struggled to his feet. Parka Jacket slammed a punch into his kidneys and he went down again. Then Parka Jacket grabbed a handful of the kid's hair and dragged him across the track, and onto the grass – making for the Range Rover. The kid's legs kicking out behind him. Not so much as a scream.

I slipped the gun back in my pocket and marched after Mrs Kerrigan.

'Ash, you old *bastardo*.' Andy Inglis stuck his hand out. Five foot four, broad shoulders, short arms, Glaswegian accent, and a collar-length sweep of grey hair surrounding a little freckly bald crown. He was wearing a double-breasted suit in a dark-blue pinstripe: playing up to the image. 'How's it going?'

His handshake was like a car crusher, making my knuckles scream.

I gritted my teeth and forced a smile, keeping my eyes on Mr Inglis. *Not* looking at Parka Jacket kicking the living shite out of the young man on the grass. 'Can't complain: no bugger would listen.'

Mr Inglis clapped his hands together and roared out a laugh, hunching his shoulders, doing a little two step, as if the ground beneath his feet was lurching. 'You remember that Russian? What was his name, Mikhail Massivesonofabitchovitch? Fists like shovels?'

The young man had duct tape over his mouth – which explained the silence – tears and blood running down his angular face, grunting every time Parka Jacket slammed another boot into his stomach, ribs, thighs, and back. He was razor-thin, with straggly brown hair and Keith Richard dreadlocks.

'Thirteen rounds!' Mr Inglis beamed. 'Man, that was a beautiful fight.'

Parka Jacket staggered back a few paces, then bent double, hands on knees, puffing, breath steaming out from inside his fur-trimmed hood.

Mr Inglis popped a couple of punches into the air. 'Right hook, jab, jab, then that haymaker! Wham!' He shook his head. 'Happy days... You hear he croaked it? Three weeks after he got out of hospital, bunch of guys – lost a lot of money on the big Ruskie – decided to recoup their investment. Used a wood-chipper.'

Lovely. 'Mrs Kerrigan said you wanted a word?'

'Man, you were something *special*...' He tilted his head on one side, eyes flicking across my face. Probably taking in the bruises and the scabbed-over scrapes. 'Let's see them golden hands of yours.'

I held them up. 'Wanted to drop off a chunk of cash. I know I've been a bit behind but—'

'Ash, what do I keep telling you?' He shook his head. Sighed. 'Gottae go in with your elbows, not your fists. Look at these knuckles. With your condition?'

'I know I'm a bit behind, but—'

'See, you use this bit.' He pressed his right fist into his right shoulder and threw the elbow out, head height, *fast*. Caught it with the palm of his left hand with a sharp smack. 'No cartilage in there, no joints to break, just a nice wee slab of bone to shatter the bastard's face with...' He frowned. Turned. 'Mrs Kerrigan?'

She appeared beside me without a sound, as if she ran on castors. Wellington boots in stealth mode. 'Mr Inglis?'

He hooked a thumb at the young man bleeding into the grass. 'Aye, what's the story?'

'This little bollox needs taught a lesson in manners. Robbin' off his employers.'

Parka Jacket straightened up, grinned from the depths of his fur-lined hood, then stomped on the T-Shirt's head a couple of times, grunting with the effort.

Mrs Kerrigan nodded. 'That should do, Timothy. Break both his legs, then yez can dump him outside Accident and Emergency.'

Parka Jacket got to work.

Mr Inglis turned his back on the beating. 'I hear you've had a wee problem with that house of yours in Kingsmeath. Place is all flooded and wrecked?'

I stared at Mrs Kerrigan. 'Council says it's "not fit for human habitation".'

'Never was, Ash. Come on: enough with the hair shirt. You got to live for the day, 'cos Mr Time's gonnae eat you up.' He curled his hand into a fist. Squeezing the life out of the air. 'Man like you shouldn't be living in a shitehole like that. How about I set you up in one of them executive flats down Logansferry? Dock-front property: got a whole heap of them sitting empty. Every bugger's broke.'

'Well, thanks, but really I can't—'

'Nah, not another word. Be my pleasure. What are friends for?'

T-Shirt screamed behind his duct-tape gag as Parka Jacket jumped up and down on his shins.

'Mr Inglis, I—'

'Mrs Kerrigan'll sort you out keys and that.' He grabbed my hand again and pumped it in his car-crusher grip. 'Don't be a stranger, OK?'

'Constable Henderson?' Mrs Kerrigan took my arm and led me away towards the exit. 'Seven hundred pound deposit, plus one month's rent payable in advance. Call it eleven hundred for cash. We can add it to the six thousand yez already owe.'

'But I don't want—'

'And just so we're clear, I'm needin' half by Wednesday lunchtime, and the rest the week after. Mr Inglis likes yez, but that doesn't mean you can do a legger on your debt.' Mrs Kerrigan stopped outside the entrance to the tunnel, the stand looming above us. She pulled out a small yellow notebook and scribbled something down, then tore out the sheet, folded it in half, and handed it to me. 'Let's not get back into arrears, OK? 'Cos if ye miss yer payment by so much as a *gee* hair, yez'll end up as dog food. And I will *personally* feed yer yockers to the greyhounds.'

'I don't want a bloody flat!'

She pulled on a tight little smile that didn't touch her eyes. 'Constable Henderson, are yez *really* spittin' in Mr Inglis's eye, when he's been nothin' but the friend of ye?'

I stared at her in silence.

She stared back. Then nodded. 'Thought not. Now if yez are lookin' for a way to repay Mr Inglis's kindness, ye could think about doin' him a favour. Brian Cowie's comin' up for trial in a couple of weeks – maybe yez'd like to lend a hand gettin' him off: names and addresses of the witnesses, copies of statements, that kind of thing.'

'A favour.'

'It'll get yez a thousand off what ye owe.' She shooed me off down the tunnel.

I stomped away into the darkness. Seven and a bit grand...

Her voice came echoing behind me. 'And one more thing: you'll feckin' regret stickin' a gun in my face. Should've pulled the trigger, Constable Henderson. Trust me on that.'

I clunked back through the turnstiles – Arabella still had her chip-pan face in her book, lips moving as she read. She didn't look up as I slumped past.

Seven thousand, one hundred pounds. Three and a half by Wednesday, the rest the week after. That weight was back, pressing down on my chest. *Seven thousand, one hundred pounds.* Everything I'd done – the extortion, the car, the jewellery, the cash – and I still couldn't see out of the pit. And Mrs Kerrigan was merrily shovelling dirt in on top of me.

My pulse pounded in my throat, lungs fizzing, fingers tingling. Jesus...

Outside the sunshine had disappeared, leaving a cold wind behind that whipped crisp packets, dust, grit, and leaves into a drunken dance. The protesters were gone and so was their minibus, but steam curled from the open hatch of Bad Bill's Burger Bar. The big man was scraping mayonnaise out of a jar and into a squeezy bottle, while Dr McDonald stood at the counter drinking from a polystyrene cup.

Seven thousand, one hundred pounds.

She looked up, saw me, and waved.

Deep breath. Straightened my back. Walked over there as if something wasn't chewing its way through my stomach.

Bill unscrewed the top from one of the brown sauce bottles. 'Still in one piece, then.'

I nodded at Dr McDonald. 'You ready to go?'

'Bill gave me some hot chocolate.' She held up her cup. 'It's got marshmallows in it.'

The big man poured a hefty measure of vinegar into the bottle. 'Katie's been telling me what a great dad you are. She's a good kid. You're lucky – my eldest is a wee shite.'

I stopped. Opened my mouth. But Dr McDonald got there first.

'That's what I keep telling Mum, but she never believes me.' Big grin. She swigged from the cup, then placed it on the counter. 'Thanks, Bill, it's been fun talking to you.'

He smiled, his chin disappearing into a roll of neck fat. 'My pleasure, darling. Good luck with university.' Then he dug beneath the counter and chucked something to her. 'Gotta keep your strength up.'

Back in the car she unwrapped the muesli bar. 'He's nice.'

I gripped the steering wheel. 'You're not Katie.'

A sigh. 'I know, but it made him happy, didn't it, and you didn't exactly disabuse him of the notion when you left me with him, did you, so I played along. It was your idea really.'

She had a point. The Renault's suspension squeaked and groaned as we crossed the rutted car park. 'How come, with me you're this rambling gibbery wreck, but with Bill you're like a normal person?'

'Are you going to tell me who this Mrs Kerrigan is?'

'No.' I took a left onto Angus Road, heading back towards Castle Hill.

28

'No. No I don't.' The flat-faced woman with the frizzy blonde hair ushered us outside. Then peered down the stairs towards the road. Wrinkled her top lip. 'And can you not do something about those horrible people?' She ducked back inside and closed the door.

McDermid Avenue can't have been much above freezing. The sky had gone the colour of charcoal, streaked with fire as the sun sank towards the hills. I stuck my hands deep into my pockets, hunched my shoulders. 'How many's that?'

Dr McDonald scored the woman's name off the list, then blew a foggy breath into stripy woollen gloves. 'Another twenty-six to go.'

Those 'horrible people' were parked in a collection of tatty vehicles on the other side of the street, the shiny black eyes of their cameras pointing at us. Carrion crows looking for a fresh kill. At least they'd stopped pestering us for quotes.

I followed Dr McDonald three doors down – to the next address on the list. A people-carrier moved along a couple of parking spaces. *Click. Click. Click.* 'You'd think they'd have something better to do with their time: catching politicians shagging their mistresses, rapist footballers getting hair extensions, D-list celebrity's secret boobs-out shame...'

Number fifty-two had a Volkswagen camper van sitting outside – gleaming paintwork, not a spot of rust, personalized number plate.

Dr McDonald marched up the stairs and rang the bell.

A man in a dark-blue anorak clambered out of the people-carrier and hurried across the road, big digital camera in one hand, some sort of Dictaphone in the other. Hairy; no chin; pointy nose. Half monkey, half rat. He locked eyes with me then froze, one foot on the pavement. Opened and shut his mouth a couple of times. A pale strip of sticking plaster crossed the bridge of his nose, a bruise leaking out from underneath. That'd be where I'd smacked him in the face with his own camera.

Frank somebody – Jennifer's photographer. Which meant she probably wasn't that far away. As if my luck wasn't crap enough already.

He took a step back. 'I...' Cleared his throat. 'I didn't want to file a complaint, it was all Jennifer's idea... I made sure they dropped the charges...'

Car doors clunked shut on the other side of the street. The murder was gathering: scenting something to feed on.

I turned and frowned up at the house. 'Who lives here?'

Dr McDonald checked her list. 'Steven Wallace?'

Never heard of him.

She rang the bell again, and the crows settled in a semicircle at the foot of the steps. *Click. Click. Click.*

Who the hell was Steven Wallace?

She shrugged. 'Maybe he's not in?'

And that's when the door opened. A slightly chubby man beamed out at us: bright-blue suit, bright-yellow shirt, blond hair jelled into spikes, a little ginger goatee, and tiny rect-angular glasses. 'Hey, hey, hey, what's all this then?' Big cheesy voice, big cheesy grin.

Dr McDonald checked her list again. 'Mr Wallace?'

He winked. 'But you can call me Sensational Steve!'

Oh Christ... Steven Wallace, host of *Sensational Steve's Breakfast Drive-Time Bonanza*. He was even more of a tosser in real life. Mugging it up for the cameras.

I flashed my warrant card. 'Can we come in, please, sir?'

'Course you can, course you can. Walk this way!' Then he turned and hobbled off down the hall, dragging one leg behind him, one shoulder up as if he had a hunch.

Dr McDonald pursed her lips. 'Right...'

I put a hand on the small of her back and *encouraged* her inside, then stepped in after her and slammed the door.

'...and that's why I think it's so important to do as much for charity as I possibly can. I mean, you've got to use your celebrity as a force for good, am I right or am I right?'

The conservatory glowed like a bonfire as the sun set. It was big enough for a baby grand piano, a leather sofa with matching armchairs, coffee table, a couple of large pot plants, and Sensational Steve's ego. He took up the entire couch on his own, arms draped along the back.

Prick.

Dr McDonald sat quietly in the other seat, batting her eyelashes at him, knees together, leaning forwards, drinking in his shite like it was nectar.

I took a sip of the weak green tea he'd served up from a china pot with his own face on it. An over-sized oil painting hung on the wall behind him – Steven Wallace posing like some eighteenth-century gentleman in front of a log fire – and a handful of teddy bears wearing 'SENSATIONAL STEVE!' T-shirts sat next to him on the couch. The piano was covered with framed photos of him grinning away with various musicians and actors. Look at me! Look how famous I am!

'And you didn't see anything?'

'What?' He blinked a couple of times. 'Oh, yes, when the girls went missing. Well ... no. Not a thing. Sorry: wish I had.' He shuffled forwards in his seat, looked left, right, then dropped his voice to a whisper. 'Seriously, how wonderful would that be? Think of the publicity: radio personality helps police catch serial killer. Don't get me wrong, I'm not complaining – I've done four interviews this week, *two* with the BBC and one with Sky News. But actually being a witness... I'd be on every front page in the country.'

He sat back again, picked up his tea and smiled into the cup. 'Next thing you know: *I'm a Celebrity... Get Me Out of Here!* I have the bone structure for TV, don't you think?'

I flipped open my notebook. 'Tell me, Mr Wallace, where were you last night?'

'Oh, some dreary fund-raiser for Cancer Research, or something. I was your host with the most, making the toasts. You should have seen it, we did a prank call live on stage – not everyone has the chutzpah for that. You have to time it to *perfection*, pick the perfect victim, or it's a disaster.'

'What about the afternoon: quarter past three?'

A pause. A frown. And then he flashed his veneers at me. 'Right, well, I was at home getting ready for the gig. I like to meditate: helps me shine.' He stood and walked to the wall of glass, looking out over his back garden towards the ivy-covered wall at the bottom. Cameron Park lurked on the other side, shadows growing darker as the sun disappeared. Three of the SOC tents were visible through the rampant bushes and jagged trees – glowing blue in the twilight. 'I have to admit: it's not easy with that going on all day and night. I have to be up at four to get to the studio and rehearse the *Breakfast Drive-Time Bonanza*.' A sniff. 'Spotlights shining everywhere, tents, generators, it's like a bloody circus out there.'

'Well, on behalf of Oldcastle Police let me *formally* apologize that our investigation into the murder of ten teenaged girls is disturbing your beauty sleep.'

Silence.

Then he turned around, that cheesy grin plastered across his creosote-tanned face again. 'Ha! Quite right. Sensational

Steve's a team player, he knows how to take one for the good guys.' He shot me with a finger. 'Don't sweat it.'

Dr McDonald squirmed in her seat. 'Your house is simply amazing, Sensational Steve, I mean it's so great, how long have you lived here, must've taken *forever* to get it looking like this.' Big acolyte eyes.

He swaggered back to the couch. 'You'd think, but I only got my hands on it eleven years ago. It was my dear old mum's house, and *her* dad's before her. It's like a family heirloom. Got a team of architects up from Edinburgh to gut the place and completely redesign it to my personal specifications.' He pointed down. 'Floor's Italian marble. They wanted to use slate, but I insisted. Told them: Sensational Steve knows what he wants.'

What Sensational Steve wanted was dragging outside and being given a stiff kicking.

'Wow.' Dr McDonald gave a little gasp. 'You know what would be great: a tour, would you show us round, Sensational Steve, I'd *love* that.'

'For you, little lady, anything.'

'And *that's* big enough for eight people.' He nodded at the Jacuzzi. 'I think we've seen the lot now.'

Dr McDonald held up a hand and counted things off on her fingers: 'Four bedrooms, one recording studio, one study, dining room, kitchen, conservatory, wine cellar, three bathrooms, living room…' She scrunched her face up like a happy chipmunk. 'It's just the best!'

Yeah, there was *nothing* better than getting a self-important tosser to show you around his house, boasting about how expensive and exclusive everything was. Great way to spend half an hour. And listening to Dr McDonald fawning over every word made it *extra* special.

Could she lay it on any thicker if she tried?

We followed Steven Wallace through to the front hall – lined with yet more photos of himself.

He pointed at Dr McDonald. 'Don't move a muscle, I'll be back in a tick.' And then he was off up the stairs, taking them two at a time. A minute later he returned with one of those teddy bears and a glossy photograph. An eight-by-ten of his own cheesy face signed in chunky black marker. He waggled the bear. 'I saw you admiring the Cuddle Crew when we were talking earlier. Here, you can hug him all night and think of Sensational Steve.'

Dear God, I was going to be sick.

She took the bear and the photo, bouncing on her toes as if she was about to wet herself. 'Thanks, they're great, I'll treasure them forever!' Then she leapt forwards, kissed him on the cheek, blushed, and ran out of the front door.

Steven Wallace preened himself, then turned the Colgate grin on me. 'And if I can be of any further assistance, you let me know, OK? Sensational Steve is *always* glad to help.'

I shifted my mobile to the other ear. 'Yes, I spoke to him. I said I would, didn't I?' Gravel crunched beneath my feet as I followed the path between a pair of huge rhododendrons – their seed heads like alien eyes on their dark bodies, leaves glistening sickly yellow in the sodium light.

On the other end of the phone, Michelle took a deep breath. *'He won't be round again? You promise?'*

'If he is, it'll be the last thing he does, and he knows it.' The path wound through Cameron Park, the edges choked with weeds. One of the SOC tents was up ahead, its walls glowing through a copse of skeletal beech trees.

'I don't want him anywhere near us, Ash. I... I can't.'

'He won't be round again.'

Dr McDonald scuffed along the path behind me.

'Thanks...' Michelle cleared her throat, forced a little cheer into her voice. *'Have you booked somewhere for Katie's party yet?'*

'Did she tell you she wants to go pony-trekking this year?'

'Have you booked somewhere?'

'Yes, I've booked somewhere. I told you last time.' I checked my watch – still time to get something organized. 'How many of her friends need to go play on the horsies with her? Four? Five? A dozen?'

'Her birthday's on Monday, *Ash: you need to get this sorted.'*

'I'll get it sorted. For God's…' I stopped on the path, rubbed at my eyes. 'How did this go from, "Thank you, Ash, you're my saviour!" to roasting my knackers over an open flame?'

Silence from the other end.

I stared up at the heavy dark-orange sky. 'OK, OK: I'll book it for six of them…'

More silence.

Then Dr McDonald was right at my shoulder, talking far too loud in a fake Glasgow accent. ''Scuse me, Constable Henderson, the guvnor wants to see youse, but.'

I looked around. There was no one there, just the two of us.

She mimed hanging up a phone, still clutching that bloody teddy bear.

'Michelle, I've got to go. Work.'

'I… I'm sorry. I do appreciate you talking to Ethan. Thank you.' And then Michelle was gone.

Dr McDonald grinned. 'Looked like you needed a get-out-of-jail-free card.'

I kept walking towards the glowing SOC tent.

'Ash?'

Still had two days left to organize Katie's pony-trekking and hire somewhere to corral a bunch of thirteen-year-old girls while they screeched their way through cake and ice cream. Two days and six hundred quid. How hard could it be?

Dr McDonald popped up at my shoulder again. 'Are you not speaking to me, I mean, you barely looked at me when we were at that last house interviewing Mrs Goddard, did I do something to—'

I jumped my voice up an octave. 'Oh, Sensational Steve, you're so sensational, I mean really marvellous and lovely, and your house is so special, and you're special, and I'll treasure this moment *forever*!'

She skipped alongside, scuffing through the gravel. 'I was pretty convincing, wasn't I?'

'The *key* to undercover work is subtlety. Not fannying about the place, overacting like a pantomime dame. It's a murder enquiry, not a game.'

'Come on, I was perfect: a devotee, a fan, an acolyte, exactly the kind of person someone like Steven Wallace loves to show off to, I mean, did you see his photo collection: there's not a single one in the entire house that doesn't feature him, he positively radiates an almost sociopathic selfishness, I mean look at this.'

She held out the bear with his face on its T-shirt.

'Who has these lying around the house, and he's got no alibi for the time Megan went missing yesterday, and he's in the media, so while he's an odious greasy little man he's a local celebrity, he's charming, he'd tell a young girl exactly what she wanted to hear: I'm famous and I can make *you* famous too. Now get in my funky VW camper van with the curtains on the windows.'

I stopped. 'You think he's the Birthday Boy?'

The little shite...

She kept going, still skipping, holding the bear by the arm, swinging it back and forwards. 'Steven Wallace is a narcissist, no one else matters but him, he's lived there since he was a little boy so he knows the area and the park, and he's got the perfect vehicle for transporting unconscious teenaged girls, why do you think I got him to give us a tour of his house?' Dr McDonald stopped, the bear hanging limp at her side. 'It's a shame there wasn't anything there...'

We cadged a cup of tea in the marquee-sized SOC tent. A diesel generator droned in the far corner, powering the floodlights that lit the place like a cold summer's day, meaning the lumpy-nosed woman in the white coverall had to shout. 'We think we've got another body: that's six.'

Five more to go.

Warmth prickled at the back of my head. What if it was Rebecca? What if they'd finally found her... My stomach clenched. There was still time: she wasn't on the list of victims, it'd take longer to identify her remains.

Sensational Steve Wallace – it wouldn't take much to make him talk. A hammer, a pair of pliers, one of those little crème brûlée torches like Ethan had...

And then what? Torture a confession out of him and the defence would tear us apart. Steven Wallace would walk out of court a free man with a big wad of compensation in his pocket.

'...Guv?'

I blinked.

The SEB tech frowned at me, then pointed over her shoulder at a fresh cordon of yellow-and-black tape. 'I said the ground-penetrating radar's acting up – we've been giving it a bit of a hammering since we found the first one – so we can't be sure till we excavate.'

Something in my throat. 'Get digging: I'll square it with Weber.'

Dr McDonald wrapped her hands around the chipped mug, steam curling out into the tent. 'Imagine lying here, buried in the cold ground for eight years, alone and afraid...'

'Right...' The woman took a step back, one eyebrow up, the other down. 'Well, I suppose these remains aren't going to dig themselves up.'

I looked out across the floodlit clumps of yellowy grass. 'Soil samples back from Aberdeen yet?'

A shrug. 'You think anyone would tell us?' Then she picked up her trowel and stomped away, ducking under the cordon.

Dr McDonald slurped her tea, watching me out of the corner of her eye. 'Do we suspect something?'

'Steven Wallace had the whole house remodelled eleven years ago. One year later the Birthday Boy snatches Amber O'Neil. If you wanted to build yourself a hidden room to torture twelve-year-old girls to death in...?'

A frown. 'The wine cellar. But we would've seen—'

'For all we know, there's a whole Josef Fritzl Bat Cave hidden behind the merlot.' I pulled out my phone, called DCI Weber and asked him about the soil samples.

'How would I know? Dickie and his Party Crashers have muscled in, we're nothing but bloody support staff now. And before you ask: they're all off at the mortuary, playing doctors and cadavers, so if you want to beg for scraps, you know where to go.'

'Who pissed in your tea?'

'Who do you think: that slimy arselicker DS Smith and his new best friend ACC Drummond.'

'So give Smith something crappy to do and don't let him dump it on one of the DCs. Tell him he's the only one you can trust. He'll love that.'

'Hmm... You want that friend's number?'

Seven thousand, one hundred pounds. 'Maybe. You know anywhere good to hold a kid's birthday party?'

29

The mortuary rang with the sound of refrigerated drawers being clunked in and out of the wall. 'Sorry about this...' Alf the Anatomical Pathology Technician ran a hand along his ponytail then tried another drawer. 'I know they're in here somewhere.'

A small set of speakers dribbled boy-band blandness into the room – the tiled walls and floor making the noise echo out of phase with itself. It complemented the eye-nipping stench of bleach.

'Where are you...?' Another drawer. 'Nightshift did a stock-take yesterday – took everyone out, cleaned the drawers, and put half the buggers back in the wrong place. Ah-ha! Here we go.'

The drawer was full of paperwork, boxes of pens, and packs of Post-it notes. Two bottles of what looked like vodka clinked at the back. 'Used to keep it all in the office, but the cleaners kept nicking stuff. Least this way we can lock it up, eh?' He selected a blue folder from the pile and handed it to me. 'One forensic report.'

Dr McDonald stood in the middle of the room, staring at the empty cutting tables, both arms wrapped around herself. 'What happens to the girls now?'

'Long-term storage; got a deep-freeze facility on this industrial estate in Shortstaine. Can't release them for burial till there's a trial – defence'll want to do their own post mortem.'

'That might be years...'

A shrug. 'Kinda depends on how long it takes you lot to catch him.'

I flicked through the chilled paperwork. A preliminary soil analysis was covered in graphs and tables of numbers. The bit at the back was in actual English. 'Says here that there's soil particulates recovered with the body that don't match the substrate it was buried in.'

Alf nodded. 'Means they were killed elsewhere and dumped in the grave.'

I stared at him. 'Yeah, because we couldn't tell that from the photographs on the birthday cards.'

Pink rushed up his cheeks. 'Well... I was ... ahem. Do you guys want a tea or coffee or something?'

Dr McDonald walked over to the wall of refrigerated drawers, and put her hand on one of the stainless-steel doors. 'All that time in the cold ground, and they still can't go back to their families.'

Just a little longer, *please*. Just long enough to get Steve Wallace. After five years, a couple more days wouldn't make any difference...

I cleared my throat, stuck the report back in the folder and returned it to Alf. 'If we can get a soil sample from the murder site they'll be able to match it. All we need's a warrant.' I pulled out my phone. The network icon blinked at me: no signal.

Alf shoved the drawer back into the wall. 'It's all the metal and pipes and fridges and being underground and that: plays hell with the signal. There's a sweet spot right outside the doors though.'

Nothing, nothing ... then the mortuary doors closed behind me and I had four bars.

DCI Weber wasn't picking up, and neither was Rhona, so I tried Sabir instead. 'Need you to do a PNC and full background on one Steven Wallace, eighty-six McDermid Avenue, Oldcastle, I.C.One male, early to mid forties.'

'PNC me arse, did I not tell youse the internet was where it's at?' A rattle of keystrokes in the background. *'Don't mean to geg, but who's this Steven Wallace when he's at home whackin' one off?'*

'Depends what you find, doesn't it?'

'...OK. This on the record, or off?'

'Like I said: depends what you find.'

The door opened behind me, and Dr McDonald slipped through into the gloomy corridor. 'Do you want to—'

I held up a finger and pointed at the phone in my other hand. 'I need enough to go in there and turn his house upside down, drag him into the station, take DNA, full body-cavity search, the lot.'

'Leave it with us. Gonna cost youse a bevvie though, right?' Sabir hung up.

I slid the phone back in my pocket. 'Sorry: business.'

'Do you fancy dinner tonight? I mean a carryout or something, Aunty Jan's off to Glasgow to see *My Chemical Romance*, and she's staying over with friends so I'm going to be on my own and maybe we could talk about the case or something. Or we could watch a film...' She bit her bottom lip and took a step back, staring over my shoulder.

I turned. There was someone on their knees in the shadows – big shoulders, grey boilersuit, scuffed trainers. The Rat Catcher. She was stroking something, holding it to her chest. One of the big plastic traps lay empty in front of her.

Dr McDonald stepped closer, tugging my sleeve. 'Is that a rat, I mean is she *actually* cuddling a dead rat?'

The Rat Catcher must have heard her, because she looked up and stared at us.

My mobile rang – the harsh noise cutting through the hum of the hospital above.

Mrs Rat Catcher didn't move.

I answered. 'Michelle, this isn't really a good—'

'The school just phoned.'

Something heavy dragged a sigh out of me. 'What's she done now?'

'Katie's been in a fight – they're keeping her in the office. Someone has to go round there and speak to the headmistress.'

Silence.

'And?'

The Miss Jean Brodie voice came out full bore. *'Well,* I *can't do it, can I? I'm stuck in a meeting till seven.'*

'Yeah, well you know what: I'm trying to catch a serial killer who kidnaps and tortures young girls. You think your meeting's more—'

'Oh, don't give me that. You had plenty of time to sneak off with your reporter whore when you were on duty, didn't you? Katie's only ever your daughter when it's convenient!'

'That's not—'

'They're talking about expelling *her, Ash. I'm stuck here till seven. Go be a father for a change.'* And she was gone.

I closed my eyes, leaned back against the wall and banged my head off it a couple of times. *Thank you, Ash, you're my saviour.*

A hand on my arm.

I looked down and Dr McDonald was staring up at me. 'Are you all right?'

Boom. The door clattered open and Alf appeared from the mortuary, shoving a big metal gurney in front of him. 'Beep, beep: mind your backs.' The door swung shut again. 'Got a client to collect from Oncology.' He stopped for a moment, banging one wheel of the trolley up and down on the concrete floor. 'Bloody thing never goes in a straight line…' He peered down the corridor. 'That you, Lisa?'

The Rat Catcher stared back, clutching the dead rodent against her chest.

Alf smiled. 'How you doing? Everything good? Yeah, perfect with me too. Keeping busy, you know?'

Blink.

'Well, better get back to it, right? No rest for the wicked.'

She stood, opened the cage mounted into her trolley and placed the rat's body inside. Her Oldcastle accent was thick and gravelly. 'Keeping busy.'

'That's the spirit.'

Lisa the Rat Catcher hunched over her trolley and scuffed away through the on-and-off patchwork of light and shadow.

Dr McDonald shuffled her feet. 'She's very... Erm...'

'Nah.' Alf gave his gurney's wheel another couple of dunts. 'Don't worry about Lisa, been working here longer than I have. Not the sharpest hamster in the cage, but she's all right. You OK to see yourselves out?'

'The school day finished a quarter of an hour ago, Mr Henderson.' The headmistress stood with her back to the room, looking out of the office window at the dirty rectangular blocks that made up Johnston Academy, classroom lights glowing in the darkness. Surveying her domain.

Her office wasn't like the ones on the telly – no wooden panelling and large teak desk with matching trophy case. Instead it was crammed with filing cabinets, in-trays and piles of paperwork. Cracked magnolia walls and a scrawl-covered whiteboard, a corkboard littered with pinned-up notes.

Two chairs sat in front of the desk. A balding man perched in one of them, wearing a corduroy jacket and a frown, hands knotting and unknotting themselves in his lap.

I sank into the other seat. No point waiting to be asked: headmasters were like detective chief inspectors – you couldn't let them get above themselves. 'You do understand what I do for a living, don't you, Mrs...' There was a wooden plinth in the middle of the cluttered desk with a brass nameplate on it. 'Elrick. We are *rather* busy trying to catch a killer.'

Her back stiffened. 'I see. Yes ... well. We need to talk about Katie.'

Captain Corduroy shifted in his chair, hands working overtime. 'Yes, we definitely do, it's simply not acceptable.'

'Your daughter is a disruptive influence, Mr Henderson. I'm afraid I have no option but to request that you make alternative arrangements for Katie's education.'

'It's simply not acceptable...'

I stared at him and he closed his mouth with an audible click.

'She's a bright kid: she's bored having to go at the slower kids' pace, if you lot—'

'Please, Mr Henderson, spare us the delusional parental ramble—'

'She's a bright kid.'

'No, she isn't: that's the problem.' A long sigh. 'Mr Henderson, your daughter isn't acting out because she's not being challenged intellectually.' The headmistress shook her head – still staring out of the window with her back to me, as if she couldn't be arsed going through the motions again. 'Sometimes that's the case, but Katie's academic track record simply doesn't support that. She underperforms in nearly every subject. Perhaps you should look on this as an opportunity to move her somewhere she can get more ... individual attention.'

Corduroy nodded. 'And it's not as if we haven't tried: we've been incredibly patient with her behaviour, given her family situation, but it's simply not—'

'What "family situation"?'

He flinched. 'It ... coming from a broken home, her sister going missing, you being a police officer.'

That was it, I was going to knock the wee shite's teeth down his throat. 'You listen up, you jumped-up—'

'Mr Henderson, we're not talking about a little backtalk, or running in the corridors. In the last six weeks Katie has been in my office twenty times. And given her attendance is appalling, that's something of a record. Quite frankly—'

'So she's a little high-spirited...'

The headmistress kept staring out of the bloody window, as if I was a badly behaved child.

I stood. 'Are you actually going to have the common courtesy to look at me when I'm talking to you?'

Mrs Elrick turned around. She was older than she'd seemed from the back: a used-looking face lined with creases, a long nose, her hair thinning at the front. A bruise stretched its way across her left cheekbone, half an inch higher and it would've been a black eye. Scratches marred her neck – four parallel lines, red against the pale skin. 'For the last three years we have put up with your daughter's lying, and cheating, and coming in reeking of alcohol – when she bothers to come in at all – the fighting and the stealing, because we know she's been struggling to cope with her sister's disappearance and your divorce. But today I found out she's been bullying the other children. Not just her peer group: the first years too.'

'That isn't true, the other kids are lying. Katie wouldn't—'

'When I tracked her down she was forcing a girl half her size to eat a handful of mud.' The headmistress raised her chin, showing off the scratch marks. 'This is what happened when I tried to stop her.'

Captain Corduroy nodded like a dashboard ornament. 'It's simply not acceptable.'

I grabbed the arms of his chair. 'SHUT YOUR FUCKING MOUTH!'

He jerked back, hands covering his face.

The headmistress folded her arms. 'Well, now we can see where she gets it from.'

'It's not true, Daddy, they're *lying*!' Katie clutched her schoolbag to her chest like a dead rat. She'd dyed her hair again – jet black and straight, tucked behind her ears, her big blue eyes puffy and pink, a metal crucifix around her neck. Her white shirt was rumpled and stained, the green-and-yellow school tie at half-mast.

'Get in the car.' I wrenched open the passenger door.

'How can you take their word over mine?'

'Get in the bloody car, Katie.'

Dr McDonald peered out from the back seat. 'Is everything OK?'

Katie slumped into the passenger seat, then turned her smile on the psychologist. Stuck her hand out. 'Hi, I'm Katie, Ash's daughter, really nice to meet you, I love your hair, it's great.'

'Thanks, I like yours too, it's very goth.'

'You wouldn't believe what's happened – the teachers never liked me in that place, it's a factory for churning out brain-dead drones – it's like a *complete* misunderstanding.'

I thumped myself in behind the wheel and slammed the door. Stabbed the key in the ignition. 'Seatbelt.' The headlights cut through the darkness.

'Honestly, Daddy, I didn't *do* anything, it's all—'

'You beat up a girl two years younger than you. Seatbelt!'

'It wasn't like—'

I stamped my foot on the accelerator and jerked the Renault out onto the road. 'Is that what we taught you? To pick on people smaller than yourself? Is it?'

'I didn't...' Deep breath. 'OK, yes, I got into a fight, but you should've *heard* her, she was going on about how all the police are fascists and racists and corrupt and why can't you catch proper criminals instead of victimizing real people. And I know for a fact it's because her dad got done for drink driving last week. I was only sticking up for you.'

'You made her eat dirt.'

Round the roundabout, leaning on the horn to shift a flat-cap-wearing corpse in his bloody Volvo.

Katie was staring at me, I could feel it.

'*What?*'

'You made Uncle Ethan eat dirt. You dragged him out into the back garden and you made him eat dirt till he was sick, then rubbed his face in it.'

'That was different.'

'You broke his nose *and* his arm.'

'You *know* that was different!' Houses flashed past the car windows as I took the rat-run through Barnsley Street. 'And he's not your bloody uncle. Don't call him that.'

'Mummy called him that.' Arms folded, bottom lip sticking out.

'Actually,' Dr McDonald's voice was a high-pitched squeak from the back seat, 'could we slow down? I mean it's a twenty zone and we're doing about forty and I really don't want to die in a car crash, so could we please—'

'Does your mother know what you've been doing? The drinking, the bullying, the fighting? Your teacher showed me letters from the local shops – you're barred for shoplifting! My own daughter's a *thief*!'

'I didn't—'

'I've been standing up for you all this time, and you... I *believed* you.'

'They're lying. They're *all* lying!'

'Look out for the bus!'

I jerked the wheel to the right as some moron bus driver pulled out without looking. Roared past him. The bastard had the cheek to flash his lights at me. 'Lying, stealing, drinking... what's next: drugs? Or are you already—'

'You can talk! You've been on drugs most of my life!'

Fuck's sake. 'It's medical, it's *different*!'

'It's always different when it's you, isn't it? "It's different." "It's different." I HATE YOU!' She thumped back into her seat: legs crossed; arms crossed; staring out of the passenger window; muscles bulging in her jaw; lips moving as if there was something bitter trapped behind them, trying to escape. A tear ran down her cheek, she didn't try to wipe it away.

Right onto Craighill Drive with its tall sandstone buildings and line of boutique shops.

Ungrateful little brat.

All this time. Playing me for a bloody idiot.

Dr McDonald cleared her throat. 'I know this seems pretty irreconcilable at the moment, but if you'd both just talk about how you really feel, I mean openly and honestly, I'm sure we could resolve it...?'

Katie kept her quivering mouth shut. I didn't say anything either.

'I know you don't really hate your father, Katie, you're hurt because—'

'Shut up, OK? Shut up. You don't know me. *Nobody* knows me.'

And that was it. Dr McDonald tried poking her nose in a couple more times, but she was pissing into the wind all on her own.

30

Katie's boots thumped up the stairs, then her bedroom door slammed.

The hall wallpaper was cool against my forehead, but it didn't stop the throbbing.

Dr McDonald closed the front door. Shifted from foot to foot. Rubbed her arm with a hand. 'It's a nice house.'

Much nicer than a condemned shitheap in Kingsmeath.

I dumped Katie's keys in the bowl in the hall, and made for the kitchen. Fully fitted – had it put in new by this guy who owed me a favour. Would have cost a fortune if I hadn't caught him nicking building supplies from a yard in town. The fridge was a shiny grey obelisk in the corner, I pulled out the milk and dumped it on the granite worktop. Scowled at it. 'You want tea?'

Dr McDonald leaned against the door frame. 'She doesn't really hate you: she's upset and she's lashing out. You've always backed her up before, but now you're on *their* side, and doesn't matter if they're right or not, it still feels like a betrayal.'

There was wine in the fridge, a bottle of gin too. Been a long time... That was the trouble with pills. I closed the fridge door and dry-swallowed a couple of Diclofenac.

'Would you like me to go speak to her, Ash?'

Stealing, lying, fighting. Pretending my teaching Ethan Baxter a lesson was the same as her beating up little girls.

Dr McDonald shifted her feet. 'OK, well, I'll go give it a go, see if I can find out what's really troubling her. It's not my field, but if I can get inside the head of a serial killer I can get inside the head of a twelve-year-old girl, after all, they're not all *that* different...'

I drank my tea, looking out of the kitchen window at the garden that used to be mine – everything turned into silhouettes in the dim glow of reflected streetlight. The jungle gym I built with off-cuts from B&Q; the cherry tree Rebecca and I planted that never produced a single cherry; the dog house that hadn't seen a dog in years; the shed that fell down the first two times I tried to put it up...

Upstairs the sounds of Katie screaming abuse came through the ceiling, each one followed by Dr McDonald saying something too quiet to make out down here. And slowly the shouting got quieter, and quieter, until they were barely murmuring.

Looked as if Dr McDonald was right about twelve-year-old girls and serial killers.

I pulled the house phone from its cradle and scrolled through the list till I got to, 'MUM: WORK'.

No reply. Of course there wasn't: Michelle was in a meeting.

I pulled out my mobile and sent her a text instead:

Katie got expelled
Been bullying little girls
Attacked a teacher
At home now (rowan drive)

Sounded like crying coming from upstairs.

I emptied the cold dregs of my tea into the sink. Put the kettle on again.

Maybe Dr McDonald would manage to fix Katie? Nice thought.

Spare me your parental delusions.

There was a packet of Jaffa Cakes hidden at the back of the tea-towel drawer – guaranteed safe from Katie. The one drawer she avoided like the plague, in case someone asked her to dry the dishes. At least some things never changed.

The house phone rang – an off-kilter rendition of a waltz. I grabbed it out of its cradle before Katie got there.

Michelle: *'Katie Jessica Nicol: how could you get yourself expelled? What the bloody hell were you thinking?'*

'It's Ash.'

'Oh... I didn't—'

'So she's Katie Nicol now, is she? I thought we agreed.'

A pause. *'How could you let them expel her?'*

'The headmistress stopped her beating up one of the first years, so Katie went for her – tried to rip her throat out. How *exactly* was I supposed to gloss over that?'

Out in the garden a magpie settled on the jungle gym, clacking and cawing.

'You tell that young lady: when I get home there's going to be hell *to pay.'*

'You're coming home now, right?'

'For God's sake, Ash, how many times: I'm supposed to be in a meeting.'

'I can't stay, Michelle, you *know* that. And she's too young to leave unsupervised. Christ knows what she'd get up to.'

'Well...' Silence. Probably chewing on her fingers. *'I'll be home at half seven, you'll just have to sort something out till then.'*

'Michelle, I can't—'

'Half seven. I'll call Mother. She can come up from Edinburgh Monday.'

'Katie'll love that.'

'Katie's twelve: she'll do what she's bloody well told. And if she thinks she's getting a birthday party next week she's got another think coming.'

'Don't worry, it'll all be fine.' The plump tweedy woman with the long grey hair patted me on the arm. 'You run along.'

'Thanks, Betty.' I left her standing in the doorway, marched down the garden path, got back in the rusty Renault and cranked it into life.

Dr McDonald was slumped in the passenger seat, arms hanging limp. 'Urgh... Thought I was done with teenage angst.'

As I pulled away from the kerb, Betty waved, then stepped back inside the house and closed the door.

Dr McDonald closed her eyes. 'She seemed nice.'

'Lost her husband twenty years ago, more or less adopted Michelle and me when we moved in.' And as long as she stayed away from the gin in the fridge, everything would be fine till Michelle got home. 'You sure you want to go back to the door-to-doors?'

'As opposed to?'

'We should be concentrating on Steven Wallace.'

'Well ... we *could* do that, but there's still a chance he's not the Birthday Boy. Fitting the profile doesn't make him guilty.'

I opened my mouth, then shut it again. Get too obsessed with Steve Wallace and the real Birthday Boy might get away. And look what happened to Philip Skinner. 'Yeah, maybe you're right.'

I headed back through Blackwall Hill, across the Calderwell Bridge, and took a right into Castle Hill. Still nothing from the passenger seat.

'Going to tell me what you and Katie talked about?'

Dr McDonald shrugged. 'Need time to process it.'

God, that was positively monosyllabic for her.

Mr Billy Wood – Flat 4, 25 McDermid Avenue

'And you're sure you didn't see anyone or anything suspicious yesterday?'

Mr Wood scratched at his beard. Dandruff drifted down onto his baggy Dundas University sweatshirt. 'Nah, was doon at ma sister's till midnight. Look, have youse got a card in case anythin' else happens? Them wee shites from over the road keep settin' fire to ma wheelie-bin.'

Mr Christopher Kennedy – Ground Floor Right, 32 Jordan Place

'Can I see the photo again?' Mr Kennedy took off his little round glasses, polished them on his shirt then popped them back on again. Peered at the photo of Hannah Kelly. 'Aye, I recognize her. She's that girl who turned up dead: it was in all the papers.' He passed the picture back to me. 'Hold on, I've got a copy of the *Post* kicking around in the living room – you can keep it if you like?'

Mrs Kaitlin Fleming – 49 Hill Terrace

'Oh, no we've lived here for donkeys: long before they threw up those bloody flats. It's a disgrace, isn't it? I mean, *why* the council doesn't evict the lot of them is beyond me.'

'Just...' I held the list up again. 'Just take another look and tell me if you saw anything unusual on any of these dates...'

'How many more?' I leaned back against a tree, looking up through its bare branches at the dirty-orange sky.

Dr McDonald checked her list. 'Nineteen.' Breath hanging around her head in a cloud of pale mist, glowing in the streetlight. She tucked her hands into her armpits and stomped her feet.

'This was your idea, remember?'

My phone rang: 'RHONA'. I jabbed the button.

'Sorry, Guv, been interviewing sex offenders all day. Got a missed call from you on my mobile – what's up?'

'Don't worry about it. Wanted you to run a PNC check on Steven Wallace, but someone's doing it.'

'Oh. OK.' A pause. *'Isn't Steven Wallace that wanker on the radio? Saw him on the telly being interviewed by STV – kidding on he's some sort of Birthday Boy expert.'*

I stared up at the branches again. Frowned. PNC checks...

'Guv?'

'You did three PNC checks on Birthday Boy victims' families.'

'I did?'

'According to the computer.'

'Oh...' Some rustling. *'Any idea when?'*

Sabir's spreadsheet was sitting on Dr McDonald's laptop somewhere, but could I remember the details? 'Do me a favour: tell Weber I won't be in tomorrow morning, we're still following up on those door-to-doors.'

'Got some sausages and bacon and black pudding in for breakfast. Anything else you fancy?'

'No, I'm...'

There was someone watching us – a hairy man in a dark anorak, pointy nose, digital camera hanging around his neck, standing next to a people-carrier parked on the other side of the street. Little bastard wouldn't take a telling.

I stepped into the road, and he flinched. Backed up a step. Then dug a set of keys out of his pocket, fumbling with the driver's door lock.

'Guv? Everything OK?'

I hung up, stuck the phone back in my pocket, balled my fists. 'Right, you little shite.'

He squealed, wrenched the door open, threw himself inside, jammed the key in the ignition.

Too slow.

Should have locked the door first.

I dragged him out onto the road.

He tried to scramble away, shoes scuffing against the tarmac, going nowhere. 'Please! It wasn't me: I'm just doing my job!'

I grabbed his camera and pulled. The strap tightened around his neck.

'What did I tell you about taking photos of me?'

'I didn't! I didn't! Ulk...' Hands flapping for the camera. 'I can show you! Please... Let go... Please...'

I let go, and the thing thumped into his chest. A couple of deep breaths, then he turned the camera over and pressed some buttons until the display screen on the back lit up with a shot of Steven Wallace's grinning face. The next one was the same, and the next, and the one after that. Then there were pictures of a TV crew interviewing local residents, then a bunch of head-and-shoulder photos of what looked like local residents. The standard pish the *Castle News and Post* liked to print alongside idiotic quotes, like: *'"Oh, I've lived here a hundred and twelve years and nothing like this has ever happened before!" Agnes Dalrymple (82)'*

Not a single picture of me, or Dr McDonald.

He switched the thing off and the screen went black. Then looked up at me, on his arse in the middle of the road. 'See?'

I stuck out a hand and helped him up. 'You OK?'

'It's not me you've got to worry about, it's Jennifer. She's on a bloody mission.' He wiped the seat of his trousers. 'Sorry about your house, by the way.'

'She been digging into that too?'

'Off the record? She's digging into everything: you and Len Murray, you and Andy Inglis, you and some pole-dancer...'

Mrs Elizabeth Dubrowski – Flat 2, 48 Hill Terrace

'I think it's that Kevin Flemming. Thirty-four and still living at home, what kind of grown man does that?' Mrs Dubrowski sniffed, top lip curled as if someone had farted. She'd squeezed herself into white stretch jeans and a white fluffy jumper designed for someone half her age, and size. 'And his mum's no better – moaning on the whole time about how her view's been ruined. As if they built these flats to spite *her*. Egotistical bitch.'

'And did you see Kevin Flemming acting suspiciously?'

Mrs Dubrowski leaned in close and enveloped me in a throat-catching reek of perfume. 'He smokes dope. And he's got a skateboard. Grown man of thirty-four!'

Dear Jesus...

* * *

The stick-thin teenager shrugged, then closed the door.

I slouched down the stairs and out onto the pavement. Dr McDonald trailed along behind me, yawning.

A misty drizzle made the streetlights sparkle.

I stuck my hands in my pockets. The small velvet box from Little Mike's Pawn Shop was still there. 'Don't know about you, but I've had enough tosspots for one day.'

'Urgh...' Another yawn. 'Chinese for tea, I mean if that's OK with you, every time I stay with Aunty Jan we always have Chinese; she's chicken chow mein mad, but it wouldn't be Oldcastle without prawn crackers.'

It wasn't far to the car, but my whole face *ached* from the cold by the time we'd clambered inside. I turned on the engine and cranked the heater up full. A whistling roar and the smell of burning dust filled the interior.

Dr McDonald's phone blared out a familiar tune – something goth, or emo – the kind of thing Katie liked. 'Ooh, no one ever calls me...' She answered it. 'Alice speaking... Uh-huh, hello, Detective Chief Superintendent, are you— ... Yes... No, I don't think— ... I see.'

I stuck the headlights on and pulled away from the kerb. 'Seatbelt.'

'Sorry.' She did as she was told. 'No, not you, Detective Chief Superintendent, I was talking to Ash... Yes he is... I... Hold on.' She held the phone against her chest. 'It's Detective Chief Superintendent Dickie.'

As if I hadn't worked that out already.

'He says Megan Taylor's mother and father got a birthday card from the Birthday Boy this morning.'

I stared across the car. 'She only went missing *yesterday*. And why's it taken them so long to tell anyone?'

Dr McDonald grabbed the dashboard with her free hand, eyes wide. 'Watch the road, watch the road!' Back to the phone. 'But she only went missing yesterday... Yes, I do... Very significant, I mean— ... OK, yes, fine, we'll be right over.'

31

Megan's birthday was on Monday, same as Katie's. She was a little shorter; a little wider; with long blonde hair hauled back from her face; eyes rimmed in red; mouth open in a frozen, silent scream; wearing the same clothes she'd had on in the CCTV footage from the shopping centre. Tied to a chair in a filthy little room with a dirt floor and exposed wooden beams.

I handed the homemade birthday card – secure in its clear plastic envelope – back to Dr McDonald. 'She isn't gagged.'

'He's tired of the silence, tired of them wriggling and grunting behind the duct tape, he wants to hear Megan scream.'

The bedroom was plastered in posters – horses, boy bands, girl bands, puppies, kittens... There was barely any wallpaper left. A single bed sat beneath the window, a computer desk with a sticker-covered laptop on the other side of the room, some books, some stuffed toys, a nineteen-inch flat-screen TV mounted on the crowded wall above an Xbox, a wardrobe full of designer grunge.

The window looked out over a triangular back garden studded with tiny lights, then a fence, then a hill topped with jagged silhouettes. Moncuir Wood. You could almost believe you were living in the country, instead of a sprawling development of identical yellow-brick houses with identical orange pantile roofs and identical built-in garages too small to take a real car.

Murmured voices came through the floor beneath my feet – DCS Dickie, a Family Liaison officer, and Megan's parents.

Dr McDonald took out her mobile and snapped a picture of the birthday card, then fiddled with the image a bit. Pressed a button. Thirty seconds later her phone rang. 'Hello? Henry, how are you? ... Yes... I know. Hold on, I'll put you on loud-speaker...' She did something with her phone and a tinny version of Henry's voice crackled into the room.

'Hello? I hate these things. Are you there? Ash?'

'Hi, Henry.'

'Right, the thing we have to consider is why he's varying his pattern. What makes Megan Taylor different to all the others? Why her?'

Dr McDonald popped the phone on the bedside cabinet, then propped the birthday card up next to it, wrapped an arm around herself and fiddled with her hair. 'She's his twelfth victim: this is the penultimate one, he's been building up to number thirteen all this time, Megan's his last chance to get it right before it really matters?'

What a lovely thought – Rebecca and all those other girls were just a dress rehearsal. They didn't mean anything.

Henry cleared his throat. *'Maybe we shouldn't be too hung up on numbers.'*

I picked a book off the shelf, flicked through the first few pages, but it wasn't a first edition. 'If Megan's number...' I cleared my throat. 'If she's number twelve, who's number eleven?'

Silence from the other end of the phone.

Henry was going to tell her, I knew it, I *never* should have trusted him. Should've kept it to myself.

A sigh came from the speaker. *'We won't know till next year, when the card arrives. It's halfway through November now; he's only taken girls twice in December; I think he's already got one under his belt. Alice is right: he's experimenting. That's why she's not gagged, and that's why the card arrived today.'*

I closed the book. 'So, he had time to grab her, get back to his place, tie her up, take her photo, print it, make the card, and get it in the post before the last collection. What's that: six ... six-thirty tops?'

'Perhaps—'

'She's on CCTV leaving the shopping centre at quarter past three. Call it fifteen minutes to abduct her, fifteen ... twenty minutes to get her home... I mean it's do-able, but it'd be tight.'

'He's been planning this for a while, refining his methods.' Silence from the other end of the phone. Then, *'And let's suppose for a moment that Megan* isn't *number twelve.'*

Fuck: here we go. 'Henry, you—'

'We're assuming that he didn't take a victim five years ago, but what if he did? What if the parents haven't come forward with the birthday card?'

Dr McDonald frowned. 'So he wasn't in prison that year, or abroad somewhere...' She twiddled her hair. 'Why wouldn't the parents come forward?'

I licked my lips. 'Maybe—'

'Perhaps they died, or left the country, or ... perhaps they think they've got good reasons for not getting the police involved. Whatever the reason, we can't discount the possibility that Megan Taylor is his thirteenth victim: thirteen girls, killed on their thirteenth birthday. Megan's not an experiment, she's his masterpiece. He needs this to be perfect, because it justifies everything he's done.'

Thank you, Henry.

It was like a valve being opened in my chest – I could breathe again. 'You think he's going to stop?'

Dr McDonald sat on the edge of the bed. 'Or perhaps this is a transformative moment for him, I mean now he's reached his target he's realized he doesn't have to stop, he can keep on going, getting better and better at what he does, that's *why* he's experimenting...'

'No, it's too significant – he's been building towards his grand finale. When he kills Megan Taylor it's going to be cathartic.'

She shook her head. 'The pattern's changed: there's no gag, the card arrived today instead of next year, it's more ... immediate.'

I put the book back on the shelf. 'I need to know if he's going to stop. Is this it? Does the bastard just disappear back into the woodwork?'

'Yes.'

'No.'

'He's been building to—'

'Henry, you don't walk away from something like this, it's an acquired taste and you've got it, you're *good* at it, and they're never going to catch you, it's time for ambition and vision, time to *feed* on what you create...' She bit her bottom lip. 'Why would he give all that up?'

'Henry?'

Silence from the phone. Then the metallic crackle of the top being screwed off a fresh bottle of whisky. *'It's about power... It's always about power.'* Glugging. *'If you're right, he'll be monitoring the media: getting off on the reports, the press conferences, the public displays of grief. "Look on my works, ye Mighty, and despair."'*

Dr McDonald stared down at her red Converse Hi-tops. 'He'll want to experience it in person ... what if we help him, I mean, we could put on a candlelit vigil, or something?'

'Yes: Ash, you need to set up one of those over-the-top affairs where everyone leaves teddy bears and flowers and football scarves. Somewhere big and impressive. Lots of public sackcloth and ashes. Get some cameras on the crowds, our boy won't be able to resist.'

She nodded. 'He'll stand in the middle and feed off the grief, knowing it was all him, he did it, he has the power of life and death...'

I picked the birthday card off the work surface. 'I'll see what I can do.'

'We've got this big party organized: bright pink stretched Humvee limo, DJ, jelly and ice cream, smoked salmon and sushi – the works.' Bruce Taylor fiddled with his tie – a black one, funereal, it went with his pallid face and bloodshot eyes. 'Is... Are you sure this is all right, I don't look threatening in a tie? Maybe I shouldn't wear a tie...?'

His wife perched on the edge of a large red sofa, still as a shallow grave. As if someone had replaced her with a waxwork dummy, eyes fixed on the middle distance, a little crease between her neatly plucked eyebrows. Mouth pinched.

'Andrea, do you think I should change?'

She didn't even look at him.

He fiddled with his tie some more. 'Maybe I should change...'

Dr McDonald placed a hand on his arm. 'Wear whatever makes you comfortable. With all the cameras, and the flash-guns going off, and everyone shouting questions, you don't want to be worrying about your tie. If you don't like the tie: screw the tie.'

A little smile twitched across his face. Then disappeared again. 'She's still alive.'

Dickie nodded. 'She's still alive. We'll put out Megan's picture, appeal for witnesses, ask him to let her go...' The DCS glanced at me. Cleared his throat. 'And we'll let people know about the candlelit vigil tomorrow.'

DCS Dickie sucked on his cigarette, cheeks hollow, the tip glowing hot orange in the dark garden. 'You're sure?'

Dr McDonald shook her head. 'We can't be, I mean we don't know enough about him to be one hundred percent, but I'm pretty certain he'll want to turn up and join in all the mourning.'

'And that helps us catch him *how*?'

I cupped my aching hands around the warm mug, steam curling up into my face. 'We film everyone who turns up. We show the footage to the victims' parents and if they recognize someone we get a warrant and drag them in for questioning.'

'Hmmph.' Dickie tapped his cigarette, sending a nub of grey flakes spiralling away into the darkness. 'Someone like Steven Wallace?'

Ah... I took a sip of tea. 'Sabir's got a big mouth.'

'Didn't think you were that kind of man, Ash. Running around behind my back: thought you were better than that.'

Dr McDonald licked her lips. 'Actually, it was my idea – I wanted him to keep it low-key, I mean we don't want to spook Wallace if he's a potential suspect...'

As if I needed protecting from the big scary Detective Chief Superintendent. I put on my best and-what-the-fuck-are-you-going-to-do-about-it voice: 'It wasn't her, it was me.'

The cigarette hissed as Dickie dragged in another lungful of smoke, staring straight ahead. 'What's this, "I'm Spartacus!" time? I don't give a monkey's arsehole who did it, you run this stuff by me *first*. Both of you.'

'Sabir say if he found anything when he ratted me out?'

'My team's going through Megan's friends. Sabir's doing the CCTV walk-through at the shopping centre. Ask him yourself.'

The cameras started flashing as soon as I stepped out of the Taylors' front door. Since we'd gone inside, someone had thrown up a cordon of police tape, keeping the press and gawkers on the pavement and out of the front garden and driveway.

The uniformed constable guarding the front door flared his nostrils. 'Bastards got here ten minutes ago, Guv. Swear they must be bloody psychic.'

One outside broadcast van, nearly a dozen photographers, a handful of print journalists... Shite: Jennifer was standing in the middle of the pack, bundled up in her camel-hair coat, auburn curls hidden under a fur hat, speaking into a Dictaphone. Her ratty little photographer shuffled about beside her. He saw me staring at him and lowered his camera. Looked away. Not wanting another smack.

A patrol car pulled up – half on the pavement, blocking the Taylors' driveway.

The door opened and Shifty Dave climbed out, camera flashes glinting off his bald head. Looked me up and down. 'What you doing here? Thought your shift finished ages ago.'

I nodded towards Dr McDonald. 'Responsible adult.' She ducked behind me, peering around my shoulder at Shifty Dave and his cheap suit.

He sniffed. 'Dickie still here?'

Flash. Flash. Flash.

'Inside...'

Jennifer squeezed her way through the collected bastards of the press, making for the edge of the driveway. Bet she thought she could buttonhole me, force the issue, wind me up and get me to say something stupid she could smear across the *News and Post* tomorrow. And she was probably right.

'Dave, do me a favour?'

He pulled his neck in, making extra chins. 'Still not got the smell out my car boot from last time.'

'Jennifer and her monkey, I don't want to speak to them.'

'Aye, life's tough.'

'I might let something slip. Like, ooh, say: personal details about some of my esteemed colleagues' love lives?'

His eyes narrowed. 'You bloody promised me!'

'Then don't be a dick.'

'You're the dick...' He chewed on something for a moment, then sighed. 'OK. But it's your own stupid fault for screwing her in the first place.' Shifty Dave turned, marched back down the drive and stopped right in front of Jennifer. He was easily big enough to block her view.

I grabbed Dr McDonald's hand and dragged her to the side of the lock-block, helped her clamber over the knee-high box hedge and into the next-door neighbour's garden while Shifty did his thing.

His voice boomed out into the cold night. 'Well, well, well, if it's no' Jennifer Prentice, how they dangling?'

'I want to speak to DC Henderson.'

'Do you, now? Bit late to fuck up *his* marriage: that boat's already sunk. Mind you, if you fancy giving mine a wee wrecking, I wouldn't say no. Your place or mine?'

I snuck across the neighbour's lawn, then down to the kerb, Dr McDonald sticking close behind me.

Shifty Dave's voice took on a sing-song quality. 'And aye, aye: who's this? If it's no' Wee Hairy Frank McKenzie. Two counts drink driving, and six months for phone hacking. Surprised any paper'll touch you since you got kicked off the *News of the World*. Relegated to camera boy now, are we?'

'I'm just doing my job...'

Two more steps and we were on the road, through the parked cars, and into the rusty Renault. She started first time. Looked as if my luck was finally on the up for a change.

32

'Shoppers are advised that the centre will be closing in ten minutes. Please complete your purchases, have a great evening, and come back soon.'

A little old lady bustled past, dragging a tartan shopping trolley behind her – a wee white terrier peering out of the zip at the top – rubber-tipped walking stick thunk, thunk, thunking on the polished marble floor.

Dr McDonald stood in the middle of Templers Vale Shopping Centre, staring up at the huge glass wall that dominated the atrium. Outside, the lights sparkled on Calderwell Bridge, Blackwall Hill rising up behind it. Kingsmeath reduced to a network of glowing points – like early Christmas decorations.

Even Kingsmeath didn't look too bad in the dark.

Friday night and Templers Vale was virtually empty. A handful of late-night shoppers drifted between the same stores that always filled places like this – Next, Dorothy Perkins, Primark, Burger King, Apple, Vodaphone, Monsoon... Three floors of high-street chains and fast-food franchises.

I pointed up to the next level. 'There he is.'

Sabir was wandering along by the glass railing, holding something out in front of him as if he was sleepwalking.

We took the escalator, gliding up to the sound of piped muzak. Sabir stopped outside a generic teenagers' clothes shop – the kind with silver mannequins in the window wearing ripped jeans, hoodie tops, and retro T-shirts. He stared up at a little white blob fixed to the wall above the shop's entrance.

I tapped him on the shoulder. 'Hoy, Judas.'

He jumped. 'Jesus... You tryin' to do us in?'

'You ratted me out to Dickie.'

'Ah, now, not really...' The thing Sabir had been holding out was a white iPad with a red cover. He clutched it against his belly. 'You didn't exactly swear us to secrecy, did youse? Dickie asked us what I was doin' and I told him.' A grin spread his large grey face even wider. 'Hey, Doc, lookin' better than you did this mornin'.'

She gave him a little wave.

'Shoppers are advised that the centre will be closing in five minutes. Please complete your purchases, and make your way to the exits. See you again soon.'

Dr McDonald peered in through the shop window. A thin bloke in skin-tight black denim and cockatiel hair was tidying a stack of hoodies.

'Hold on a tick, I just need to nip inside and get a few things...' She ducked through the door.

'So what did you dig up on Steven Wallace?'

Sabir pointed at the lump above the entrance. 'They've gorra hidden camera, right there. Most of them's out in the open where you can see them, but there's this network of sneaky buggers like this one 'ere. So when the sketchy shopliftin' bag'eads are casin' the joint, they think there's these tasty little blackspots where they're safe – they've no idea it's all on film.'

A large rectangular planter sat about eight feet away, with a mini jungle sprouting out of beige pebbles. There was something familiar about it... I turned, frowned at the shop Dr McDonald had gone into, then walked around to the other side of the planter.

'This is where she was: Megan Taylor, on the CCTV footage.'

Sabir pointed over my shoulder. 'Camera's behind youse.'

I turned, and there it was – like a glossy black egg fused to the ceiling.

'So if you were watchin' a bunch of kids, and maybe *one* kid in particular, and you didn't wan' anyone to know about it, you'd stand in one of the blackspots, right? Only they don't exist, do they?'

'If you find Steven Wallace on those tapes I will bloody kiss you, Sabir. Even if you do look like a mouldy Weeble.'

'Cheeky get...' He pawed at his iPad. 'Steven Wallace, AKA: Sensational Steve – youse can tell he made up his own nickname, can't you? Born in Oldcastle; boarding school at Glenalmond College; dropped outta Edinburgh Uni after two years of Law; had a trial with Hibs, didn't make it; gorra gig on hospital radio at Edinburgh Royal Infirmary; then a little community station. Most of that's from the bio on his website. In other news: he was married; one kid, but she died in a car crash – drunk driver took out the family Vauxhall; got divorced; moved back to Oldcastle when his old lady died and left him the house on McDermid Avenue.'

'Convictions?'

'Nothin'. Done for speedin' a couple of times, but only three-point jobs. Licence is clean now. Made a complaint two years ago 'cos some bird was stalking him, other than that, he's squeaky.'

Sabir lumbered over, holding his iPad out, tilting the screen so I could see it. Grainy black-and-white CCTV footage whizzed backwards until Megan Taylor was sitting on the planter in front of us.

'Did you work your internet-search-magic on her?'

'Facebook, Twitter, and Hotmail. All just bollocks really: moanin' about school, droolin' over boy bands, wonderin' how old you have to be to go on *Britain's Next Big Star*... Nothin' sayin', "Oh, I'm meetin' that slimy prick off the radio tomorrow and he's gonna tie us to a chair and take me picture." I'm runnin' the lot through pattern-recognition software, see if there's anythin' that matches up with the other birthday girls.'

'Customers are advised that the centre is now closed. Please make your way to the exits.'

Dr McDonald bustled out of the trendy-teen shop carrying two large red paper bags with string handles. 'Have we started yet?'

Sabir held a finger over the play button. 'Perfect timin', Doc.' He poked the iPad. Megan and her chunky friend sat on the edge of the square planter. The four boys milled around them, strutting, laughing, shoving each other.

Dr McDonald peered over Sabir's massive forearm at the screen. 'Classic mating pattern: males displaying for the females, showing off and boasting ... they're not really interested in Megan, they're interested in her friend, the one with the boobs, she's very well developed for a thirteen-year-old.'

Sabir pointed. 'That's Brianna, she's Megan's BFF. And that's Joshua, Brandon, Tyler, and Christopher.'

Brianna got up and straightened out her miniskirt – no sound on the footage, but her lips moved. Asking a question? Megan curled her top lip. Whatever the reply was, Brianna stood there with her mouth hanging open while everyone else laughed. Then she stuck her nose in the air and marched off on too-high-heels, leaving Megan with the boys.

Dr McDonald dumped her bags on the ground, wrapped an arm around herself. 'Brianna's my best friend, but I really, *really* hate her. I mean *look* at her: she's a fat cow, but everyone loves her because she's got *breasts*. Morons. Fawning over *her* when they should be paying attention to *me*.'

Megan took a draw on her cigarette.

'Why can't they see I'm *much* more sophisticated and grown

up than she is? Than *any* of them. They're just boys, children, but…' A frown. 'Look at her fidgeting.' Dr McDonald narrowed her eyes. 'But I've got a secret… Something I'm dying to tell everyone, but I promised…'

The security guard turned up, pointing and shouting.

'Shut up, you jumped up little dick in your crappy uniform. Couldn't even be a real policeman, could you? What a *loser*. Not like me, I'm going to *be* somebody, somebody special…'

The Coke went flipping end over end, then exploded on the marble floor.

'Outahere, Grandad; place is shit anyway…'

Megan ran, and Sabir lumbered after her, making for the escalators down to the ground floor. Dr McDonald went with him, still staring at the screen as the picture jumped to another camera.

'Got places to go, people to see…'

I grabbed the bags and followed.

The footage was a long shot of Megan running, laughing. She barged past an overweight woman wrestling a pushchair onto the down escalator.

'Outta the way, you old bag! Fuck you. And fuck your screaming brat. None of that shit for me: gonna be *famous*.'

We rode down to the ground floor, Sabir pressing pause again so that we arrived at the bottom as Megan leapt off the escalator. New camera angle: she was running for the exit, ponytail trailing behind her like a banner. Jinked around another of the centre's big rectangular planters. Then bang – she collided with an old man, sending his shopping flying. What looked like a bottle of wine exploded in black-and-white.

'Fuck you too.'

She pirouetted, then out through the front doors, face stretched wide in an animal grin.

'Fuck the lot of you!'

A hunched old man with a mop and bucket stopped to stare at Dr McDonald as she spun around on the spot – giving the shopping centre both middle fingers.

'I'm gonna *be* somebody!'

'More crispy seaweed?' I held the plastic container out and Dr McDonald scooped a mound of crunchy green slivers onto her plate.

The house on Fletcher Road was huge inside – the dining room big enough to seat a football team, so we camped out in the lounge, spreading a Chinese carry-out from the Blue Wok on Keep Street across a large wooden coffee table. A real fire crackled in the hearth, casting flickering shadows across the ceiling.

Dr McDonald was on the floor, sitting cross-legged, shovelling in special fried rice with chopsticks. Talking with her mouth full. 'You sure you don't want to come down here, it's *much* more authentic?'

'At my age? I'd never get up again.' The chilli beef wasn't bad: crispy and spicy.

Dr McDonald stared into her rice for a moment. 'It's not your fault.'

OK...

'What isn't?'

'I mean, she's really lucky to have you as a dad.' Still not looking up.

I put my fork down. 'Dr Mc—'

'My father left when I was fourteen months old.' Deep breath. 'I would have killed to have a dad like you.'

I couldn't help smiling. 'Thought I was a "man of violence"?'

'My mum had a load of boyfriends after he left, I don't remember most of them, but the last couple were horrible. One broke her arm and her nose. The next one put her in hospital for a fortnight.' Dr McDonald picked up her Irn-Bru and ran her fingers around the blue-and-orange tin. 'It wasn't the same after that… She needed someone to protect her and my father wasn't there. Didn't care.' Dark brown curls covered her eyes.

'Yeah, well my dad was a prick.' I jabbed a sliver of deep-fried beef. 'Swore I wasn't going to be like that. I'd be a good dad to Katie and Rebecca…' Yeah, and that worked out *so* well, didn't it?

The beef didn't taste quite so nice any more.

I put the plate down, picked up my jacket and dug the big paper bag out of the pocket. Placed it on the coffee table in front of Dr McDonald.

She shovelled in another load of rice. 'More prawn crackers?'

'Open it.'

A shrug. She peered inside, then pulled out the fluffy puffin. 'Is this…?'

'For you.'

A grin split her face. 'Really? He's lovely!' She gave the thing a squeeze. 'I'll call him … *Wilberforce*, does he look like a Wilberforce to you, I think he looks like a Wilberforce. Thank you.' She tucked the puffin into the gap between her crossed legs, smiling down at his orange and black beak. 'Would you like some rice, Wilberforce?'

OK, so it was meant to be Katie's present, but after today she didn't bloody deserve it. And it was nice to see Dr McDonald so happy, pretending to feed Wilberforce special fried rice, like she was six.

I took another mouthful of chilli beef. Didn't taste too bad after all. 'So: Steven Wallace?'

'What was Katie like as a child?'

'Katie? Happy, cute, bright… Every night we'd sit in her room with the lights turned down, reading the Brothers Grimm. She *hated* the Disney versions, said they took out all the good bits. Other kids were drawing stick-figures in nursery, she was drawing severed heads.' The smile was back. 'Used to call her "Daddy's Little Monster". Couldn't have been more different from her sister if she'd tried.'

'She really is sorry about today. It's been ... *difficult* for her since Rebecca ran away.'

'We went to the beach once. Michelle was beautiful, and we sat in the dunes and ate sausage rolls and egg sandwiches. Rebecca had her head in a book, and Katie had this black skull-and-crossbones kite and an eyepatch. And she spent the whole time running up and down the beach, making pirate noises. "Avast me hearties!" "Shiver me timbers!" Giggling.'

'Katie thinks it's her fault Rebecca left – they had a fight the night Rebecca ran away. And if Rebecca hadn't run away, you and Michelle wouldn't have got divorced, so that's Katie's fault too.' Dr McDonald's hand was warm on my knee. 'She didn't mean to let you down.'

'It wasn't her fault. It wasn't anyone's fault.' I stared at the little curls of meat on my plate. 'Sometimes shite things just happen.'

'And there's *loads* of mineral water in the fridge.'

Rhona's flat was immaculate, everything hoovered and dusted and tidied, like something out of a magazine. She opened the door to the spare room. A pile of my clothes lay neatly folded on the double bed. 'Didn't have time to get an alarm clock, but I can easily give you a shout when breakfast's on the go.'

I picked up a shirt from the pile. Perfectly smooth. 'You did my ironing?'

'Sorry I couldn't get the rest done. I'll stick another load on tomorrow.' She cleared her throat. 'You ... want a cup of tea or something?'

'So Shifty says, "You can get a cream for that."' Rhona threw her head back and laughed – a throaty gargling noise that went in jagged heaves. Showing off her pearly beiges. '"Cream for that..." Priceless.'

The living room was every bit as tidy as the rest of the house. A pristine oatmeal carpet, a white leather couch with one matching armchair, two Ikea bookcases and a boxy coffee table.

I put my mug back on the tray. Covered my mouth for a yawn. 'Sorry: been a long week.'

A little frown pinched the skin between her eyebrows. 'Oh, before I forget...' Rhona picked herself up off the couch and left the room. She came back a minute later and dumped a cardboard shoebox on the coffee table. The thing was full of police-issue notebooks, all lined up in neat rows.

Rhona pulled one out and flipped it open. 'I had a trawl through my notes. You wanted to know about me doing PNC checks on Birthday Boy families?'

'You really didn't have—'

'Here we go: "Ran full PNC on Arnold and Danielle Burges – first of October". That was two years ago. ACC Drummond asked me to do it: same for Sophie Elphinstone's parents and Amber O'Neil's. Lazy bugger never does his own computer searches. Kevin's always moaning about having to pick up his dry-cleaning and stuff. Like we're his personal bloody slaves or something.'

'He's a bit of a tosser, even for— Sodding hell.' My phone was blaring its old-fashioned ring. The screen said 'Dr McFruitLoop.'

I pressed the button. 'Is Wilberforce not behaving himself?'

Her voice was a high-pitched whisper. '*Someone's trying to get in the house! Ash, I'm scared! What if they get in?*'

Shite. 'I'll be right over.' I stood, grabbed my jacket. Put my hand over the mouthpiece and nodded at Rhona. 'Call the station: tell them we've got an attempted break-in at Eighteen Fletcher Road, right now. Householder is in residence.'

Her mouth fell open, then she shut it. Nodded. 'Right, Guv.' She grabbed the house phone and dialled. 'Aye, Marge, who've you got near Fletcher Road? Get a patrol car up there pronto...'

'Dr McDonald, I need you to stay calm.' I barged out of the flat, taking the steps two at a time down to the building's entrance hall.

'What do I do, what do I do, what do I do?'

I banged out into the cold night. 'Is there anywhere in the house with a door you can lock?'

'Aunty Jan's study?'

'Go. Lock the door. Stick a chair or something under the handle so it can't open.' I jumped into the Renault, cranked the engine over, and floored it.

33

PC Sheila Caldwell rolled the dusting brush back and forward over the back door, the bristles barely touching the gouged wood, leaving a layer of powdery white. She was getting it all over her black fleece too – and the matching fluorescent-yellow 'Police' waistcoat, and black bobble hat. She turned and peered at me through a haze of dust. 'Not looking good, Guv...'

The security light clicked off again. I waved my arm across the sensor's path. Crack – we were bathed in a searing white glow. Shame it wasn't as warm as it was bright. Bloody freezing out here.

The wood around the lock was gouged and scratched, the damaged wood clean and raw against the blue paint.

I looked up at the house. Light glowed from a window up near the top of the building, a face peering out through the glass.

Rhona shuffled through the bushes, one hand deep in her pocket, the other clutching a huge torch, breath trailing out behind her like a steam train. 'Long gone. Think they came in over the back wall. Ground's frozen solid: no footprints, but there's some broken branches and stuff.' She sniffed, wiped her hand across her top lip. 'Your psychologist come out yet?'

'Nope.'

Rhona puffed out her cheeks, then slid the torch beam up the wall until it spotlit the study window – Dr McDonald ducked away from the glass. 'Her highness is a bit nervous isn't she?'

'Be fair: someone did try to jimmy the back door open with a screwdriver.'

'And the first thing she does is call her knight in shining armour. Not nine-nine-nine or anything *sensible* like that.' Another sniff. 'I'd have gone out and kicked his arse for him.'

Sheila straightened up, then slipped the cover back over her brush. 'Sorry, Guv. There's nothing here. Little sod must've worn gloves.' She popped the brush into the SOC kit box. 'Probably just a junkie – a pro would've brought a crowbar or a claw-hammer. Screwdriver's great for chibbing your scumbag mates, but not so good for getting through a Yale lock.'

Rhona squinted at the powder-covered door. 'You made a right dog's breakfast of that.'

'Bite me. Every SEB bugger's off digging up skeletons.' Sheila wiped a hand across her face, making a clean patch in the dust. 'Think you can do better?'

Rhona gave a lopsided shrug. 'A monkey could do better.'

'Oh, ha, ha. It's cold, I've been on since seven this morning, and I'm not in the bloody mood.'

I held up a hand. 'All right, that's enough. No fighting.'

They scowled at each other.

God help us. 'Sheila: do me a favour and make sure a car cruises by every hour or so, OK?'

'Yes, Guv.'

I left her to pack up, and followed Rhona back around to the front of the house, torchlight picking a path through the darkness.

More sniffing. 'You don't think it's a junkie, do you?'

'Depends where Sensational Steve Wallace was tonight.'

The front door opened as we got there. Dr McDonald stood on the threshold, one arm wrapped around herself, pressing Wilberforce the stuffed puffin to her chest, the other hand fiddling with her hair. 'Is he gone?'

Rhona took out her notebook. 'You see someone?'

A nod, sending brown curls bouncing. 'It was dark: I didn't see his face, but he was wearing a thick coat and a woolly hat, and what if he comes back?'

'Patrol car'll swing past through the night. Now, if there's nothing—'

'Ash, will you stay, please, I mean there's plenty of spare rooms and I really don't want to be stuck here on my own if he comes back, Aunty Jan's got the dogs with her and what if it *wasn't* a burglar, what if it was ... someone after me?'

Rhona squared her shoulders. 'Think you're really special, don't you?'

'I'm only—'

'You think the Birthday Boy's after you, 'cos...' Rhona put on a big theatrical voice. 'You're the only one who can stop him!' A snort. 'Seriously?'

'It's not—'

'That kinda thing only happens in the movies, Princess. Serial killers don't stalk the investigating team, they stay the hell *away* from the police.'

Dr McDonald took a step back. 'Oh...' Bit her bottom lip. Looked away.

'All right, Rhona, that's enough. Not her fault she's scared.'

'Oh, come on, for all we know she's making it all up to get attention. Could've scratched the back door herself, and the description's not exactly—'

'I said that's *enough*.'

Dr McDonald gave the puffin a squeeze. 'Please, Ash?'

'Come on, Guv, I'm just saying: it wasn't the Birthday—'

'*Please*?'

* * *

I lay flat on the bed, in the dark, in an unfamiliar room, watching a sliver of light sweep across the ceiling – headlights on a car outside, going by.

All this time with nothing and then Steven Wallace comes along. Let it be him. Let the bastard be the one.

I ran my fingers over the surface of the small velvet box Little Mike gave me. Rough in one direction, smooth in the other, a sunken line where the lid and the base fitted together.

Let Steven Wallace be the fucker that killed Rebecca.

Four years of looking, and lying, and waiting. Four years of everything *broken*. Four years praying for a chance to catch the bastard: to be there when he confessed, to watch him go down for the rest of his miserable life. To tell Rebecca that I got him…

A knock on the door.

'Ash?'

I stuck the box under my pillow. 'Hello?'

The door opened. A silhouette in flannel jammies stood in the hall outside, head shrouded in curls. 'I wanted…' She cleared her throat. 'Thank you for staying.'

'Try and get some sleep, OK?'

'You're a great dad.' She closed the door, leaving me alone in the darkness again.

I wrapped my hand around his throat and squeezed.

Saturday 19th November

34

The smell of sizzling bacon drifted through the house as I pulled my socks from the pile of clothes on the floor. Sniffed them. Good enough for another day. Have to pop past Rhona's at some point and pick up clean clothes, though. Goosepimples rippled across my bare skin, still damp from the shower.

One sock on, and my phone rang: 'MICHELLE.'

I closed my eyes, took a breath. Perfect way to start the day. I answered it anyway; tried to sound cheery. 'Is she giving you any more—'

'What the buggering fuck *do you think you're playing at? Raising* your daughter *on my own is tough enough without you undermining me every two minutes!'*

I sank onto the edge of the bed and dragged out the other sock. 'Good morning, Ash, how are you today.'

'Don't you bloody start with me, Ash Henderson: you know fine well Katie's grounded. Honestly, how am I supposed to maintain any kind of discipline when you pull shit like this?'

Dr McDonald's voice came from somewhere downstairs. 'ASH? BREAKFAST'S NEARLY READY. DO YOU WANT TEA?'

'I'm hanging up, Michelle.' Pulled on the other sock.

'That's your bloody answer to everything, isn't it? Run away. You can't take Katie and not tell me!'

'Take…? I didn't take anyone anywhere. What the hell are you—'

'—irresponsible arsehole. Why did I think you could change?'

'Katie isn't with you?' Something curdled deep inside my stomach.

'I don't know why I even bother, you—'

'Michelle! Will you shut up for *two* seconds. Where's Katie?'

A pause. *'She's staying at your house.'*

'No she isn't.'

'Her note says she's—'

'My place is all boarded up: flooded, I've not been back since yesterday morning. How could you let her out of your sight?'

'Ash?' Something went thump on the other end of the phone. *'Oh God, what if she's run away? What if she's run away like Rebecca? What if we never see our baby ever again?'*

No. Not this. Not again. I swallowed. 'You said she left a note.'

'Oh God, Ash, what if she's gone?'

'The note, Michelle – what does it say?'

'I shouted at her when I got home. What was I supposed to do, she got expelled!'

'She's… She's probably just sulking: punishing us for not taking her side against the school. Katie'll be at one of her friends' houses.' Please, *please* let her be at one of her friends' houses. 'Now read me the bloody note!'

'I shouted at her…'

'Michelle, will you calm—'

A knock. Then the door swung open, and there was Dr McDonald, standing in the hall: a blue pinny tied over her usual stripy top and jeans. Holding a cup of tea. 'Thought you might…' Pink rushed up her cheeks and her eyes widened. Staring at me.

Wearing nothing but a pair of socks, the phone clamped to my ear.

'Oh.' She spun around, facing back the way she'd come. 'Sorry... I... Breakfast is on the table...'

I dragged my trousers on. 'Answer the bloody phone!'

The other end rang, and rang, then: *'Oldcastle four nine six, zero three two seven?'* A man's voice, rough with cigarettes.

'Is Katie there? Katie Henderson?'

The voice became sharper. *'Who is this?'*

'Her dad. I need to speak to her, *now*.' Who the hell did she think she was kidding? Pulling the same trick twice in one week, as if we were idiots.

'You're her dad, are you? Well done: what a sterling job you *did. Last time she was here she had fifty quid out my wallet – lucky I didn't call the police!'* It wasn't the same Tennent's Lager Tory I spoke to on Wednesday.

'Where's Ashley's father?'

'And another thing – if she doesn't stay away from my daughter, I'll—'

'Where is he?'

'Right here. I'm *Ashley's dad, and she's doing a lot better at school now your sodding Katie's not dragging her down.'*

I stared at my mobile. 'But ... she was there Wednesday night.'

'She's not been near our Ashley for three months. And it's staying that way, or so help me...'

He slammed the phone down.

Three months.

I hauled my shirt on. Dialled Katie's mobile again. Come on. Come on...

Voicemail. Same as the last three times I'd tried. 'Katie, it's your dad – where the hell are you? Your mother's worried sick!'

Struggled into my shoes, grabbed my jacket and hurried down the stairs.

Dr McDonald was waiting at the bottom, still wearing her

pinny. 'Is everything OK, only I made you an omelette, you like omelettes don't you, it's got ham and mushrooms in it and some cheese, and there's bacon and orange juice and croissants...'

I kept walking, buttoning up my shirt on the way to the door. 'I have to go.'

'You don't like omelettes: I knew I should've made pancakes, I can make pancakes, it'll only take a minute? Ash?'

Outside, it was still dark – the sky a heavy lid of slate and dirty-orange, hanging over the city, streetlights like flickering candles buffeted in the driving rain.

Dr McDonald followed me out into the downpour, stopped beside the rusty Renault as I fought with my keys. Wringing her hands. 'What did I do wrong?'

I yanked the car door open. 'Katie's missing.'

She stood there, staring at me, the rain battering the curls around her head. 'Oh God, that's *terrible*...' She tore off her apron and chucked it over her shoulder, then sprinted back to the house. Slammed the door.

By the time I'd got the engine started she was clambering into the passenger seat. 'You drive, I'll call the police.'

The city flashed by the car windows: the dirty sandstone tenements of Castle Hill giving way to rows of Sixties concrete boxes. Silver and gold shimmered back from tinted glass as the sun peered through the gap between the surrounding hills and the bruised sky. Rain bounced off the bonnet, the windscreen wipers going full tilt.

'...yes... No, you'll have to speak up... No, no I don't...' Dr McDonald clutched the phone to her chest. 'Where are we?'

'Tell the useless bastard to get a patrol car over there now!'

Back on the phone. 'I don't know, coming up to a big bridge over the river... Yes. Ash says... Oh, you heard that. Right... And?'

The Renault's back end shimmied as I hurled her around the corner and onto Epsom Road, right in front of a bus. An outraged squeal of brakes and horn. Then up onto Calderwell Bridge.

Blackwall Hill loomed before us, still wrapped in shadow.

'He says they're sending Bravo Three, should be there in five minutes, do you want them to start broadcasting?'

'Yes, of course I bloody do: all the surrounding streets. I want every patrol car he's got out looking for her.'

A pause. 'Uh-huh... Uh-huh... He says they're doing everything they can.'

I tightened my grip on the steering wheel, overtaking a boxy little Berlingo van with 'DREADNAUGHT BAKERY' down the side.

'Fuck, fuck, fuck...' A line of traffic cones cut the lane in half, sickly yellow lights flashing on top. Why couldn't the bloody council fix the potholes at night when no one needed to use the sodding roads?

Left at the roundabout, skirting Montgomery Park – sunlight flaring on the boating lake and river beyond, then right, under the railway line and up into Blackwall Hill, the speedo hitting fifty.

Dr McDonald pointed through the windscreen. 'There.'

A patrol car raced across the road in front of us, two junctions down, lights flashing, siren blaring.

It was sitting outside the house as I pulled into Rowan Drive, a pair of uniformed constables clambering out into the rain. I squealed the Renault to a halt and followed them up the path.

Michelle had the door open already, holding onto the frame, eyes darting up and down the street. 'Did you find her?' Her blonde hair was plastered flat to her head, cheeks hollow, eyes red. Fingernails chewed to ragged stumps.

One of the Uniforms took out his notebook, the rain pattering on the brim of his peaked cap. 'If we can start by taking a few details, it— Hey!'

I shoved past. 'Have you tried all her friends?'

Michelle blinked, then backed into the house. I followed, Tweedledum and Tweedledee bringing up the rear.

'Have you called Katie's friends?'

A nod. 'Soon as I spoke to you... Oh God, Ash... Not again. I can't take it again!'

Tweedledum took off his hat. 'Do you have a recent picture? Any idea what she's wearing?'

The front door clunked shut, and there was Dr McDonald. She gave me a little wave, her mouth pinched in a tight line.

I put a hand on Michelle's shoulder. 'It'll be OK. It'll be fine. We'll find her.'

'I don't... It was night. I was asleep.'

Tweedledee tried a big Cheshire smile. 'Not to worry, teenagers run off all the time. They're usually back soon as they're hungry...' He licked his lips, staring at my bunched fists. Then up at his partner who was making throat-slitting gestures. 'Ah, right... Sorry, Guv, we only... It's what we're supposed to say... I didn't mean...'

Michelle stood at the kitchen sink, staring out into the back garden, shoulders slumped, a cup of tea going cold on the work surface next to her. 'How can we be such *horrible* parents that both our girls run away?'

'We're not horrible parents.'

'How can we *not* be? Rebecca walked out on us, and now Katie... What did we do wrong?'

'Michelle, we're going to find Katie. It's going to be OK.' My stomach lurched, acid burning at the base of my throat. *Please* let it be OK. Don't let it be like last time.

The sound of a loudhailer blared outside – Tweedledum and Tweedledee driving slowly around the area broadcasting Katie's name and description.

I scrubbed a hand across my face. *Think.* 'And she didn't say anything?'

'Lots of things. None of them nice.' Michelle's shoulders drooped a little further. As if someone had chained another weight to her arms. 'She used to be such a sweet girl… Bloody Rebecca! This is all *her* fault – she poisoned *everything* when she abandoned us.' The mug crashed into the sink, sending shards of china clattering back in a spray of murky brown liquid. 'Selfish little bitch…'

Tea dripped down the kitchen window.

I closed my eyes. Dug my hands into my pockets.

Tell her. Just come clean and tell her everything.

It wasn't Rebecca's fault.

My fingers traced the edges of the small velvet box. I pulled it out, opened it.

The diamond ring inside sparkled, even after all this time.

A noise behind me. Dr McDonald – her reflection distorted in the dark glass door of the microwave. She stood there for a couple of beats, then cleared her throat. 'Is it all right if I take a look in Katie's room, see if I can find some clue where she might have gone?'

I nodded.

A pause. Then Dr McDonald patted me on the shoulder, and backed out of the room. Her feet creaked the stairs up to the landing. The muffled clunk of a door closing.

Silence.

I brushed a bit of fluff from the box's silk lining. 'Do you remember the morning we got engaged?'

'What if she doesn't come back?'

'You'd been throwing up in the toilets at that Wetherspoons on Beech Street, so we went to Boots and got that pregnancy test…'

'What if she disappears like Rebecca and we never see her again?'

'We were happy, weren't we?' I stood, went over to the sink. 'It all went to shit, but we *were* happy.'

A smear of red was mixed in amongst the shards of broken

mug. Blood dripped from the end of Michelle's middle finger. 'I don't think I can go through all this again.'

I put the open box on the work surface.

She stared down at it for a bit. Then picked the ring out of the box. 'My engagement ring! Granny gave me this – it was her mum's. I thought I'd lost it...'

'Found it when I was clearing my stuff out of Kingsmeath. In one of the boxes. Thought you'd want it back.'

After all, what was one more lie?

Dr McDonald flinched when I knocked on Katie's bedroom door. She shut the book in her hands and placed it on the bed beside her. Stood. 'Sorry, I always feel guilty reading someone else's diary...'

The room was a tip, same as always: the carpet barely visible between the discarded socks and pants and jeans and T-shirts and hooded tops. A stack of *Kerrang!* magazines teetered by the bed, a couple of books poking out from underneath the dirty washing. Posters on the wall of emo, goth and death-metal bands, a Disney's Little Mermaid given the Tim Burton treatment with biro scars, sunken eyes, and gaping ribcage.

A couple of drawers on the bedside cabinet were pulled out. Stripy socks and pants with little skull-and-crossbones on them. A single training bra.

I stayed where I was. 'She left her diary.'

'Well, it means she's not really planning on being gone long, I mean she wouldn't leave that behind if she was going to run away really, and it doesn't look like she's taken much in the way of underwear, and there's a toilet bag still in the wardrobe, I'm sure she'll be back soon... Ash?'

Oh God.

Not again.

I picked my way through the debris and sank down on the edge of the bed. Stared at Disney's Little Zombie. 'What about the note?'

'A bit confused, like she's making it up as she goes along, spontaneous rather than something she's planned and worked on, she's sorry for being such a disappointment, it's not her fault, ever since her sister disappeared it's all gone wrong for her, and nobody understands, and she hates everyone, but she loves them too, and why won't anyone listen to her side of things any more?'

Maybe Dr McDonald was right.

Rebecca never left a note…

Maybe Katie hadn't really run away; she hadn't been snatched; she wasn't tied to a chair, in a basement, waiting to die. She was off sulking somewhere trying to prove a point. She'd be back any minute.

Dr McDonald sat down next to me. 'That was a nice engagement ring.'

From downstairs came the rattle-clack-rustle of the mail hitting the front mat.

'What…' I cleared my throat. 'What about the diary?'

She put her hand on the book's cover. Keeping it shut. 'The usual teenage stuff.'

'Katie lied to me: said she was staying at her friend Ashley's house on Wednesday night, but Ashley's dad told me she'd not been there for months.'

'Ah…' Dr McDonald picked up the diary and held it against her chest. 'It's never a good idea to—'

'I *need* to know.' I looked down at my fists. 'Does she talk about Steven Wallace?'

A pause.

'Steven Wallace? No, no … there's no mention of Steven Wallace, or Sensational Steve, or anything like that, why would she talk about Steven Wallace?'

'Then who the hell was she staying with?'

35

I scooped all the post up from the mat, flicking through the envelopes. Two bills, a couple of circulars for hearing aids and stair-lifts, and a handful of birthday cards, all addressed to Katie.

Dr McDonald peered around my shoulder. 'Are you OK?'

None of them looked like the ones that wound up in my PO box once a year, but I tore them open anyway.

'Happy 13 Today!', 'It's Hormone-City From Here On In!', 'I Hear You're Getting Older!' Every one of them was shop-bought: kittens, teddy bears, grinning cartoon characters, all scribbled inside with best wishes from friends and family. A five-pound note in the one from Michelle's mother.

No homemade card with a photo of her tied to a chair, eyes wide with terror.

He didn't have her. It wasn't the same as last time. Katie really had run away.

Oh thank Christ…

I rested my head against the front door, blood thumped in my forehead. Deep breath.

He didn't have her. She'd run off to stay with the prick she was sleeping with. My little girl. Twelve – years – old.

'Ash? Ash, are you OK?'

Now all I had to do was find the boyfriend, get Katie back, and then batter the living shite out of him.

I dumped the cards on the little table by the stairs and pushed outside into the hammering rain.

It took four of Katie's friends before we found someone who knew where the little bastard lived.

Millbank Park towered eighteen storeys above the surrounding council estate. A set of three square high-rise blocks, strung together with walkways, paths, and corridors. Some public-spirited arsehole in the Housing Department had decided that what three big hulking lumps of concrete needed was a bright paint job. Most of the colour had worn off over the years, leaving nothing but various dirty shades of brown and grey.

A chain-link fence surrounded the car park, buckled and full of holes. A couple of battered Transit vans were abandoned over by the exit, a Fiesta up on bricks, a pair of matching VW Polos with more rust than paint.

I parked next to the Transit vans, then chucked the keys across to Dr McDonald. 'Lock the doors. Anything happens, put your foot down: don't look back, don't get involved. Anyone asks, I made you come.'

'But that's not—'

'I *made* you come.' Wind tried to tear the door from my hand as I climbed out. Rain crackled against my back.

Jesus it was cold. I clumped across the car park, through the broken gate, across a glass-strewn concrete path, and under one of the walkways linking Millbank East and North.

The double doors to Millbank North were propped open, one pane of glass spiderwebbed through with cracks, criss-crossed with duct tape. I walked into the eye-stinging reek of bleach and disinfectant, the tiles wet beneath my feet. Graffiti tags covered the walls. A drift of soggy takeaway leaflets slumped in one corner, dumped by some delivery boy that couldn't be arsed delivering them. Probably no point trying the lift, but I did anyway.

Waited.

A groaning creak, a clunk, then the lift doors squealed open. A baking urinal stench slumped out into the hallway.

Screw that.

I took the stairs.

According to Katie's friends, Noah McCarthy was seventeen and lived on the fourteenth floor with his mum, a nurse at Castle Hill Infirmary. That was lucky, because her little darling would need some medical intervention by the time I'd finished with him.

Katie wasn't even thirteen till Monday, and the bastard was *seventeen*.

I took the stairs. They opened out onto a featureless concrete balcony on each floor, cold morning air diluting the stench of stale piss. I kept going. Climbing higher, lungs burning in my chest.

When I reached the fourteenth floor I stepped out onto the balcony. Wind whipped along the concrete walkway, turning the rain into shotgun pellets that raked the flats' front doors.

I counted my way along the row: Fourteen-Ten, Fourteen-Eleven, Fourteen-Twelve, Fourteen-Thirteen, then around the corner. The wind died down, blocked by the building's bulk. Fourteen-Sixteen was almost dead centre, looking out over the concrete quadrangle between Millbank East, North, and West. Rain hammered the walkways below.

The sound of something cheery came from next door, a woman's voice singing along with the radio inside.

I took a couple of steps back, until I was up against the balcony railing, then kicked number sixteen's door off its hinges. BOOM.

Deep breath. 'NOAH MCCARTHY: GET YOUR ARSE OUT HERE, IT'S FUCKING JUDGEMENT DAY!'

In. I hauled on my leather gloves. No one would bother

running DNA for a wee shite like Noah McCarthy. As long as he was still breathing.

The hallway was just big enough for two doors on either side and one at the end. The nearest one burst open and a spotty young man staggered out, pulling up a pair of baggy jeans over his boxers.

Bow-legged, big red trainers that weren't laced up properly, tartan shirt with the sleeves torn off worn over a Korn *'Issues'* T-shirt. Shiny black hair, ring through his eyebrow, another through his nose. He looked me up and down, teeth bared. 'The fuck you think you're doin', old man?'

'You Noah?'

He buttoned his fly. 'Gonna unleash a world of fuckin' hurt on you, Grandad, comin' in here...' His mouth fell open. 'What did you do to our fucking door?'

It was him – the voice on the phone pretending to be Ashley's father. The prick who told me they'd stayed up late eating pizza watching Freddy Krueger slash his way through central casting.

'Where is she?'

'That's our door! Mum's gonna go *mental* when she finds out.'

'WHERE IS SHE, YOU LITTLE PRICK?'

He backed up a step. 'She's ... at work?'

'Not your mum: Katie. Where's my daughter?'

'Oh *fuck*...' He turned and ran, back into the bathroom, slammed the door behind him. 'Oh fuck, oh fuck, oh fuck...'

A little clunking noise, like a teeny bolt being slid home.

I opened the nearest door on the right: small kitchen, the surfaces littered with pizza boxes and discarded remains of microwave meals, a pyramid of empty lager cans arranged on the floor.

Next door: a double bed littered with clothes, a small dressing table turned into a shrine to face cream, perfume, and makeup.

The door at the end opened on a living room with a big telly in one corner, a brown sofa, and a coffee table – a heaped ashtray sitting next to a pack of Rizla, a pouch of rolling tobacco, and a half-inch block of Moroccan.

Another bedroom lurked behind the fourth door, smaller than the first, the walls adorned with the same kind of posters as Katie's. Only Noah didn't have a Disney's Little Mermaid, she'd done him a zombie Tinkerbell instead. Rumpled duvet cover, jeans, T-shirts, socks, and boxer shorts were scattered across the floor… And a pair of red panties with little white skull-and-crossbones on them.

I checked the wardrobe – no Katie.

Back to the bathroom.

A muffled voice came from inside. 'Denny, you fuckin' spaz: answer the fuckin' phone!'

The bathroom door came off its hinges even easier than the front one. It crashed down into the bath, ripping the shower curtain from the rail.

He squealed, scrabbled back until he was standing on the toilet lid, mobile phone clutched against his chest. As if that was going to save him.

'Noah McCarthy?'

'I… Whatever she told you, it's a fuckin' lie, OK? I never—'

'She's *twelve*, Noah. You're seventeen, and my little girl is twelve. AND HER PANTIES ARE IN YOUR FUCKING BEDROOM!'

A medicine cabinet was fixed to the wall above the sink. I grabbed it and pulled. The whole thing creaked and rattled, then pop – the rawlplugs holding it to the wall gave and everything slid around inside. Heavy enough to do some decent damage. I hurled it at him.

'Aaaaaaagh!' Noah ducked, arms covering his face, as the medicine cabinet smashed into him. The door flew off, pills and toothpaste and cotton buds going everywhere.

I took a handful of his baggy jeans and hauled.

He crashed down against the cistern, the back of his head leaving a smear of red where it bounced off the tiles above the toilet.

Noah struggled, but I didn't let go: I twisted his leg halfway around and shoved it against the lip of the bath. Leant my full weight on it till it snapped. Another scream. A kick in the balls shut him up. Then a knee in the face. Stamping on his ribs till I felt a couple of them break. Then all the fingers on his right hand.

I staggered back, breathing hard.

Noah slumped on the floor against the toilet, blood trickling down his face from a broken nose, right hand curled against his chest, left leg bent in a way nature never intended. Sobbing.

Good.

'Where is she?'

'Ah ... God...'

'How does it go, Noah? After forty days and forty nights, he sent forth a dove to see if it could find land. Something like that?' I grabbed his other leg – the unbroken one – and pulled.

More screaming.

Out into the hall. He snatched at the doorframe, but I stamped on his elbow. It did the trick. He cried and moaned and pleaded all the way to the front door.

I dragged him onto the balcony, then flipped him over onto his front. Took a hold of his collar in one hand and the waistband of his trousers in the other. 'Katie's *twelve,* you raping paedo piece of shit. TWELVE.'

'I'm sorry, I'm sorry, I didn't—'

I shoved his head forward, banging it off the concrete railing.

'Where is she?'

'I... I don't know, please...'

'I'm going to send *you* forth, Noah.' I hauled him up until his top half was out over the railing. 'Think you'll be able to find land when I let go?'

'I don't know! I don't know! She was here Wednesday night, but that's it! Jesus… Honest: I don't know!'

Liquid trickled across the concrete at my feet. It wasn't rain.

I heaved Noah's damp arse up higher, and he screamed.

Someone barrelled around the corner and skidded to a halt on the balcony, grabbing onto the handrail. Dr McDonald. Her mouth fell open. 'Ash?' She glanced back over her shoulder – towards the stairs. 'Ash, what are you doing?'

'Noah here's going forth to find land.' I gave him a shake. 'Look, Noah, it's right down there, can you see it?'

'PLEASE HELP ME!'

'Ash, you can't do this, it's—'

'She's twelve!' I let go of his collar and slammed a fist into his kidneys. Fire and ice burst inside my knuckles. So I did it again.

Noah screamed.

The lady next door turned up her music.

'Please don't kill me! Please!' He waved his good arm at Dr McDonald. 'Help me!'

She licked her lips. Looked away. 'Katie's only twelve.'

Good girl.

I gave him another shake.

'AAAAAGH! Please, I didn't mean it! I didn't know! *Please!*'

'WHERE IS SHE?'

'Ash, we've got to get out of here – Dickie's on his way up, he's got the big hairy one with him, they're looking for you.'

'Not till this piece of shit tells me where Katie is.'

'I don't know! I don't … I don't know…' The words getting more and more mushy, broken up with jagged sobs.

'Ash, we have to go!'

'He's been screwing my twelve-year-old daughter!'

'We have to go *now*!'

'Bye, Noah. Say hello to the ground for me.'

'PLEASE!'

A man's voice boomed out from the other end of the balcony. 'Officer Henderson!' Didn't need to look to know it was Dickie. 'Ash: put him down.'

I stayed where I was. 'Should've said, "Let him go." Would've been funnier.'

'DON'T LET HIM KILL ME!'

Dickie walked towards us, hands up, as if I had a gun on him. 'Ash, this isn't helping.'

Behind Dickie, DS Gillis puffed and panted to a halt, leaning on the handrail and wheezing. 'Christ on a bike...'

'Ash, I need you to put Mr McCarthy down.'

No chance. 'How'd you find me?'

'Katie's friends. Come on, Ash, it's over, you can't do this.'

'He's been *fucking* my little girl.'

'We'll do him for it: we'll lock him up with the other dirty kiddie fiddlers. Now haul him in.'

No.

'Ash, please. We need to talk about Katie.'

'He knows where she is!' I gave Noah another shake.

'I don't! I don't know anything!'

Dickie put his hands down. 'Michelle called the station. She got a card from the Birthday Boy.'

'You're a lying bastard: I checked the mail before we left.'

He reached into his jacket and pulled out a smart phone, pressed a couple of buttons and held it out. A snapshot filled the shiny screen – a homemade birthday card with a photo of Katie on it. Tied to a chair. A gag over her mouth, eyes wide, cheeks streaked with mascara.

I let go of Noah.

36

'I'm sorry.' Dickie leaned on the windowsill, looking out into the rain.

The lounge stank of cannabis, cigarettes, and armpits. Noah was sobbing in the kitchen – the sound seeping through the paper-thin walls as DS Gillis tried to patch the dirty little fucker up before the ambulance got here.

Dr McDonald lowered herself onto the couch next to me, put a hand on my knee. 'We'll find her.'

I ran a thumb over the smartphone's screen, bringing it back to life before it went into sleep mode. Staring into Katie's eyes... 'You can't tell anyone about this.'

'Ash, it's not—'

'They'll take me off the case. You *know* that.'

Silence.

Dickie sighed. 'Ash, we can't. She's still alive; it's not her birthday till Monday, there's still time. We need to throw everything we have at finding her.'

'I can't sit at home and do nothing!'

He ran a hand across his face, his back to the room. 'We *can't*. You could've killed that boy—'

'He was screwing my twelve-year-old daughter!'

Dr McDonald squeezed my knee, brought her chin up, and

stared at Dickie. 'I was with Detective Constable Henderson the whole time. When we arrived Noah McCarthy had clearly been taking drugs. Ash asked him about Katie and McCarthy flew into a rage. He attacked me. Ash had to intervene.'

Dickie shook his head. 'And the balcony?'

'McCarthy was obviously confused. He ran out of the flat and tripped. Ash caught him and saved his life. He was pulling him to safety when you arrived.'

The only sound was Noah crying in the other room.

Dickie nodded. 'Stick to your story. No deviation when Professional Standards come asking questions.' He turned and perched a buttock on the window ledge. 'My team's speaking to all of Katie's friends. Then we'll start on her teachers and classmates.'

Katie stared at me from the phone's screen. Pleading. Terrified.

I couldn't look any more. 'We pull Steven Wallace in, and we tear his house apart till we find her.'

Dickie glanced at Dr McDonald for a moment. 'Would you excuse us, Doctor, I need to speak to DC Henderson in private.'

She gave my knee another squeeze, then left the room. Closed the door behind her.

He folded his arms. 'We've got nothing on Steven Wallace; we need probable cause before we can—'

'Fuck probable cause. He's got Katie.'

'Ash, I understand: you're hurt, you're upset, you're—'

'You understand? What? What *exactly* do you understand?' On my feet now, trembling. 'How many daughters have *you* lost to a serial killer?'

'She's not…' He closed his eyes for a moment. 'Ash, go home: Michelle needs you. Be there for her.'

'I'm not—'

'And stay away from Steven Wallace, he's … he's not the only suspect, OK?'

I stared back. 'Who else? Who's a suspect?'

'Ash, we can't—'

'Who's a fucking suspect?' I took a step closer.

'You nearly killed Noah McCarthy. What are you going to do if I give you a list of names and addresses: go round and make them a nice cup of tea?'

'She's my *daughter*!'

'Ash, we'll find her. You have to let us do our jobs.'

Pretty much the same bollocks I'd told Lauren Burges's dad in Shetland. The same bollocks I'd been telling myself since Rebecca's first Birthday Boy card slithered through the letter-box four years ago.

I put Dickie's phone down next to the heaped ashtray. 'Right. Like you found Lauren Burges, and Amber O'Neil, and Hannah Kelly, and—'

'We'll *find* her.' He ran a hand through his greying ginger hair. 'Trust me on that, Ash. Hell or high water, we'll find her.'

Detective Constable Gillis hauled on the handbrake and turned off the engine. The Renault groaned and pinged, rain thudding into the roof, drumming on the bonnet. 'Pfffff...' His breath reeked of old cigarettes. The smell got worse when he scratched at his beard. 'No offence, but your car's a piece of shit.'

I held out my hand. 'Give me the keys.'

'Dickie's only trying to look out for you.'

A scarlet Alfa Romeo sat opposite my... Opposite Michelle's house, the driver's window wound down a crack, two figures inside – blurred and indistinct through the rain-spattered windscreen. Jennifer and her photographer, Frank.

The Oldcastle CID grapevine strikes again.

Looked as if none of the other media had got wind of it yet: if they had, the whole place would've been swarming with the bastards.

'—have to do, OK?'

I blinked.

'Yeah.'

Gillis dropped the keys into my open hand. 'I mean it, anything you need – you let me know. Well ... if I can.'

'Why?'

Gillis sniffed, pursed his lips, making his moustache bristle. 'Keep trying to imagine what it'd be like if the bastard snatched one of my kids.' He shook his head, dirty yellow curls bouncing around his bald patch, then pointed at the big black BMW pulling up on the other side of the road. 'If there was *any* way Dickie could keep you on, he would. You know that, right?'

I opened the car door and climbed out into the rain.

He followed me. 'And don't worry about the Noah McCarthy thing: I saw you trying to save him.'

Gillis turned up his collar and hurried through the puddles to the waiting BMW. Dr McDonald peered out from the back seat, fingers spread on the window, biting her bottom lip as the car pulled away from the kerb. Down to the end of the road – the brake lights flared, then a right and they were gone.

Cold water trickled down the back of my neck as I stood there, staring after them.

It was too early to pay Steven Wallace a visit. Have to wait till it was dark and he was at home and everyone was asleep. And Dickie would have him under surveillance by now... So it wasn't as if I could just march up to the front door and kick it in.

But what if it wasn't him? What if Steven Wallace *didn't* have a hidden room built into his refurbished wine cellar so he could torture twelve-year-old girls to death?

It wasn't worth the risk.

I looked up at the house.

Dickie was right: I should go in and be with Michelle. Play the supportive ex-husband. Pretend it'll all be OK. Sit in the dark and wait for them to find Katie's body.

I got back in the car and pulled out my phone.

Sabir picked up on the eighth ring. *'Better be important, I was havin' a crap!'*

'I need the names and addresses of every suspect you've had for the last seven years.'

Silence.

'Sabir?'

'Ash... I'm dead sorry about Katie. But Dickie's been on to all of us: we can't give you nothin'. I can't. Look, we're doin' our—'

I hung up. Tried Henry instead.

His mobile rang, and rang, and rang, then went to voicemail. 'Henry, it's Ash, I need you to call me back. It's urgent.'

The windows were steaming up. I drummed my fingers on the dashboard. Waited.

Tried again. Got the same recording telling me to leave a message after the beep. Hung up.

'Fuck!' I slammed my palms against the steering wheel. Took a deep breath. 'FUCK! Fucking, shit-fucking ... FUCK! AAAAAAAAAGH! FUCK!' Spittle flecked the windscreen.

My throat burned, pulse throbbing in my forehead, little sparks of light glittering behind my eyes.

A knock on the driver's window. I looked up, but the glass was opaque with fog. I wound it down.

It was Jennifer, standing there underneath a black umbrella, all huddled up in her camel-hair coat, eyes pinched. She leaned forwards. 'Erm... Ash, are you all right?'

'No comment.'

She looked down for a moment. Then back again. 'I know we... Look, it's not important what happened between you and me, is it? What matters is Katie.'

'I said, no comment.'

'Ash, I want you to know the *Castle News and Post* will do everything we can to help get Katie back. You could put out a personal appeal?' She licked her lips. 'We could make the Birthday Boy see what kind of pain and damage he's doing. Maybe run a photo of Katie's room, a couple of quotes from her mother...?'

'It's Saturday. Her birthday's on Monday.' I turned the key

in the ignition. 'By the time he reads anything in your rag she'll already be dead.'

HM Prison Glenochil – an hour and a half south of Oldcastle. A couple of rusty hatchbacks huddled in front of the bland, slab-faced reception building, but other than that the car park was empty.

I tried Henry's number one more time: bloody voicemail again. Then called Weber instead. At least *he* was answering his phone.

'Hello?'

'It's Ash.'

'Ah...' A breath. Then a muffled, *'Excuse me, I have to take this...'* A clunk, some rustling, and Weber was back. *'Where are you?'*

'I need the names of all the suspects Dickie's got—'

'Don't be an idiot. ACC Drummond's crawling all over me, and that slippery shite Smith is right behind him, taking notes. I want to help, you know *that, but they're—'*

'I want a couple of names, not a fucking kidney!'

'I know, I know.' Sigh. *'Look: where are you?'*

'Doing what you should be doing.' I killed the link and pocketed the phone; clambered out of the car and marched towards the prison.

'Right, here's the rules.' The prison officer ran a finger along the side of his long, hooked nose, as if they were written there in Braille. 'You do not pass the prisoner anything. You do not accept anything from him. He *will* be strip-searched at the end of your visit. You have fifteen minutes, then he's back in his cell.'

I nodded. Placed my notebook and pen on the table in front of me.

The visiting room looked as if it'd been set out for an exam – Formica tables with a chair on either side, arranged in eight rows, spaced out just enough to afford a little privacy and give the security cameras a good line of sight.

Scuffed blue carpet tiles covered the floor, crime-scene stains marking the death of spilled coffees.

A buzz sounded, then the heavy metal door at the far end of the room swung open. Another prison officer shuffled in, stepped to one side, and there was Len.

He was about a head taller than his escort, a fringe of neatly trimmed grey hair around a big bald crown, round glasses, and a grey goatee with a handlebar moustache. He'd lost a bit of weight, broadened out a bit. Probably been spending a lot of time in the prison gym.

Len settled into the seat opposite and nodded, as if we hadn't seen each other since the morning briefing, instead of two and a bit years. 'Ash.'

'Chief.'

A smile. 'Not any more.' His voice was deep enough to make my plastic cup of water tremble on the tabletop. 'Or shall we play yesteryear: I'll be Detective Superintendent Murray, and you'll be DI Henderson?'

'I need to know who the Birthday Boy suspects were. All of them.'

'I'm fine, thanks. A lot better now they've taken the stitches out. Talk about *itchy*.'

'Len, I'm serious.'

'Still, ex-Constable Evans will be taking his food through a tube for the next six months, so I suppose I win.' He took hold of the bottom of his sweatshirt. 'Want to see the scar? It's pretty spectacular?'

I closed my eyes, gritted my teeth. 'He's got Katie.'

'Came at me in the library with a razor blade stuck in the end of a toothbrush.' A frown. 'Ever seen your own innards, Ash? They're not as pretty as you might think.'

'The Birthday Boy's got Katie and they're locking me out of the investigation!'

Len sighed, tilted his head to one side. 'Two years, eight months, three weeks, and fifteen days. That's how long I've been in here, and you haven't visited once. Not until you want something.'

'He's got Katie...'

'You said that already.' He picked up my water and sipped at it. 'I thought we were friends, Ash.'

'He's got my little girl.'

Len leaned back in his chair. '*You* got a slap on the wrists. I got eighteen years. I think I'm due a little conversation first, don't you?' He pursed his lips, glanced up at the ceiling. 'Who do you fancy this afternoon: Warriors or Aberdeen?'

'For God's sake, Len.' I checked the clock on the wall. 'I've only got twelve minutes till they kick me out.'

'Like I said: I've got eighteen years.' He smiled.

'Fine. Aberdeen.'

'Really? I think we're in with a chance this time. Bob Eason's bought a couple of good players this season – might look like Gollum in a tracksuit, but the little sod knows his football.'

I curled my hands into fists. 'Len, he's going to kill her!'

'See, that's what I've been trying to figure out: why her? Why you?' He teased the end of his goatee into a point. 'Why target someone on the investigation? Why make it personal? It's too risky, too flashy, like something out of a movie. Doesn't happen in real life.'

'I saw the birthday card. He's got her.'

'Hmmm...' Silence. Then, 'Maybe you've spooked him? Maybe you've been running your sticky fingers through his dirty laundry, and he needs you ... distracted?'

'Who was a suspect?'

'Philip Skinner's mum writes to me, did you know that? Every month I get this big wodge of paper through the post telling me what she's been up to, and what's happening on *Coronation Street*, and what her grandchildren are doing.

Course she's not *really* writing to me, she's writing to Skinner...'

'Len, *please*.'

He put the water down. Sighed. 'Well, there was a sergeant with Northern Constabulary, but I think he hanged himself... Turned out he was into kiddie porn – I'm pretty sure they found the bin in his study full of crumpled up printouts of the birthday cards, covered in spunk. We thought it was part of a ring, but you know what the Tartan and Shortbread Brigade are like. Then there was that journalist with the *Aberdeen Examiner*...' Frown. 'Tolbert? Talbert? Talbert – but we couldn't get anything to stick. Or Harriet Woods? She was a private investigator in Dundee. Ended up moving to Dubai.'

I scribbled names and details in my notebook.

Len sat forwards, huge hands on the tabletop. As if he was the only thing holding it down. 'Skinner confessed: how was I supposed to know?'

'Anyone else?'

'The profile was a perfect fit. Henry Forrester was in on the interview, he *said* Skinner was our man.'

'I know.'

'Those little boys: raped and cut up into little bits...'

'Len was there anyone else?'

He stared at the table for a while, mouth pinched, a deep crease between his eyebrows. 'Couple of nut-jobs: Ahmed Moghadam, Danny Crawford, some woman who thought Jesus lived in her basement...' He tapped his finger on the tabletop: tap-tap-tap, tap, tap, tap, tap-tap-tap. 'Some nights I can still hear him screaming.'

37

'Get out the way!' I jammed the mobile between my ear and shoulder and leaned on the horn again, but the prick in the Subaru refused to budge from the outside lane. 'Come on, Henry, ANSWER THE FUCKING PHONE!'

Finally the prick drifted into the other lane, and I could put my foot down again. Kidding on I didn't see him give me the finger in my rear-view mirror.

Voicemail. 'Henry, where the *fuck* are you? Call me back.'

I tried Rhona.

Fields ribbed with poly tunnels whipped by on either side. A green sign: A90, Dundee 9, Forfar 23, Oldcastle 34, Aberdeen 75.

'Guv? Jesus, I heard about Katie, are you OK?'

'Finally someone answers the bloody phone!'

The speedometer needle edged up to eighty-five.

'...I didn't—'

'I need you to run some PNC checks for me, but you can't tell anyone, OK?' I pulled out my notebook, pinned it against the steering wheel, and flipped through the pages. Then read her the list of names Len gave me. Made her repeat them back. 'I mean it – you tell no one about this. Not Weber, not Dickie, not even Shifty Dave.'

Nothing.

'Rhona?'

'Why didn't you call me *first? You said no one was answering their phone, why didn't you call me? I would've helped. I* always *help. I ironed your shirts!'*

As if I didn't have enough to worry about... 'Rhona, the Birthday Boy's going to kill my little girl on Monday, OK? I've got other things on my mind.'

The needle hit ninety and my foot was flat to the floor – that was it, the Renault didn't have any more. I tossed the notebook onto the passenger seat. Roared past an eighteen-wheeler with 'SCOTIABRAND TASTY CHICKENS LTD. THEY'RE FAN-CHICKEN-TASTIC!' on the side.

On the other end of the phone, Rhona cleared her throat. *'Sorry. I didn't mean—'*

'It's OK. I'm...' Deep breath. 'I appreciate your help. It's ... not a great day.'

PC Julie Wilson spun around on one of the swivel chairs, pointing at the ceiling tiles, long blonde hair trailing out behind her. 'Twoooo ni-ill, twoooo ni-ill...' She stopped. Closed her mouth. Shifted on her seat. 'Sorry, Guv.'

The CID office was half empty. A little radio sat on the table by the kettle, crackling out the Warriors–Aberdeen match. *'And it's Morrison to Chepski, Chepski to Woods...'* The roar of the crowd chanting, *'You're going home in a tasty casserole...'*

Julie jumped to her feet, straightened her black T-shirt. 'We're all really sorry about Katie... I didn't meant to... Will someone switch off that fucking radio?'

One of the other PCs flicked the switch.

Silence.

She stared at her feet. 'Sorry, Guv.'

I marched through to Weber's office.

He was sitting behind his desk, face all pinched and lined.

No prizes for guessing why – ACC Drummond sat stiff-backed in one of the visitors' chairs, DS Smith-the-Prick in the other. They both turned to stare at me.

Weber took off his glasses and polished them on a hanky. 'How's Michelle holding up?'

'I…' I hadn't even bothered to ask, just ran off to see Len. 'Have you hauled Steven Wallace in yet?'

'We were talking about the candlelit vigil. Obviously we'll add Katie to the—'

'Have you hauled him in, or haven't you?'

The Assistant Chief Constable brushed fluff from his trouser leg. 'I was saddened to hear about your daughter, Constable Henderson. But I'm a little concerned about what happened with this…' He raised an eyebrow at Smith.

'Noah McCarthy, sir.'

'Thank you, Sergeant. He's made a complaint. Claims you assaulted him and tried to throw him off a fourteenth-floor balcony?'

'Fuck him.' I stared at Weber. 'Steven Wallace.'

Weber sighed. 'I've got every patrol car we have scouring the streets for Katie, and everyone on day shift's—'

'Why the hell haven't you hauled him in?'

ACC Drummond stiffened even further. 'Because, Constable, we don't "haul people in" without a warrant, and we can't get a warrant without probable cause.'

'Dr McDonald says he fits the profile!'

'Dr McDonald is barely out of nappies, Constable.' Drummond stood. 'The Procurator Fiscal needs slightly more than your little doctor's word before we start waterboarding members of the public.' He picked up his peaked cap and tucked it under his arm. 'Now, if you'll excuse me, I have to brief the Chief Constable. DS Smith will be taking your statement about this morning's unfortunate events. I expect you to give him your utmost cooperation.'

The ACC paused on his way out the door to pat me on the

shoulder. 'We'll do everything we can to get your daughter back.' And then he was gone.

Lucky I didn't break every finger on his bloody hand.

Smith levered himself out of his chair. Smiled. 'Why don't we go somewhere a bit more comfortable?'

Interview room three smelled of feet and cabbage.

DS Smith drummed his fingers on the tabletop, marking time for the tape whining around in the recorder. 'And that's how Oldcastle CID likes to do business, is it? Beating the crap out of suspects?'

'I told you what happened. *Twice.*' I sat forwards. The chair stayed rock solid on the floor, held there with four thick bolts. Not like the seats on the other side of the table: where the police officers sat. 'Do you need me to use smaller words, or does shagging sheep make you go deaf?'

The uniformed PC standing behind me snorted. Then tried to turn it into a cough.

Smith narrowed his eyes, lips pursed beneath that long pointy nose. 'Are we having a problem, Constable Dawson?'

Another cough. 'Something in my throat, sir.'

Dawson – he was on the list Sabir emailed through when we were in Shetland.

I turned in my seat. 'It's Tim, isn't it?'

'Yes, Guv.' He smiled, showing off a mouthful of squint teeth – it went with his squint nose and lopsided ears.

Smith stared at the ceiling tiles. 'How many times...? Constable, we do *not* address detective constables as—'

'You ran a PNC check on the Birthday Boy victims' families, didn't you?'

A blink. 'Yeah. Couple of times, why?'

Smith rapped his knuckles on the chipped tabletop. 'That's enough, *Constable*. DC Henderson, do you have any idea how much damage you caused Noah McCarthy? He—'

'Why did you do the search?'

'Dunno, Guv. Think it was one of the high-heejins... Yeah, definitely – the ACC got me to do it for him.'

'Constable! This is a serious enquiry into a complaint of police brutality, not a bloody knitting circle.'

I pulled out my phone and called Shifty Dave – he was on the list too. Asked him the same question.

'Fucking Drummond, wasn't it. Starched wee bawbag never does his own dirty work. Why?'

I hung up and tried another couple of names, while DS Smith sat bug-eyed on the other side of the table – going a lovely shade of trembling pink.

Every single one of them blamed Assistant Chief Constable Drummond.

Smith banged his hand down on the tabletop. 'Officer Henderson, I must *insist*—'

'Interview terminated at fifteen thirty-two.' I slid out from my immovable chair and stood. Grabbed my jacket. 'Thanks, Tim.'

'Officer Henderson, this interview isn't over till I say it's... Officer Henderson!'

I slammed the door behind me.

'...wait, no! He's in a meeting, you can't go in!' Nicola made it halfway out of her seat before I barged through into ACC Drummond's office. 'Officer Henderson!'

It was huge – lined with wood panelling, lots of teak furniture, an expanse of deep-red carpet, picture windows overlooking Camburn Woods. Not a single filing cabinet or whiteboard.

Drummond stood with one hand behind his back, the other holding a large whisky, a golf-course grin frozen on his cadaverous face. 'Is there a problem?'

Nicola stomped to a halt beside me, all rumpled cardigan and scarlet nail polish. 'I'm sorry, sir, he barged past...'

A tall white-haired man in a dark-blue suit was lounging

on Drummond's leather sofa, legs crossed, an avuncular smile on his tanned face, a cut-crystal tumbler of whisky dangling from his fingertips. 'Trouble in the ranks, Gary?'

Colour flushed high on Drummond's cheekbones. 'Peter, this is Detective Constable Henderson. Henderson, this is Lord Forsyth-Leven.'

The man unfolded himself from the sofa, put out his hand for shaking. 'Your friendly local MSP.' The smile faded from his face. 'I heard about your daughter on the radio, I'm dreadfully sorry. If there's anything I can do, please don't hesitate to—'

'You can bugger off.'

His eyes widened. 'Oh...'

Nicola grabbed at my sleeve. 'Officer Henderson, come on, we'll get you a nice cup of—'

'You!' I jabbed a finger at Drummond. 'All this time we've been trying to figure out how the Birthday Boy knows where to send the cards. Turns out the only place you can get all the families' details is the Police National Computer.'

'I'm sorry about this, Peter.' Drummond placed his drink on a coaster, then folded his arms. 'And?'

'You've been getting everyone to do it for you, haven't you? You get PCs and DCs and all the lower ranks to do PNC searches, because you know they won't ask questions.'

A smile tugged at the corner of Drummond's mouth. 'Are you *actually* suggesting that I'm the Birthday Boy?'

Nicola tugged at my sleeve again. 'I'm sorry, sir.' Dropped her voice to a whisper. 'Come *on*, Ash, you're making an arse of yourself.'

'Detective Constable Henderson, I'm hardly likely to run my own PNC searches, am I? Not when I have a station full of dogs to bark for me. For your *information* the Chief Constable and I request these details throughout the year so we can take strategic decisions about resources and deployment on the victims' birthdays; managing the media; providing support services to the families.' He stretched his arms out, as if he was finishing a magic trick. 'This is how intelligence-led policing works. Would you rather we just *guessed*?'

Oh... I cleared my throat. 'I see.'

'Now, if you don't mind, Nicola will see you out. And Professional Standards will be expecting you in their offices first thing tomorrow morning.'

'Ash?'

I looked up from my cold coffee and there was Dr McDonald, standing on the other side of the pub table. She smiled, gave me a little wave, then looked around her. 'This is ... nice.'

'No it isn't.'

The Monk and Casket wasn't a big place: barely enough room for five or six tables and a pair of fruit machines pinging and chattering like Technicolor magpies. Red vinyl upholstery on creaky wooden seats and rock-hard benches. The bar was nearly as sticky as the cracked linoleum floor. One door back out to the outside world, and one on the other side with a faded sign: 'Toilets, Telephone And Function Suite.'

She pulled out a chair and sat. 'DCI Weber said you'd be here.'

I held up my hand. 'Hoy, Hairy: same again and a large white wine.'

Hairy Joe looked up from his *Daily Mirror* and grunted. About a dozen earrings clinked on either side of his broad, furry face as he cranked up the coffee machine.

There were a couple of regulars in: Weird Justin with his long black hair and scabby baseball hat; the Donahue sisters, both of them far too old to be making a living selling blowjobs in darkened doorways; and in the corner, the manky skeletal figure of Twitch and his mate, Fat Billy Partridge.

No one that would want to talk shop with a police officer. Even one like me.

Dr McDonald made scritchy Velcro noises with her Converse

Hi-tops on the tacky floor. 'Is it true you told a Member of the Scottish Parliament to bugger off, and accused ACC Drummond of being the Birthday Boy?'

I stared into the milky scum floating on top of my coffee. 'Welcome to my world…'

She reached across the table and took my hand. 'You did what any good father would do. Katie's lucky: you won't give up till you find her.'

Yeah, because I did such a great job with Rebecca.

'Dickie won't bring Steven Wallace in for questioning.'

'I know.'

'Hoy, lovebirds.' Hairy Joe loomed over the table, mug in one hand, big glass of wine in the other. 'You OK with Pinot Grigio, sweetheart? Only I'm all out of Sauvignon Blanc till Monday. Had a run on it during the footie. You two want to see the menu?'

'Er … no, that's perfect thanks.' She took a sip. 'Mmm…'

He shrugged and lumbered off.

I wrapped my other hand around the fresh, hot coffee. 'What am I supposed to do now?'

'You could go and see Michelle, I mean she's going to be all on her own and worried and scared…?'

Sit in quiet painful silence, trying not to fight.

'I don't—'

My phone blared its harsh old-fashioned ring. 'HENRY' flashed on the screen.

I hit the button. 'Where the hell have you been?'

'None of your business.' A sniff. *'Come on then: all your messages say phone you back, so I'm phoning you back.'*

'He's got Katie. The Birthday Boy's got her.'

Silence.

'Henry?'

'What time is it? Four… I'll be there as soon as I can. The airport's closed with the snow, but I think the ferry's still running.' Clunking noises came from the earpiece. *'Have you told anyone?'*

'Michelle called the police.'

'Thank God for that: it'll make things a lot easier. Get Dr McDonald to fax everything she's got on Katie through to Lerwick police station, mark it for my attention. I'll throw some stuff in a case.'

'Henry—'

'What does Dr McDonald say about Rebecca?'

I turned away from the table. 'She doesn't know.'

'Ash, it doesn't matter any more – you need to tell her. If the Birthday Boy's got Katie, maybe Megan Taylor wasn't number thirteen. Maybe number thirteen is Katie. It's important.'

'I'm not—'

'Ash, they know about Katie – it's over. Tell her.'

38

The sharp smell of vinegar filled the car, the blower's gentle roar keeping the windows from steaming up with chip-shop fug as the rain hammered down.

'...candlelit vigil organized for six-thirty this evening at St Jasper's...'

Dr McDonald frowned. '"St Jasper's" is a weird name for a church, I mean there *isn't* a Saint Jasper, I checked on the Catholic websites, what sort of city names churches after made-up saints?'

The Castle car park was empty, just us and the pay-and-display machine. There wasn't much left of the battlements, or the keep, or the main building, but the ruins were lit up with coloured spotlights. As if that would make them look any better.

'...we spoke to Megan Taylor's father earlier today.'

From up here, on the tip of the sharp granite blade, Oldcastle was spread out like a blanket of stars. Streetlights flickered in the downpour, reflections sparkling back from the twisted black snake of Kings River.

'...want to ask whoever took our daughter to please give her back.' Bruce Taylor sounded as if he was reading it off a bit of paper, the words stilted and unnatural. *'Megan's a wonderful girl who brings hope and joy to everyone that knows her...'*

Dr McDonald broke off another piece of battered fish, blew on it, then popped it in her mouth. Crunching. 'Great batter.' Eating by the glow of the dashboard lights.

'Told you.' Two fish suppers from the Blisterin' Barnacles Chip Shop, one with a couple of pickled onions, the other with mushy peas – microwaved, and served in a Styrofoam cup with a tinfoil lid.

'I'm asking you as a father, please...'

She dipped a chip into the lurid-green mush. 'I spoke to Dickie, he's got the whole church wired with cameras, if the Birthday Boy turns up at St Jasper's we'll get him on film, then Sabir's going to run facial-pattern analysis on all the CCTV footage from the shopping centre when Megan went missing, if he shows up we'll get him.'

'Hmm.' My fish tasted of cobwebs and cardboard.

'...as police continue to hunt for Katie Nicol, daughter of Detective Constable Ash Henderson of Oldcastle CID...'

Even the Irn-Bru was tasteless.

'We'll find her, Ash, we're closer than we've ever been.'

'Katie Nicol is the Birthday Boy's thirteenth victim, and only the second one to receive a card the day after she was kidnapped...'

'Fucking moron.' I switched off the radio. 'It's not a kidnap unless there's a ransom demand. She was abducted...' I stared at my chips, then closed the blue-and-white cardboard container and shoved it back in the plastic bag it'd come from.

'Are you sure you don't want to go to the vigil?'

A gust of wind raked the Renault's bonnet with rain, the droplets sparking off the dirty paintwork, caught in the headlights of a hatchback as it pulled into the car park. Stopped as far away from us as possible.

'Ash, I—'

'Katie used to like it when I told her bedtime stories.'

'OK...'

'Once upon a time there was a paedophile called Philip Skinner. Philip had two kids, and a wife that loved him very much, because she didn't know what he was up to. At that time, a dark plague fell upon the kingdom and three little boys were found in black-plastic bin-bags all over the city. They'd been raped and stabbed, then cut into fifteen pieces. Then he wrapped each individual bit in clingfilm, like he was trying to keep them fresh.'

The other car's lights went out – its driver and passenger turned into silhouettes by the glow reflected back from the castle. They moved closer until their heads were touching.

'The police called in a brave knight called Dr Henry Forrester, and the knight examined the chopped-up little boys and drew up a profile of the monster responsible. The police hunted high and low for someone who fit: they found Philip Skinner. Turned out Skinner had done time in a Belgian prison for aggravated assault and child porn in the Nineties. So they dragged him in for questioning.'

The napkin disintegrated as I wiped the chip grease from my hands. 'But Philip Skinner had a good lawyer who got him out on a technicality. The brave knight was convinced Skinner was guilty and one of the policemen, a big bruiser called Detective Superintendent Len Murray, believed him.'

The other car started rocking on its springs.

'So they recruited a young DI called Henderson, and they watched Skinner whenever they could, taking turns to keep the dirty wee bugger under surveillance. Only they couldn't watch him all the time, and then another little boy turned up, cut into bits and wrapped in clingfilm. So they decided Philip Skinner had to be stopped...'

I took a scoof of Irn-Bru, rolling the fizzy orange chemicals around my mouth. 'Turns out it wasn't Skinner who'd raped and killed and dismembered the little boys, it was a young man called Denis Chakrabarti. Worked as a butcher's assistant at the big Gardner's supermarket in Blackwall Hill. The profile was wrong. He killed two more boys before we finally caught him.'

Dr McDonald tore off another bit of fish. 'What happened to Philip Skinner?'

'You were right about me: I *am* a man of violence. I'm good at it.' I flexed my hands into fists. The knuckles grated – swollen and aching. 'Even with the arthritis. I've beaten the truth out of people, intimidated, lied, stolen, taken money to look the other way, cheated on my wife...' More Irn-Bru. 'When Rebecca.... When she went away we did what parents do – we tramped the streets, we put up posters everywhere from Thurso to Portsmouth, posted a reward, hired private investigators, did radio appeals. Cost a fortune, more than we had, I got into debt... A *lot* of debt.'

I drummed my fingers on the steering wheel, watched the rain make ribbons on the windscreen. 'Things weren't going so well any more. I spent too much time with this journalist called Jennifer: to begin with it was about keeping Rebecca's name in the papers, stop people forgetting, but... Someone told Michelle, and she caught us, kicked me out, got herself a live-in boyfriend who turned the house into a minefield. And that's when they asked me to help keep an eye on Philip Skinner.'

I swigged back the last mouthful of Irn-Bru then crumpled the tin in my hand, knuckles like hot gravel. 'Still think Katie's lucky to have me as a dad?'

The blower grumbled, the rain thrummed on the roof.

Dr McDonald fiddled with her chips. 'Aunty Jan isn't really my aunt, before she was a vet she was a social worker, she looked after me when I got fostered out to this family in Dumfries. I told you my mum wasn't the same after she got back from the hospital... She waited three weeks, then she climbed into a hot bath and slit her wrists, right the way up to the elbows.'

'I'm sorry.'

'I was six. I'd been outside playing with my best friend, Maureen, and I came in because I needed the toilet...' A crease appeared between her eyebrows, two more slashing down from the corners of her mouth. 'The water was so *red*; and my rubber duck was bright, bright yellow; and her skin was enamel white, like the bathtub; and I sat on the lid of the toilet and held her hand till she was gone…'

Outside the car, the wind howled.

I reached across the car and held Dr McDonald's hand. Greasy with chip fat, and a little sticky from the Irn-Bru.

She sniffed, eyes glittering in the dashboard lights.

My phone rang again, tearing the silence into jagged shards. 'Sodding hell…' I pulled it out: Rhona.

'You OK, Guv? Smith the Prick's storming about like someone put Tabasco on his buttplug. Word is: you called him a sheep shagger.'

'Not a good time, Rhona, so—'

'Had to wait till shift-change to do your PNC searches. Your journalist, Talbert, got bottled in a bar fight two years ago, bled out before the ambulance arrived. Harriet Woods's private investigator licence was suspended five years ago, she moved to Dubai and got a job with a private security firm. No idea where she is now. Danny Crawford went missing from Aberdeen eighteen months ago. Ahmed Moghadam is in a secure psychiatric ward in Dundee. And Emilia Schneider's doing eight years in Peterhead for the illegal imprisonment and torture of two Jehovah's Witnesses.'

'What happened to Danny Crawford?'

'No idea…' The sound of two-fingered typing. *'Erm… OK: reported missing by his mother; he'd been off his medication for a fortnight; threatened his parole officer with a kitchen knife; and that's it. No sightings since he got on the train for Inverness a year and a half ago.'*

So Steven Wallace was still the best bet.

'Guv?'

Blink. 'Thanks, Rhona.'

'Are you going to be wanting that bed tonight? You know, after the service: I've still got all your washing…?'

A bed for tonight.

'Hang on a second.' I pressed the mute button. Turned to Dr McDonald. 'Your aunt: she's coming back today, isn't she? You won't be on your own?'

A nod.

I took the phone off mute. 'Sounds good, Rhona.' I smiled at my reflection in the driver's window. 'See you at the church?'

'Cool.'

I hung up. Let the smile slide off my face.

Dr McDonald ate her fish and chips in silence as the rain battered down. She finished, sooked her fingers, wiped them on a napkin, then stuffed the empty box back in the bag with mine. 'That was great, thanks, I mean the fish must be really fresh, good peas too, and is it OK if I borrow your phone for a minute, I need to check what time Aunty Jan's getting back from Glasgow and mine's got no battery left?'

I handed it over. 'Give me the rubbish.'

She passed me the plastic bag.

I lurched out into the rain. There was a bin next to the pay-and-display machine. I ditched the remnants inside, turned up my collar, and sploshed across the car park to Shand Street – with its quaint collection of Victorian teashops, tourist tat, and high-street brands. Two doors down, past Boots and Poundgasm, was a wee off-licence.

I nipped in for a litre of gin, some tonic, two bottles of red wine, and two of white as well. Paid with cash, then headed back to the car, the booze clinking in purple plastic bags.

The other car had stopped rocking. Cigarette smoke curled out of the driver's window.

I dodged the puddles and clambered back in behind the wheel of the Renault. Stuck the bags in behind the seats. Then pulled out one of the whites and held it out to Dr McDonald. 'Here.'

She smiled at me. 'You didn't have to do that, but thanks.' Then gave me back my phone. 'Aunty Jan's already home, so that's great, except I'm going to have to explain why the back door's all scratched.' She cuddled the wine. 'Do you think...' Twiddled with her hair. 'Do you think it was *him*?'

'Put your seatbelt on.' I eased the ancient Renault out of the potholed car park. 'Sheila was right: probably just a junky. Fletcher Road's a prime target – there isn't a house on that whole street that's worth less than a million and a half. And your aunt's got the dogs, right?'

'Who needs Dobermann pinschers when you've got a Staffordshire bull terrier and a wheezy Jack Russell.' She hugged the bottle tighter. 'I'll be fine...'

39

The priest's voice crackled out of speakers bolted to the granite walls: *'Let us pray.'* He held up his hands and the people around me bowed their heads.

St Jasper's was packed, the pews overflowing, people standing in the aisles and at the back, desperate to be part of the public grieving. The church ceiling curved high overhead, grey and ribbed, like being inside a fossilized whale. Spotlights made the stained glass glow in grimy shades of red, blue, and yellow. A miserable bloody place full of fucking ghouls.

'Dear Lord, hear our prayer for Megan Taylor and Katie Henderson…'

Michelle reached over and squeezed my hand, chin on her chest, eyes screwed tight shut as if God wouldn't let us have our daughter back if He caught her peeking.

I stared straight ahead.

Dickie's mob had done a decent job of hiding the security cameras in amongst the twiddly carvings; by the time the prayer shambled to a halt with a communal 'Amen' I'd only managed to spot eight of them. If the bastard was here, they'd have him on film.

The priest fiddled with the white-and-gold scarf draped around his neck, amplified voice all boom and echoes. *'Now we're going to hear from some of Megan's friends. Brianna Fowler has bravely volunteered to go first. Brianna?'*

Sitting on the other side of me, Dr McDonald tugged my sleeve as the chunky girl from the CCTV footage clambered up to the microphone. 'Are you OK?'

'We should be out there looking for her, not in here pissing about wasting time.'

Up on the stage, Brianna cleared her throat and got a whistle of feedback from the speakers. *'Megan was... Megan* is *my best friend...'*

Dr McDonald glanced back over her shoulder. 'Sabir's already running footage through his software: we're not wasting time, we're springing a trap.' A small frown. Then she fidgeted in her seat. 'Are you sure you don't want to say anything?'

I clenched my jaw. 'Trust me, none of these bastards wants to hear what I've got to say.'

The crowd milled out through the huge wooden church doors. Up by the lectern, Dickie shook Bruce Taylor's hand, said something to Megan's mother, then stalked over to where Michelle was sitting.

She hadn't moved since the last hymn, just sat there, sobbing quietly.

Dickie stopped, clasped his hands in front of his groin, as if he was taking part in a penalty shoot out. 'Mrs Henderson, I want you to know that my team is doing everything it can to—'

I poked him in the chest. 'Is Steven Wallace here?'

Dickie blinked. Looked up at me. 'Sorry?'

'I said, is – he – here?'

A sigh. 'We're monitoring everyone.'

Dr McDonald tugged at my sleeve. 'Maybe we should get Michelle out of here, go home, and get a nice cup of tea or something?'

'Dickie: is the bastard here, or isn't he?'

The chief superintendent ran a hand across his eyes. 'Megan's parents invited him. Apparently she loved the radio show, never missed it.'

I stared back towards the entrance. 'I'll see you outside.'

The marble floor clacked beneath my feet.

Halfway down the aisle, a baldy wee man in a corduroy jacket stood and stuck his hand out. Mr It's-Not-Acceptable from Katie's school. 'Constable Henderson, on behalf of everyone at Johnston Academy I want to extend our sincere...'

I kept on walking.

Outside, the rain had turned to drizzle, flaring in the television camera lights: tossers doing pieces to camera, fake sincerity oozing from every word. 'Sensational Steve' Wallace was talking into a Channel 4 microphone, eyebrows pinched, nodding as whoever it was asked him a question. 'Oh yes, there's no doubt in my mind, we *can* get the girls back if we all pull together as a community and dig deep.'

A nod from the woman holding the microphone. 'That's great, we'll probably put it out on the next bulletin. Have you signed the release forms?'

Steven Wallace looked up from the paperwork, saw me, and waved. Then marched over, still wearing his graveside face. 'Constable Henderson, you can't believe how sorry I was to hear about Katie. How's your wife holding up? It must be a terrible shock.'

I stared at him. Didn't shake the proffered hand.

'Yes, right.' He shifted from foot to foot. 'Anyway, look, I thought seeing as how Megan was such a big fan of the show – well, you know I also do the *Sunday Morning Lie-In Lovefest* – how about I dedicate tomorrow's show to her and Katie? I could play their favourite music, maybe get some of their friends to phone in...' He licked his lips. 'Maybe you and your wife would like to come along, around ten-ish? Say a few words to the people, make an appeal to anyone who might have seen something?'

He'll stand in the middle and feed off the grief, knowing it was all him, he did it, he has the power of life and death...

Hit him. Grab the bastard by the throat and tear out his lying tongue, right here on the church steps. Paint the fucking world with his blood.

'Ash?' Dr McDonald. 'Ash, what's happening?'

I blinked. 'Yes, that would be good. We've got to get the message out. Let the Birthday Boy know that we're coming for him.'

Steven Wallace clapped his hands. 'Right, it's settled. Do you know how to get to the station, or shall I get a car to pick you up?'

I smiled at him. 'Oh, don't worry: I'll find you.'

Dr McDonald stood next to me as Steven Wallace hurried off through the drizzle to a waiting taxi. 'Ash?'

The taxi's lights flared in the darkness as it performed an illegal U-turn and headed off down Jessop Street.

'It's not him. Steve Wallace isn't the Birthday Boy.'

'We need to—'

'He didn't push himself into the middle of things, he was invited. He was at that charity cancer thing when Megan Taylor was abducted. It's not him.'

Dr McDonald shifted her red Hi-tops on the wet granite steps. 'Are you sure?'

'We need to look for someone else.' Brought my chin up. 'Katie's still out there.' Laying it on thick.

Dr McDonald looked up at me, little wrinkles at the sides of her eyes, lips pursed. Then she nodded. 'I understand.'

No she didn't. Because if she did, she would have stopped me.

Forty minutes later I pulled up outside Rhona's place – parking down the road a bit, rather than in the designated spaces behind the building. I grabbed the purple carrier-bags from the back of the car – leaving the ones from B&Q behind – and headed on up.

She answered the door wearing jeans and an Oldcastle United sweatshirt, her hair lank and wet.

I passed over the clinking bags. 'You're not *still* supporting those losers, are you?'

'Yeah, yeah.' She hefted the booze. Grinned with her big beige teeth. 'Steak OK for tea? I got some chunky ribeyes, do some chips, bit of sweetcorn?'

Getting low on ice. I chucked a couple of cubes in then added a hefty measure of gin. Then a splash of tonic.

The kitchen door opened and Rhona came back in, a bloom of pink colouring her pale cheeks and nose. I handed the G&T to her.

'Pfffff...' She blinked a couple of times, then took it. Smiled. Knocked back a mouthful. 'Ahhh... Can't remember last time we got hammered. Can you? I can't...'

'Plenty more where that came from.' I picked up my own drink and clinked it against hers. 'Fuck the lot of them.'

'Fuckem!' Another swig. Then a frown. 'Look at the time, got to get the steam on.' Blink. 'I mean steak. Got to get the steak on.' The pink in her cheeks got darker.

'Nah, plenty time...'

Two thick ribeye steaks sizzled in the hot pan, butter foaming up around the edges. The smell of caramelizing meat and roasting black pepper filled the kitchen. Two bottles of red breathed on the worktop.

Rhona leaned back against the sink, sipping her gin and tonic, smiling, eyes focused somewhere about a foot and a half in front of her face. She ran a hand through her hair, making it stick out in little tufts. 'Can't believe ... believe we've spanked half a bottle of gin.'

'Steaks'll need to rest for five minutes.' I tipped them onto a warm plate and poured the pan juices over the top. 'Do you want to check on the chips?'

'Chips? Chips, yes, chips.' She shook her head for a moment. Smiled again, then lurched over to the oven and peered in through the glass door. 'Yup. Those are chips all right.'

I stuck the sweetcorn in the microwave.

'See the thing is ... the thing people don't unnerstand about you is ... is you're a *great* cop.' She held a hand up, as if she was stopping traffic. 'No, I mean it. You're a great cop, and they ... and they're jealous.' Another mouthful of wine. 'They are, they're *jealous*.'

I topped up her glass. 'How's your steak?'

'Is ... It's great too. You're a great cook. I ... people don't get that, but *I* do. I get it...'

'...so I said ... I said, "No, fuck you, you gap-toothed hairy wee bastard." And he ... he burst into tears!' Rhona threw back the last mouthful of wine from her glass and grinned. 'Right there ... right there in the court.' A frown. 'Back inna ... inna minute...'

She levered herself out of the couch and wobbled for a moment, before stomping off stiff-legged to the toilet.

I topped her up again. Then went through to the kitchen and fetched the second bottle of wine.

'No, you gotta ... you gotta listen to this: you'll love this...' She sat on the carpet in front of the stereo, pulling CDs out of the rack and dumping them next to her. 'Where the buggery... Ah, ah – found it! You'll love this...'

The second bottle was already two-thirds gone.

'Here...' She fumbled with the CD case, then wobbled the shiny disk into the machine, one eye squinted shut, the tip of her tongue sticking out the corner of her mouth.

Music swelled from the speakers.

'Listen ... listen, no, listen you'll love it...' Then she started to sing.

'My gates are open wide,
but she stands outside,
consu-ooooooo-oo-oo-oomed by pride...'

She should have sounded like a football crowd bellowing from the terraces, but she didn't. Rhona's voice was soft and lilting, perfectly in tune.

I glugged more wine into her glass.

'No, I *mean* it!' Rhona blinked at me, her left eye not opening all the way, held down by a droopy lid. She ran a pale tongue across her wine-stained lips. Head nodding round on a bobbling circular path. 'You're the ... the only policeman in ... in that place ... worth a shit. A *shit*!'

The last of the red disappeared, except for the dribble that splashed onto her sweatshirt. 'You're a great ... a great ... an' I love you, Ash – no I mean it! I love you...' She threw her arms wide. 'There ... I've said it, I've said it...'

More blinking. Then she peered into her glass. 'All gone.' A jaw-cracking yawn full of teeth. 'Pffffff....' Bink. Blink. Then her eyes stayed closed, chin resting on her chest.

The wine glass wobbled in her hand, and she jerked upright – eyes wide. 'M'wake...'

'No you're not.'

'You've barely touched ... barely touched your wine...'

'You have it.' I took her glass and poured mine into it. 'Not really in the mood.'

Two more sips and her chin was on her chest again, breath slipping into a deep rhythmic drone.

That should do it.

I picked her glass out of her hand and put it on the table. 'Come on, let's get you to bed.'

A warm fuzzy smile spread across her face. 'Yes please...'

* * *

Snoring rocked the walls. Rhona lay spread out like a scarecrow on top of the bedclothes – she'd managed to get the sweatshirt off, exposing a bright-red lacy bra, but the jeans had defeated her. They were bunched around her knees, socks making her feet look twice as long as they were.

I grabbed an ankle and hauled her jeans off, then fought with her pale limbs until she was under the duvet. Went off to the kitchen, came back with a basin and put it by the side of the bed, covered the carpet around it with newspaper. Then slipped out and closed the door.

Checked my watch. Ten to midnight.

Soon be time to pay Mr Steven Wallace a visit and see how sensational the little bastard felt coughing up blood.

40

McDermid Avenue was dead. Parked cars lined the road, tarmac glistening in the streetlight. The houses lay in darkness. Ten past one, and I'd been sitting here long enough for the cold to burrow into my joints, making them ache.

The rain had given up half an hour ago, leaving everything slick and wet. Clouds scudded across the dark sky, stars twinking through the gaps.

Dickie's surveillance team were in an unmarked VW Polo on the other side of the road, about three doors down from Steven Wallace's house. Close enough to keep an eye on the place, far enough away to be inconspicuous. Sort of. The driver's window was open, cigarette smoke curling out into the cold night. Might as well have stuck a big neon arrow on top of the car.

Should've done it properly and parked two hundred yards away, like I had.

The Polo was facing the wrong way to see me climb out into the night.

Christ it was freezing – especially without a jacket. My breath trailed behind me like a pale ghost as I went around to the boot and pulled out the bags from the DIY superstore in Shortstaine.

It's perfectly innocent, Officer: I'm planning on doing a bit of decorating. My house was vandalized and flooded. Nothing suspicious about that, is there? What? Why don't I have the DIY supplies I was seen purchasing at B&Q? Someone must have stolen them from my car when I left it outside Rhona's house. It's not the best of neighbourhoods, after all. I certainly didn't burn them to destroy any trace evidence. And besides: I was with Rhona all night, drinking wine and putting the world to rights. Ask her if you don't believe me.

Not exactly perfect, but it'd do.

I walked away from Steven Wallace's house – even if the surveillance team *had* spotted me, I wasn't going anywhere near their target. I kept walking till I reached a gap between two of the buildings. A dirt footpath led away into Cameron Park. The four surrounding streets were full of them, all sealed off with blue-and-white 'POLICE' tape.

I ducked through onto the path. The low clouds reflected back a dim jaundiced glow, just enough light to keep me from stepping in anything as I pulled on a set of dark-grey decorator's overalls. Would've gone for a white Tyvek SOC-style all-in-one suit, but it wouldn't exactly have blended in on a dark night. Next: plastic overshoes on over my boots. I tucked my hair into a shower cap – the thin plastic kind that looked like a condom, given away free in hotel-room bathrooms – then hauled on a dark-blue woolly hat, safety goggles, and a face mask. Nitrile gloves over my leather ones.

The Scenes Examination Branch might not bother collecting DNA when a wee shite like Noah McCarthy got a beating, but by the time they found what was left of Steve Wallace... Well, that would be another matter.

I stuffed all the plastic packaging back in the bag, scrunched it up and put it in my pocket. Then walked down between the buildings, past the brick-walled back gardens, under another strand of 'POLICE' tape, and out into Cameron Park.

One of the SOC tents glowed in the distance, nearly obscured by bushes and trees. No chance anyone would see me. I picked my way along a track that ran along the back of the gardens – sticking close to the eight-foot-high wall – until I could see the ridiculously massive conservatory stuck onto Steve Wallace's house.

A tall wooden gate was set into the brick, tendrils of ivy snaking around it. I tried the handle: locked. Fair enough. I scrambled over the wall and dropped down into the garden.

Silence.

For a minute I just stood there, not moving, scanning the backs of the houses for twitching curtains...

Nothing.

I started towards the conservatory and a security light seared the garden with eye-watering brightness. I kept on walking. That's the thing about security lights – by the time the owners notice you've set one off, you can be right up against the house. They look out, see nothing, curse next door's cat, and go back to bed.

Click. The garden plunged into darkness again.

No sign of an alarm box on the back of the house, but that didn't mean the place wasn't wired. A couple of planters sat by the conservatory double doors. I looked underneath both. No spare key. Ah well – worth a try.

One brand-new flat-head screwdriver and three sharp taps from a brand-new hammer, and the door lock was buggered enough for me to twist the mechanism. Clunk.

I opened the door and stepped inside.

No screaming alarm. No flashing lights. No irate householder.

That'd change.

'Say cheese.' I raised the camera, let the autofocus whirr, then pressed the button. The flash turned the wine cellar monochrome for a moment, then everything faded back into gloom.

Steven Wallace blinked at me, breath hissing through his

nose, tears streaming down his cheeks, mumbling words behind the duct-tape gag.

The cellar was a good size – probably bigger than the whole ground floor of my ruined house – lined with wooden shelves, piled high with wine.

'Where is she, Steve?'

He wriggled, but the cable-ties didn't budge – holding him tight to the wooden dining chair, rumpling his silk pyjamas. The bruise on his cheek was beginning to darken.

I turned, ran my hands across the rack of bottles. 'It's here, isn't it? Your secret torture chamber? Hidden away…' I hauled at the shelving and bottles crashed to the flagstone floor, red white and rosé shattering, soaking Steve's slippers.

A muffled shriek. Then nervous giggling.

'Oh, you think this is *funny*, do you?'

He shook his head.

'Where is she?'

More mumbling.

I yanked another set of shelves off the wall. Still no sign of a hidden door.

'WHERE IS SHE?'

He closed his eyes and trembled. I slapped him.

'Look at me, you little shite!'

He turned his head away, so I slapped him again.

'LOOK AT ME!'

He did what he was told. 'Mmmmmmphnph…'

'You see what I'm wearing, Steve? The mask, the goggles, the outfit? They're not so you won't recognize me: they're so I don't leave any forensic evidence behind when I carve you into little fucking bits.'

I pulled a birthday card from my pocket – Rebecca, the number five scratched into the top-left corner – and held it under Steven Wallace's nose. Let him drink it in. 'Look familiar? Helpless, tied to a chair in a basement, gagged, terrified?'

I cleared a shelf of Rioja with a sweep of one hand, then reached into the B&Q carrier-bag.

'You're already dead, Steve.' I pulled a pair of pliers out and placed them on the shelf, then a claw-hammer, braddle, Stanley knife, heavy-duty scissors, and a little blowtorch. 'Tell me where she is and I'll make it relatively quick.'

'Mmmmph... MMMPHNPH!'

I smiled at him. 'What, you think I'm going to use *these* to make you talk?' The pliers felt nice and solid in my hand – I snapped the jaws half an inch from his left eye. 'Where is she?'

'Mmmmmmph! Mnnnphnmmph!'

'WHERE IS SHE?' A shelf full of burgundy exploded on the flagstones.

'MMMNNNPH!' The sharp tang of fresh urine joined the heady tannin stench of red wine.

'She's near, isn't she? When you had this place renovated, you got them to put in a secret room, didn't you? Somewhere you could take people's daughters. Where is she?'

'Mmmnphnnnmmmnnn...'

I grabbed a corner of the duct tape and pulled.

'Aaaaaargh... God... I don't ... I don't know. I don't, I *swear*.'

I put the pliers back on the shelf. 'Wrong answer.'

'HELP ME! SOMEONE! PLEASE DEAR GOD HELP ME! HELP—'

I slammed my elbow into the murdering bastard's face, catching him above the left eye. A nice solid smack. His head snapped back, thumping into the wine rack behind him, making the bottles clatter against each other. Got to hand it to Andy Inglis: when it came to beating the shit out of people, he knew his stuff.

'Where is she?'

Steven Wallace blinked a couple of times, I grabbed his hair and forced the bastard's head back, staring into his eyes. Dilated pupils.

'I didn't do it... I don't know anything...'

'What are you on: amphetamines, ecstasy, cocaine? Smoke a few joints before bedtime?' The skin above his eye was already starting to swell up. 'Nah, it's coke, isn't it? Nothing else is showbiz enough for a prick like you.'

I dragged him and his chair into the middle of the room. Put a foot on his chest and pushed. The chair tipped over, crashed to the floor amongst the broken bottles, pinning his arms underneath him.

A grunt.

'Don't go anywhere.'

I was back two minutes later with a couple of hand towels.

Only took three kicks to get the cellar door off its hinges. I carried it over to one of the wine racks and propped the top end up on the second shelf from the bottom, then hauled Wallace and his chair on top of the door – still flat on his back, feet up, head down.

'Where is she?'

'You can't do this to me, I *know* people!'

'Pliers and blowtorches are for amateurs, Steve. The field of torture has come on leaps and bounds since the Spanish Inquisition.'

I pulled one of the bottles from the rack. An '84 Bordeaux. No idea if it was any good or not. Didn't really matter. I smashed the neck against the wall: red splashed across the bare stone.

'Where is she?'

'They're gonna find you and they're gonna pay *you* a visit.'

'Grow up.'

'Gonna cut your cock off and make you eat it!'

'You've got nice towels in that spare bathroom. Very soft and fluffy. Very absorbent.' I draped one over his mouth, then upended the wine into the towel, saturating it. Then another bottle. I put my foot on his forehead, pressing down hard enough to stop him moving his head. Poured more Bordeaux over his mouth and up his nose, filling his sinuses. He shuddered in the chair, knees and shoulders jerking, making muffled screams through the sodden fabric.

I pulled the towel off his face. He spluttered and retched.

Dirty murdering little fuck.

'Where is she?'

'Gahhh... Jesus... SOMEBODY HELP ME!' Eyes blinking, red wine running down his face and onto the tilted door. 'HELP ME!'

Pliers were old hat, but waterboarding was a different matter. Thank you ACC Drummond for the suggestion.

'Basement wine cellar, remember? No one can hear you. But that's why you had it built, isn't it?'

I flipped the wet towel back over his mouth, picked a '96 Pinot Noir, and stood on his forehead again. 'Where is she?'

'Mmmmphmmnnnnphpnnnn!'

'Glug, glug, glug.' I emptied the contents over his face.

More struggling, more screaming.

Someone once told me that the CIA's best covert operatives – the ones specially trained to resist torture – can put up with this for about fourteen seconds. The trachea, larynx, sinuses, and throat all fill up with liquid and the body goes apeshit. The brain's not in control any more. Panic, gag reflex, terror. Of course the lungs are above the high-tide mark, but the body doesn't care. Help me, I'm drowning, I'm *dying*.

I dropped the empty bottle.

Wallace's eyes were wide open, tinged with pink and wet with red wine. His whole body shook as if he was having a fit, the wet towel sagging into his open mouth as he gasped for air that wasn't there.

Bet no one in Guantanamo Bay got waterboarded with a '96 Pinot Noir.

I flipped the towel away.

He kept shaking, jerking against his restraints. I tipped the chair over onto its side.

Red wine gushed out of him, a deep sucking breath, then a spray of vomit onto the broken glass. I let him heave until there was nothing left but bile.

'You having fun yet, *Sensational* Steve? Cause you've got what ... two, three thousand bottles down here? We can do this all night.'

'I don't... I don't know where she is. I swear! If I did, I'd tell you! I don't know: I never touched her... Please...' He closed his eyes, banged his head against the wet door. 'Please, I didn't touch her...'

'Don't believe you.'

'I didn't touch her, I didn't!'

'Prove it: where were you Friday night?'

'Dundee. I was in Dundee... I was in Dundee doing a leukaemia thing...'

I shoved him over onto his back again and pulled another bottle from the shelves. 'How does a Lengs & Cooter reserve shiraz sound to you – 2001's a good vintage to drown in, isn't it?' The glass neck shattered against the wall and Wallace screamed.

'God, *please*... I was with my boyfriend! I was with my boyfriend! I was in Dundee with my boyfriend...' Wallace screwed his eyes tight shut. 'He's married. I didn't touch your daughter, I swear!'

I stuck the towel back over his mouth and rested my boot on his head. 'Let's double check that, shall we?'

Cue muffled screaming.

I pulled out Steven Wallace's mobile phone, found his boyfriend's name in the list, and pushed the button with my gloved finger.

It rang. And rang. And rang. And then a man's voice, throaty and muzzy. '*What... Hello? Steve? God...*' Rustling. The clunk of a door being shut. '*Jesus, Steve, it's two in the morning: Julia was right there in bed with me... Steve? Hello?*'

I put on an English accent, hamming up the Mockney: asked him where he was last night. Told him I'd send photos to his wife if he didn't tell the truth.

Then swore and hung up.

Looked down at Steven Wallace's shivering sobbing body.

Ah…

I rolled up the overalls and dropped them into the flames. Held my hands out and absorbed the heat. Oldcastle Industrial Estate was a bit of a shithole, but at quarter to three on a Sunday morning it was perfect for a little tidying up. Boxy warehouses were locked away behind chain-link fences, streetlights standing guard over deserted cul-de-sacs.

The old Belbin's cash-and-carry was boarded up, its car park littered with plastic bags, leaves, and assorted crap: the charred skeletal remains of a burnt-out Ford Fiesta; a trailer with a broken axle – the wheels sticking out at sixty degrees to the vertical; a little pile of buckled shopping trolleys, mattresses, and bin-bags.

And an oil-drum brazier.

I tossed the hammer and screwdriver in with the overalls, then dropped the woolly hat and shower cap on top. Pulled out Steven Wallace's mobile phone and dumped that into the flames too. Watched the whole lot burn.

Katie…

No going back now.

Sunday 20th November

41

'And then she threw up all over Sergeant Roberts' back, right there in the briefing room.' Charlie wiggled his hips, twisted his shoulders from side to side, and lowered his head. 'And it's this for a birdie...'

Plink. The golf ball trundled across the carpet tiles, then up into the little horseshoe-shaped thing with a hole in it, sitting on the floor by the far wall. He held the putter above his head and made fake crowd noises. 'And it's in! The young officer from Oldcastle is *romping* home at Gleneagles today.'

He handed me the club, then settled into his office chair and ran a hand across his head, making sure the dyed brown comb-over was still in place. A splodge of what looked like brown sauce stained the breast pocket of his white shirt, black uniform jacket hanging over the back of his seat, its superintendent's epaulettes in need of a good clean.

The horseshoe thing spat the ball out again.

Charlie stuck out a finger and traced an invisible path around the cluttered office. 'It's a par three with a dogleg around the wastepaper basket.' Another mouthful of bacon buttie.

Outside the tiny office window, the station car park was nearly empty. The occasional sweep of headlights broke the gloom, illuminating a high brick wall topped with razor wire. Twenty past seven: the sun wouldn't be up for nearly an hour yet.

I rolled the ball onto the tee – a Tennent's Lager beer mat – and lined up the shot. Nice and casual. Nothing out of the ordinary here... 'Well, Rhona did get a bit bladdered last night.'

'You know I'm supposed to give you a kicking, don't you?'

'Yup.'

Plink. The ball rolled under the desk and bounced off the skirting board.

'Oh, good shot. Can we take the bollocking as read, then? I really can't be arsed, and you're not going to give a toss anyway.'

'Yup.' I lined up the next shot. 'Any progress on the door-to-doors?'

'But come on, Ash: the Assistant Chief Constable? Could you not have picked a bigger toss-pot to accuse of being the Birthday Boy?'

Plink... The ball clanged into the wastepaper basket.

'And telling our beloved MSP to bugger off? Really?'

'Lucky I didn't knee the greasy little bastard in the balls. So: door-to-doors?'

'They not talking to you, eh? Join the club – no one tells us poor sods in Professional Standards anything. I have to guess what the soup is most days.'

'No one likes a clype.'

Charlie checked his comb-over again. 'Ash, I'm really sorry about Katie.'

'I need to be in on the investigation.'

'It's such a horrible thing...' Sigh.

'I need to know what's happening.'

'This isn't the movies, Ash: you can't get twenty-four hours to crack the case – not with the media camped out on our doorstep. You should be at home with Michelle... Everyone's doing their best.'

Plink. Bloody ball went wide, ended up in the gap between the filing cabinets and the visitor's chair.

I tightened my grip on the club, knuckles going white. 'So I'm out.' Not exactly a surprise, but still... 'He's got my *daughter*.'

'I know, Ash, I know.' Charlie pulled a sheet of paper from his pending-tray and held it out. 'I'm sorry. The ACC wants you taken off active duty for the duration of the investigation, and the Chief Constable agrees.'

'Suspended.'

'With pay.'

As if that bloody mattered.

He looked down at the makeshift office golf course, the piles of paperwork on his desk, the remains of his bacon buttie – everywhere but at me. 'I'm truly sorry, Ash. But we don't have any choice.'

The CID office printer groaned and creaked in the corner churning out reams of reports. The only other noise was the clink and thump of me hurling the contents of my desk drawers into a cardboard box.

'Are you OK?' Dr McDonald sidled in from the corridor outside. Her hair was different: flatter, and darker too. The usually stripy grey top had been replaced with a black long-sleeved one with a red and black striped T-shirt over the top. A cross hung around her neck on what looked like a string of rosary beads. Black jeans. But the shoes were still bright-red Converse Hi-tops, the toecaps unnaturally white. What, did she put on a new pair every morning?

I dumped a stapler and a two-hole punch in with the assorted crap. 'Everyone fucked off soon as I produced the cardboard box.'

'More honour among thieves than police officers?'

'Suspended till the investigation's over. Eight years and they've got nowhere. Eight *years*...' I jammed the desk tidy in on top of all the half-used pads of Post-it notes. 'Her birthday's tomorrow.'

'Maybe we don't need a warrant to question Steven Wallace, maybe we could—'

'I told you last night: it's not Steven Wallace.' A knot of black cables, attached to a variety of plugs, lurked at the back of the bottom drawer – rechargers for phones I hadn't had for years. I packed them anyway. 'He's got an alibi.'

She perched herself on the edge of a desk, little red shoes dangling two feet above the carpet tiles. 'We need to work out why he's targeted Katie, I mean perhaps Henry was wrong and the Birthday Boy didn't take someone else before Megan Taylor, perhaps *Katie's* number thirteen... Unless he really did take a year off, which would make her number twelve...' A crease formed between her eyebrows. She stared at her hands, clasped in her lap. 'I'm sorry, I'm *trying* to help, but I know I can be a bit—'

'It's not your fault.'

'I didn't mean to talk about her like she was just another victim, she's your daughter and—'

'Doesn't matter.' I rammed a handful of old notebooks in on top of the cables. 'Anything that helps get her back.'

'OK.' A nod. 'Henry's ferry got in half an hour ago – he wants to meet us at the burial ... at Cameron Park.'

I stared into the box. All that time, and what did I have to show for it? No house, a shitty little Renault, and a cardboard box full of crap. 'I'm not on the case any more.'

'Are you going to let that stop you?'

Was I hell.

A queasy groan came from the door. 'Never, *ever* again...' Rhona – pale as a mealie pudding, with the skin texture to match. She leaned against the door frame. 'I'm dying...'

'Then go home and lie down.' I dumped the last of my stuff in the box.

'No chance. Katie's birthday's tomorrow – I'm not going

anywhere till we find her.' Rhona slumped into the nearest chair, covered her face with her hands. 'Oh God…'

'Anyway,' Dr McDonald swung her little red feet, 'we should probably get going, Henry won't be—'

'Hold on a minute, Princess.' Rhona surfaced from behind her fingers. 'What's with the new look?'

'Do you like it, I had a bit of an accident in the shower this morning: grabbed Aunty Jan's hair-product stuff and it went all straight, but I think it—'

'Yeah, and the clothes – they an accident too? You really think you can replace Katie by dying your hair and nicking her clothes?' Rhona curled her top lip. 'You're fucking sick.'

I blinked. Frowned. Stared at Dr McDonald. The hair, the clothes, she did look—

'I'm not replacing her: I'm trying to get into her head, I mean when I saw what had happened to my hair, I thought, OK, let's go for it, sometimes it helps me piece together connections and points of contact, and don't you think we should be doing everything we can to—'

'God, enough!' Rhona buried her head in her hands again. 'Do you *never* stop talking?'

I picked up my box and headed for the door.

Dr McDonald hopped down from the desk and pattered out ahead of me. 'I think your friend might be a little hungover.'

No wonder she came top of her class.

I slammed the CID office door behind me.

I parked the Renault on McDermid Avenue – opposite the alleyway I'd used last night to get into Cameron Park – clambered out into the gloomy twilight and marched over. Ducked under the 'POLICE' tape. You found my DNA, Officer? Well, of course I was there: five to eight on Sunday morning, with Dr Alice McDonald. Saturday night? No, you must be thinking of someone else…

Dr McDonald padded along beside me. 'Brrr, it's cold, isn't it cold, I'm cold.'

Cameron Park was a monochrome blur, disappearing into the mist. The SOC tent from last night shone like a lighthouse in the gloom. Dew dripped from jagged trees and drooping bushes. We followed the path, then cut across to the entrance.

Henry's ancient Volvo estate was parked on the grass outside – Sheba had curled up in the back next to a suitcase and a couple of file boxes, twitching, her grey muzzle resting on her paws.

A voice behind me: 'She's not well...'

I turned and there was Henry.

He nodded at the steaming mug in his hand. 'Before you ask, it's just coffee.'

Dr McDonald stood on her tiptoes and kissed him on the stubbled cheek. 'Thanks for coming, I—'

'We need to talk about the order of victims.'

She stepped back. Nodded. Then wrapped an arm around herself. 'Well, it really depends on whether or not the Birthday Boy took a year off, and—'

'He didn't.' Henry took a sip of coffee. The mug trembled in his hand. 'I know for certain there was a victim five years ago, but the parents didn't come forward.'

She stared at him, head on one side. 'How do you know they—'

'The father told me.' He gazed off into the mist. 'They don't want to be involved.'

'That makes Katie number thirteen, she's the one he's been building up to.'

'Fuck...' I sat on the bonnet of Henry's car. Cold leached through my trousers.

He smiled at Dr McDonald. 'You look frozen, Alice. Why don't you nip in and get yourself a mug of tea? Maybe see if they've got a detailed map of the area while you're there?'

She backed up a step. Looked from Henry, to me, and back

again. Then nodded. 'OK.' Her red Hi-tops squeaked through the damp grass as she disappeared into the SOC tent.

The only sound was the diesel generators powering the spotlights inside.

'Thanks for coming, Henry.'

'You have to tell her.'

'I don't want—'

'Ash, she needs to know. She's not playing with a full deck and you won't let her see all the cards.'

'No.'

He put a hand on my shoulder. 'I spoke to Dickie – they put you on compassionate leave. It doesn't matter any more.'

'It matters to me!'

'Why? For God's sake, Ash, you're—'

'Because it's *mine*. OK? That's why.' I pushed away from the car, hands curled into aching fists. 'It's been mine for four years. Rebecca's not public property, she's my daughter. I'm not having bastards picking her life apart and telling me she's *dead...*'

Henry's voice was barely audible. 'I'm sorry, Ash, but Rebecca—'

'She's not dead. Not until I get that card...'

A glow spread through the mist, peach and gold and blood red. The sun must have made it up over the hills.

I stared down at my fists. 'And yes: I know what that sounds like. I've never...' Deep breath. 'It's mine.'

Dr McDonald emerged from the SOC tent, something tucked under her arm and a steaming mug in both hands. 'Ash, did you want coffee, because I've got you a coffee and there's doughnuts but they look a bit stale so I didn't bother, unless you want me to go back...?' She handed me a mug. 'Got the map too.'

Henry spread it out on the Volvo's bonnet. It was fairly high detail, big enough to take in the park and the surrounding streets. Someone had marked the burial sites – a red 'X' for each girl recovered. 'Right: if he cared about the bodies he'd keep them close.'

Off in the distance, the sound of a car engine and crunching gravel came through the mist. Getting louder.

She leaned on the bonnet. 'But he doesn't. Given the deposition sites, it looks as if he's simply throwing them away.'

'Exactly. So he's not going to want to carry them too far…' Henry produced a pencil. 'Have you done any geographical profiling? These days it's all computers and statistical analysis, but we used to do it with brainpower.'

A battered Astra pulled up on the other side of the SEB Transit. Dickie clambered out of the driver's seat, a smile putting extra wrinkles in his cheeks. 'Henry! Henry Forrester, you old sod, they said you were here, but I didn't…' He stared at me. 'Ash.'

I stared back. 'Dickie.'

Dr McDonald smiled. 'Isn't it great: Henry's agreed to assist the investigation.'

Dickie didn't even look at her. 'Yeah, that's great. Ash, you can't be here.'

'She's my daughter.'

'I *know* she's… Look, you're on compassionate leave: I promise we'll keep you up to date, but you – can't – be – here.'

I took a step towards him. 'Her birthday's tomorrow, do you *really* think I'm—'

'Don't make me get someone to escort you home, Ash.' He closed his eyes, rubbed at his forehead. 'Please.'

Sun sliced through the clouds, sparkling back from the wet streets as I creaked the Renault onto Rowan Drive. Weber must've pulled a few strings, because there was a police cordon cutting off the road a good hundred feet from the house, keeping the journalist scumbags at a reasonable distance. Giving Michelle some privacy.

I pulled into the kerb, behind a BBC outside broadcast van.

Should really drive down there and see how she's coping. Give her some support. Lie to her and pretend this isn't what happened to Rebecca…

Maybe Henry was right: maybe it didn't matter any more. They'd booted me off the investigation anyway, who cared if everyone found out?

The steering wheel was cold in my hands, the plastic coating creaking as I squeezed.

I cared.

Blink.

Why couldn't it have been Steven Wallace?

Blink.

I screwed my eyes closed and squeezed the steering wheel till my arms trembled.

My phone rang, the noise too loud in the quiet car. I pulled it out – 'NUMBER WITHHELD'.

'Who is this?'

'Ash, you old bastardo…' Andy Inglis, Mrs Kerrigan's boss. He cleared his throat, then dropped his voice to something less cheery. *'I heard about your daughter, I'm really sorry.'*

The driver's window was cool against my forehead. 'So am I.'

'Look, I was gonnae give you a call, give you the usual "If there's anything I can do," bollocks, then I thought: why not lend a hand instead? Put out some feelers for you.' I could almost hear him grinning. *'So I did. And guess what: man I know says another girl went missing a couple of months ago: got a card and everything. Her parents said fuck all about it, 'cos her boyfriend's connected, you know?'*

A couple of months ago: the twelfth victim. The one before Megan Taylor.

Nothing that would help me find Katie before tomorrow. 'I … appreciate the effort, but it's—'

'The boyfriend said he saw the bastard.'

I sat up straight. 'He *what?*'

'*Said he was there when she was lifted. Wasn't meant to be, but he was. Saw everything.*'

'And he didn't tell anyone? How could he not—'

'*His dad's allergic to police officers. Now: you got a pen for the address?*'

I pulled out my notebook. 'What's it going to cost?'

'*Fuck all. Public-spirited citizen, that's me. Make sure the bastard gets what's comin' to him.*'

42

'…and that was … that was Coldplay and "Fix You".' A cough rattled out of the car radio. *'Sorry folks, had a bit of a rough one last night.'* A shuddering sigh. *'Right, OK: you're listening to* Sensational Steve's Sunday Morning Lie-In Lovefest *and … and now here's another of Megan Taylor's favourite songs…'*

The fields and little towns raced by as I hammered down the M74 – accelerator flat to the Renault's filthy carpet, phone to my ear, swearing as the other end rang and rang and rang. Then put me through to voicemail again.

'Henry, for fuck's sake: answer your bloody phone!'

I hung up and tried again, for the fourth time in twenty miles.

Lockerbie was a blur in the rear-view mirror when I finally gave up on Henry and tried Dr McDonald instead. She picked up first time.

'Ash, are you OK, I mean I know you're not OK, with everything happening and now you can't be on the team and I'm … we're worried about you.'

'When does he kill them?'

'On their birthdays, is there—'

'No: does he kill them in the morning, in the evening, lunchtime, when?'

'I don't… It's hard to tell, there's nothing in the photographs to give us time of day, it's all indoors under artificial light, so—'

'If you were him, when would you do it?'

I swung over into the outside lane and roared past a coach full of ugly children.

'I don't think that's a healthy thing to focus on, if we—'

'When – does – he – kill – them?'

A sigh. *'It's impossible to tell, I mean I* think *it's important to kill them on their actual birthday, and Professor Twining said it took Lauren six or seven hours to die, so he can't have started later than six o'clock… I think he works, so he can't start torturing them before he goes off in the morning in case something happens and they die while he's not there, so it's after work.'*

'That means we've got till five o'clock tomorrow.' I checked my watch. 'Thirty hours till he… Till Katie.'

There was silence on the other end of the phone.

'What?'

'Or he might have taken Monday as a holiday so he can spend the whole day on—'

'Don't, OK? Just … don't.' I scowled at the dual carriageway. 'Is Henry there?'

'He's with the SEB search team, he worked up probable deposition sites for the other victims from the map, he's very good, Ash, I mean he's scarily *good.'*

One step closer to them finding Rebecca…

'Call me soon as he gets back.'

'Hello? Hello? Can you hear me?'

'I hate these things…' Henry cleared his throat. *'You're sure no one can hear us?'*

'Henry it stinks *in here.'*

'Sheba can't help that. Wind the window down if it bothers you that much.'

Nearly a quarter-tank of petrol left, still a bit to go before I had to stop. 'Will you two shut up? There's another victim.'

'What?'

'A couple of months ago, a girl in Bath: the family got a card but they hushed it up.'

Someone whistled.

Dr McDonald: *'You know what this means, it means Katie's not number thirteen, she's number fourteen.'*

A pause.

Henry's voice was barely audible over the engine's roar. *'I was wrong.'* A deep breath. *'I was wrong, Ash. He's not been building up to his thirteenth victim. It's not going to stop...'*

'Ash, if Katie's number fourteen then he's escalating: one a year for seven years, then two the next year, another two last year, and now three, that means there's going to be more of them, soon.'

'He's escalating...'

'How does that help us find Katie?'

Dr McDonald got even faster than usual. *'Ash, he can't keep this up, he's operating at full stretch, running from victim to victim, and we should issue a statement telling everyone who's got a daughter coming up to her thirteenth birthday to keep her under lock and key.'*

'There'll be a panic.'

'What else can we do, Henry, he's one step away from going on a spree, we can't not *tell people, what if it was your daughter?'*

'Hrrmph. My daughter can't wait for me to drop dead so she and her husband can get their hands on my money. Apparently I'm "a selfish old man drinking her inheritance"...' A sniff. *'I'm sorry, Ash. I got it wrong.'*

A fluorescent-yellow speed camera wheeched by, the flash going off as I overtook a mini. 'The victim's boyfriend said he saw the Birthday Boy.'

Dr McDonald sounded as if she was bouncing up and down in her seat. *'Ash, that's* great, *we'll get Dickie onto Avon and Somerset Police, get them to take a description and—'*

'No: no police. The boyfriend wouldn't talk to them anyway. I'm on my way there now.'

'But—'

'No police!' I hung up and jammed the phone back into my pocket.

One hundred and seventy miles to go.

I clambered out of the car, groaned, then tried to rub some life back into my spine. Twenty past three. Seven hours from Oldcastle all the way to Bath. Got pulled over outside Carlisle for doing ninety, but once they'd checked my warrant card, that was it: I'm sorry to hear about your daughter. Do you want us to escort you down the road a bit, blues-and-twos all the way?

They had to give up at junction 37, but at least it was something.

Of course, I could have flown into Bristol and saved myself three hours, but airport security tended to get a bit twitchy when you tried to take a gun onboard.

I pulled out my notebook and double-checked the address I'd got from Andy Inglis. This was it: number twenty-six, a third of the way along a narrow street of terraced houses. Green and brown streaks made dirty shadows under the guttering. Dirty, rust-coloured pantiles, small gardens, the pavements solid with down-at-heel Hondas, Fords, and Citroëns.

Not the fanciest bit of Bath by a long shot.

I squeezed the Renault in behind a van and climbed out into the afternoon. It was a damn sight warmer down here than back home, and it wasn't raining either.

The wooden gate creaked as I pushed through into the garden. Football blared out from a TV somewhere inside: the crowd roaring, the commentator sounding as if he was about to wet himself with excitement.

I rang the bell.

A muffled voice: 'OK, OK, I'm coming... Jesus... Couldn't wait till half-time, could you.' A little man with a big nose and curly hair opened the door. He wasn't smiling. 'Better not be one of them bloody born-again tossers.'

I stared at him.

He fidgeted with the buttons on his polo shirt. 'What?'

'You didn't go to the police.'

He shuffled an inch backwards, licked his lips, started to ease the door shut. 'I didn't. I said I wouldn't and I didn't...' He looked down to where my foot was jammed in the door, stopping it going any further. '*Honestly*: we didn't say anything.'

I took out my warrant card and held it up for him. 'Why?'

His mouth fell open, and then he sniffed. 'I'm very busy, so if you'll *excuse* me...'

A woman's voice came from the hall behind him. 'Ron? Is it Mrs Mahajan? I've got her casserole dish.'

Ron glanced back into the house. 'I'll take care of it, you go back to the kitchen.'

'Ron?'

'I said I'd take care of it!' He squared his shoulders, still peering around the door. 'You've got no right coming round here, harassing us. Nothing happened, I've got nothing to say, now go away.'

'The bastard got your daughter, didn't he: the Birthday Boy?'

His jaw clenched. 'Nothing happened, now please—'

'I know how you feel.'

He slammed a fist into his own chest. 'You know *nothing* about how I feel.'

'He took my daughter.'

'Ron? What's going on?'

I dug back into my wallet and came out with a photo – Katie dressed in funeral black with a huge smile on her face. Heading off to see Green Day at the Aberdeen Exhibition and

Conference Centre. Her first big gig. 'She went missing Friday night. We got the card on Saturday.'

He blushed, then lowered his head. Stared at his shoes. 'I'm sorry, but I don't know what you're talking about. Now you have to go.'

I reached in, took a handful of his shirt, and pulled, banging his forehead off the door. 'Pin back your lugs, you little shite: he's got my daughter, her birthday's *tomorrow*, and I will tear your fucking head off if I think it's going to help me find her. Are we crystal clear on that?'

'Ron?'

'They made me promise...'

We sat in the lounge while Ellie Chadwick poured tea from a red teapot. She was a slight woman in a pair of bright green jeans and a pink fluffy jumper. Her hair was tucked behind her ears, the fringe spirit-level straight; wearing enough makeup to get a job on the counter at Debenhams. Couldn't have been a day over thirty.

Ron sat on the other side of the coffee table, scowling at a slice of Battenberg. 'We *promised*.'

She put down the teapot and picked up the photo of Katie. '*You* promised, Ronald Chadwick, not me.' Ellie traced Katie's hair with a finger. 'Your daughter's pretty.'

'She's a pain in the arse ... but she's mine.'

'Our Brenda was the same. Always getting into trouble.' Ellie turned, opened a drawer in the TV unit and pulled out a small photo album. Flipped to a page near the end, then placed it on the table in front of me. A young girl with glasses, and hair like her mum's, grinned up at me from a funfair somewhere – the carousel horses out of focus behind her. She had one arm around a thin boy with floppy blond hair and a big gap between his front teeth.

I pointed at the picture. 'This the boyfriend?'

'Dawson Whitaker. He lives over in Newbridge – it's

probably the poshest bit of Bath, you should see the houses... To start with we thought she'd done really well for herself, his family's loaded, but—'

'Ellie, that's *enough*!' Ron banged his hand on the table, making the crockery rattle.

'Oh shut it, Ron. Christ... You're just like my mother.'

'You got any idea what that bastard'll do to us if he hears we've been talking to the cops?'

'I don't care, Ron, OK? I'm sick of it: I'm sick of being scared all the time. I'm sick of hiding Brenda's pictures and pretending she doesn't exist. She was our *daughter*.' Ellie took the album back, then slipped the funfair photo out from behind the clear plastic sheeting and handed it to me. 'She disappeared four days before her birthday. Then that ... *card* arrived, and it was exactly like the ones in the papers...'

Ron scowled. 'Ellie, I'm warning you...'

She took a deep breath. 'That's what he does, isn't it? He tortures them, and he kills them, then he sends you these sick birthday cards.'

'Have you still got it?'

Ron snorted. 'Have we still got it?'

Ellie shook her head. 'Dawson's dad took the card when he came over. The only time we've ever met him. He said if we told anyone about what happened, if we got the police involved, someone would burn our house down with us in it.'

Ron picked the marzipan off his Battenberg. 'Don't forget the rape first, that's the *best* fucking bit.'

'He was only trying to scare us.'

'He did a bloody good job then, didn't he? He's a drug dealer, Ellie, he kills people all the time. It's what they do.' Ron wadded his marzipan into a ragged ball. 'I don't want to be raped...'

The school was a fancy collection of sandstone buildings on the southern outskirts of Bath, with a coat of arms mounted above the gates and a lodge house. Windows like a cathedral, crenellations, and ten or twelve acres of sweeping parkland, all hidden behind an eight-foot-high wall. Very imposing. Very exclusive. And very expensive.

Dawson Whitaker's dad must have been shifting a hell of a lot of drugs.

I parked my crappy Renault behind a line of Range Rovers and BMW four-by-fours, none of which looked as if they'd ever seen so much as a muddy puddle. A rugby pitch was laid out in the grounds, and a group of about thirty kids sprinted up and down, passing the ball back and forth every time a bloke in a black tracksuit blew his whistle.

My phone rang. I pulled it out and read the screen: 'PARKER'. I pressed the button. 'This important?'

Silence from the other end. Then, *'Embers… Fuck man, I just heard. You OK?'*

'What do you think?'

'Shite… Anything I can do? You want me to go see Michelle, or something?'

Maybe someone should. 'She doesn't like you, Parker.'

'Aye, I know, but she's family. Katie's family. Can't sit on my arse and do nothing.'

'It's not—'

'I'll get her flowers or something, yeah?' A pause. *'I'm really sorry.'*

A woman appeared at my shoulder, wearing a dark trouser suit with the school crest on the breast pocket, silver hair immaculately coiffured. 'Think we're going to win next week, don't you?'

I hung up on Parker, put the phone back in my pocket.

'Which one's Dawson Whitaker?'

A little frown. 'I'm sorry, I don't think we've met. Are you a parent?'

Until five o'clock tomorrow. I pulled out my warrant card. 'I need to speak to Dawson.'

'Ah, I see… Is he…?'

'No: potential witness.'

'Well, in that case I'm sure Mr Atkinson will be happy for you to have a word. Do follow me.'

Down the hill and across to the pitch. The massive white 'H' of the goal posts glowed like honey in the setting sun, the sky a deep and crystal blue.

The whistle blared and the kids changed direction again, getting slower. The guy in the tracksuit made a megaphone with his hands. 'Come on, pick up your feet! Five more! Jenkins, don't cuddle it: it's a rugby ball, not your teddy bear!'

This close it was easy to pick out Brenda Chadwick's boyfriend: still skinny; still with floppy blond hair; mouth hanging open, showing off the gap between his front teeth.

'One second, please.' My guide walked over to the man with the whistle. Talked to him in a low voice, pointing back at me.

He shrugged, then gave an extra long blast on the whistle. *Phweeeeeeeeeeeeeeeeeep*. 'Whitaker, over here, at the double! The rest of you: laps!'

Dawson trotted over, all elbows and knees, a rugby ball tucked under his arm. 'Sir?' Posh-boy accent, his voice doing that uncomfortable teeter between a wee kid's and a proper grown-up's.

The children thundered past, puffing and panting and groaning. Off in the middle distance, Mr Atkinson and the woman in the trouser suit shared a joke. Giving us a little privacy.

Dawson shrugged, an exaggerated gesture that seemed to haul his arms up at the elbows. 'I don't know. It all happened really quickly, we'd been arguing – she wanted to go to the new Disney film on the Wednesday for her birthday, I'd got tickets to an Ingmar Bergman retrospective at the Watershed. It was nothing serious. I mean the relationship *and* the argument.'

Relationship? He was thirteen; since when did thirteen-year-old boys call it a *relationship*? 'But you saw him, right? The man who took her?'

'It was only ever a casual thing, but she got a bit clingy. Truth be told, I was going to break it off after her birthday. Didn't want to spoil the day.'

Yes, because nothing said HAPPY BIRTHDAY! like an evening watching Swedish existential cinema.

I pulled out the photo of Katie. 'She's my daughter.'

He raised an eyebrow. 'Very gothic.'

'The Birthday Boy's got her and he's going to kill her *tomorrow*. Did – you – see him?'

Dawson closed his mouth, looked away over my shoulder. 'My father doesn't like me talking to police officers. You shouldn't have come here.'

'He's going to kill her.'

'I'm sorry. I really, genuinely am.' A small shake of the head.

And then a hand landed on my shoulder. Big hairy one, attached to a mountain of muscle in an expensive-looking suit. Sunglasses, bullet-shaped head with a crew-cut and a diamond earring. 'This bloke botherin' you, Dawson?'

'Genuinely sorry.' The kid backed away a couple of steps. 'I have to get back to practice.' He turned and jogged away on an intercept course with the rest of the team.

I curled my hands into fists. 'Move your paw, or I'll break every finger on it.'

'You hear that, Ed? Haggis here's gonna break my fingers for me.'

A rumble, like a bear in an echo chamber. 'Don't think so.' Ed stepped in close. His face was a knot of scar tissue tied around a boxer's nose, hair greying at the temples.

Shit – two of them. What was the point of taking the gun all the way to Bath and leaving it in the bloody car?

Up above, the sky turned the colour of blood, shadows stretching across the playing field like claws.

One last try at being civilized before the violence started. 'I just want to know what the boy saw, that's all. I don't give a toss about your boss.'

A third voice. 'Yeah, well, he gives a toss about you.'

They frogmarched me across the car park to a Range Rover with blacked-out windows.

I tried a couple of steps towards my manky Renault. 'Need to get something from the car.'

'Don't be fuckin' stupid, Haggis.' The one with the hairy hands plipped open the Range Rover's locks. 'Now, you gettin' in nice and quiet, or do we have to traumatize the little kiddies by stompin' on your head?'

'I don't—'

'Either way, you're gettin' in the car.'

Chin up, head high. I climbed into the back of the Range Rover. Hairy Hands got in behind the wheel. His mates piled into the back, one on either side of me. The throat-catching reek of aftershave was almost overwhelming.

The car drifted out through the gates, onto the main road.

'Where are we going?'

'Shut it, Haggis. You talk when I tell you to, understand?'

Five minutes later we were parked on a tree-lined country lane surrounded by scrubby green-and-brown fields. Not a single house to be seen.

Hairy Hands turned in his seat, and looked me up and down. Smiled. 'Ed...?'

A fist slammed into my stomach, fast, hard, sending shock-waves of fire rippling through me. I folded forwards, the air hissing from my lungs as the ache spread. Couldn't breathe in again. Should've been ready for it... *God...*

'Search him.'

Hands fumbled through my pockets.

Ow...

'Ho, ho, what we got here then?'

'Warrant card: our jock really *is* a cop. Fuck me, thought you bastards would be smarter than that.'

'Nice chunk of cash in here too. What's that look like to you: four hunnerd? Five?'

Finally, air rushed back into my lungs.

Hairy Hands pocketed my wallet. 'You're well off your patch, Haggis. Hasslin' Mr Whitaker's son, pokin' your nose into stuff what doesn't concern you, causin' trouble. Not very bright, are you?'

A gurgly laugh from Ed. 'Not very bright.'

Yeah, they were probably right.

43

The Range Rover's engine changed pitch – we were slowing down. A trickle of sweat ran down the side of my face. It was hot in here, under the black hood, the fabric puffing out with every suffocating breath.

Blood pounded behind my eyes, swirled in my ears. Keep breathing. Deep, calm breaths.

The Range Rover purred forwards, bumped over something, then came to a halt. They killed the engine, leaving nothing but the whine of an electric motor, then a clunk. 'Here we go, Haggis, home sweet home.'

Someone yanked the hood off my head.

I blinked. Coughed. Dragged in a lungful of cool air.

It was a double garage, big enough for the Range Rover and an Audi R8 – stone walls, shelves of stuff in boxes, and a flickering strip-light.

Hairy Hands turned and grinned at me. 'We ready?'

'Why don't you go and—'

A sharp, stinging pain exploded across the back of my head. The world went yellow, black rushed in from the corners in jagged waves.

'Gllk...'

Couldn't move my arms and legs. Nothing worked.

Ed dragged me out of the car, holding me up so I wouldn't fall and make a mess on the garage floor. He was talking to Hairy Hands, but the words were all jumbled and out of synch.

Don't be sick. Don't be sick...

They hauled me down a flight of stairs: bare wooden beams on the ceiling, more buzzing strip-lights, the smell of damp and mould.

And then everything—

'Gah...' Cold water rushed down my throat, spilled out the sides of my mouth and soaked into my shirt.

'There we go. Feelin' better, Haggis? Thought Ed'd lamped you a bit hard there for a minute.'

I blinked, spat, coughed – every convulsion was like someone inflating my brain with a bicycle pump full of burning oil.

Why couldn't I move...?

Shite. I was sitting in an ancient-looking wooden dining chair, ankles cable-tied to the legs, arms behind my back, fastened to the supports. So this was how Steven Wallace and Ethan Baxter must have felt: completely screwed.

It was a windowless room with a dirt floor, bare walls, and a single light bulb swinging from the ceiling. Looked as if I wasn't the only one getting screwed in here – a grey dustsheet was draped over someone sitting in another wooden chair, a single bare foot poking out from the folds. The skin scuffed, bruised and filthy. The dustsheet was flecked with brown stains – dried blood.

Fuck, fuck, fuck, fuck...

The dining table that went with the chairs was against the wall, right in front of me – the surface stained and scratched. Hairy Hands settled back against it and folded his arms. 'You know the rules here, right? Or do you need me to repeat them?'

'I know the rules.'

A nod. 'Why you poking about in Mr Whitaker's business?'

'I'm not. I told you: I don't give a toss about your boss, I just want to know—'

Ed's fist slammed into my stomach again. At least this time I had time to clench. Still stung like a bastard though.

I wheezed in another breath.

Hairy Hands tutted. 'Said you knew the rules, Haggis. No porkies. Is there an investigation goin' on? That why you're down here from…' He pulled out my warrant card. 'Where the fuck's "Oldcastle"?'

'The Birthday Boy's got my daughter. I need—'

Another punch drove the air from my lungs, set fire to my stomach muscles, made me retch.

'Ghhhh… Will you stop doing that!'

Ed grinned. 'Not very bright.'

'So come on, Haggis, what they investigatin'? Someone been talkin', have they? Tellin' stories out of school?'

'The Birthday—'

My head snapped to the right. Blood roared in my ears, pins and needles spreading across my cheek. Like being stung by a six-foot-tall bee with a face like a dog's arse.

'Not buyin' it, Haggis.'

'The Birthday Boy's got my daughter. He got Dawson's girlfriend. Dawson saw him. He—'

Back to the stomach again. I curled up as far as I could and let it wash over me, breathing through gritted teeth. 'Call the … call the station and *ask*.'

'Nah, this is much more fun.'

I nodded. 'OK, OK. I'll tell you the truth. I'm part of a special task force investigating drug trafficking in the area. The local cops are compromised so we're using out-of-towners. My movements are being monitored and they know where I am right now. The whole building's wired.'

'And who told you about us?'

I glanced at Ed, and back again. Licked my lips. 'I can't tell you that.'

A slow clap came from somewhere behind me. 'Oh, *bravo*.' A woman's voice, soft and flowing. 'I loved the bit where you looked at Edward. Like you were trying not to drop him in it? Very smooth.'

She walked over to the table. Tall, elegant, wearing a black dress and high heels, long brown hair spilling down to the small of her back. High cheekbones, eyebrows plucked to a delicate line, dark-red lipstick on a small delicate mouth, diamond earrings. A plain gold wedding ring on her finger. 'Eugene, be a darling: take the gentleman's credentials away and check them out. Oh, and while you're there, let's have the party starter kit.'

'No problems, Terri.'

She leaned back against the wood, gave me a dazzling smile.

Dawson Whitaker's dad must've been doing better than I thought if he could afford a trophy wife that good.

'You didn't *really* learn about our little operation from Edward, did you. You were having Eugene on.' The smile faded a little. 'I do so hate deception, don't you?'

'They wouldn't believe me when I told them the truth.' I tensed, ready for Ed's fist, but it didn't come.

Terri reached over and took hold of the dust sheet, then whipped it off: as if she were performing a magic trick.

A woman was tied to the chair, in her bra and pants, her torso covered in bruises, swollen mouth crusted with blood. Broken nose and two black eyes. The hair hacked off on one side of her head.

'Take Virginia here. Virginia's a post-operative transsexual, she works as an escort: the kind that negotiates optional extras. For a fee you can fuck a woman who used to be a man.' Terri ran a finger along the battered woman's collarbone. Virginia flinched...

Terri raised an eyebrow at me. 'Would you like that? Would that be something new and exciting for you?'

'No.'

'Only Virginia isn't really a post-operative transsexual, is she? She's just an ugly *whore*.' Terri's hand flashed out and Virginia's head rocked back. Fresh blood dribbled bright red from the corner of her mouth. 'Pretending she used to be a man. Conning her clients. Taking their money and *lying* to them.'

Paging Mrs Psycho...

'Can you believe anyone could be so dishonest?' A frown marred Terri's smooth forehead. 'To lie like that...'

Virginia hung her head, shoulders trembling, making little gasping sobs.

'Oh, stop whining you little bitch, it's your own fault. Kenneth paid you good money for your filthy lies, how could you take advantage of a man IN A FUCKING WHEELCHAIR?' Face scarlet, spittle flying.

A thump behind me and a draught of cool air on my back, then Eugene Hairy Hands appeared, holding a sports bag in one paw and a cheap-looking mobile in the other. A burner. Pay-as-you-go. The kind of phone that could be used and ditched. He placed the bag on the table.

Terri straightened up, wiped a hand across her chin. 'Eugene?'

'Detective Constable Ash Henderson, Oldcastle Police, used to be a DI but got busted down 'cos some paedo got killed. And the Birthday Boy really did grab his daughter. My mate says it's all over the jock papers.'

Finally. 'That's what I've been telling you!'

The frown was back, but this time it came with a little pout. 'So all that nonsense about a task force and everyone knowing where you are... That was a *lie*.'

'They wouldn't believe the bloody truth! What was I supposed—'

A left to the face, hard enough to make the chair groan beneath me. Everything tasted of blood. I spat out a mouthful of scarlet.

'Yeah.' Hairy Eugene dumped my wallet beside the holdall. 'And that's not the only thing: he's bent. Works for some local hood called Andy Inglis.'

'Oh, don't look so glum, Constable Henderson, we're only teasing you.' Terri smiled. 'We've been expecting you all day.' She held out a hand. 'Eugene: phone, please.'

Eugene handed it over and Terri punched in a number. Waited.

'Hello, Maeve? ... How are things up there in sunny Oldcastle? ... Yes... That's right...' She looked at me. 'Yes, he did: thanks again for the tip-off... I know... He does a bit. Do you want a word?' A nod. 'OK, here you go...' She handed the phone back to Eugene. 'Maeve would like a word with our guest.'

Eugene grabbed a handful of my hair, then stuck the phone against my ear.

'Are ye enjoyin' the party I laid on for yez?' Mrs Kerrigan.

'Fuck you.'

'Oh now, don't be like that, Officer Henderson. Did I not tell yez I'd claim ye, ye little bollox? This is what ye get for stickin' a gun in me face. Told yez ye should've pulled the trigger.'

'You sent me down here for *nothing*? The bastard's got my daughter and you're fucking me about, wasting my time in fucking BATH?'

'Listen up, gobshite: Mr Inglis went out of his way to get that lead for yez. He was doin' you a solid. This little hooly yer havin' now? That's a gifter from me. Enjoy.' She hung up.

Terri smiled. 'All done?'

'Whatever she's told you, it's a lie.'

'I don't think so... Eugene?'

He took the phone from my ear. 'Sorry, Haggis.' Hammered his fist into my stomach again.

Fuck…

Terri unzipped the holdall. 'Maeve tells me Pitbull sent you all the way down here to talk to my Dawson. Imagine that? And I thought we'd got past the whole rat-poison-in-the-heroin thing. So tell me, Constable Henderson, what did Pitbull tell you to do?'

I spat another mouthful of blood. 'I don't work for Andy Inglis. I … owe him some money, that's all.'

Eugene sucked in a breath, sounding like a car mechanic preparing to bend someone over the service desk. 'Our mate here's got six hunnerd notes on him.'

'Constable Henderson: are you holding out on poor Pitbull?'

'I'm not… I… You heard your monkey – my daughter was snatched. Dawson saw the Birthday Boy when Brenda Chadwick was abducted, I need to know—'

This time the punch was hard enough to send the whole chair crashing over onto its back.

Ahhh. *Fuck…* It was like being stabbed in the ribs with broken glass.

The ceiling was bare joists, and cables, then the floorboards of the room above. Like the one in the birthday cards.

'You're awash with lies and deceit, Constable Henderson. That's not good for the soul. You need to perform an act of atonement, like Virginia here.'

I coughed. Little droplets of red pattered back down on my face. 'I just want my daughter back…'

'Brenda Chadwick was a cheap whore who tried to get her hooks into my son. Only twelve and she thought she could *screw* her way into my family. Imagine that?' Terri frowned down at the table. 'You can't believe how delighted I was when Dawson came home and said she'd been abducted.'

'He saw the Birthday Boy…'

'Eugene: how much money did you say Constable Henderson had?'

'Six hunnerd. Well, five hunnerd and eighty.'

'Good, that's more than enough.' She picked my wallet off the table and counted out a wad of cash. 'Twenty, thirty, forty, fifty, sixty, seventy, and eighty. That's enough to rent a gun for … oh, let's call it fifteen minutes.'

I blinked. 'I don't want—'

'Of course you want a gun. You want to be saved don't you?' Back into the wallet. 'Eighty for the gun and twenty for a bullet. But that's not rental – you get to keep that.'

Oh fuck.

'Edward, help Detective Constable Henderson assume the position, will you?'

Ed dragged the chair back upright, then cut the cable-tie holding my right wrist to the back of the chair. He grabbed my forearm in his huge scarred hand and hauled it up in the air, as if I was asking to go to the bathroom.

'He's all set, Terri.'

She reached into the holdall and pulled out a freezer bag, the clear plastic kind with a zip-lock fastener. There was a gun inside, something big and black and deadly. She held the bag out. 'Eugene, do the honours, will you?'

'Pleasure.' He snapped on a pair of blue nitrile gloves, then took the gun out of the bag. 'Bul Cherokee: nine millimetre, double action semiautomatic pistol; as used by the Israeli security forces.' He drew the slide back and it stayed there. 'Weighs seven hundred and five grams unloaded.' He pressed a little black button on the black handgrip and the magazine slid out. Eugene caught it in his other huge hand. 'Magazine takes ten rounds. You get one.'

He picked another zip-lock bag from the holdall. This one had a rectangle of black foam rubber in it – about the size of a box of kitchen matches – studded with little shiny dome shapes. He popped open the bag and dug something out of the foam: a bullet; it glittered like polished gold. 'Nine-mill Luger, one-twenty-four grain, full metal jacket.' He thumbed the thing into the top of the magazine and slapped it back into the handgrip. Released the lock and the slide clacked forwards again. 'Ready to roll.'

Terri smiled. 'Eugene likes guns, what can I say?'

I couldn't take my eyes off the thing. 'Look: I only want to know what Dawson saw, I swear, I don't—'

Ed clamped his hand across my mouth, thick fingers digging into my cheeks. Eugene marched over, took my wrist from his mate and wrenched my arm down, pulling me forwards until my chest was against my knees – left arm still fastened to the chair.

Ed leaned on my back, holding me in place, his other hand still clamping my jaws shut.

Bastards... Struggling did nothing: Ed was too heavy.

Eugene pressed the gun into my hand, forcing my fingers around the handgrip. 'This little lever's the safety catch.' A click. 'And you're good to go.'

Fine I'll blow your head off you big hairy... My whole arm trembled with the effort, but he wouldn't let go. He shoved the barrel of the gun over my right foot, forcing the end against my shoe.

Terri raised her arms. 'It's time to atone, Detective Constable Henderson.'

Fuck that.

'Pull the trigger.'

No way in hell was I pulling the trigger.

'Either the bullet goes in your foot, or it goes in your head. Your choice.'

Ed's spit flecked the back of my neck. 'DO IT!'

Eugene's spattered against my cheek. 'FUCKIN' DO IT!'

'Your time's running out, Detective Constable.'

'DO IT!'

'PULL THE TRIGGER, HAGGIS!'

'You've only got the gun for another eight minutes.'

'PULL THE FUCKIN' TRIGGER!'

'One way or another you're taking that bullet with you.'

'DO IT!'

'PULL THE TRIGGER, OR I'M GONNA SHOOT YOU IN THE FUCKIN' HEAD!'

'Not much of a choice really, is it?'

Did they really think I was going to shoot myself in the foot? Like I was a bloody idiot?

Get stuffed.

Eugene shook his head. 'He don't believe us. Haggis here thinks we're kiddin' about.'

'Hmm...' Terri picked up the grey dust sheet and draped it over Virginia's battered body again. 'What can we do about that, Eugene? What can we do to convince Constable Henderson?'

Eugene tore the gun out of my hand, stood, aimed, and pulled the trigger. A sharp crack boomed around the room, reverberating off the stone walls. Virginia's head jerked back under the dustsheet, the fabric billowing out behind her. Red spread like a field of poppies, seeping into the dusty material.

Jesus... Right there, in front of me...

'Thank you, Eugene, that'll do nicely.' Terri took two more tens out of my wallet. 'But now Detective Constable Henderson needs another bullet.'

He killed her, right there...

Terri sighed. 'Oh don't look so shocked: as if I was going to let the lying bitch live after what she did to my Kenneth.'

Eugene loaded the magazine, then pressed the gun back into my hand and forced the soot-streaked barrel against the top of my shoe again. 'Last chance, Haggis.'

'Your rental time's running out, Constable Henderson.'

'PULL THE FUCKIN' TRIGGER!'

'It goes in your foot, or it goes in your head.'

What choice did I have?

'DO IT!'

I squeezed the trigger.

44

The harsh crack reverberated around the room, deafeningly loud.

Nothing – no pain. The bastards were winding me up, using blanks. It was all a big...

FUCK.

Fire ripped up my leg, radiating out from my right foot like an earthquake of molten metal. AAARGH, fucking FUCK... I jerked in the chair, trying to get away, but the pain was still there, following me. Screaming into Ed's huge callused hand.

Eugene took the gun from me and dropped it back in its zip-lock bag.

Fuckers...

Ed let go and I grabbed the seat, my whole body rigid. 'FUCKING ... SHIT! AAAAAAAARGH! BASTARD.' I slumped forwards, clutching my right foot. 'AAAAAAGH, BASTARDING FUCK!' The hole in the top of the shoe was tiny – ringed around with flecks of grey, like a dark sunburst. 'JESUS!' The underside was wet, covered in grit from the floor. Bright red dripped through my fingers, pattering onto the dirt. 'AAAAAAAAARGH...'

'All right, that's enough self-pity.'

'Self-pity? You fucking bastards! You fucking shit-eating *wankers*!'

'Now, now, Detective Constable.' Terri held up my wallet again, gave me a dazzling smile. 'You've got more than enough money here; would you like to buy another bullet?'

NO!

I shook my head, clenched my teeth, hissed the breath in and out, in and out.

Oh dear Jesus that *hurt*...

'Would you like something for the pain?'

'Yes.' Forcing the word out like a gallstone.

Fuck, fuck, fuck, fuck, fuck...

'Ed, would you be so kind as to fix Constable Henderson up?'

'Pleasure.' He grabbed my arm, held it out and twisted clockwise, so the elbow was locked, palm up. Ed dug his thumb into my skin, making a vein stand out, then pulled the safety cap off a syringe with his teeth.

'I don't want—'

'Shhh, it'll make everything all better.'

'No, it...'

The needle slid in. A small sting as he pressed the plunger.

'There we go.' Terri counted more money from my wallet onto the table. 'That should be enough to cover our heroin starter kit. Don't worry – it's rat-poison free.' She smiled. 'Now, why don't we give you a lift out of town?'

Warmth sizzled through my body, radiating out from my heart. Making the walls pulse. As if the room was breathing...

Terri's mouth was moving, but the words didn't make any sense, making far-off muzzy noises in the gloom.

Foot didn't hurt any more.

'Right, Haggis, you got everythin'?' Eugene stuck his hands under my armpits and levered me out of the Range Rover.

Got me upright. Let go ... then grabbed me again as the ground wobbled beneath my feet. 'Whoa there, still not got your sea legs, eh?' He leaned me back against the side of a wheelie bin.

It was a lay-by, somewhere in the darkness outside Bath. Not even on the main road – traffic thundered somewhere off in the distance, just audible over the hissing in my ears.

'Mmm'OK.' Mouth wasn't working properly. Numb, like the rest of me.

'Right, I'm lettin' go...'

This time I stayed upright.

'Good stuff. Open your hand.'

I squinted at him, but he wouldn't stay in focus. 'Nnnn... Gnn shoot me gen.'

'Don't be daft.' Eugene dragged my hand up then tipped two little shiny things into my palm. Bullets. He squeezed my fingers around the gleaming brass casings, then took the bullets back and dropped them into a clear plastic freezer bag. Zip-locked it shut. 'There you go. We get these, and you get this.' He slid a plastic pencil case into my jacket pocket, then slapped me gently on the cheek. 'Catch you later, Haggis.'

Eugene peeled off his blue nitrile gloves, disappeared behind the car and climbed back in behind the wheel.

Terri buzzed the passenger window down. She'd changed out of the dress into a yellow shirt, black denim jacket, and baseball cap. 'Well, it's been fun, but in case you're thinking of hopping off to the nearest police station to file a grievance: please remember, yours are the only fingerprints on the gun.'

I stared at her. Blinked in slow motion.

'We have a dead slut with your bullet in her. And who *knows* where the gun will turn up next: armed robbery, dead cop, series of murdered prostitutes...?' A wink. 'You take care of that foot.'

The Range Rover growled away from the lay-by, taillights glowing like the eyes of an evil cat. Shrinking. Then gone.

All alone.

All alone in the dark.

Got to get back to Bath: find the car. Go *home*...

My right foot dragged across the tarmac. Pins-and-needles wrapped in silver duct tape, wrapped in a towel, wrapped in more duct tape, wrapped in a heavy-duty bin-bag. Step, scuff... Step, scuff... Step, scuff, stumble. The ground rushed up to catch me. THUMP.

Fuck.

I lay on the road, in the dark and the cold, panting. Swearing.

Katie...

Crying.

A thin frigid drizzle settled onto my face.

'BASTARDS!'

Deep in my pocket, my mobile rang. Took me three goes to drag it out. 'DR MCFRUITLOOP' flickered on the screen, then disappeared. Gone to voicemail.

My legs wouldn't work.

I fumbled with the buttons for a while, and finally her recorded message crackled out of the speaker. *'Ash? Hello, it's Alice, Alice McDonald? OK: so Henry was right about everything – the Scenes Examination Branch have dug up all the spots he marked on the map and they've found the other bodies. All of them.'* A pause. Somewhere in the distance, a fox shrieked. *'We've got eleven sets of remains in total – so there really* was *another victim five years ago. I wanted... I thought you'd like to know. Call me back when you get this... Please?'*

'End of message. To delete this message, press three.'

They'd found Rebecca.

I covered my face with my hands and sobbed. All these years, and my little girl was finally dead. Rain soaked through my hair, into my clothes, cold and damp on my numb skin.

Katie and Rebecca...

No.

Get up: still got till five o'clock tomorrow.

Get up.

'AAAAAAAAAAAAAAAAAAAAAGH!'

Up. NOW.

I hauled myself onto my knees, then up onto my jittery feet. Step, scuff… Step, scuff… Step, scuff…

Find him and kill him… Step, scuff… Step, scuff… Wrap my aching fingers around his throat and squeeze… Step, scuff… Step, scuff… Tie him to a chair in the basement… Step, scuff… Step, scuff… Carve shapes into his skin, listen to him scream… Step, scuff… Step, scuff…

Headlights glittered in the darkness, getting closer.

Step, scuff… Step, scuff…

The car slowed, then rolled to a halt, right in front of me.

Step, scuff… Step, scuff…

The driver's door opened, and a light came on inside. 'Are you all right?'

I blinked, rubbed a hand across my eyes.

It was a kid: skinny, blond floppy hair, big gap between his front teeth. Dawson Whitaker, Terri's son.

I screwed up my face till the car came into focus too. A shitty Renault with dents down the side. My car. 'That's my car.'

'I'm sorry.' He opened the passenger door, hurried over and took hold of my elbow.

Step, scuff… Step, scuff…

'Watch your head.'

I collapsed into the seat. 'Want to go home…'

Dawson licked his lips, fidgeted for a moment. Then got back in the car.

'It wasn't my fault.' The kid changed down, drifting into the outside lane to overtake a motor home. 'I knew something was up – Mum won't let me go to rugby practice without protection, not after what happened to Dad… But it's usually just Eugene, or Ed, or Derek, never all three…'

A motorway sign loomed out of the darkness: South Wales M4; Bristol (West), South West, Midlands (M5); Bristol M32.

Dawson drove past the junction. 'Can't take you into Bristol – Mum does all her business there, if we show up at A&E she'll know in fifteen minutes. We're going to Gloucester.'

I sagged further back into my seat. 'No hospitals…'

'You should settle down. Try to sleep or something.'

Fat chance. 'How did you find me?'

He kept his eyes fixed straight ahead. 'What happened to your foot?'

'An act of atonement.' I made a gun from my fingers and pointed it at him. 'Bang.'

'Mum always dumps them on the way to work. I thought… Well, if you were still alive…' Streetlights sparkled in the distance. We overtook a scabby Transit van. 'Did the Birthday Boy really take your daughter?'

'You drive pretty good for a wee boy.'

'I'm *thirteen*. I'm not a child.'

'Right.'

He tightened his grip on the steering wheel, twisting his hands as if he was trying to wring its neck. All he needed was arthritis, a dead daughter, and a hole in his foot.

The steering column's plastic casing was cracked open like a big grey pistachio nut. Wires stuck out, their shiny copper ends twisted together. 'You hotwired my car…'

Dawson took a deep breath. Then the words came out in a rush, like a shaken can of Coke. 'The Birthday Boy didn't kill Brenda.'

I sighed. Let my head fall against the cool glass of the passenger window. 'It was your mum, wasn't it? She didn't approve.'

'Thought she was a gold-digger, but Mum's *wrong*.'

'So she killed Brenda.'

Silence.

'No. Because I got there first.'

The street was quiet and dark as Dawson pulled the Renault off the road and onto the square of gravel behind a bland concrete building: three storeys tall, lights glowing in the windows.

I blinked. Arms were like lead, legs too. Probably lost a fair bit of blood.

He half helped, half dragged me out of the car. 'Can you walk?'

'Isn't... Yeah.' Step, scuff... Step, scuff...

He lifted my arm and hooked it over his shoulder. 'Not much further.'

The back door opened with a Yale key and we hobbled along a narrow corridor to a flight of stairs, going down. Bloody hell, why did it have to be stairs?

Step, thunk... Step, thunk... Using my heel to take the weight.

A blue door lay at the bottom with a letterbox in it. Dawson took out his keys again, fiddled with the locks, and we were through into a little basement flat filled with the sticky warm smell of baking.

He closed the door and locked it again – three heavy deadbolts, and a metal rod that hooked into a big steel plate on the door and an eyelet in the floorboards.

We had cannabis farms back home with weaker security.

Dawson took off his coat and hung it on a hook. 'Bren? Bren, it's me.'

A voice from down the hall. 'How was practice?'

He led me through into a little kitchen, painted a cheery shade of yellow. A young girl stood in front of an electric cooker, stirring something in a pot. 'Fish fingers and apple crumble, if you're...' She turned – long blonde hair, with a razor-sharp fringe like her mum.

The smile on Brenda Chadwick's face disappeared. She dropped her wooden spoon and cupped her swollen belly with both hands. 'Who's this?'

Dawson held up his hands. 'It's OK, I can explain.'

'You'd better!'

A cup of hot milky tea and a plate of fish fingers, mash potato, and spaghetti hoops sat on the table in front of me. Congealing while Dawson and Brenda wolfed down their dinner.

Brenda scooped up the last of her hoops, then sat back – stroking the top of her bulge. 'So you see, we couldn't stay. If Dawson's mum found out I was pregnant she'd kill our baby. *And* me.'

'Could've run away.'

Dawson shook his head, wrapped an arm around her shoulders. 'You don't know Mum. She'd find us, wherever we went.'

Brilliant. I pushed my plate away. 'But not if she thought Brenda was already dead.'

'That's why I said I saw Bren getting grabbed.' He stared down at his hands. 'Mum didn't used to be like this, it's only since they crippled Dad…'

Just a working mother looking after the family business.

Brenda stared at me. 'It was my idea. They printed that Inverness girl's card in the papers, and we made our photo look like that.'

'You faked the abduction, you faked the card, and you got a flat in Gloucester to hide in.'

Dawson nodded. 'A man takes care of his family.'

A pair of thirteen-year-olds playing house. Yeah, *that* was going to last.

Brenda smiled up at him. 'I know it's not much, but it's ours. Dawson skims a little from his mum every week: enough to pay the rent and buy things for the baby.'

'I'm saving up for a deposit. We'll have a real home soon.'

My phone rang. Dawson and Brenda flinched. I let it go through to voicemail. 'What about your mum and dad?'

She lowered her head. 'This way, she won't hurt them either.'

After dinner, Dawson helped me through into the bathroom. I sat on the edge of the toilet while Brenda cut away the scuffed black-plastic bag, then the duct tape underneath. The towel was stained dark red – it splatched down into the yellow bathtub, sending little droplets of blood up the sides.

'Oh dear…' She licked her lips, rubbed the fingertips of her Marigold gloves together. Stared at the dripping mass of duct tape and leather. 'Do you want me to pull the shoe off, or should I, you know: cut it?'

Now the bathroom smelled of fireworks and black pudding.

'Cut it. It's ruined anyway.'

I closed my eyes and gritted my teeth. Bits of shoe clattered into the tub.

A clunk. A hiss. Then warmth spread across my foot.

I peeked.

Brenda played the shower head back and forth, washing off thick slugs of congealed blood. She puffed out her cheeks, brows creased. 'Come on, Bren, you can do this…'

Pink appeared through the red and black, then pale flesh. The whole thing was swollen and distended, like a massive wasp sting, centred around a dark circle – not much bigger than a garden pea – an inch from where the foot became toes. The starburst of black that had marked the shoe was there around the bullet hole too. Little black flecks of powder tattooed into the skin. Tiny slivers of cream poked out of the swollen mess. Bone.

Pink oozed out, staining the water.

She looked up at me. 'My sewing's not very good, but I've got disinfectant…?'

'Clean it up and bandage it. It'll be fine.' I tried for a smile while I bled into her bathtub. 'You're doing good. You'll make a great mother.'

Gangrene wasn't fatal any more, right?

Rain drifted down, shimmering in the streetlights. Dawson shuffled from foot to foot. 'I'm sorry, I really am. You came here because of us, and I'm sorry we can't help save your daughter.' He dug into his pocket, and produced a clear plastic bag with a dozen little round pills in the bottom. 'Amphetamines: they'll help keep you awake. And I've put a full tank of petrol in the car.'

I took the pills, slipped them into my jacket. 'You can't keep skimming product from your mum, someone's going to notice.'

His chin came up. 'A man's got to provide for his family.'

'Parents fuck you up.' I climbed in behind the Renault's wheel. 'You're a good kid, Dawson: don't turn out like your mum.'

He grinned at me. 'Don't worry – I look shit in tights.'

Headlights streaked past on the other side of the motorway, leaving glowing trails behind them that crackled and pulsed in time with my throbbing foot. Wasn't easy working the accelerator and brake with my left, but it was do-able. Just.

Bloody heroin was wearing off. My jackhammer heart wouldn't slow down, no matter how much I ground my teeth. Bloody amphetamines. And the high blood pressure wasn't exactly helping the hole in my foot either. But at least I was still going…

The windscreen wipers groaned and squealed back and forth in the drizzle, sounding like angry crows waiting to tear out my eyes.

Have to stop soon and get petrol. Take some of the Naproxen, Diclofenac, and Tramadol I'd rescued from the house. Keep the pain down far enough to drive.

According to the dashboard clock it was a little after half ten. An hour and a half till midnight. Seventeen hours from then till five o'clock Monday evening. One and a half plus seventeen was… I ground the heel of my hand into my eye. Why did the headlights have to be so sodding bright? Eighteen and a half.

Eighteen and a half hours until the Birthday Boy started cutting chunks off my little girl.

I shifted my left foot slightly, keeping the Renault at a steady seventy up the M6. Flashing my warrant card might have worked on the way down, but that was before I had pupils like huge black buttons and a bullet hole in my foot.

Preston went by on the left-hand side, nothing more than lights in the darkness and a name on a sign that glistened with rain.

Eighteen and a half hours.

My phone blared in my pocket. I dug it out: 'HENRY'. I pressed the button.

'Is … isn't working any more…' The words were all slurred, running into one another.

'You found Rebecca.'

'I've been … I've been trying to think… But it's so … difficult… I'm so sorry, Ash, so … so sorry.' Unbelievable: I'd seen him down a whole bottle of Bells in one sitting and *still* look completely sober. *'I want to … want to save her, but it… I can't get… I don't know what he wants…'*

'Henry, how much have you had to drink?'

'I can't do it any … any more. I'm… Should have stayed in Shetland. Ash, why … why did you make me come?' A little sob. *'She's dead… It isn't… I can't.'*

'Fuck's sake, Henry…' I tightened my grip on the steering wheel. 'You're not the only one having a shite day, OK? Grow up.'

Something roared past me in the outside lane, making the crappy little Renault lurch.

'I should … should've caught him … years *ago. Is all my fault. Is … no.'* Slurping, gulping, then a hissing breath. *'I didn't mean to… I'm sorry, Ash, I'm sorry. Is all my fault…'*

'Put the bloody bottle down, you useless drunken old bastard: I need your help! Katie's still out there. There's still time. We have to *find* him.'

'Stupid, uselessssss ol man… Should've … should've died years ago.'

'Henry!'

'Everyone I know … everyone's dead.'

A clunk, and then muffled crying.

Thanks, Henry. Thanks a fucking heap.

Monday 21st November

45

Cold…

I coughed, shivered. Opened my eyes. It was still dark. 'Urgh…' Everything ached from the base of my skull all the way down to the tips of my toes. I was in the passenger seat – reclined back as far as it would go – my coat draped across me as a makeshift blanket, breath hanging in front of me like fog in the gloom.

The Renault's windows were all steamed up.

I scrubbed a hand across the chilled glass, making it cry condensation tears.

Outside, the sky was blue-black; no sign of any stars. The massive bulk of an artic lorry sat in the space next to mine, facing the boarded-up services. A sign hung on the temporary security fence: 'CLOSED FOR REFURBISHMENT, BUT DON'T WORRY, WE'LL BE BACK SOON!!!'

Moving sent burning needles tearing up my right leg. I gritted my teeth. Tried to ride it out. But it wasn't working.

Ah, *Jesus*…

Then someone started pounding a hammer into my foot: thump, thump, thump, in time with the blood in my ears.

Tramadol and Diclofenac: I popped three of each out of their blister packs and dry-swallowed them.

Come on, come on, work. *Work.*

The breath hissed out of my mouth, taking a shower of spittle with it.

Fuck...

I slammed a punch into my leg.

'WORK!'

Banged my head back against the seat.

Not going away...

God.

Hauled in another breath.

The pills weren't working...

I fumbled Eugene's junky starter kit out of my coat pocket and unzipped the shiny plastic with trembling fingers. It looked like an exchange pack – the kind that chemists gave away free, trying to keep intravenous drug users from infecting themselves or anyone else. The only bits that looked as if they hadn't come from Boots were the three tinfoil wrappers, the cheap plastic lighter, and the instruction sheet. A step-by-step how-to guide to forever fucking your life up.

I followed it to the letter.

Only a half-dose this time. That'd be safe, wouldn't it? Enough to take the pain away and not leave me a dribbling wreck.

Nothing. Nothing... And there it was – the same rushing warmth from last night, forcing down the stabbing, throbbing ache. I sagged back into the seat as if my joints were made of jelly. Brain all muggy. The sound of distant church bells. Melting...

Maybe Dawson's mum was telling the truth? Maybe there wasn't rat poison and caustic soda scouring its way through my veins, killing me from the inside out. Just the heroin.

Get up you lazy bastard. The Birthday Boy's got Katie.

I blinked at my watch, squinting to get it into focus. Nearly half-six in the morning.

Get up...

I knocked back a couple of Dawson's little white pills, then lay back and waited for them to work their magic. Heroin and amphetamines for breakfast. Most important meal of the day.

There was a slightly gamey smell in the car, as if something in the fridge was on the turn. Not rancid, but heading that—

Oh God… My stomach rolled and boiled. Lurched.

I scrambled out into the morning, fell on my knees, and heaved.

A swirl of sour steam wafted up from the puddle of vomit. I spat, wiped the string of spittle from my chin with my sleeve.

Foot felt a lot better now. No more throbbing.

I limped across the car park, past the dark and silent lorries, to the garage at the end. Its forecourt and pumps were all lit up like Las Vegas. Even had a wee shop attached where you could pay for your petrol.

I wobbled in, bought six bottles of water, a couple of Ginsters pasties, and a packet of extra-strong mints. The guy behind the counter looked at me as if I was about to bite him.

I paid in cash. Turned. And stopped. Frowned. There were dark-red streaks on the grey terrazzo floor, as if someone had dragged a chunk of fresh roadkill across it. Didn't notice them on the way in. Too focused on getting something to drink.

Cheeky bastard: staring at me like I was some sort of freak, when *he* was the one with the filthy bloody floor.

More streaks on the faded tarmac outside.

Place was a pigsty.

I limped back towards the car.

The water was ice cold; I gulped down a whole bottle, scrunched up the plastic and dumped it in a forecourt bin. Then tore open the ham-and-cheese pastry. Wasn't really hungry, but heroin and amphetamines probably weren't a great idea on an empty stomach. I drained the second bottle and started in on the cheese-and-onion slice, getting flakes of pale gold all down the front of my shirt.

I brushed them away. Frowned again. My shirt was all stained with something reddish-brown. That wasn't right… Oh, sodding hell: Big Ed's fist in my face. My tongue found the gap at the side where those two loose teeth used to be, jagged stumps sticking out of the gum.

You'd think it would hurt more.

'Ash?'

Must be the drugs.

'Oh, Ash, what *happened* to you?'

Raising my head was like dragging an anchor through mud. Getting her in focus was even harder. 'Dr McDonald?'

It was: it was her. She was standing beside the Renault, wearing a big thick parka jacket, both arms wrapped around herself. No glasses, but lots of black eye makeup, lipstick so dark it was almost black, straight black hair, just like Katie… She looked beautiful.

She rushed over and threw her arms around me, buried her head against my chest.

I dropped my shopping and hugged her back.

My little girl.

'Ash? Ash, there's another sign for the hospital…' The morning was dark as a funeral. A heavy lid of grey hung over the three lanes of motorway, tiny flakes of delicate white sacrificing themselves against the Renault's windscreen, holding on for a moment before they melted, or the wiper scraped their corpses to one side.

'Ash?'

I blinked, squinted. All the motorway signs were perched on top of concrete lintels spanning the road, glowing orange lettering telling Dr McDonald to 'BE A COURTEOUS DRIVER', 'USE YOUR MIRRORS', and 'SPEED KILLS'.

Especially when you mixed it with heroin.

'Ash, I said there's another—'

'No hospitals.'

She bit her bottom lip, that little crease denting her forehead between her eyebrows. 'You need to see a doctor, they—'

'It's a gunshot wound, they have to report it by law. Soon as they do, that's it: the police turn up, I can't leave, and Katie's dead.' I rested my head against the cool window. 'Anyway, *you're* a doctor.'

'No I'm *not*. I mean I am a doctor, but not that kind of doctor, I don't know anything about bullet holes, I've only ever seen them on dead bodies…' She reached across and put a hand on my leg. 'Please don't—'

'Oldcastle. We have to go to Oldcastle.' I took another swig of water.

'Thirsty…' I rubbed a hand across my gritty eyes. Squinted out at the snow. It was heavier now, still not enough to lie on the ink-black road, but working on it. The traffic crawled in front of us, corralled into one lane by a regiment of orange cones, yellow lights flashing.

'You're awake.' Dr McDonald reached behind her seat and came out with a bottle of mineral water. 'How are you feeling?'

I screwed the top off and drank. Downed half the bottle and surfaced again with a gasp. 'Where are we?'

'Coming up to Stirling. Traffic's horrible.'

'Stirling…' A smile pulled at my face. 'Rebecca loved the Wallace Monument. Every time we went south we had to climb the bloody thing… All the way up to the top so she could see everything.'

'Ash, I'm worried about—'

'Katie hated it.' I drained the rest of the bottle. Frowned. 'How did you find me? I turned round and there you were…'

'You need someone to look at your foot.'

'In the car park, at the services, there you were…'

'We had fish and chips in the car on Saturday night: you let me borrow your phone because I told you my battery was dead… I knew something was going to happen, I was worried about you and everything was going wrong, so I downloaded an app onto your phone that would track where you were.' She hunched her shoulders, getting closer to the steering wheel. 'Don't be angry with me.'

'Dr McDonald—'

'*Alice*. Why can't you call me Alice? *Please*.'

I nodded. Alice. Not Dr McDonald. 'Alice: thank you for coming to get me. Thank you for not making me go to hospital. And thank you for helping me find Katie.'

She turned and beamed at me. 'We'll find her, won't we?'

Ten o'clock. We had seven hours.

'Have to stop…' Something was eating my foot, chewing through the flesh and sinews and bone with sharp metallic teeth. 'Stop…'

Alice looked across the car at me. 'You should sleep.'

'Can't…' The River Tay was a flat grey smear on the far side of the dual carriageway, a long line of skeletal trees standing guard in front of it. Waiting to drag us down into the frozen earth. 'Hurts. Need my medication.'

'You shouldn't…' She flexed her fingers around the steering wheel. 'Ash, it's poison.'

'It works. I tried Diclofenac and Tramadol: barely made a dent in it. We have to stop…'

Alice licked her lips. 'Can you hold out till Dundee?'

Burning petrol surged up my leg, blue-tinged fire that crackled and fizzed, eating away the muscles and charring the bone beneath.

'Ash?'

I screwed my eyes tight shut. Gritted my teeth. Nodded. 'Dundee.'

'Need to stop for petrol soon anyway.'

Warmth spread out from the middle of my chest, forcing the shredding blades down into my leg, then my shin, then my foot… then gone. The car's headrest was like a warm lap beneath my head.

A cool hand on my brow, stroked the pain away.

'You're burning up.'

'Mmmm…' I let go of the syringe – the other half of this morning's wrapper – let it fall to the grimy carpet.

'Do you want a sandwich, or I bought some crisps?'

'M'not hungry.'

'Ash, you have to eat something, and you have to drink lots of fluids, and you can't keep doing this, we have to go to hospital.'

'Need Henry…'

She bit her bottom lip. Sat back in her seat. Looked down at her lap. 'He's not answering his phone.'

The engine purred into life, and we were moving again, falling through the snow, fat white flakes like starbursts in the cold morning light.

There was an egg sandwich in my lap. I stared at it, but it didn't do anything. 'Rebecca liked egg sandwiches. She had this … this imaginary friend when she was wee, she said he was a cereal killer. Every time we found all the Sugar Puffs gone, it would be Naughty Nigel's fault. Wasn't so keen on Bran Flakes though.' I rested my cheek against the passenger window, cool and smooth. 'It's been… such a long time.'

'I'm sorry she ran away.'

'She didn't run away. He took her.'

The Kingsway was busy, cars and buses carving their way across Dundee's back, avoiding its vital organs. Off to the right, the retail park where the Party Crashers had camped out on the fifth floor of a chain hotel drifted by at fifty miles an hour. Only a week ago, but it might as well have been months.

I cradled the egg sandwich against my chest like a baby. 'We didn't know what happened to her… Michelle still doesn't. One day Rebecca was there, and we were planning this big party, and the next she was gone. No note, no word. I got the first card on Rebecca's fourteenth birthday. Happy birthday! The number one scratched into the top corner, so I'd know there'd be more to come.'

The heroin tingled in my fingers and toes, as if they were going to break free and fly away. 'I keep them all in this cigar box Rebecca gave me for Christmas when she was six. Don't know where she found it, but she painted it and covered it in sequins and glitter... And that's where I hide them.'

'But why didn't you—'

'They would've taken me off the case. I'd have to sit on my arse and watch them screw it all up. Never told anyone, not even Michelle. At least this way she gets to hope.'

'Ash, she needs to know or she can't move on, she—'

'Sometimes it's better not to know.' A shrug. 'Doesn't matter anyway: they found Rebecca yesterday, remember? The extra body in the park, with all the others. My little girl in a hole in the ground, her bones stained the colour of old blood.'

'Oh, Ash.' Alice squeezed my arm. 'I'm so sorry.'

'Me too.' I turned back to the window. Stared out at the snow. 'He won't use Cameron Park any more, not now we've crawled all over it... We'll never find Katie's body.'

Everything was getting heavier, gravity hauling my body down into the seat. Pulling my eyelids shut. So difficult to move.

'Ash?'

Should've taken another one of Dawson's stolen amphetamines.

'Leave me alone...' Cold wrapped its arms around me and heaved. Dragged me out into the snow. I looked up into a grey sky turned almost white. Soft icy kisses on my cheeks.

A face peered down at me. A woman's voice. *'I don't like this. Alice: he needs to go to the hospital.'*

'Please, Aunty Jan, we have to.' Alice stroked my forehead. *'He needs me.'*

'I must be mad...' A big, heavy sigh. *'All right, all right: grab his feet. But if he dies, you're the one explaining it to the police, understand?'*

'Thanks, Aunty Jan.'

I blinked up at a white ceiling; kitchen cabinets lurked around the edges; the sound of a kettle boiling. I was ... inside... How did I get inside? Got to get up and find Katie.

'Will you bloody hold him still! This is hard enough as it is.'

Something heavy on my arms and legs.

'Sorry.'

'Christ, what a mess...'

Someone was kicking me in the head. I peeled an eye open, but the bastard was invisible.

Up above me the ceiling was dappled with animal-shaped shadows, slowly rotating around a hazy sun. My mouth was two sizes too small for my head, the inside of my cheeks lined with sandpaper, tongue forced inside a cage of teeth. Something sticky on my face.

I put a hand up to scratch it away, but someone caught my wrist.

'No.' Alice pushed my arm back down by my side. 'How are you feeling?'

Like I'd been hit by one of those tankers they used to empty septic tanks. 'Thirsty.'

'Here.' She pressed a bottle to my lips and I drank, gulping it down, getting half of it all over my chin and neck. Not caring.

'Aunty Jan fixed you up.'

A face loomed over me – the same one from the kitchen. Bobbed hair jelled into spikes on one side, a face pinched around narrowed eyes. 'Lucky you didn't lose that foot. What were you *thinking*?'

'Told you she's a great vet.'

I held out a hand and Alice hauled me up till I was sitting in a single bed. My stomach lurched. I gritted my teeth, swallowed hard. Held onto the mattress in case it soared away. Looked down.

My right foot was encased in professional-looking bandages, wrapped so tightly I couldn't feel a thing.

Alice's aunt folded her arms. 'I've done a nerve block – lidocaine, epinephrine, and a corticosteroid. The whole thing will be numb below the knee, but that doesn't mean you can go out and run a marathon. The bullet sheared through your second metatarsal, right now the only thing holding your toe on is skin and some stitches. You'll need a bone graft.' A nod. 'Keep that foot elevated or you're going to end up with an oedema, septicaemia, and probably gangrene. That sound like fun to you?'

Didn't hurt at all. 'You're a genius.' I swung my legs out of bed and the room whooshed around my head, doing a lap of honour. 'Christ…'

'You need to rest. And shower. You absolutely *reek*.'

'What time is it?'

'You've lost a lot of blood, you need to—'

'What's the bloody time?'

Silence.

Then Alice held up her watch. 'Two o'clock.'

Three hours.

46

The Snooze-U-Like Inn on Martyr Road was a Rubik's cube, where all the sides were the same colour: grey. Henry's ancient Volvo estate was the only thing in the car park until Alice slid the Renault in next to it.

She looked up at the bland frontage with its little square windows. Snow drifted down from the gunmetal sky. 'Still nothing?'

I fidgeted with the collar on my borrowed shirt. Everything Alice's uncle owned was just a bit too big, but at least it didn't stink of blood and sweat and vomit. 'Come on, Henry, answer the bloody phone…' It rang through to voicemail again. I hung up.

She hopped out of the car, breath pluming around her head. 'I'll go get him.'

Five minutes later and there was still no sign of her.

I climbed out into the cold.

It took me a dozen steps to get used to the cane Alice's aunt Jan had lent me – leaning on the polished mahogany handle every time my right foot touched the ground, lurching from side to side as I hobbled towards the hotel entrance.

The nerve block was great – couldn't feel a thing.

I pushed through into the reception area. Scuffed carpet tiles, faded wallpaper, dusty plastic pot plants, and a bored-looking man behind the desk.

The receptionist glanced up from his copy of the *Daily Mail*. 'You got a reservation?'

Fucking thousands of them. 'Henry Forrester: where is he?'

'Room seventeen, first floor.' Mr Daily Mail pointed towards a set of double doors. 'Lift's out of order.'

Brilliant, more stairs.

I puffed and panted up to the first floor, paused for a second to catch my breath, then limped into a dingy corridor. A door at the far end lay open, the number 17 picked out in brass on the scuffed brown paint, a 'Do Not Disturb' hanging from the handle.

Television noises oozed out into the hall – some snooty woman's voice banging on about the interest rates.

They were watching the bloody news, as if we had all the time in the world. As if he wasn't going to kill my little girl at five.

For fuck's sake.

I lurched down the corridor. 'Henry Bloody Forrester, get your lazy drunken arse downstairs, now...'

Alice appeared in the doorway, both arms wrapped around herself, bottom lip trembling, a drip shining on the end of her nose. 'Ash...'

I stopped. 'Where is he?'

She stared at the threadbare carpet. 'He's gone.' A tear sparkled in the dim light, then plopped onto the toe of her red shoes.

'What do you mean, he's...' No. I pushed past into the room.

Sheba was on the bed, on her side, completely still. Henry lay beside her, dressed in his funeral suit, an empty Macallan bottle at his fingertips, a clear plastic bag over his head – the sides streaked with condensation.

He was cold to the touch, no pulse. The ancient dog was the same.

She's dead... It isn't... I can't.

And I'd called him a useless drunken old bastard.

Alice shuffled in behind me. 'These were on the bedside cabinet.' She held out a small white pill tub.

Fluvoxamine. The antidepressant he was taking in Shetland.

She sniffed. Cleared her throat. Rubbed a hand across her eyes. Took a big shuddering breath. 'He left a note.'

Sodding hell: she'd found her mother in the bath with slit wrists. And now this.

Henry, you stupid selfish old bastard.

'...thoughts and prayers are with the families at this time. Both girls' birthdays are today and we can only imagine how their parents are feeling.'

'Do you think Megan Taylor and Katie Henderson are already dead?'

'Well, we have no concrete evidence that the so called "Birthday Boy" kills his victims on their—'

I switched off the car radio. 'Are you OK?'

A shaft of sunlight broke through the clouds, making the wet road sparkle. The streets were arranged in neatly ordered rows: old-fashioned houses with four-pane windows and gardens out the front. Beech trees in cast-iron cages dotted the pavements.

Alice wiped at her eyes, smudging the black makeup even further. 'I'm fine.'

'It's OK to be—'

'We should have called the police.'

I softened my voice, put a hand on her shoulder. 'Henry won't mind waiting. We've only got two and a bit hours. He'd understand.'

She sniffed, wiped her eyes again. 'Right, yes, I'm being silly, I mean he's already dead... We've got a job to do.' A little shudder. Then she peered out through the windscreen. 'Are you sure about this?'

ACC Drummond's house sat back behind a beech hedge and a small granite wall – two gateposts either side of a gravel driveway. But then the Wynd was that kind of neighbourhood.

'Think about it: Drummond says he needs the families' addresses so he can plan the work roster, but why spread the PNC searches out across so many people? Why not give the whole lot to Weber, or one of the DIs? Why divvy up the work himself? He doesn't want anyone to know what he's up to.'

I opened my door.

She put a hand on my arm. 'Ash, you've been shot, you've been taking drugs, you've lost a lot of blood, and … Henry. Maybe you're not thinking all that straight, and—'

'You got any other suspects lurking up your sleeve? Drummond's the only game in town.' I got out, clunked the door shut, pointed at the house.

The cane crunched on the gravel as I hobbled up the driveway, pulling on my black leather gloves. A double garage sat off to one side, no sign of any cars. Better safe than sorry: I rang the doorbell and a high-pitched *trrrrrrrring…* sounded inside.

No answer.

Tried again.

Still nothing.

I looked down at my right foot, wrapped in bandages and stuffed into one of Alice's uncle's trainers – no chance I was kicking the door in. Besides, this was a neighbourhood watch area. Some nosy old bat in twinset-and-pearls might hear and call the police.

Have to try around the back.

Alice scrunched up behind me. 'Maybe we should come back later?'

A path led along the side of the building, to a cast-iron gate with an elaborate catch and no padlock. Looked as if Drummond needed someone to pop along and give him a talk about home security.

I slipped through into the back garden, then closed the gate behind Alice.

Big, lots of flowerbeds, bushes, trees, a hammock, huge greenhouse. Shadows already starting to lengthen across a neatly trimmed lawn.

The back door was part-glazed, with some sort of utility room on the other side. I stood and stared up at the building: no sign of a burglar alarm. Nothing around the front either. Drummond really *did* need that talk.

I grabbed a flowerpot and smashed one of the door's glass panes. Reached in and unlocked the door.

Alice shifted from foot to foot on the threshold. 'This is now officially breaking and entering, right?'

'Told you to stay in the car anyway.'

Inside it smelled of fresh washing and oranges. The utility room opened on a large kitchen.

She crept in behind me, voice lowered to a whisper. 'What are we looking for?'

Through the kitchen into a hallway with the usual assortment of jackets and keys, some shoes, a pair of long leather riding boots, a pile of mail lying on the mat. A flight of stairs heading up.

Alice tried a door – it swung open on a living room with a couple of stripy sofas and a lot of wood panelling. 'Is he married? Because if he's married he's not likely to keep Katie here, is he, what if his wife found out, it'd—'

'Why aren't you wearing gloves?'

Her eyes went wide, then she grimaced. 'Sorry.' She wriggled her hand into the sleeve of her long-sleeved top and wiped the door handle. 'I've never done this before.'

Really?

We tried all the other doors on the ground floor: garage,

dining room, reception room, one bathroom, one toilet. Stairs led up to the upper floor.

Bollocks.

Had to take them one at a time, one hand leaning on the walking stick, the other on the handrail. One of the doors up there was ajar. I raised the stick, placed the rubber-tipped end against the door, and pushed.

It opened on a study lined with bookshelves and framed photographs. A desk sat opposite the door, a laptop and flat-screen monitor on top, an office chair, computer tower unit and a half-height filing cabinet underneath.

Alice slipped through into the room. 'Maybe we can find out if he's got another house, or a lock-up or something?' She tucked her hands into her sleeves again and pulled at one of the filing drawers. Locked. 'Oh...'

'Try the computers.' I went back onto the landing and checked the other rooms. No sign of Katie. According to my watch, it had just gone three: two hours left.

Back in the study, Alice was perched on the edge of Drummond's executive leather chair, mobile phone clamped to her ear. The flat-screen monitor in front of her displayed the Windows log-in screen. 'Uh-huh... No I tried that... OK, hold on...' She dragged around her satchel, pulled out her laptop and stuck it on the desk. Pressed the power button. 'Yes, it's booting up now.'

'No joy?'

She jerked around, one hand on her chest. 'Don't sneak up on me like that! You know I'm nervous enough as it...' A frown. She shifted her grip on the phone. 'No, not you, Sabir, it's ... my aunt. Right, my machine's ready.' Alice poked at the keyboard.

I took a tour of the bookshelves. A large SLR digital camera sat between a set of P.D. James novels and a copy of *Sexual Homicide: Patterns and Motives*. I took the camera down and played with the switches until the thing beeped and the screen on the back lit up.

'Uh-huh... That's it downloaded. Connecting it with the USB cable... OK, here we go.' She drummed her fingers on the desk. 'It's running.'

Looked as if Drummond had a thing for photographing people walking their dogs. I flicked through them. Kings Park, Montgomery Park, Camburn Woods.

'We're in! Sabir – you're a genius...' Alice grinned. The flat-screen monitor changed to an almost empty desktop with icons along the bottom. 'No, I don't know how Aunty Jan managed to forget her log-in details... Yes, I'll make sure she writes them down this time, thanks, Sabir.'

Alice hung up and went to work with the computer mouse, clicking on things – filling the screen with folders and documents.

I kept going through the photos. More dog walkers: Moncuir Woods, the Bellows.

What if Drummond wasn't the Birthday Boy? What if he was just like Steven Wallace?

Two hours left; it *had* to be him. Because if it wasn't, Katie was dead.

Alice cleared her throat. 'Ash...?'

A woman walking a Dalmatian through the rain, her yellow umbrella glowing like a slice of the sun. Next photo...

'Ash?'

The camera trembled in my hands as I stared at the little screen. 'Jesus.'

'Ash, you have to see this.'

A little girl – couldn't have been more than three or four – naked, lying on top of a double bed, crying. A man wearing nothing but a Homer Simpson mask stood next to the bed, playing with himself. The next picture was worse.

'Ash, Assistant Chief Constable Drummond's computer is

full of child pornography. There has to be *thousands* of images here, videos too.'

I switched the camera off. Put it back on the shelf. Pulled out my phone and dialled the station.

'Ash? What are we—'

I held up a hand. 'Shh...'

'Assistant Chief Constable Drummond's office, how can I help you?'

'Nicola, it's Ash. Ash Henderson. Is he in?'

Her voice cooled. *'Officer Henderson, I'm sorry about your daughter, but I don't think it's really—'*

'I want to apologize for my behaviour yesterday. I... It's been difficult for us. I wanted to say sorry.'

A pause. *'One moment, I'll see if he's free.'*

Bland, innocuous hold music, then, *'I've cut you a lot of slack, Detective Constable, given your situation, but this is unacceptable. Steven Wallace claims you broke into his home last night and subjected him to—'*

'I know.'

'So you're not denying it? Have you any idea how much trouble—'

'No. I mean I know about *you*.'

A pause.

He put a little metal in his voice. *'And exactly* what *do you know?'*

'Everything.'

More silence.

'I have no idea what you're talking about.'

'No? Is that a friend of yours in the Homer Simpson mask, or did you put the camera on a timer?'

Alice raised her eyebrows and mouthed, 'Homer Simpson?' at me.

I waved a hand at her.

ACC Drummond cleared his throat. *'I see... And what do you want?'*

'Guess.'

Muffled scrunching noises came from the other end of the phone – Drummond putting his hand over the mouthpiece. *'Nicola, clear my schedule for the afternoon. I have to go out.'* Then he was back. *'Neutral territory: Moncuir Woods, the parking area by the sculpture trail. Half four.'* He didn't wait for confirmation, just hung up.

ACC Drummond's blue beamer turned onto the gravel driveway and crunched to a halt in front of the garage. He climbed out and scurried over to the front door.

I stepped back from the bedroom window.

The sounds of keys and locks echoed up from below, then the front door slammed shut.

'OK.' Alice took a deep breath, keeping her voice low. 'What's the plan, I mean we do have a plan don't we, he's going to—'

'We've *got* a plan...' I reached into my pocket and pulled out the gun.

Footsteps on the stairs: Drummond taking them two at a time.

She stared. 'Ash, is that... Well, of course it is.' Alice shrank back against the wardrobe. 'Is that what happened to your foot, you accidentally shot yourself with your own—'

'I did *not* shoot myself.' I blinked. 'It's complicated. And it wasn't this gun.' I tucked it into my belt, at the side on the left, where my borrowed jacket would cover it. 'And it wasn't an accident.'

'You did it on *purpose*?'

My gloves squeaked on the door handle. 'Are you coming or not?'

Through in the study, ACC Drummond was on his knees in front of the desk, hauling CDs out of a black zip-up case and dumping them into a carrier-bag while the computers powered up.

I knocked on the doorframe. 'Problem?'

He jumped, spun around, eyes and mouth wide. His lips twitched, then he scrambled to his feet. 'You have no right coming in here! This is private property.' He cleared his throat. 'I'm... I'm placing you under arrest.'

'Where is she?'

'I don't know what you're talking about.' He squinted over my shoulder. 'Dr McDonald? I... I want you to phone the police: Constable Henderson has become a danger to himself and others.'

The walking stick was a good sturdy model. I jerked it up into the air, caught it by the bottom and swung it like a crowbar, smashing the head into one of Drummond's pictures. The glass shattered – the ACC and some bloke off the television crashed into the carpet. 'WHERE IS SHE?'

He flinched. Opened and closed his mouth a couple of times. Then put on his sergeant major's voice: 'Officer Henderson, I insist—'

Another picture exploded off the wall.

'Where is she, Drummond?'

Alice squeezed past me into the room. 'You should really tell him, Assistant Chief Constable, he's been under a lot of stress recently, and I don't think Ash is too worried about the consequences of battering your brains out right now.' She settled into the office chair. 'Where's Katie?'

'I don't know anything about—'

The cane's head battered into his cheek, hard enough to make my arm shake. He staggered against a shelf, sending law books thumping to the ground. Stood there with a hand pressed against his face, groaning.

'Where – is – she?'

'I don't—'

I went for the side of his knee this time and he yelled, then doubled over – clutching at the joint. So I cracked the lying fuck on the back of the head too. Blood and hair stuck to the handle.

Drummond screamed and curled into a ball, arms wrapped around his head. 'I don't know, I don't know!'

Alice shoogled the office chair closer to the desk. 'It's my professional opinion that Officer Henderson is suffering from post-traumatic stress disorder as a result of what's happened, he's not responsible for his actions, it'd certainly count as temporary insanity if he beats you to death.'

'I don't know where your daughter is!'

I held the gun in front of his face, hauled the slide back and racked a round into the chamber. Then stuck the gun against his forehead. 'Give me one reason, you sick little shite.'

'You're crazy, you've lost your bloody mind!'

Alice nodded. 'That's what I've been trying to tell you. I think it was all your child pornography that finally pushed him over the edge.'

'It... It's evidence in a case, I was only *holding* it until—'

The gun made a dull thunk when I slammed it into his head.

'Aaaagh...' Blood seeped out of the gash in his scalp.

'You made everyone at the station do PNC searches.'

'It's not my fault!' He covered his head with his arms again, scarlet soaking into the sleeves of his white shirt. 'He found out about everything... What was I supposed to do, let him tell the world? It'd ruin my family – my wife, my children, my friends...'

'*Who* found out?' I forced Drummond's head back. Jammed the gun barrel into his cheek. 'WHO FOUND OUT? WHO DID YOU TELL?'

'It wasn't—'

'I'LL BLOW YOUR HEAD OFF, YOU PIECE OF SHITE!'

The words came out high-pitched and fast: 'A journalist, I give them to a journalist! Every year, three weeks before each girl's birthday, I have to give him the family's address.'

A journalist...

I let go and limped away. Stared out of the study window

at the shining street. The clouds ate the sun, and everything went grey and gloomy again. All this, just so some tabloid scumbag could get at the story. So they could doorstep Lauren Burges's mother and ask her what it felt like to know her only child's bones had been dug up in a dilapidated park. Maybe stick a camera in her face: 'GRIEVING MOTHER CRIES FOR POOR LAUREN – EXCLUSIVE!'

I leaned on the windowsill. 'Who was it?'

'I didn't have any choice, he was investigating the death of a … colleague in Inverness.' The ACC coughed. 'He found out about our little group.'

'Drummond, I swear to God I will put a bullet in you.'

Alice nodded. 'Temporary insanity.'

'He's…' Deep breath. 'He's called Frank McKenzie; he's a freelance journalist.'

'No he isn't, he's a fucking photographer on the *Castle News and Post*…' I frowned down at the front garden.

Outside Megan Taylor's house – when Jennifer and her cameraman were waiting to ambush me – Shifty Dave taking the piss: *'If it's no' Wee Hairy Frank McKenzie. Two counts drink driving, and six months for phone hacking. Surprised any paper'll touch you since you got kicked off the* News of the World. *Relegated to camera boy now, are we?'*

Got kicked off a London-based paper. London: the only place other than Oldcastle where the Birthday Boy had taken more than one victim. Frank McKenzie: always there whenever we turned around. Every time there was a press conference, or an appeal from the parents, there he was with his camera, recording it all. Preserving it. Soaking up the grief.

I thrust the gun into Alice's hands and lurched for the door. 'If the bastard moves, shoot him.'

Down the stairs – my right heel thunking into every step – then out the front door, hirpling along, the cane thumping against the wet tarmac.

Shadows lengthened across the street, everything painted

copper and gold. I unlocked the Renault and hauled the driver's door open. It was in here somewhere... Not in the door-pocket. I knelt on the damp pavement and peered under the seat.

There it was – lying next to two empty water bottles, some scrunched-up receipts, an empty crisp packet, and the discarded syringe.

I reached in and plucked the SD card from the debris, blew the dust off it, and hobbled back to the house.

Alice slipped the SD card into the slot on Drummond's laptop. 'What are we looking for?'

'You're the psychologist, figure it out.'

She fiddled with the mouse for a bit, and a window appeared, full of thumbnail images. Alice scrolled through them: half a dozen pics of a grinning ginger kid holding an oversized cardboard cheque; another half-dozen of a car on Dundas Road with the front end caved in and a smear of what might have been blood on the dashboard; a series of random faces grinning at the camera; thirty or forty shots of the press conference in Dundee – DCS Dickie sitting up on the platform with Helen McMillan's mum; a few arty shots of the Oldcastle skyline; and that was it.

I breathed out. Nothing there.

Alice opened up a web browser and started clicking away at things.

'What are...' Drummond cleared his throat. 'I have money.'

I turned on him. 'You want to buy your way out of it? Flash a few grand and we'll forget all about your collection of kiddy porn? *Seriously*?'

'I can... You want to be a DI again? I can make that happen. DCI even.'

'Ash?'

'I'm going to throw your arse to the wolves, Drummond.'

'Come on, be reasonable.'

'Ash!'

I grabbed the gun and ground it into his forehead. 'You want reasonable?'

Alice tugged at my sleeve. 'Ash, you need to look at this.'

She pointed at the laptop screen. A girl I didn't recognize was tied to a chair in a filthy basement room, her bare skin covered in bruises, head shaved, three gouges across her chest leaking scarlet onto her pale skin. The next image was the same again, only worse. In the one after that, her throat hung open and dark.

Alice double-clicked on the first image, filling the screen with it. 'I downloaded a program to find deleted files on the card...'

Little bastard. Little *fucking* bastard. I turned, stared down at Drummond, snivelling away on the study floor. 'You piece of shite.'

'I... I didn't...'

'Ash, I know her: she's one of the missing girls the Party Crashers are looking for.'

'You gave him their addresses!'

'It... McKenzie was... Blackmail. I didn't have any choice! I didn't know!'

'YOU HELPED THE FUCKING BIRTHDAY BOY!' I grabbed Drummond by the hair again, banged his head against the desk. 'Open your mouth.' He stared up at me, eyes wide and full of tears. 'OPEN YOUR MOUTH!'

He did. I jammed the gun barrel inside.

'Gllllk...' Hands up, palms facing out, whole body trembling.

'We could've caught him. We could've caught the bastard years ago! HE'S GOT MY DAUGHTER!'

47

'One second, I'll check for you.' Hold music warbled out of my phone.

The back end of Drummond's BMW crept into his garage, reversing light glowing. I held up a hand and the car rocked to a halt.

Alice clambered out from behind the wheel and popped the boot lid. 'Anything?'

'They're looking.'

'Hello, Assistant Chief Constable? Yes, Mr McKenzie isn't in today, he's putting his mother's house in storage – poor dear has to go into a home. Dementia. I can take a message if you like?'

I didn't. I called Rhona instead and asked her to do a PNC check on Frank McKenzie and his parents.

'Is... Is everything OK, Guv? Only... Well, you didn't come home last night and I made curry and—'

'Please, Rhona. I need those details soon as you can.'

'Oh... OK.'

'Call me back.' I hung up, stuck the phone in my pocket. 'You ready, Alice?'

A nod.

Together we heaved ACC Drummond into the boot of his BMW: arms cuffed behind his back, face a mass of bruises and seeping red cuts. A knotted shirt acting as a gag. Alice dumped the laptop and tower unit in beside him, then went back through the door to the house for the CDs.

I reached in and slapped the filthy little bastard.

He blinked up at me with puffy, bloodshot eyes.

'Listen up, Drummond – if anything happens to Katie, I'm parking this car in the middle of Moncuir Woods and setting fire to it. With you in the boot.' The lid made a satisfying clunk when I slammed it shut.

And then Rhona phoned back. She read me Frank McKenzie's criminal record – it was pretty much identical to the version Shifty Dave had reeled off outside Megan Taylor's house the other night – then gave me an address in Cowskillin.

'What about the mother?'

'Couple of complaints from the neighbours a few years ago: playing loud music in the wee small hours, standing in the back garden in her nightie screaming at the seagulls, that kind of thing. You want the address?'

Christ's sake… 'Please.'

'Mrs Dorothy McKenzie, thirty-two McDermid Avenue, OC15 3JQ.'

I waved Alice towards the car. 'Rhona, I owe you a big one.'

'What's this all about, Guv? Do—'

I hung up and clambered into the passenger side of Drummond's BMW, jammed the walking stick into the footwell. 'Drive.'

The clouds were fringed with violent pink and orange as the light faded. Twenty past four on a Monday afternoon and McDermid Avenue was virtually empty. No sign of a removal lorry.

I climbed out, stuck the gun in my waistband, and hobbled across the road. Alice scurried along behind me. Number thirty-two looked like all the other buildings on the sandstone terrace – three storeys high, bay window on one side of the panelled door.

No wonder the little bastard was always lurking about when we were here.

I leaned on the bell, but nothing happened – it was dead. So I pounded on the door instead. BOOM, BOOM, BOOM.

The room with the bay window was stripped bare, nothing left but dusty rectangles where pictures once hung.

Alice stood so close she was pressed against me. 'Shouldn't we call Dickie and the team? I mean we know it's him, we should get a SWAT team down here or something…'

'You any idea how long it'll take to get a firearms team authorized and organized?' I hammered on the door again. 'He's been in there all day, with Katie…'

BOOM, BOOM, BOOM.

'Well, I could phone anyway and they can back us up and—'

The door opened a crack and a single eye peered out. Frank McKenzie, face shiny with sweat, breathless as if he'd been running. 'Go away. Go away, or I'll call the police.'

'Open the door.'

'I've got nothing to say to you. This is harassment.'

'OK, OK.' I held my hand up, backed away a step… And lunged. My shoulder slammed into the wood and the door crashed open. I couldn't stop: my right foot wouldn't take my weight, bloody thing gave way and I thumped full-length on the hall carpet, sending up a cloud of dust. It was empty – like the front room – the only light coming from the open front door, making everything dark and grey.

McKenzie was flat on his back, hairy arms covering his head, legs flailing.

I hauled myself up. 'It wasn't Mrs Kerrigan, was it? *You* wrecked my house looking for this…'

He stared at the SD card in my hand. 'It… I…' Scrambled to his feet. And he was off, running down the hall.

I limped after him, the cane thumping against the dusty carpet, the gun cold and heavy in my hand.

Alice barged past, going at full tilt, black hair streaming out behind her, red Hi-tops flashing in the gloom. 'Come back here!'

McKenzie battered through the door at the end of the hall – a glimpse of an old-fashioned kitchen – and then out the back into the garden with Alice closing the gap.

Halfway down the hall I froze...

Muffled screams came from behind one of the doors.

Katie.

It opened on a windowless corridor, the bare floorboards disappearing into darkness. A cord, hung from the ceiling – I pulled it and an overhead strip-light blinked and flickered into life. The corridor took a right turn about four or five feet in, heading towards the back of the house. I limped up to the corner: another short length of corridor with a door at the far end.

Locked.

More screaming.

I braced myself against the wall, taking as much weight as I could on the walking stick, and kicked out with my left. Twice. Three times. On the fourth go the lock ripped its way free of the surround, and the door jerked open. The stench of rancid meat slithered out into the corridor.

Six stone steps led down to a large dirt-floored room, the walls covered with pink rockwool insulation. Not a basement at all, some sort of outbuilding. It was divided into small rooms by plasterboard-and-stud partitions that didn't go all the way up to the ceiling – like the set of some twisted horror film. It was colder in here than outside; my breath fogged in front of my face.

I shoved my way into the middle room: where the screaming was coming from.

Megan Taylor froze. She was strapped into a wooden chair, legs fastened at the ankle with cable-ties, arms behind her back. Her eyes went wide, then the screaming got even louder.

'It's OK: police. I'm the police.' I stuck the gun back in my waistband and limped over. Then stopped, turned, and looked back towards the door I'd just come through. 'Oh shite...'

Megan wasn't the only one in here. A digital camera sat on a tripod, but behind that was another girl, tied to another chair. Blood covered every inch of skin ... where there *was* skin. Naked, head shaved, throat open in a thick dark slash.

My stomach churned.

It wasn't Katie. It was the girl in the photographs – the ones on the SD card. What looked like an old kitchen table was against the other wall, its wooden surface laid out with knives and hammers and chunks of flesh.

'Jesus...'

I backed up, knocked over the tripod. The camera crashed to the ground.

She'd been here at least a week.

Behind me, Megan kept on screaming.

'Alice.' Shit – Alice was chasing him on her own. I turned and yanked at the cable-ties holding Megan to the chair. Solid. I took one of the serrated knives from the table and hacked through the plastic. Dropped the knife at my feet. 'You're OK, it's over.'

Megan tipped out of the chair and fell to the dirt floor, grabbed the knife, and scrambled back into the corner, holding the blade in both trembling hands, pointing it at my face.

'I'm not going to... For fuck's sake, I don't have time for this shite!' I backed out of the room, tried the one next door – empty, except for the stains on the floor. The third one was the same.

'Listen to me, Megan: I have to go. Someone's going to come for you, OK?' I backed up the stairs and into the corridor. 'Try not to kill them.'

I shoved through the back door into the garden. The pale looping bones of a giant honeysuckle loomed in the growing darkness. The garden wall was eight feet tall, red brick, with a gate at the bottom. A private entrance into Cameron Park. It hung open.

The wet grass grabbed at the walking stick as I lurched through into the park. Everything was jagged shadows and indistinct shapes in the gloom. I stopped... No idea which way to go.

Shouts came from somewhere to the left. 'Hoy, you: come back here!'

I limped past a copse of trees and there was one of the SOC marquees, glowing like a carnival, a cluster of white-suited techs standing around the entrance, a couple running off deeper into the park – bobbing white shapes against the dark.

By the time I reached the tent, the crowd had thinned a bit – Alice was sitting on the grass, holding a hand to her head, someone on their knees beside her, stroking her back.

'Where is he?'

Alice looked up at me. One of her eyes was already starting to swell, the side of her mouth too – a line of blood trickling down from a split bottom lip. 'I tried...'

The Scenes Examination Branch tech helped her to her feet, then ripped off his facemask revealing a huge moustache. 'Who the hell was that?'

I pointed back the way I'd come. 'House over there: gate's open. Megan Taylor's inside...'

The SEB tech stared at me.

'Why are you still here? Go take care of her, you idiot! Call an ambulance, backup, preserve the scene. And watch out: she's got a knife.' I hauled Alice to her feet. 'Come on.'

I turned to hobble after the two SEB techs chasing Frank McKenzie, but she wrenched her hand free and sprinted towards a mud-spattered SOC Transit van instead. Pulled open the driver's door and climbed in behind the wheel. The headlights snapped on, then the engine roared into life, the front wheels spinning. Mud and grass spattered up the sides of the cab. The wheels caught and the van slithered forwards onto the path, pulled up beside me and stopped. The window buzzed open. 'Get in.'

I clambered into the passenger seat and she put her foot down.

The Transit van surged forwards, then lurched off the path onto the grass again, bucking and slithering through the bumps.

Up ahead, one of the SEB tripped and went sprawling, but the other one kept going, his SOC suit glowing in the van's headlights.

We crashed through a knot of brambles and out the other side.

The park's boundary wall loomed into view. In the middle distance, the twin chimneys for Castle Hill Infirmary's incinerator reached towards the heavy sky, warning lights twinkled at their tips turning the billowing steam to boiling blood.

The SEB figure slowed to a trot, then a walk, then stopped – bent double with his hands on his knees, back heaving as we roared past. The headlights caught someone up ahead, running, hairy arms pumping. Frank McKenzie.

He ducked through one of the park's arched entrances, and Alice swung the van after him. Closer. Closer.

'Oh, shite...' We were never going to fit. Not in a Transit van. I clutched at the grab handle above the door.

She didn't slow down. The brick arch exploded above my head as we smashed through. BANG, and the windscreen was an opaque mass of cracks. The van's bodywork squealed, sparks flying in the gloom.

Alice stamped on the brakes and the Transit screeched to a halt in the middle of the road. 'Bastard!'

I tore off my seatbelt, dragged my left leg up, and kicked. The shattered windscreen buckled. Another two kicks and it was clear, crashing down onto the road. Only one of the headlights was still working, peering myopically into the darkness.

Alice jabbed a finger through the hole where the windscreen used to be. 'There!'

A screech of tyres and we jerked forwards. I fumbled my seatbelt back into its buckle.

McKenzie was heading for the hospital.

'Run the bastard down!'

Alice almost had him, but he leapt over a short retaining wall and legged it across the grass towards the west wing of Castle Hill Infirmary. She swung the van around at the junction, taking the road marked 'MATERNITY WARD, EYE HOSPITAL, OUT PATIENTS, RADIOLOGY'. Only halfway down she swung right, mounted the kerb and bounced onto the grass, making a straight line for McKenzie's back as he shoulder-charged his way through an emergency exit into the building.

48

Alice sprinted off down the corridor while I lumbered along – falling further and further behind, forehead peppery with sweat. Clenching my teeth every time my right foot hit the cracked linoleum. The thunk, thunk, thunk, of the cane's rubber tip was like an icepick in my lungs.

What was the point of a nerve block if the bloody thing wore off?

Thunk, thunk, thunk.

A trail of scarlet dots speckled the floor. Fresh blood, red and glistening in the fluorescent lighting. Frank McKenzie might have got away from Alice in the park, but it looked as if she'd done some damage first. The trail led through a set of double doors and into another two-tone institution-green corridor.

No sign of Alice.

A pair of nurses were helping an old lady up from the floor, glancing back over their shoulders. 'For God's sake, someone should call that girl's parents.'

'Come on, Mrs Pearce, let's get you back into bed.'

I clumped past, breathing in time with the cane.

My phone blared. I dragged it out, cutting the thing off mid-ring.

'Ash?' It was Alice. *'Where are you?'*

'I'm ... I'm going as fast ... as I can...' Thunk, thunk, thunk.

'He's gone downstairs to the basement.'

'Don't go after... Hello? Alice? Hello?'

She'd hung up.

Why did no one ever bloody listen?

Through another pair of doors. My phone went again. I jabbed the button. 'I told you not to follow him! Wait for—'

'Guv, where are you?' Rhona. *'We got a call from the SEB – they've got Megan Taylor, she's alive. We can—'*

'Get a firearms team down to Castle Hill Infirmary. Full lockdown. No one in or out unless I say so.'

'But—'

'The Birthday Boy is Frank McKenzie: tell Dickie. And get that bloody firearms team down here now!' With any luck it'd be too late to stop me beating the fucker to death. I stuck the phone back in my pocket and lurched through one more set of doors.

The corridor opened out onto a hallway. Signs hung from the ceiling: 'RADIOLOGY', 'ONCOLOGY OUT PATIENTS', 'NUCLEAR MEDICINE', pointing in three separate directions. On the right was a hospital lift, flanked by stairs – one lot going up to 'CARDIOLOGY' the other down to the basement.

The trail of blood snaked off into the depths, shiny red spots on the grey concrete steps.

Screw that. I limped over and pressed the button, my back wet with sweat. *Ding.* The lift doors slid open.

Going down.

The air reeked of mildew, mingling with a metallic tang. Not the hot coppery smell of blood, something older. Industrial.

I stopped for a moment – rested my head against the cool concrete wall.

Deep breaths. Ignore the pain. Ignore the pain. Didn't hurt... Didn't hurt at all...

Load of shite, it *burned*.

The wall was rough against my skin. No sound of footsteps, or shouting, or a struggle, just the buzz and hum of unseen machinery somewhere in the depths.

Where the hell was she...?

A light up ahead crackled, flickered, then died – altering the patchwork of light and dark.

I pulled out my torch and clicked it on. Flicked the beam across the floor until it picked up the trail of glittering red droplets. They crisscrossed the black line painted on the concrete, leading off towards the mortuary.

Told Alice not to follow the bastard down here.

Move.

I hobbled on, leaning heavily on the cane, sweat running down my face. Every step was like someone hammering a burning nail into the sole of my foot.

Sodding tunnels were a maze.

Deeper into the gloom.

Another T-junction. I paused, panted, wiped a sleeve across my face. Blinked.

Left or right? The line to the mortuary stretched off to the right, the other direction led away down a corridor more dark than light. No more blood.

Bastard...

I dug out a couple of Tramadol and forced them down.

Where the buggering hell was Alice? Why did everyone—

A scuffing noise from somewhere down the left-hand corridor. I brought the torch up. And there she was – Alice, in her black and red stripy T-shirt and long-sleeved black top, a length of metal pipe clutched in her hands.

I limped towards her, keeping my voice low. 'Alice?'

She spun around, eyes wide. Then a pause. Then a smile, twisted out of shape by the swollen cheek and black eye. 'Sorry...'

She shifted her grip on the pipe and nodded at a door a couple of feet away: 'AUTHORISED PERSONNEL ONLY'.

'I told you not to go after him!'

'Why do you think I'm standing out here, when he's in there? I'm delightfully quirky, not stupid.' Frown. She reached up and touched my cheek. 'You're absolutely sodden.'

'How long's he been in there?'

'Three, maybe four minutes?'

I wiped my hand across my face – slick with sweat. 'Right.' The gun seemed to weigh a ton as I dragged it out. 'You go back down the corridor and you wait in the mortuary, understand? Backup's on its way.'

Alice nodded. 'Ash, don't...' She stood on her tiptoes and kissed me on the cheek. 'Be safe.' Then turned and crept back to the junction, then on to the mortuary. She paused on the threshold, peered back at me, then disappeared inside.

I shifted my grip on the gun. Limped over to the 'AUTHORISED PERSONNEL ONLY' door and tried the handle. It wasn't locked.

It swung open on a dark room – the only light a faint red glow coming from overhead. Like emergency lighting.

A row of metal shelving units blocked the rest of the room from view – stacked with boxes of rubber gloves, big tubs of bleach, rolls of bin bags, and bottles of disinfectant. Hot in here, the sharp stink of ammonia overlaying something foul and earthy. Like peanut butter and raw bacon.

I raised the torch and ran the beam across the shelves. 'I know you're in here, McKenzie. It's over.'

Scuffing noises. Something small: scrabbling.

I kept my back to the wall and limped down to where the units stopped. 'Shite...'

One wall was covered in metal cages – stacked floor to ceiling. Hundreds of red eyes shone in the torchlight. Rats. A couple of the little bastards hissed at me.

I swung the torch around, and there was Frank McKenzie: back pressed up against another set of shelves, trembling. His nose would never be straight again. Blood made a Rorschach inkblot on his shirt.

I brought the gun up. 'Where's Katie?'

He flinched back, staring at his feet, hands spidering along the shelves. 'I don't—'

'WHERE'S MY FUCKING DAUGHTER?'

'It wasn't me, she made me do it, they—'

'Where is she?' I hobbled closer. The rats turned to stare at me. Scaly pink tails writhing.

'I...' He shrugged one shoulder. 'They took her away. They dug her up and took her away.'

They dug her up? Something solid wedged in my throat, cutting off the air... Rebecca: they'd dug *Rebecca* up with all the others.

'Not Rebecca: Katie. Where's Katie? She wasn't in your torture porn dungeon. WHERE IS SHE?'

He looked up at me, frowning. 'Katie? We didn't... Who's Katie?'

'Katie Henderson. Katie Nicol. My bloody daughter!' I hauled my wallet out, held it up so he could see her photo. 'Katie!'

'I don't know, I've never seen her before, it—'

I jammed the gun against his forehead.

McKenzie squealed, hands flapping against the shelves, sending cartons and tins clattering to the concrete floor. 'I didn't do anything, I just took the photographs, it was all her! I didn't want to! It—'

'WHERE IS SHE?'

'I don't know, I've never even—'

The gun barked like a pit bull.

McKenzie screamed, clutched both hands over the hole where a big chunk of his left ear used to be as the boom echoed back and forth from the breeze-block walls.

He sank down onto his haunches, blood oozing out through his fingers.

'Where is she?'

'I DON'T KNOW!'

I backhanded him with the gun, and he clattered back against the shelves.

'Aaaaaagh…'

'Katie Henderson: your fourteenth bloody victim.'

He blinked up at me, eyes wet with tears. 'Fourteen?'

There was a sink in the corner, by a mop and wheelie-bucket. The bucket was full of greasy grey water. Wasn't exactly a '96 Pinot Noir, but it'd do.

'Last chance.'

'I don't understand…' He stared at me, eyebrows pinched together, mouth turned down, blood trickling down his cheek. 'Why would we need *fourteen*?'

Have to find something to tie the bastard down to. The door was too heavy – couldn't kick it off the hinges anyway. The shelves would do though. I grabbed the nearest set and hauled them away from the wall – toilet roll and bottles of cleaning fluid bounced off the floor as it smashed into the concrete.

McKenzie screamed, both arms wrapped around his head. 'I didn't touch her!'

'Ever been waterboarded? Because you're…'

A noise behind me.

God's sake: why did no one *ever* listen? 'Alice, I told you to wait in the mortuary.' I turned. Froze.

It wasn't Alice. It was the Rat Catcher. She was huge, shoulders hunched, staring down at me. Her eyes shone in the torchlight, like the rats' in their cages… She bared her teeth. 'Leave my little brother ALONE!'

The fist came from nowhere – sparks exploded deep inside my head, making everything fuzzy as the floor rolled beneath my feet. Then another one.

I lurched back, stumbled over something, went crashing against the wall of cages. Hissing, rattling, snapping yellow teeth.

The next punch drove all the air from my lungs, and wrapped barbed wire around my chest.

Fight back. Fight back, you useless bastard.

I swung for her face. Missed. Got another punch in the stomach for my troubles.

Knees wouldn't work any more.

She grabbed me by the lapels, pulled me forwards, then slammed me into the cages again.

Screeching rats. The stink of piss and droppings.

Gouge her eyes out. Bite her. Kick her in the crotch. DO SOMETHING!

She curled her fist back and grinned at me. 'You've been naughty.'

Bang.

I blinked. How...? I was on the floor, lying on my back, looking up at a network of wires and pipes. Ringing in my ears, black dots swirling in front of my eyes. 'Unnngh...'

Voices in the red-tinted gloom.

McKenzie: 'Who's Katie Henderson?'

Rat Catcher: 'Dunno.'

'He thinks we took fourteen girls, I mean, why would we take fourteen girls? It doesn't make any sense.'

'I'm tired.'

It took three goes to haul myself up onto my elbows. I blinked again, tried to shake the black dots away. My head throbbed.

The pair of them were sitting on the concrete floor, the wall behind them full of glowing eyes.

McKenzie brushed the hair back from his sister's face. 'It's OK. Soon be time to go home.'

'All finished.'

He smiled. 'All finished.'

'Your ear looks sore.'

It looked like a chunk of chewed bacon.

I grabbed the tipped-over shelving unit and used it to pull myself up, until I was sitting with my back against the sink in the corner. Panting, sweating, every move fanning the flames. My foot throbbed and burned, my back crackled, my head filled with boiling smoke.

The Rat Catcher pointed at me. 'He knows.'

McKenzie nodded. 'Everyone knows, now.'

'We should kill him. Kill him and put him in the incinerator.'

'Fuck... Fuck the pair of you.' I reached into my jacket... But the gun wasn't there.

McKenzie held it up. Shook his head. 'No.'

'We kill him and we put him in the incinerator.' She stood, towering over both of us.

'Lisa, we can't. *I* can't.' He stared at the gun in his hands. 'We need to go away, before more people come.'

'We can't go away till we see to Andrea.'

'They've got her. They came to the house. They've taken her away.' He looked at me. 'Haven't you?'

I wiped the sweat out of my eyes. 'It's over.'

'It's not over.' The Rat Catcher curled her dirty hands into fists. 'We get her *back*. We get her back and we make the bitch pay for what she did to us! The blood, the screaming, the photographs. We get her back.'

'There's a firearms team on its way down here right now. You're not going anywhere.'

'We get her back and we tear her apart, just like all the others.' She stepped forwards. 'We kill him and we put him in the incinerator.'

I grabbed a bottle of bleach from the debris on the floor. Fumbled at the lid with my aching fingers. What stupid bastard invented child-proof caps? Come on...

She grabbed me by the throat and dragged me to my feet.

Ulk— Her hand was a noose around my neck, tightening, cutting off the air, making the blood thump in my ears.

I scrabbled my hands at her creased face, pulled at her fingers. They wouldn't budge.

The bleach bottle thunked to the floor.

A door creaked.

'We kill him and we put him in the incinerator.' Her breath reeked of Parma Violets.

I blinked – staring over her shoulder.

Alice stood in the middle of the room, clutching that section of pipe as if she was up to bat. 'HEY, UGLY!'

The Rat Catcher turned, eyes narrow and dark. She opened her mouth and screamed through brown teeth, spit flying in the dim light. 'Kill them all!'

The pipe ripped through the air, battered into the side of her head. Hair and scraps of skin flew out in a spray of blood.

Her hands went slack around my throat, then she lurched sideways a couple of steps, then crashed to the floor like a fallen tree. Twitched a few times, then lay still, stretched full length, her eyes open, blood trickling out of her nose and mouth.

Alice dropped the pipe. It rang and clanged against the concrete, echoing through the little room. 'Is she...? I didn't mean to... It... I didn't have any choice...'

I limped across the cluttered floor to Frank McKenzie. Held out my hand. 'Give me the gun.'

He didn't even look at me. 'It's not Lisa's fault. It was Andrea... It was always Andrea.'

'Give – me – the gun.'

He held it up and stared into the barrel. Then pressed it against his temple. Closed his eyes. Hissed a breath out between his teeth, sending a shower of spittle down the front of his bloodstained shirt. Trembling. Crying.

I reached down and took the gun out of his hand.

49

Frank McKenzie cradled his sister's battered head in his lap, stroking her blood-soaked hair. 'Shh... It's all OK, it'll all be OK.'

I slumped back against the sink. The gun felt like an anvil in my hand, pulling my arm out of its socket.

Alice shifted from foot to foot, both arms wrapped around herself. 'I'm sorry, I'm so sorry...'

The gun weighed less in my pocket, but not much. 'You didn't take Katie?'

He shook his head. 'We only ever took Andrea. All the girls were Andrea.' A sniff, then he wiped a hand across his eyes, leaving a smear of dark red. 'She left us. She ran away and left Lisa and me alone with *him*. I was five...'

'Ash, I didn't mean to kill her, I just wanted her to let you go.'

'I know.' I held my arms open and Alice shuffled forwards into them, rested her head against my shoulder and cried.

'She was our big sister, she was supposed to protect us.' He leaned forwards and kissed the Rat Catcher's forehead. 'He hit Lisa so hard... She was never the same; something came loose inside her head. She just wanted someone to love her.'

'You killed my daughter. Her name was Rebecca. She was only twelve.'

A nod. 'Thirteen years ago Andrea turns up in Oldcastle again. She's pregnant. She's got herself a husband and a new house in Shortstaine; only she's not Andrea *McKenzie* any more, she's Andrea *Taylor*. And Andrea Taylor's seen Father's obituary in the paper...' McKenzie laughed. 'All those years and she comes back to tell us Mother has to go in a home: we have to sell the house so she can get her share. Said the old bastard owed her for everything he did. Owed her? What about us?'

Alice gave a long shuddering breath then stepped back, scrubbed a sleeve across her face. Brought her chin up. 'So you decided to get your own back – make her suffer for abandoning you, make her life as bad as yours. You started abducting her...' Alice fiddled with her hair. 'Amber O'Neil looked like her, didn't she? Enough to make it feel right: you turned her into Andrea and punished her for abandoning you. And it felt so good you went out and did it again, only Hannah Kelly didn't have Andrea's hair, so you dyed it for her. Made her fit the mould. Then you did it again, and again, turning them into Andrea so you could shave their heads and burn them and carve lines into their skin, so you could torture and mutilate and—'

'I didn't.' He kept his eyes on the floor. 'I just ... took the photographs. Lisa did everything. She ... you saw what she's like: she made me.'

'And then you used the birthday cards to punish the parents. You made them wait and worry for a whole year – what did they do wrong, why did their little girl run away – and then you rubbed their noses in it: look what happened to your daughter! You turned the girls into Andrea as she was back *then*, when she abandoned you. Then you turned their parents into Andrea as she is *now*, torturing her with the birthday cards. Two for one. Practising. Building up the fantasy. Waiting until Megan was old enough to do it all for real.'

I stared at him: sitting on the floor, holding onto his dead sister. 'Is that it, McKenzie? Is that all Rebecca was to you, a dress rehearsal?'

He shook his head. 'It wasn't like that, it...' A little shrug. 'I don't know.'

Alice turned her back on him. 'Henry was right: it was all about Megan Taylor. Thirteen girls killed on their thirteenth birthday.' She nudged a fallen bottle of bleach with her toe. 'Oh, I'm not saying they would've just given up – the thrill of torturing Megan and Andrea would have worn off eventually and they'd just keep on going, more girls, year after year.'

I let my head thunk back against the wall. 'They didn't take Katie.'

'No.'

But I saw the card: Katie tied to a chair in the Birthday Boy's room...

I ground the heel of my hand into my eyes. 'Then where is she?'

'Excellent work, Ash, excellent.' DCI Weber rubbed his hands together. Then frowned. 'Well, perhaps not the dead body – they'll make us have an enquiry about that – but everything else...' He clapped a hand down on my shoulder. 'Are you all right? You look a bit peaky.'

The mortuary doors banged open and Alf backed into the room, ponytail swinging from side to side as he pulled a hospital gurney after him. Lisa McKenzie lay on the shiny metal surface, glassy eyes staring blindly. He wheeled her over to one of the cutting tables. 'You know, that has to be the shortest trip to the mortuary in existence.'

Weber checked his watch. 'Right – press conference in half an hour, and as ACC Drummond is playing hard to get, I'm up with DCS Dickie and the Chief Constable. He wants you there to take the credit.'

I gritted my teeth, leaned on my walking stick and limped out the door. 'Fuck him.'

Weber hurried after me. 'Look, about Frank McKenzie's ear—'

'He fell down the stairs.'

'Right, stairs, yes. Only he claims you threatened him with a gun, then shot him.'

'He's a psycho, ask Dr McDonald.'

The corridor was cordoned off with 'POLICE' tape – a group of SOC-suited figures clustered on the other side, in the gloom, waiting for the OK to get started.

Weber stopped at the mortuary door. 'So I should tell the SEB they won't find any gunshot residue on him or the walls or a bullet or anything?'

'Tell them what you like.'

Alice was waiting for me at the main doors. She stared at the toes of her little red shoes. 'Did they say anything about...'

'They'll have an enquiry, but you're in the clear – you hadn't hit her with that pipe I'd be dead by now. Probably give you a medal or something.'

She smiled, then hooked an arm through mine, doing a little hop-jump to get in step as I hobbled out into the drizzly evening. 'Do you want me to pinch a wheelchair, I mean you're all sweaty and it's a big walk back to the car?'

'Taxi.' I pointed at the rank on the other side of the entrance.

'This is good news, you know – that they didn't take Katie. The obsession with killing the victims on their thirteenth birthday thing is specific to *their* psychosexual behaviour, whoever took Katie doesn't have that, the fact that they aped the Birthday Boy's modus operandi suggests they're more interested in you than her.'

I limped across to the rank. 'So it's my fault.'

'We need to work through everyone who's got reason to hate you, does anyone have reason to...' She coughed. 'Yes, well, let's make a list.'

'I don't need a list. I know who it is.'

Drummond's BMW purred into the Westing's car park. Monday wasn't a race night, but the whole place was lit up.

Alice parked by the entrance. Hauled on the handbrake. 'Right.'

'You're ... you're staying ... here.' Bloody seatbelt wouldn't unfasten, the plastic was all slippery under my fingers. Sweat trickled down my back. My right foot *burned*.

'Ash, look at yourself, you can barely move.'

I blinked at her. 'I'm fine...'

'No, no you're not.' She bit her bottom lip, then reached into her leather satchel and pulled out Eugene's pencil case. 'Still got one wrapper left.'

Silence.

I reached for the junkie starter kit, it shook so much the zip wouldn't work. 'I can't.'

Alice nodded. Took the case back, opened it up, and laid the contents out across the dashboard. Then unfolded the instructions. 'OK...' Deep breath. 'If ten-year-old Neds can work it out, so can I.'

Warmth oozed through me, squeezing the pain away until there was nothing left but a vague tingle. I breathed out. Then in. Someone was singing deep inside my head.

'Ash?' A gentle slap on my cheek. 'Ash, I've only given you a third, OK? That should be enough for an analgesic... Ash?'

I scrubbed a hand across my numb face. Rubbed some life back into my brain. 'Right.' The walking stick was rough beneath my fingers, the surface all scratched and dented from battering the pictures off ACC Drummond's walls. 'If I'm not back in—'

'No chance.' She clambered out into the rain, looked back at me. 'Do you *really* think I've done all this just to sit out here in the car like a good little girl? I want to be there when you get Katie back.'

Fair enough.

It wasn't bucketing down, but it was steady enough: droplets bouncing off the neon sign like tiny fireworks. I went around to the boot and slammed my palm on the lid. 'Still there, Drummond?'

Some scuffing noises.

Must've hurt when Alice took all those speed bumps at full tilt. Good.

I limped for the entrance tunnel, Alice walking slowly beside me. 'Should we not have handed Drummond over to Detective Chief Inspector Weber?'

'No.'

Arabella was still in her little cage, still reading about vampires perving on teenage girls. She didn't look up. 'We're closed.'

I slipped a twenty through the little slot at the bottom.

'Still closed.'

Another twenty.

She reached over and pressed the button.

The walking stick's thunk, thunk, thunk echoed down the tunnel. There was light at the end of it – coming from the massive spots mounted on the stadium roof, making the race-track glow. I kept going.

Andy Inglis's Range Rover sat in the middle of the grass, the sides smeared with mud. He stood beside it, dressed up like a country squire in tweeds and a flat cap, an elderly black Labrador at his feet. Two men trotted a pair of muscular greyhounds up and down in front of the car.

'Put the bitch up first...' Mr Inglis turned, saw me, and threw his arms out. Beaming. 'Ash, you old bastardo! I hear you caught the Birthday Boy: that deserves a drink. Got a couple bottles of Veuve Clicquot in the office, eh?'

'Where's Mrs Kerrigan?'

'She sort you out with the key for your new flat yet?'

One of the guys walked over to the starting gates, the greyhound loping along beside him.

Inglis pointed. 'See that? That's a twenty-second dog or I'm a scabby arse. She'll—'

'For God's sake, Andy: is Mrs Kerrigan here or not?'

He threw back his head and roared out a laugh. 'Caramba, you're obsessed, aren't you. Fine: she's in the office. Tell her to crack open the bubbly.'

I limped up the stairs, ignoring my phone ringing in my pocket.

Alice looked back at the racing track. 'Ash, we do have a plan, don't we, I mean a better plan than we had at ACC Drummond's house, we're not going to march in and—'

'Same plan.' I pulled out the gun, checked the magazine. More than enough bullets to kneecap the bitch.

My phone went silent, then blared out its old-fashioned ring again.

'There's three people down there who've seen us go up to the office, if you shoot her someone's going to notice and—'

'She's got Katie.'

Whoever was trying to call hung up. Then Alice's phone started ringing instead. She pulled it out. 'Dr McDonald? No... Is it? ... Yes, we did, he was a photographer with the local paper...' She put a hand over the mouthpiece. 'It's Sabir.'

The Westing's main office had a panoramic window overlooking the track. The lights were on... And there was Mrs Kerrigan, standing in the middle of the room with her back to the door, a phone clamped to her ear.

I hobbled up the last flight of stairs, shirt sticking to my back.

Alice slowed, hanging back. 'Did he? All thirteen of them? That's great... No: a confession's perfect... Uh-huh...'

The office door swung open on creaky hinges.

Mrs Kerrigan didn't turn around. She leaned over a desk and shuffled through some sheets of paper. 'Yez've got to be kiddin'. I'm lookin' at the figures now, and there's no way... Naw, this whole thing's a ball of shite.'

Two hobbling steps and I was right behind her.

'No: *you* listen to *me*, you little bollox, if I don't see three grand by Friday, your—'

I cracked the gun off the back of her skull. She dropped the phone and grabbed the desk, knees buckling. So I hit her again.

Mrs Kerrigan crumpled to the carpet, both hands on her head, blinking hard, teeth bared. 'Aya feckin' bastard...'

I pointed the gun at her stomach. 'You said next time I should pull the trigger.'

Alice grabbed my sleeve. 'Ash? Sabir says DC Massie needs to speak to you.'

'I'm *busy*.'

'Yer feckin' dead is what ye are!'

'Ash, she says it's urgent...' Alice held the phone up to my ear.

'Hello?' Rhona's voice crackled out of the speaker. *'Guv, we've got something! Someone phoned the hotline: said they saw Katie getting into a Silver Mercedes on Friday night! Didn't get the number plate, but she was certain it was a man driving – chunky, balding at the front, long hair at the back. Dickie's putting out an appeal for them to come forward.'*

I swallowed. 'I see.'

Mrs Kerrigan glowered up from the carpet at me. 'I'll hack yer balls off and shove them right up yer gobshite arse. Yer feckin'—' Her head snapped back, blood spurting from her nose.

Alice hopped from foot to foot, clutching her right hand. 'Ow... That always looks so much easier in films.'

Mrs Kerrigan wobbled twice, then keeled over flat on her back and stayed that way.

Oh fuck.

I stared down at her, lying there, unconscious and bleeding. That nose was definitely broken.

Oh, *fuck*.

Silver Mercedes; chubby; receding hairline, but long at the back. It was Ethan Baxter.

50

The front door wasn't even locked. I lumbered down the hall. 'ETHAN FUCKING BAXTER!'

The silver Mercedes sat outside – rescued from K&B Motors.

'WHERE ARE YOU, YOU LITTLE SHITE?'

The kitchen door was open. I barged in.

Ethan was sitting at the table, sobbing away to himself. The fibreglass cast on his left arm was cracked and filthy, smeared with dark-red stains. A half-empty litre of Belvedere lay on its side in front of him, next to a small white plastic tub – the kind that came with a child-proof cap and doctor's directions printed on a sticker. Like Henry.

He looked up at me, eyes red and watery. 'I didn't mean to…'

'Where is she?'

'I'm so sorry…'

I leaned on the table, looming over the little bastard. 'WHERE IS SHE?' Flecking his face with spittle.

'Oh no, not *again*.' Alice picked up the plastic container. 'Triazolam – sleeping pills.' She put a hand on Ethan's forehead and levered one of his eyes wide open with her thumb. 'How many did you take?'

He squealed when I grabbed him by the throat and hauled him out of the chair. 'WHERE IS SHE?'

'I didn't mean to!'

'I will break every fucking bone in your body, you—'

'Downstairs, she's downstairs... I'm sorry.'

'You will be.'

He staggered along the hall to a door, opened it, and flicked a switch. A flight of stairs led down into the basement. 'I didn't mean to... I didn't.'

He'd built a mock-up of the Birthday Boy's torture room. Not all of it – just three walls, identical to the ones in the cards. Enough to fake up a photo. Katie was sitting in the middle, on a wooden chair, her ankles fixed to the legs with cable-ties, her hands behind her back. Slumped forwards in her seat, long black hair hanging over her face.

Not moving.

'I didn't... I didn't mean to hurt her, it was an accident.' Ethan leaned back against the wall, breathing hard. 'She wouldn't stop screaming...'

Alice brushed Katie's hair away from her face.

Her eyes were open above a rectangle of silver duct tape, throat covered in bruises. The left side of her forehead was torn and bloody, distorted, as if the bone underneath had caved in.

Oh God...

The walking stick fell to the basement floor, sending up a little puff of dust.

Katie...

'Didn't... Didn't mean... Only meant to get my own back... Make you ... make you...' Ethan slumped against the wall, clutching the cast on his shattered left hand. 'Never hold a pencil again...'

No...

He sank down until he was sitting on the ground, eyes half shut, breath heaving in his chest like an aqualung.

Not again...

I lurched forwards, fell to my knees, and put two fingers against Katie's throat. Pulse – there had to be a pulse. *Something*. Her skin was cold. 'No. Katie, no, no, no, no, no... *Please*!'

'Didn't mean to...'

'Oh, Ash, I'm so sorry.' Alice knelt beside me, wrapped her arms around me and squeezed. 'I'm so sorry.'

I don't know when Alice let go, but one minute she was there, and the next I was on my own looking up into Katie's blue eyes.

Retching noises echoed around the room from somewhere behind me. I turned.

Alice had Ethan bent over her knee, sticking her fingers down his throat. His back heaved and stinking yellow splashed against the basement floor. And again. And again. 'Come on, get it all up.'

Bitter-smelling vomit flecked with little white pills.

I stood. 'Leave him alone.'

'He's going to die if I don't—'

'LEAVE HIM ALONE!'

She stared at me, then dropped him, backed away from the little fuck who killed my daughter.

The gun sang in my hands. One loud, *deafening* note that echoed around the room, back and forth, and back and forth, slowly fading to nothing.

Ethan lay on his side with a tiny black hole in his face, half an inch below his cheekbone. The back of his head was wide open, the contents making a scarlet peacock's tail up the wall.

Alice eased the gun from my fingers. 'Shh... it's OK. It's OK.'

She wiped it clean on her stripy red-and-black T-shirt, then placed it in Ethan's hand, pointed it away from herself and pulled the trigger. Another echoing bang.

She let go and Ethan's arm flopped across his chest. Alice

stared at him for a bit. Then nodded. 'He's got a hole in his head, gunshot residue on his hand, and a bloodstream full of sleeping pills.' She straightened her top. 'He was ranting and raving when we came in. He threatened us, then he shot himself.'

I cradled Katie's head against my chest.

'Ash, this is important: if anyone asks we have to be on the same page – he threatened us with the gun, then he shot himself.'

Katie...

Tuesday 22nd November

The curtain slid back.

Katie was lying on her back, on the other side of the viewing room window, eyes closed, hair brushed, a sheet pulled up to her chin – covering the bruises on her throat – hair arranged over her battered forehead. Hiding the damage. It looked as if she was sleeping. As if she'd wake up at any moment.

Michelle stepped forwards and put a hand on the glass, lips trembling.

The uniformed constable cleared his throat. 'Is this your daughter?'

A nod. Eyes shining and wet. 'Yes…'

Alice put an arm around Michelle's shoulders. 'I'm sorry.'

I stayed where I was. Not breathing until the curtain slid shut again.

We stepped out into the car park. A knot of journalists jockeyed for position outside the hospital's main entrance, waiting for the photogenic moment when Megan Taylor was reunited with her parents.

Michelle stared as Andrea Taylor walked out through the doors and waved. 'It's all her fault, isn't it? She made those two bastards what they were…'

Alice shook her head. 'Their father made them, she was just the catalyst.'

'She gets her daughter back and I get Katie's body.'

'I know,' Alice gave Michelle a hug, 'it's horrible and it's not fair.'

Two figures broke away from the pack and marched towards us: DCI Weber and DS Smith, both dressed in funereal black.

My phone rang. I dragged it out, answered without really looking. Operating on automatic.

A nasal Irish accent blared in my ear. *'Two times ye had the chance, an ye bottled it.'* Mrs Kerrigan.

'Fuck off, I'm not in the mood.'

'Wanted to let yez know – no hard feelin's. In fact, I've gone and got you a present. Hope ye like it.' A little laugh, and then she hung up.

Weber stopped six foot away, cleared his throat, licked his lips, looked down at his feet. Smith's mouth twitched, struggling to contain a smile. Triumphant little shite.

I straightened my shoulders. 'Michelle, why don't you go wait in the car? I'll only be a minute.'

Michelle walked away, head down, chewing at her fingernails. 'She gets her daughter back.'

'Ash...' Weber cleared his throat again. 'I'm going to need you to come down to the station with me.'

'Why?'

Smith stuck his chest out. 'We've found your brother, Parker. He was shot twice in the head.'

I stared. Pins and needles spread out across my chest. 'He can't ...'

'We found a gun at the scene: a Bul Cherokee, nine mill – very popular with the Israeli security forces.'

Cold followed the pins and needles, freezing the breath in my lungs. Bul Cherokee: it was the gun from Bath, the one Terri rented out to me so Mrs Kerrigan could have her revenge. 'They killed Parker...?'

'Your fingerprints are on the gun, and the bullet casings.'

I've gone and got you a present. Hope ye like it.

Oh God. 'You can't believe I—'

'Ash.' Weber couldn't even look at me. 'Please don't make this any more difficult than it already is...'

Alice grabbed my hand and squeezed.

Wednesday 23rd November

The MV *Hrossey* eased itself into dock with one last growling roar. Then clanks and clangs reverberated around the harbour. Half past seven in the morning and the sky was a deep, dirty orange, fat flakes of snow drifting down over Holmsgarth Terminal, the lights of Lerwick twinkling in the darkness.

Arnold Burges tucked his hands into his coat pockets.

Seemed to be taking them forever to get the thing tied down and the bow open. But it was OK. He'd waited seven years, another ten minutes wasn't going to kill him.

The gangway shuddered and groaned as the last section swung into place against the ferry's hull. Didn't take long before bleary-eyed passengers were shivering out into the cold morning. Some would get the bus into town, some would get lifts home, some would catch a taxi, and everyone else would head down to the car deck to collect their vehicles.

Finally: the bow creaked up in a barrage of klaxons and warning lights.

One by one the cars and lorries grumbled out into the snow, trailing plumes of exhaust fumes behind them, until the only thing left was a blue BMW.

Arnold walked into the hold, sticking to the yellow-hatched path.

He had a quick check to make sure no one was watching, then ran his fingers along the rough underside of the front wheel arch on the driver's side. A little metal rectangle – about the size of a matchbox – was stuck to the surface. Magnetic. He pulled it free and slid it open. There was a BMW key inside, like the text message promised.

Plip. The indicators flashed and the doors unlocked.

Took a bit of doing to get the seat adjusted so he could fit behind the wheel – like a little girl had driven it last – but it started with a refined purr. Nice motor, shame it'd end up as a burned-out wreck, dumped in the sea off the west coast of Shetland.

The BMW slid out of the hold and onto the quay.

Fifteen minutes later he pulled into a lay-by, flanked by mountains on both sides, a grey sea loch reaching away into the distance, the faint wash of twilight just beginning to creep above the horizon. Arnold popped the boot.

Stank of shit and piss in there.

A man lay curled up on his side in the boot, hands cuffed behind his back, surrounded by shiny CDs, a laptop, and a desktop computer. Shivering.

Arnold nodded. 'You Drummond?'

The man hissed at him from behind a duct-tape gag.

'You helped the bastard who killed my Lauren. You told him where we lived...' A smile cracked across Arnold's face for what felt like the first time in years. 'I'm going to enjoy this.'